Milly Johnson is a very short but damned attractive writer of novels and greetings-card copy. Half-Glaswegian, half-Sassenach, her hobbies include eating Star Bars, singing in the car – where she is word-perfect at 'Mr Boombastic' – and, in the name of research, hanging around with big wrestlers.

She lives bang in the centre of Barnsley, South Yorkshire, across the road from her mam and dad, with her two fast-growing sons, her goldfish Gene Hunt and the battalion of cats which are obligatory for a single, middle-aged woman.

When she isn't trying to raise the awareness of bullying in the workplace or locking horns with the council over a much-needed Dodworth Road pedestrian crossing, she can be found in the wine aisle in Morrisons, cruising in the Med or scrubbing at ketchup stains on small boys' school shirts (because washing powder commercials lie). She can currently speak 150 words of Italian – mostly flavours of ice cream.

Milly's website is www.millyjohnson.com

A Spring Affair is her third novel.

Also by Milly Johnson

The Yorkshire Pudding Club
The Birds and the Bees

A
Spring Affair

Milly Johnson

POCKET
BOOKS

LONDON · SYDNEY · NEW YORK · TORONTO

First published in Great Britain by Pocket Books, 2009
An imprint of Simon & Schuster UK Ltd
A CBS COMPANY

3 5 7 9 10 8 6 4 2

Simon & Schuster UK Ltd
1st Floor
222 Gray's Inn Road
London WC1X 8HB

www.simonandschuster.co.uk

Simon & Schuster Australia
Sydney

A CIP catalogue record for this book is available
from the British Library

ISBN 978-1-84983-501-5

Typeset in Bembo by M Rules
Printed by CPI Cox & Wyman, Reading, Berkshire RG1 8EX

For my boys – Terence and George,
because I love you.

Acknowledgements

As usual I would like to give thanks to a few people here for helping me produce this book, both directly and indirectly. To my super-agent Darley Anderson and his gorgeous angels, and everyone at my publishers Simon & Schuster – in particular the lovely Libby Vernon for being a truly cracking editor and Suzanne Baboneau for being the best and sweetest Head Honcho I could wish for. Thanks also to the Essential Joan Deitch.

To my mam and dad for bragging mercilessly to their mates about me and pushing my sales up. To my sons Terence Johnson for plot consultations and George Johnson for allowing me to use his creation 'Shirley Hamster'.

To my buddies – old ones and new ones, big ones and small ones, wrestling ones and non-wrestling ones, bright ones, beautiful ones, wise ones and wonderful ones. Especially the stalwarts – Paul Sear, Alec Sillifant, Catherine Marklew, Maggie Birkin, Tracy Harwood, Rachel Hobson, Debra Mitchell, Chris and Judy Sedgewick – and, as always, my dear SUN Sisters – Pam Oliver, Helen Clapham and Karen Baker. And of course, official moggy suppliers – Colin and Sara Atkinson at www.haworthcatrescue.org

To the fair and fantastic Stuart Gibbins at www.newMedia4.com for creating the best website ever for me and explaining techno things in such a way that even thicko me can understand them.

To a wonderful set of clever-beggar authors – Sue Welfare, Lucie Whitehouse, Lucy Diamond, Matt Dunn, Louise Douglas, Jayne Dowle, James Nash, Katie Fforde, Stephen Booth, Mel Dyke and Jane Elmor for their friendship and unerring support.

To *Heeleys Skips* in Barnsley – for filling me in on all sorts of details. And starting me off on an adventure by taking away my own rubbish and clearing up my life in the process. Trust me – it really does work like magic.

To my old mucker Superintendent (congratulations!) Pat Casserly and his family for lending me the perfect name for Lou.

Grazie bella Franca Martella at BBC Radio Sheffield for being both my Italian guru and an all-round top bird.

Bacì – to all my Italian friends at *Corbaccio* and around the dinner-tables and coffee pots of Milan. You made my smile extra wide whilst I was writing this story.

. . . And to Signor Marco Pierre White – for treating my little boy so nicely, for agreeing to feature as Lou's fantasy man, and for being, like her, someone who simply 'loves to cook'.

Prologue

Spring-Clean Your Life!

Life feel too heavy and cluttered sometimes? Feel like you're going nowhere? Did it ever cross your mind that all those little unwanted items in your cupboards are controlling you, draining your energies and anchoring you to the past? If you think all this sounds far-fetched, check out Mavis Calloway's report on page 14 and see just how simple acts of clearing out some rubbish can put you on a path to your whole life moving forwards.

Women by Women, Contents page, March edition

Chapter 1

Sometimes the cosmos goes to a lot of trouble to help shift a life from its rut. On this occasion, for instance, it held up the dental technician on the M1 roadworks, gave the Practice secretary some tricky double bookings to cope with, and lumbered the dentist, Mr Swiftly, with a particularly awkward extraction that made his appointments run over by more than half an hour. All this so that the ante-room would be extra packed with bored people whiling away the time with the magazines in the rack, leaving just one tatty copy for Mrs Elouise Winter. And not just any mag, but *Women by Women* — *the* mag for women whose once-young and carnal energies were now ploughed into studying variations on hotpot and various crafts which were a bit too fuddy-duddy for Lou, despite the fact that, at thirty-five, she was starting to edge dangerously close to the chasm of middle age. Still, it was better than staring into space or reading posters about plaque. So she grabbed it and slotted herself into the only vacant seat, between a woman nervously tapping her foot and a pensioner who looked like Ernie Wise.

Lou turned to the recipes first but there was nothing

to excite. *Five delicious ways to serve a leg of lamb.* She shuddered. Not even a naked Marco Pierre White carrying a sheep limb in on a platter with a red rose between his teeth could make *that* sound attractive to her. She could never think of lamb without picturing rubbery seams of fat and mint sauce and being six years old, sitting alone in the school dining room, pushing it around her plate, willing it to get smaller and disappear so she could join the others and go out to play. She remembered how Lesley Jones's mum had written to the school demanding that her child should not be forced to eat butter beans, but Lou's mother Renee had refused to do the same for her with a lamb-avoiding note. Tagged onto the end of that memory was the still-fresh feeling of relief when she discovered a kindly dinner lady who would scrape away the odious lamb into the slop bucket and release her from the sad agony of the impasse.

Lamb was her husband Phil's favourite, although she had hardly ever cooked it for him before things went wrong between them, before his affair. Since those dark days, three and a half years ago, it had appeared quite a lot on her menu, as it would this very evening as a direct result of that little comment he had made last night about her putting some weight on. Lou had tried to shut it out of her mind, but it had continued to rotate in there like a red sock in a whites boil wash – destructive and unstoppable. Just when she had started to believe that she was on rock-solid ground, he had to go and make a comment about the size of her bottom.

Lou carried on flicking through the mag, desperate to find something to divert her thoughts, because she would go half-mad otherwise. There was a pattern for a

crocheted lampshade that had a certain kitsch charm –
except that Lou's crocheting foray had begun and ended
on the same afternoon when, aged eleven, she had made
a succession of long tapeworm-like chains from some
white wool. She never could work out how to do the
turn onto the second and subsequent lines required to
make the intricate tea-cosies or granny-square blankets
that her sister Victorianna (or 'Torah' as she referred to
herself these days) could so effortlessly make. Then again,
Victorianna could always turn her hand to anything, as
their mother boasted to unfortunate visitors when showing off her younger daughter's accomplishments. '*Except
to ringing home when she doesn't want something or to asking
you to visit*,' Lou had wanted to snipe. But didn't. It
wouldn't have made any difference anyway. Victorianna
had been on her pedestal for so long, not even a nuclear
explosion would nudge her off it.

*Top ten dressing-gowns. Write your own will. Spring-clean
your life!* Jeez, is this what is waiting for me around the
age corner? thought Lou. It was looking more and more
as if, one day, her interest in shoes and nice handbags
would suddenly be diverted to mastering the art of
laughing safely without causing a small Niagara Falls in
the knicker area, or dislodging one's false teeth. The
dressing-gowns were dire, unless you liked the sort of
nylon quilting that could give you a free perm if you
happened to brush past something metallic, and she had
already written her will – not that she had any Picassos to
leave to anyone. Nevertheless, there were at least three
people in front of her to see Mr Swiftly, so there was
nothing for it but to try and be interested in having a
good clear-out.

The article explained how *unburdening your cupboards of those unwanted and unused knick-knacks will lighten your spirit to a degree you would not think possible. How liberated you will feel, burning all those recipes you cut out from magazines and never tried, not to mention throwing away those garments in the wardrobe which are four sizes too small – the clothes you hoped you'd slim into and never did.*

The clothes bit in particular struck a chord with Lou. How long had those grey check, size eight trousers been waiting for her super-slim bum to rematerialize? She did a quick tally and was horrified to discover they had clocked up twelve years on both pre-marital and post-marital coat-hangers. In fact, she had gone up nearly two stone since deciding once and for all that she was going to slim down into them, and if Phil was to be believed last night, she was getting even bigger.

She had lain awake in the wee small hours, thinking how she needed to throttle back on the calories – she didn't even dare to imagine what would happen if Phil's eyes started wandering again. To thin women. She needed to get a grip. Quickly.

Clear your house and clear your mind. Don't let life's clutter dictate to you. Throw it away and take back the control! the article cried, and some blind, lost part within Lou Winter lifted its head as if sensing light. She couldn't remember the last time she had thrown anything out that wasn't everyday wheelie-bin rubbish, and yet her cupboards were full to bursting. At worst it would give her something to do that might divert her thoughts from where they had started to go.

Wearing her best 'nothing to declare' face, she slipped the magazine into her bag when it was her time to be

called. It wouldn't be missed, she decided, and it would-
n't have withstood another reading. To compensate, she
had a huge pile of magazines at home that she would
bring over and donate in its place, when she began her
so-called 'miraculous' clear-out.

If only she could start by clearing out her husband's
comment from her head . . .

Chapter 2

At eight-thirty that evening, Philip Michael Winter, thirty-eight years old, owner of *P.M. Autos* as well as the first sign of a paunch and a bald patch which was becoming harder to hide with every passing day, sat back in his chair and let rip with a long fruity burp of approval.

'Fantastic that, love.'

Lou smiled and he basked in the fact that he had made that smile happen. Never let it be said that he was one of those blokes who didn't compliment his wife. Oh no, he always shared the feeling of satisfaction in his belly with Lou. She deserved to know when he had enjoyed his dinner. Lou was a good wife – the best. He never had to hunt around for a fresh shirt, the house was always clean, she cooked like an angel and she never turned him down in the bedroom. She was the perfect 'surrendered wife' – well, she was now, after a bit of training. Although, let's face it, Lou was pretty lucky to be married to *him*. He had put a nice four-bedroomed roof over her head and, thanks to the success of his used-car lot, they had all the latest mod-cons, decking in the garden and plasma TVs in three rooms.

Lou had been with him from the beginning, when

all he had were dreams of running his own car lot, the drive to see them through and an appointment with the bank manager. *P.M. Autos* was a family business, and as such he liked Lou to do all the accounts for him because no one was more trustworthy than his wife and she was bloody good at number-crunching. There was plenty of money in the bank so she could pay all the bills. He even encouraged her to have a little part-time job so she could have some independence and extra money for shoes and make-up and other women things. But only part-time – he didn't want anything that might tire her too much, or interfere with his coming home every evening to a meal made by his own personal chef. He saved a fortune on restaurants. What was the point in going out? No one could cook like Lou and she would rather do it herself than have an inferior meal in fancy surroundings. He'd had the dining room and kitchen made into one huge cooking area for her and built a beautiful conservatory onto the side of the house in which to feed up and seduce potential business contacts with his wife's superior fare. And she was more than happy to do that for him. He knew this, although he hadn't actually asked her. But to be fair to him, had she ever said, 'Let's go out for a change'? Well, not since his diversion from the straight and narrow she hadn't, anyway.

Tonight's offering was melt-in-the-mouth pink lamb cutlets, mange tout, sweet apple potatoes and caramelized carrots (which he would desecrate with half a pint of home-made mint sauce) – and it was his absolute favourite. There were no sharers either, for he knew Lou and lamb went together like Dracula and garlic cloves. She had a small, bland egg salad herself, he noted with a little twisted smile. It was amazing how many ripples he could cause just by slapping his wife's backside as she climbed into bed and saying oh-so-innocently, *'Putting a bit of weight on again, aren't you, old girl?'* The merest hint that she might be letting herself go and Lou was thrown back to that place of insecurity which he considered it healthy for her to visit occasionally – just to keep her on her toes and make her appreciate what she had.

To an outsider that might have sounded hard – borderline sadistic even – but Phil Winter would have argued how wrong they were. He cared about his marriage – and needed to be reassured that his wife felt the same and was prepared to put her share of the effort in as well. He didn't want Lou falling down the slippery slope of not caring what she looked like and ending up like his business colleague Fat Jack's wife Maureen who hadn't just gone downhill, she'd travelled there on a bobsleigh.

And now, whilst Lou had a Muller Light, he shovelled down a toffee-apple crumble with calvados cream and Lou poured him out a whopping great brandy to follow. If he wasn't too tired, he thought he might even initiate some hanky-panky this evening, knowing that Lou would be more than grateful for a bit of sexual security. A woman on the edge tried so much harder in bed, as he had found. For Phil Winter, life couldn't have been better.

But it could have been better for Lou Winter, even though she did have what her mother would have said was a very good thing going on, what with her nice house, healthy bank account, holidays abroad and a husband who worked hard. One of Phil's most attractive features in his wife's eyes was how much he enjoyed his food. She could never have married a man who was picky.

In saying that, her unmarried fantasies had been more about staring into the eyes of Marco Pierre White, the candlelight between them emphasizing his saturnine glower as he savagely ripped up hunks of garlic-heavy ciabatta to feed to her, his lips glistening with traces of oil, balsamic vinegar and a blood-red Shiraz. He was the only man she and her old friend Deb would ever have fought over. Lou didn't really go for tall men like Deb did, but he ticked so many other boxes on her list that she would have overlooked that aspect − if she'd been given the opportunity. A passionate, food-adoring Yorkshireman−cum−Italian . . . oh, especially the Italian part . . .

The thought of Deb brought a smile to her lips and an unexpected lump to her throat. She coughed it away and turned her attention to Phil. The image of his shiny chin and satiated grin didn't have quite the same effect on her as the *enfant terrible* of gastronomy − but that was real life for you. Her dreams were long gone.

Lou cleared up the plates and slotted them into the dishwasher, slamming the door on the sickly, minty smell. No one could ever guess how much she hated lamb, what misery it stood for. She pressed the button and the machine whirred and sloshed into action. The suds hit the pans and the plates and the cutlery, obliterating all traces of the meal, just like the dinner lady did, all those many years ago. But this time there was no sense of the freedom that had sent her skipping into the playground, and no tidal wave of relief that her ordeal, at least for now, was over.

Chapter 3

Lou dropped her bag at the side of her desk, eased out of her overcoat and prepared to fortify herself with a coffee from the swanky new machine in the staff canteen. It looked very strong, very black, and had what looked like spit floating on top of it.

'Who goffed in your coffee?' said Karen, her work partner-in-crime currently sticking her chin over Lou's shoulder. 'Yuk! What *is* that?'

Lou smiled. Their relationship wasn't the deep alliance that she had shared with her once-best friend, Deb. It probably wouldn't have survived outside the workplace, where age gaps and living distances, different focuses and commitments would have got in the way. But Karen was a true comrade in the office. She worked, as Lou did, job-share Monday, Thursday and Friday. Although their office manager had tried to alter that to split them up, she had failed. Karen made Lou laugh lots with her irreverence, her warmth, her gorgeously plummy accent and her big snorty chuckles. Plus their banter coloured the days that their common enemy, Nicola 'Jaws' Pawson, did her best to reduce to monochrome.

Nicola was a weird one, that was for sure. Pretty and

slim, she looked quite benign until she opened her mouth to reveal a gobful of metal that would have made her an indispensable tool to a plumber. There had been a lot of crude jokes about what she was supposed to have done to the Chief Accountant Roger Knutsford in the lift at the Christmas party with that mouth, especially when he lost his voice in the New Year and started talking like a eunuch.

In stark contrast Karen was a dark-haired farmer's daughter, built like an Amazonian warrior with shoulders that would have scared off Jonah Lomu in a scrum, but she had the most beautiful posh husky voice, thanks to good genes, old money and a grandmother who had been a private elocution teacher. Karen wore the brightest colours in the spectrum and the reddest lipsticks in House of Fraser, and decorated her largeness with no attempt to hide anything she had. In fact, the combined ingredients of Karen Harwood-Court cooked up to make one hell of a sexy woman. It wasn't hard to understand why she was the object of so much male office-leering – not that Karen was interested in a relationship at this point in her life. But then, men were always drawn to what they couldn't have.

'You seem in an extra relaxed mood today,' Lou said, taking a sip of her drink and wincing as it punched the back of her throat.

'Nicola's off. Can't you tell? The room temperature's up twenty centigrade and there aren't any thunderclouds above us.' Karen's eyes floated around the room as if feasting on a tangible lightness.

Stan Mirfield, the oldest office administrator, bounded in and threw his briefcase on the desk as if it were an

Olympic finishing line and every nano-second counted, which with Nicola in charge, it did. He lived out in some country place and didn't drive. That hadn't been a problem until the last few months when the council had farted around with the timetables and the first bus of the morning got him into the town centre at ten to nine, leaving him with a paltry ten minutes to get to the office by nine. He was a physical and a psychological wreck by the time he'd reached the accounts floor.

Huffing like an old asthmatic steam engine, Stan wiped frantically at the sweat on his face.

'Chill, Stanley, she's not in,' called Karen.

'You what, love?'

'She's not in – Jaws. She's away today.'

'Ill, I hope,' said normally kind-hearted Stan.

'Apparently so. One of her cloven hooves has fallen off.'

Stan punched at the air with a 'yes'.

Karen leaned into Lou. 'Is it worth getting himself in a state like that for? He'll have a heart-attack before he gets to his pension,' she said, with some anger on Stan's behalf. They both watched him go through his normal routine before settling down to work. He would graft quietly and efficiently at his desk like a well-oiled machine all day, without loitering around coffee-machines and circulating jokes from the internet, as did a huge percentage of the staff.

'If I ran a department with people like him in it, I wouldn't give a bugger if they were a few minutes late,' Karen went on.

'Has he had a word with HR to give him some leeway?' asked Lou.

'*She* has, apparently,' said Karen, sneering on the 'she'. 'Stan said she told him that Bowman said it wasn't an option.' She pulled back her top lip, exposing the maximum teeth for her to do a Nicola impression: '"*Human Resources have made it quite clear to me that the original contract you signed says you start at nine. By not starting at nine you are in breach of that contract.*" Or words to that effect. Enough to dangle the sack over him as per normal.'

'Poor old Stan,' tutted Lou, torturing herself with another slug of coffee. 'I bet she never told them that the guy hardly ever takes his full lunch-hour.'

'No. Instead, she told him that he should take part-time hours, but that would affect his pension so he can't – although she knows that, of course. Right, must get on,' said Karen, rubbing her hands together in preparation.

'Hmmm, that looks exciting,' Lou said with sarcasm as she pointed to an enormous bound set of computer print-outs taking up most of Karen's desk.

'I have an anomaly to find. Rogering Roger has lost twenty thousand pounds somewhere in here and he can't find it, so he gave it to lucky old me to do it for him.'

Roger Knutsford had acquired his nickname in deference to his reputation for appreciating figures – of the young, female variety more than the numeric.

'So much for being the big cheese. You should ask him for some of his salary,' said Lou, adding slyly, 'Course, you could always aim to be a senior accountant yourself . . .'

'Shut up, Lou, and lend me your ruler,' Karen sighed.

Lou opened up her drawer, which was a veritable

Aladdin's cave of disorganized stationery. After five minutes of foraging and mumbles of, 'Hang on, it's in here
somewhere,' she handed over her rather grubby ruler.

Clear that clutter.

The thought came to her as surely as if someone had
whispered it softly and seductively into her ear.

'What on earth are you doing?' Karen asked five minutes
later as Lou wrestled with the drawer, heaving it out
from the body of the cabinet under her desk. Then she
turned it over and emptied the contents out onto the
carpet, dropping to her knees by the small mountain of
detritus. She had had no idea her drawer could hold so
much. It was like a Tardis. She would probably have her
hand exterminated by a lurking Dalek in a minute.

'Well, seeing as Jaws is not in,' Lou panted, 'I'm having
a springclean.'

'You've timed it perfectly. It's March the twenty-first –
the first day of spring today,' said Karen, tapping her desk
calendar.

'Yep, and I'm going to do something on this first day
of spring that is long overdue.'

'You're NOT going to burn that burgundy suit at long
last, are you?' asked Karen, laughing hard at her own sarcasm.

'Ha ha. No, I'm going to clear out some rubbish,' Lou
replied.

'Same thing.'

'You really are a cheeky sod – there's nothing wrong
with my suit.' Lou put her hands mock indignantly on
her hips. The suit cladding them was functional, if a little
old-fashioned, but she felt nicely inconspicuous in it.

Twenty-somethings had a different clothes agenda. They didn't want to melt into the background and couldn't understand why anyone else would want to be there either.

'It messes about with your shape. Makes you look dumpy.'

'I am dumpy,' said Lou. 'Plus at thirty-five I don't think anyone is looking to me to be a fashion icon.'

'Good job.'

'Don't mince your words on my behalf,' Lou huffed.

'I mean it, Lou. Whoever sold it to you should be shot at dawn. In fact, why wait? Shoot them immediately for a crime as severe as that.'

'Oh go and boil your head.'

Karen twisted around in her chair to give Lou her full attention.

'Lou Winter, you have great hair, great tits, and eyes that make you look about sixteen. Didn't anyone ever tell you about diamonds and settings? If I had your attributes I'd be pushing them in everyone's face. You just don't appreciate what you've got.' She stared down wistfully at her own A cups. 'You are such an attractive woman. Why the hell do you insist on hiding yourself away?'

'I'm not hiding myself away. But at thirty-five—'

'Listen to yourself! Thirty-five isn't old.'

'You're twenty-five – you're supposed to say I'm ancient.'

'You have an outstanding talent for not making the best of yourself, you know. You push everyone onwards but yourself.'

'Keep your horses on,' said Lou, but Karen was on a

roll and had no intention of stopping now, not even to take the rise out of another of Lou's Lou-isms.

'You could have had Jaws's job if you'd applied for it. So really it's your fault we're all so bloody miserable, if you think about it. We'd all much rather have worked for you than Sheffield-Steel Face. It makes me so cross to see ability go to waste.'

'Oh, is that so?' countered Lou, with the confidence of a defence barrister who has just discovered a loop-hole the size of Brazil in a key prosecution witness's evidence. 'Well, whilst we're on the subject of "making the best of ourselves" . . .' She walked on her knees over to her handbag, humming, 'Hi ho, hi ho . . .' then got out a leaflet and rustled it at Karen. 'Here. I got you this.'

'What is it?' Karen took it tentatively.

'Accountancy courses. I picked it up for you when I passed the college.'

'Oh, I haven't got time for all that education stuff.' Karen dismissed it immediately.

'One day a week, that's all.'

'When would I do my housework?'

'Sod the housework.'

'And what about the children?'

'They're at school, as you well know.'

'And what do I do in the school holidays?'

'Well, the college will have the same holidays, won't it, twerp? And your mum and dad would have the chil-dren at the farm, you know that.'

'What about the cost?'

'You could go down to Human Resources. They're always harping on about courses so they must have a decent budget for them. If not, this is a big investment in your future — you could do it. It would be a pinch but you could do it. Beg, steal, borrow it — you'd recoup your costs when you qualify.'

'*If. If* I qualify.'

'Come on, Karen! Roger Knutsford is sending stuff down to you that he won't give to his own team. You won't have the slightest problem. You're a natural with numbers and you know it.'

'You're better than I am with numbers. Why don't you go and do it yourself?'

'Because I have no interest in carving out a career in accountancy like you do,' Lou volleyed. 'God may have given me a bit of ability with numbers, but my heart belongs to pastry.'

Karen stamped down on the smile that was forcing itself out of her. 'You've got all this worked out, haven't you?' Lou was so comical sometimes. Really nice and funny and such a warm person. She would have made some kid a fantastic mum.

'Seriously, you would walk this course,' said Lou with conviction. Slyly she tickled Karen's Achilles heel. 'And think of what you could do with a qualified accountant's wage. You could dress your two boys in all the latest designer gear, give them a private education, buy them elocution lessons so they could drive their own office managers insane with jealousy one day . . .'

'Unfair!' said Karen. But Lou had a bulldog hold on her interest now.

'You could work from home, get an au pair in . . .'

'You really are a dreadful manipulative old bag, Lou Winter!'

'No Jaws to contend with and your own coffee-machine coughing away in the background . . .'

'Oh, pur-lease!'

'Or you could be running this place, making Stan's life less of a misery, getting Zoe through a day when she wasn't in tears.'

'OK, OK, I'll read it. *If* . . .'

Lou knew what was coming, but was resigned to it.

'Go on, say it then. Have your moment.'

'You burn that suit.'

Lou laughed. 'You enrol on that course and I'll burn all my suits and replace them with crop-tops and mini-skirts.'

'That I'd just love to see,' said Karen, opening up the college leaflet. 'Now, I'm interested.'

The magazine article had promised that clearing out unwanted items would dramatically improve her mood and energy levels. By four o'clock, Lou wasn't quite convinced that clearing out a couple of drawers had been wholly responsible for her having had such a really good day. It could have been because Nicola wasn't there, which had everyone in a mood jollier than *The Sound of Music* nuns, or because it was a Friday – and no ordinary Friday either, but one preceding a week where she had booked the Monday off to use up some holiday. But she had to admit it had made a weird contribution to her happy mood and sense of real achievement.

There had been a healthy satisfaction in seeing all her paperclips and staples in their organized compartments, dead memos in the bin and the foolscap files in the drawer now emptied of all outdated paperwork. She had transferred all the information scribbled down on scrappy notes into her desk diary then she had wiped down her desktop and her computer screen and raised her eyebrows at the dirt residue on the cloth – shame old Tin Teeth didn't have jurisdiction over the cleaners. And when she came to do some actual accounts work in the afternoon, the tidiness of her workspace somehow made her feel extra efficient.

At the end of the day, she put everything she usually left out on her desk inside her drawer. It looked so fresh it almost made her want to sit at it and start working again.

'Good God,' said Karen, poking her head round Lou's section. 'I need my sunglasses on to look at your desk. Have you sold all your stationery on eBay?'

'Wouldn't know where to start doing that.'

'Too technical for you pensioners, eh? At least you should get a cleaning job here.'

Lou smiled. 'Clean as a flute, if I say so myself.'

'*Whistle*, Lou – *clean as a whistle*.' Karen smiled. Lou should never have been given unsupervised charge of the English language.

'You can put in a good word for me when you're a qualified accountant and running the place.'

'Knickers, darling,' said Karen, breezing out of the door, like the Queen on a day off. 'Have a lovely long weekend and I'll see you – without your burgundy suit, I hope – next Thursday.'

Chapter 4

Phil liked a curry on Friday nights after he had been for his usual workout at the gym, so the kitchen had a warm and exotic air as Lou stirred a selection of her own mixed spices into the pot of chicken which was bubbling away in its garlicky tomato marinade.

Her text alarm went off. It was from her friend Michelle. OFF OUT TO SNARE DAVE. WISH ME LUCK That came as a bit of a surprise to Lou, as the last conversation they had had was that he was a complete dickhead and Michelle wouldn't have him back if he walked across hot coals to deliver armfuls of rare orchids to her. Lou texted back GOOD LUCK! She knew in her heart of hearts though, that Michelle was heading for disappointment and would probably be on the phone tomorrow in tears.

Michelle had fancied rugged builder Dave for ages and had got lucky one night, two months ago, when he was exceedingly drunk. However, since then, he had made polite but hurried exits from her company. Michelle had convinced herself that the more she was in his face, the more he would realize she was the woman for him, and thus pursued him at every turn possible. He was apparently the most gorgeous man she had ever met, although she had said the same about Colin – and Liam and John and Gaz and Jez, two Ians and a Daz. That wasn't counting Death Row Dane she hooked up with on the internet (who was also a 'kind, gentle soul in need of loving from a good Christian woman' and had been falsely accused of slaughtering six gas-station owners). Lou's advice to her that maybe she should be less keen had been interpreted in Michelle's own special way, and now whenever she had managed to seek poor Dave out, she proceeded to ignore him – laughing loudly and flirting outrageously with anyone nearby. It was the sort of thing Lou had done with Andy Batty when she was fourteen. But then Lou was hardly an expert at relationships and, as such, in no place to preach.

The opening notes to *Coronation Street* played out on the portable TV in the corner, signifying the time that Lou called 'wine o'clock'. She always had a glass of red whilst she was cooking, but when she went to get the corkscrew, it was as if she was looking at the cutlery drawer for the first time.

Lordy, this could do with a clear-out, she thought, looking down at the strange gadgets she had bought to experiment with and never used, including the miracle potato peeler abandoned at the first attempt and ancient spatulas she never used since Phil bought her a new set of them as part of his last Christmas present. She opened the drawer beneath it too – the one she used for scraps, string, Sellotape, nail clippers and all the motley collection of familiar bits and pieces which didn't belong anywhere else. She picked out the old green scrunchie stained with ink from a leaky pen, a rusted-up padlock and key which had been there for ever, and a pamphlet for the Indian takeaway in town which had been closed down last Christmas after maggots had been found in the bhajees. She dropped them in the bin and wondered why on earth she hadn't done such a simple and easy thing as that before.

She pulled open the bottom drawer. It needed an extra tug because it was so crammed with cloths made from Phil's old vests and cut-up tea towels. Did she really need so many? The timer buzzer went then, demanding her attention, and Lou closed all the drawers.

'Tomorrow,' she decided.

At the car lot, Phil shook his head in disgust and prepared to be in pain.

Sharon Higgins, the sum of two hundred and fifty pounds.

Whenever he wrote out the wording on these cheques his mind always whirred into calculations that plunged downwards like a big spoon and stirred up the contents of his stomach. Ten years of £200 per month was £24,000, plus another eight years of £250 per month brought the total to £48,000. Not counting the fact that the bitch might ask for another increase at some point. Then there was the possibility that they might carry on in full-time education until they were twenty-two. Or longer, if they were going to be doctors or something extra brainy. It was lukewarm comfort that he'd received no surprise letter from the CSA, who would demand a hell of a lot more money from him. He could only guess that she was on some sort of benefit fiddle. *Forty-eight thousand quid!*

He had only laid eyes on the leech children once,

when he and Lou were shopping one Christmas at Meadowhall five years ago. They had literally bumped into Sharon and her mother and the kids outside the Father Christmas grotto. No words had been exchanged. Sharon had whipped the kids away with a sort of panic that suggested he might immediately bond with them, although nothing could have been further from the truth. To him, they were just two small, ordinary, dark-eyed, blonde-haired kids who he hadn't felt a thing for then, or since. Nothing positive anyway, only resentment that they were probably going to take at least £48,000 out of his bank account – and that wasn't including interest. He groaned.

Two nights he had spent with Sharon. One of which he couldn't remember at all, he was so drunk. But apparently they'd done *it* three times, *which would work out at sixteen thousand pounds per shag!*

He first met her on a night out in Chesterfield a couple of years before Lou came on the scene. Sharon was the clichéd twenty-year-old bimbo barmaid with long legs, massive tits, blonde hair and eyes like big blue sapphires. She was a bit weighty around the hips but that was easily forgiven in view of all her other attributes. He hypnotized her easily by flashing a bit of cash, and three posh meals, a silver bracelet, a four-foot teddy bear and two bottles of champagne later, she was in his bed.

She had said that the champagne was too dry (why didn't the silly cow tell him that in the first place and save him fifty quid then?), and had a Diet Coke instead, so he was lumbered with it, and he wasn't going to waste it at those prices despite the fact that it didn't sit happily with the lager and the vodkas already sloshing around his system. She assured him he had been fantastic though.

The second time, he made sure he was stone cold sober but the sex had been a bit of a let-down, to say the least. She might have had a lovely bod, but she was one of those annoying types who wanted cuddling and hours of foreplay before he could get anywhere near the main target area. The conversation was like wading through treacle in concrete boots. Plus it didn't help when he'd pleasured her and she refused to reciprocate in the same way because apparently she didn't do blow jobs. He was, quite frankly, bored by the morning and decided, over their post-coital Little Chef breakfast, that she had to go. He had a feeling she might have turned out to be too clingy and expensive if he didn't sever it, although he didn't realize just how expensive until she turned up unannounced at the car lot that he managed five months later waddling like a fat duck and supporting her back, not only pregnant with one sprog, but two. They were his apparently, without a doubt. There was a history of twins in the Winter family which added immediate credibility to her claim. But anyway, she had a supporting ultrasound-scan picture for proof.

To his insurmountable relief she said she didn't want him to assume any responsibility, he wouldn't be named on the birth certificate as father and she didn't want him in the twins' life and confusing them with periodic duty visits. Then she undid all her good work by saying she expected him to contribute to some *costs*. She dropped the word into the waters of their conversation like a two-ton pebble and he felt the ripples all the way to the bank. She named her price – £200 per calendar month.

Payment on the dot and she would promise to keep the CSA out of it. It was at that point that he asked her if she was sure he was the father.

She spun on him like a Tasmanian Devil.

'What do you think I am!' she screamed as he tried desperately to shush her up. 'You seduced me with lines like "you've got the most beautiful blue eyes I've ever seen"' (which he remembered saying), 'and "we don't need to bother with condoms because I've had the snip!"' (which he couldn't remember saying at all)!

'You used me,' she spat, 'then when you got what you wanted, you buggered off and didn't want to know me. I believed you so much about the snip, it never crossed my mind I could be pregnant – and when I found out I was, it was too bloody late to abort. So this is all your fault, you lying tosser.'

She might have been thick as pigshit for believing that line, presuming he did use it, but Phil did actually have a stab of guilt at that point, especially when she started crying, although it didn't stop her ranting. If he wanted proof, she had no worries about getting DNA samples and going down the CSA route, she raved. She threatened him with her uncles, her dad, the newspapers, Jerry Springer . . . He pacified her with a coffee and a Kit-Kat and the promise of a taxi home, and made a mental note never to have casual unprotected sex again.

He got a birth announcement seven and a half months after the shag he couldn't remember. It was a perfunctory note with her bank details at the bottom. The babies were premature but doing well, she said. The unsaid message was: *start the payments*. Though he would never admit this to anyone, Phil secretly hoped they were premature enough to slip quietly away and free him of at least eighteen years of cheque sending – plus the stamps (it all mounted up!). He didn't hear anything from her again until the children were ten, when she asked for fifty pounds more per month. He complied because it wasn't worth rocking the boat over, especially as the business was doing so well and the CSA payments would have been sickening. In fact, until he and Lou had bumped into Sharon in Meadowhall that Christmas, he didn't even know that she'd had one of each. Sharon hadn't changed much; she was a bit harder-looking in the face maybe and she'd lost the lard off her arse. He remembered no details about the kids except for their eyes, which were round and brown like a pair of fledgling owls, or should that be cuckoos. Bloody evil cuckoos nesting in his bank account, open-mouthed, demanding and insatiable, bleeding him fucking dry.

The Sharon and kids episode had been a great shake-up for Phil. He'd had a charmed life until then. When Phil and Celia, his sister, were very small, their parents split up and compensated their children by spoiling them rotten with the best things money could buy. The Winter children had grown up with an inflated sense of their own worth, a habit of getting all their own way and an obsession with hard cash. They smoothly entered adulthood under the impression that they were invincible – which was compounded when business success and money gravitated to them. Their confidence helped them attract the attentions of the opposite sex, but Sharon's outsmarting of Phil had knocked his self-belief and shaken him to the core. Since then he had striven for bigger and better deals than anyone else, to prove to himself that he was once again top dog and he clung on for grim death to all he owned. Nor did he ever again get out of his depth when flirting with a woman. Everything that happened to Phil Winter, Sharon Higgins excepted, had to be on Phil Winter's terms. That included pulling the rug from under his wife's feet every so often. That she never failed to climb back on it for him was the biggest indication he had that he was back on the right track.

Just as he had sealed the envelope and thumped a second-class stamp on it, Bradley, his second-in-command, popped his head around the door and grinned, waving a log book.

'Got it!'

'The MG?'

'Yep. Daft old cow took the twelve hundred cash, and young Colin's taking it over to Fat Jack's in the morning.'

'You bloody star! Nice bonus for you this week, cocker.'

Not too nice, though – a hundred quid was fair, especially as he himself had more or less made the deal and it was only up to Bradley to do the formalities and get the dithering owner to stick her signature on the paper-work. Twelve hundred in cash, for a vehicle that would be worth four times that by the time it came back from Fat Jack's body shop. And that wasn't counting the best bit – the personalized number-plate that was worth at least ten grand. The pensioner who sold it thought she was getting a good deal, too. Which she was, since by taking away that 'old banger' of hers he had effectively freed up a big space in her garage and relieved her of the worry of taxing and insuring it. Plus she probably wouldn't live long enough to spend twelve hundred quid anyway.

Maybe there was a God after all. A good old capitalist God Who helped those who helped themselves.

Chapter 5

As Lou snapped on her Marigolds on Saturday morning, the phone rang. It was exactly eight o'clock on a fine March laundry day for anyone with beds to change – i.e. bright and breezy. The frying pan was still hot from Phil's cooked breakfast, the man himself was barely out of the drive and Lou didn't need to check the number display to know it was Michelle.

'Hello, how are you?' said an over-chirpy voice.

'I'm OK. You're up early. You all right?'

'Yes, I'm fine,' although the crescendo of sniffs told otherwise.

'Sure?'

'Nooo . . .'

Michelle was never all right. Well, that wasn't quite true, for she had been quite all right three years ago when they had first met at the Advanced Indian Cuisine course, on which Lou had enrolled to please Phil. This was at a time when she was desperately seeking to make herself more indispensable in his eyes – and in the absence of an Advanced Blow Job course, that was the next best thing.

Lou and Michelle seemed to be the only ones capable of boiling an egg in the class, and the constant exasperations of their easily inflamed Indian tutor with his strange half-Asian, half-broad Barnsley accent, sent them into flurries of giggles which they carried to the college coffee-bar after class. They swapped phone numbers and met outside class a couple of times, and the increasingly frequent calls between their houses were as light and frothy as a six-egg sponge cake. There was a big fat space waiting in Lou's heart for a friend after Deb had gone from her life, and Michelle filled it perfectly. Well, in the beginning anyway. The foundations of their budding friendship had been so strong that Lou hadn't really noticed the first cracks appearing. Cracks that quickly seemed to deepen to fissures, and before long there were Grand Canyons springing up everywhere.

Sometimes Lou was ashamed that she felt so drained by Michelle's constant depressions, especially when she thought back to the giggles and the fun they'd had in their cookery class, before their friendship had been tested by any outside traumas. Then again, she remembered her own neediness in those awful months when Deb was there to listen to her, often in the middle of the night when she couldn't bear the thought of going to sleep and dreaming distorted dreams. When she woke up to find herself in a huge, empty, cold bed. When she felt half-insane: selfish, self-obsessed, unable to see anything past her own pain. When she thought her head would explode from the questions that tormented her. When she grabbed at anything that might fill some of the great hungry hollow inside her. She had clung to Deb like a vine, as Michelle now clung to her. True friends stuck around when the going got tough, so how could Lou even think of turning her back on Michelle in her hour (well, many hours) of need?

'Well, I got to the pub,' snuffled Michelle. 'And Dave was there.'

'Yes?'

'All I said was, "Hello there".'

'I'm listening.'

The dénouement was coming; Lou could feel the sobs crescendo-ing.

'And he turned around in front of everyone,' more tears and sniffs, 'and he said . . . he said . . .'

'Go on,' urged Lou.

'And he said, "Stop stalking me, get a life and piss off, you bunny-boiling bitch!"'

Lou cringed on her side of the phone. What on earth would be the right thing to say to that? She decided, unwisely in retrospect, to respond with: 'Oh well, that's that then.'

'Is that all you can say?' Michelle half-screamed at her.

'I . . . I didn't mean . . . mean it like that,' Lou stuttered. 'I just meant that now you're in no doubt that . . .' *He's not interested*, she was going to say. 'He's not the man for you,' sounded kinder. 'Now you can finally move on.'

'But what if this morning he's thinking, God, I was a bit hard on her last night – and now he feels guilty and really sorry for me?'

'Do you really want a man who feels sorry for you?'

'I don't care, I just want him.'

'Michelle, let him go,' Lou said as warmly and supportively as she could. 'Maybe you should stay totally away from men until you have given yourself some time to get strong. Are you really in the right place to fall in love again?'

'I'm not the sort of person who can survive without a man. Some people aren't. I'm not meant to be alone!' Michelle bleated.

'You don't want just any man though, do you? You're giving out signals that say, "Hello, idiots of the world! Come and get me – I'm vulnerable"!' said Lou.

'Nobody loves me though, Lou. I'm so lonely,' said Michelle, snorting back tears. 'Anyway, men like vulnerable women and no one is more vulnerable than me.'

Oh, how Lou wished she had the courage to say, 'Please grow up, Michelle,' after twelve exasperating loops of the same conversation, but she could no more have said it aloud than lap-danced in front of Prince William.

'Isn't loneliness a little better than being tormented like this?' said Lou eventually.

'How do you know what loneliness is? You're married!' Michelle cried. Which was so funny, Lou almost cried herself.

'Look, Lou,' said Michelle, after another ten minutes of the same self-pitying rant. 'This is silly, wasting money talking on the phone. Why don't you come round for a bit and I'll cook lunch?'

'I can't this morning,' said Lou. 'I've got stuff to do.'

'Like what?' Michelle replied with a little huff.

'Well, domestic things, then I'll be making Phil's lunch,' Lou said, wondering why she was explaining but still doing it all the same.

'Phil, Phil, Phil – all you think about is Phil,' Michelle

snapped, which Lou thought was a bit rich, coming from someone who had just been called 'a bunny-boiling bitch'. But Lou also knew how easy it was to slip into obsession until it felt like normal daily behaviour.

'I'm sorry – that was mean,' said Michelle, dissolving again. 'I'm such a horrible person. No wonder I'm by myself.'

'Don't be silly, you aren't horrible at all and you'll find someone lovely one day very soon, I'm absolutely sure of it.'

'OK, I'll go now then.'

'Listen, I'll ring you later. Go and do something nice. Cheer yourself up by buying something frivolous in town.'

'Yes, I will,' Michelle wobbled.

'Chin up – he wasn't worth it. You can do *so* much better,' said Lou, although she did happen to think the bloke had been remarkably patient in the circumstances. Being stalked by a middle-aged woman in a leather mini-skirt and anaemic-white legs wasn't exactly a popular male fantasy.

'Bye then, Lou,' Michelle snuffled.

'Bye, Mish.'

'See you when you're not so busy dusting.' The phone went down hard at Michelle's end. *Ouch*, thought Lou, although she didn't have time to wallow in guilt, as the phone rang again in a breath.

'I had you on ringback – you've been ages,' huffed her mother.

'I was talking to Michelle.'

'Oh, *her*,' said Renee Casserly disapprovingly. 'When are you going to the supermarket?'

'Well, not this morning anyway, I've got stuff to do.'

'Victorianna wants to know if your email's broken. She's written to you but she's not had a reply yet so she's told me what she wants instead.'

Lou crossed her fingers and lied. 'No, I don't think anything's arrived yet.'

Lou had heard from her sister and it was another Victorianna classic. Her email had said, *Hi there, weather fab here as usual. I'm now a size zero, can you believe, and it feels just great. How's your diet going? Can you help mum to send a couple of things over?* (Diet? Little bitch!) There followed a shopping list longer than a giraffe's leg, and no please or thank you, as usual. Most of the stuff on the list she could get in the States anyway. She just wanted the kudos of getting a 'home-parcel'. Victorianna liked the point of difference her Englishness gave her. She played Lady Muck with Oscar-winning skill.

This was the umpteenth 'hamper' she'd sent for. Lou had received a T-shirt by way of a thanks once that would have fitted around a small infant school. The words 'thank you' weren't actually said. Victorianna would have spontaneously combusted, had she had to say them. Her mum got a framed photo of Victorianna posing formally with live-in lover Edward J.R. Winkelstein the Third and his expensive hairweave, which wasn't dissimilar in texture nor colour from Shredded Wheat. Victorianna looked like a younger, more glamorous version of Renee. He looked the way Lou would expect an Edward J.R. Winkelstein the Third to look.

'Well, let me know when you're going and I'll come with you. She's got a dinner-party soon and wants some

of the stuff for then. I've got the mint chocolate disc
things.'

'OK, Mum. How about Tuesday?'

'Yes, but no later otherwise she won't get the stuff in
time.'

How tragic, thought Lou.

'We could have been and gone in the amount of
time you've been talking to that Michelle. You must
have been on half an hour. And you want to check that
email thing of yours. Your sister said she wrote two days
ago.'

'Well, I do have other things to do besides jump when
Victorianna asks, Mum. And a please and thank you and
a cheque for you wouldn't go amiss. Doesn't she realize
how much you spend on these flaming hampers?' said
Lou. 'You could have taken the stuff over yourself for
how much it's cost you in postage and packing.' *If your
beloved daughter ever had the decency to invite you over there,*
she stopped herself from adding.

'I *am* her mother. I don't expect anything in return,'
said Renee pointedly.

'Yes, but it's not as if she's poor. She's always bragging
about how loaded she and Baron Frankenstein are.
Surely there's room for you in one of the twelve bedrooms?'

'Jealousy won't get you anywhere, Elouise,' said
Renee, totally missing the point.

Lou surrendered. 'Tuesday then Mum, definitely,' she
said with a sigh.

'Don't go to any trouble if you're busy. I can get a bus
down.'

If you can get someone to unnail you from your cross

first, thought Lou. 'It's no trouble, I'll pick you up Tuesday at nine,' she said wearily.

She put the phone down and vowed she wouldn't answer it again. Everyone she seemed to speak to on it made her feel unreasonable and selfish. She badly needed this clutter-clearing session to make her feel as good as she had done cleaning out her drawer at work.

'Right, to business,' she said to herself with a big smile and a clap of the hands, and shook open a large black binliner in preparation.

The spatulas were the first to go, then some tongs that had gone rusty in the dishwasher, then some grimy-looking toothpicks that had wriggled out of their packets. She aimed the old ice-cube tray that she never used into the bag. Used lolly sticks – what the hell had she kept those for? A broken melon-baller, a stencil brush, a once-used rice ball and a blunt vegetable peeler joined them.

Be ruthless, the article had said. *Ask yourself, 'Have I used it in the last six months (seasonal goods – allow one year? Am I likely to ever use it in the future?' If the answer is no, can it go in a recycling bin, or to charity, or to a car-boot sale or be sold on eBay? No? Then throw it away without a second glance.*

Some things she questioned, such as the ancient can-opener that looked more like a medieval instrument of torture. It hadn't worked for years, but had a handy bottle-opener at the top. But as she couldn't remember the last time she had opened a bottle with it, she launched it at the binliner with the accuracy of a seven-foot-tall basketball player.

When the drawer was completely emptied, she

scrubbed it down, washed the utensils she was keeping and slotted the whole thing back. It was crazy how something as simple as throwing out some old rubbish gave her such a sense of accomplishment.

Next she tipped out the odds and sods drawer, suspecting she might be putting very little of it back. A broken mirror, five combs (none of which had a complete set of teeth), some grubby Sellotape, cheap pencils that had needed sharpening for about four years, a yellowing pattern for a cricket jumper she would never knit, an incomplete set of playing cards, sixteen CDs and DVDs given away as freebies with various newspapers, cracker novelty prizes from last Christmas . . . Into the bin went everything but the scissors and a pair of tweezers that she thought she'd lost months ago. She collected all the loose paperclips into an empty matchbox that she also found in the drawer and took them to the desk in the small study next door.

Clear and redeploy as you go, the article dictated. And the newest disciple to the religion of clutter-clearing obeyed.

Next she tackled the cloth drawer, throwing out all the old vest bits and tatty floorcloths because she had just found three new packets of J-cloths that had been hidden under everything. She had just got on her knees for the under-sink cupboard, when the doorbell rang.

She hoped it wasn't Michelle, then felt immediately mean and treacherous. She had really started to enjoy herself and just for once didn't want to talk over and over about what a man *really* means when he tells you to piss off because you're a bunny-boiling bitch. Then again, it could have been the postman. She stole over to the window and sneaked a look. It was a lot worse than Michelle and her mother combined. It was Mr Halloween himself – her brother-in-law, Des.

'Oh knickers,' Lou said, and quickly stepped back against the wall, confident that she hadn't been seen.

Luckily for Lou, there was no detectable sign that she was in – no TV or radio on, and her car was safely hidden away in the garage so, to all intents and purposes, she didn't look at home. She waited in the silence until she was pretty sure he must have gone – then, to her anger and amazement, she heard the key in the lock, the door opening and footsteps in the hall. She really would kill Phil when he got home. He'd obviously done what she told him never to do again, and lent Des his key There was nothing for it now, no place to hide. And even worse, she'd got the old white T-shirt on that made her boobs look massive.

Lou braced herself, burst into the hallway and, hands going to her chest, feigned a big shock to try and get the point across that this really wasn't on, without actually daring to spell it out directly. Lou was just too soft for confrontations these days.

'Oh Des, it's you. What are you doing? You scared the life out of me.'

'I knocked,' said her brother-in-law in his nasal mono-tone drawl, thumbing back to the door, 'but I didn't think you were in. I called in to see Phil at the garage. He lent me a key in case you had gone out shopping.'

'Oh, right then,' said Lou, who really wanted to say other things that weren't so polite. 'So, what is it that you wanted?' she urged after waiting in vain for Des to explain. He had no gene that allowed him to feel awkward in long silences but a big one that gave him the ability to make Lou's flesh creep.

'I just came to borrow Phil's golf clubs.'

'Ok,' said Lou. 'Did he say where they were?'

'No,' said Des helpfully. Not.

Lou took the quick option and rang Phil's mobile, only to get the message that his mobile had not responded and could she please try later.

Oh, how Lou wished she were one of those people who didn't feel obliged to be so polite and could just usher him out to come back when Phil was in. She was forced to go from room to room with Des following behind her in that way of his that had no respect for personal space. Phil said he was just stupidly insensitive, but Lou sometimes wondered if he got kicks from being such an unsettling presence.

Des Winter-Brown arriving at your door could make you think it was Trick or Treat night. Tall, skinny and corpse-pale, his shoulders were rounded from stooping and his hair was lank and black from over-zealous dyeing. He had regular enough features, but there was just something about his strange quietness and the way he would turn up close beside Lou without a clue of his approach that made her dread the mere hint of his visit. She hated the way his eyes dipped to her chest. She disliked his long skinny hands with their long skinny fingers most of all. God knows what his toes must look like.

When Phil had lent him a key to get something from the house on a previous occasion, Lou had been in the shower when she heard activity downstairs. She broke the world record for drying and dressing herself when she heard Des's, 'It's only me!' drifting up the stairs.

'It was just Des, Lou. He only popped in for a hammer, not a screw,' was Phil's laughing response when she countered him about it later.

'Why didn't you tell him to come back later when you'd be in?'

'You're getting this totally out of perspective,' Phil said, failing to see any problem.

'You shouldn't be giving him a key to our house!' said Lou crossly.

'Well, excuse me, but I think you'll find it says *my* name on the deeds,' said Phil then, with a dangerous degree of impatience. 'You're forgetting this house was mine long before you came on the scene.'

'I think *you'll* find that since we're married, it's *ours*,' said Lou, her voice firming as much as Lou's voice could.

'I think *you'll* find if you want to push it, we can carry on with our original plans to split up and find out exactly what the law says about it!'

Lou hadn't argued any more then.

Lou flicked on the cellar light. 'You don't have to come down here, Des. It's a bit dusty,' she said.

'No, I don't mind. I'll help you look,' Des said. He was one step behind her all the way down. She felt like Flanagan with Allen.

God, it's a mess down here, she said to herself. If she hadn't read that damn article her eyes would have just flicked over the stuff they kept down there 'just in case'. Now her new rubbish-alert radar had already spotted twelve things that they would never use again and which should be thrown out.

'Nope. They're not here,' said Lou, returning as

quickly as she could back upstairs, hoping his eyes weren't glued to her bum. That bloody husband of hers! She knew he'd given Des the key so Des would have come and gone by the time Phil came home for lunch. Her husband relished his brother-in-law's company almost as little as Lou did.

There were only the garages left to check, and the loft – but Lou wasn't going up there.

She pressed the electronic opener for the garage door, which slowly slid up and over, and checked there, quickening her step to put a reasonable distance between herself and Freddy Kruger.

Thank God, she thought. Relief washed over her as she saw the clubs poking out from under some dust-sheets, next to the old cracked plastic garden chair and grimy table-set that would never see sunshine again, and the skeleton of a broken umbrella that looked like a long-dead giant spider.

Des left her to heave it out by herself because his mobile was ringing. It played 'Sex Bomb', which was a joke in itself. The 'Funeral March' would have been more appropriate.

'Hello, baby,' he said to the caller.

Yeuch, thought Lou.

'I'm at Phil's . . . Yes, he is but I'm with Lou,'(he winked over and Lou shuddered). 'Golf clubs . . . I'm going to have a cup of tea here then I'll be off . . . Oh, you are? See you in about quarter of an hour then.'

Lou really hoped she hadn't filled in the missing gaps correctly. That would be too horrible to contemplate. She also pretended she hadn't heard the bit about the tea.

'Well, that's great you've got the clubs! Right well, I'll leave you to it, Des. Got to dash — loads to do.'

'Celia thought she'd pop in,' said Des, as he heaved the clubs into his car. 'She's just coming from Meadowhall with the children, so I might as well have a cup of tea and wait here for her.'

'No, get lost, I want to clean my cupboards out. I don't want your wife looking down her nose at me and showing off her new Prada handbag, I don't want your kids prying into my cupboards and I don't want you breathing down my neck every time I flipping turn around!' But whilst Lou screamed this in her head, aloud she said in that damned nice polite way of hers: 'Oh right. Well, I'll put the kettle on then.'

She ripped off her rubber gloves with anger that should have been directed at Phil for putting her in this position, at Des for creeping so close behind her, at Celia for thinking that she could just expect Lou to drop everything and listen to her latest impressive buys and name-dropping 'Jasper Conran' into every other sentence. But most of that anger was directed at herself for letting everyone walk over her with their unthinking, unfeeling hobnail boots.

She wished she'd gone supermarket shopping with her mother now. Even searching for posh pickles in Sainsbury's was infinitely better than a house full of the Winter-Brown family. She stood over the kettle whilst it boiled, only to find that Des had appeared silently and without warning at her back, staring out of the window with some lame comment about the lawn looking good. He would have made a fantastic ghost for some creepy mansion.

Ludicrously, in a kitchen as big as hers, she found

herself in the position of having to squeeze past him to get the milk and the cups. She half-wished he would grope her, just the once, then she could have the excuse to belt him across the chops and ban him from the house. Then she thought of those long fingers actually making contact with her skin and she shivered. Maybe not.

There was a knock on the back door.

'Come in!' shouted Des.

Cheeky swine, thought Lou.

In spilled the twins. Well, Hero spilled in, pretending to be a plane, and Scheherazade waddled in behind with a puppy-fatted belly poking out of a Bratz crop-top. Celia huffed behind them, laden with posh carriers that she could have left in her boot and complaining that Meadowhall was mad. She dumped the bags on the kitchen table and, barely acknowledging Lou, started gabbling on to Des about some shirt she had bought for him that cost more than Lou's car. She had just got it out to show him when Phil put in an early appearance and Lou didn't know whether to kiss him or kill him.

He ignored the withering look his wife gave him because he had had a very profitable morning and was feeling so full of top quality beans that not even the presence of his slimy brother-in-law, his show-off sister and the 2.4 brats, presently nosying in the drawers of the kitchen dresser, could bring him down to earth.

'You are looking at one successful mother,' he beamed, threw his arms wide and sang the first four opening lines to 'Simply the Best' very loudly.

'Mum, I'm hungry,' said Scheherazade, sticking her fingers in her ears.

'I think that tea's probably brewed now,' hinted Des.

'I'm sure Auntie Elouise will get you something if you ask nicely,' said Celia.

'What's for lunch then?' said Phil.

'I'm hungry too,' said Hero.

'Lou, sort us out, love!' said Phil.

And Lou silently got out the bread from the crock, the butter from the fridge, and from her niche in the background, she abandoned her own plans for the day in order to make lunch for a room full of people.

Chapter 6

The next morning, Phil stood in front of the mirror and put on his standard work uniform: a crisp white shirt, a heavy splash of a very expensive after-shave, a blue tie that complemented the shade of his still-sparkly bright-blue eyes, and a perfectly cut navy suit jacket with a subtle *P.M. Autos* stickpin in his buttonhole. He was wearing well and he knew it (well, except for that monk-hole in his hair). He smiled at himself and eighteen thousand pounds' worth of cosmetic dentistry work smiled back at him. It was *simply the best* investment, for a crooked, tortoiseshell smile would have been terminal for business. Women customers, especially, were very judgemental about bad teeth and oral hygiene, Phil had learned. They knew bugger-all about cars and looked for other indicators that they weren't about to be sold a duff. Women *so* wanted to trust you.

Fat Jack had given him the name of his dentist. The latter had been expensive, but worth it, and now Phil had a set of gnashers that weren't so perfect they looked false, but they sent out a clear signal that Philip M. Winter was a man who took a lot of pride in himself and his business.

He had a quick read of the *Sunday World* newspaper whilst he was fortifying himself for the day ahead with one of his wife's extra super-dooper Sunday grills that he would burn off with some serious gymwork later. Then he fired up his Audi TT and set off for the car lot, practising his friendly 'of-course-you-can-trust-me' smile in the rearview mirror.

When Phil had left, Lou had a banana and a yogurt in the conservatory-cum-dining room. She'd hoped to get away from the lingering smell of Phil's bacon in the kitchen that was making her stomach growl in jealous protest. He had gone off to work, whistling like a lottery-winning budgie because of some exciting find in an old widow's garage and his plans to start up another new business with Fat Jack selling exclusive classic cars. She had been eavesdropping yesterday whilst he was showing off to Des about it – anything but listen to Celia's boring commentary about her latest Karen Millen acquisitions, although she hadn't heard the whole story as she'd had to go and locate the children who were poking worryingly around the house, as usual. She was pretty sure Celia would have something to say if Lou went into *her* bedroom and started rooting nosily through *her* drawers.

Phil hadn't pestered her to make love that morning, which he sometimes did on a Sunday. Luckily for him, too, because she was still really angry about the Des-and-key incident. Phil, however, didn't notice. The matter was closed as far as he was concerned. Well, the matter had never really been opened as far as Phil was concerned.

Lou cleared away the breakfast things then locked all

the doors – and bolted them, just in case – then she excitedly set to work on the jobs she had been going to do yesterday, before she was so rudely interrupted.

The phone rang as she was snapping open some bin-bags. The caller display announced that it was Michelle. Lou's hand twitched dutifully towards the receiver, but she was strict with herself. Today was her day, just for once. Michelle left a brief message to say thanks for her ear yesterday and that she was feeling much brighter. Michelle's brighter patches never tended to last very long, though, Lou reflected. Shorter than a bright patch in a British summertime.

The under-sink cupboard was disappointingly full of currently useful bottles and tins, and there was nothing but some dried-up shoe polish to get rid of, but the remainder of Lou's kitchen cupboards more than made up for it. She hadn't realized just how many forgotten cans and packets lurked there – pickled onions on the top shelf that had a best-before date of eight months ago, jars of herbs and spices well past their use-by time, a can of cashew nuts so old that the shop it came from had been knocked down and replaced by a gym. She also found twelve tins of chopped tomatoes – admittedly all but one still in date. There were never-to-be-used bulk supplies of Trimslim milk shakes, which had tasted like melted-down Play-Doh, and cardboardy Trimslim biscuits. As for the quantity of Trimslim soups . . . in tempting flavours such as 'cheese and swede' and 'exotic leek'! There were glasses that Phil had got free with his petrol years ago, a beer-making kit which he had dabbled with once, novelty cruets, a fondue set, an egg scrambler and a never-opened doughnut-maker that Phil had bought her last birthday. Not to mention the Thrush Kit, as Deb used to call it – an unused yogurt-making machine and another one of her husband's 'romantic' presents. She couldn't really throw away something he had bought her, could she? She referred to the article for guidance. It said that one had to beware of sentimentality, but cowardy custards who had serious misgivings about items could put them in a bag, date it and label it to be looked through in another six months' time. If it hadn't been used it by then, then chances were it never would and should be removed from the house.

Lou knew she had no use for these things and decided to be a hard-liner. Getting out a huge green garden refuse bag, she wrote *Heart Foundation* on it and put the electrical contraptions in there. After her dad died, all of her charity donations had gone to them. Well, them and the Barnsley Dogs Home.

The kitchen, including the under-stair cupboard, yielded a startling eight full rubbish bags, plus the big green bag which was now full and ready for the charity shop.

She rang Phil at work. 'Where's the nearest dump?' she asked.

'What on earth do you want to go there for?'

'I'm clearing out the cupboards.'

'How much stuff is there, for crying out loud?'

'Too much for the wheelie-bin to cope with.'

'Go down Sheffield Hill, past the *Miner's Arms* and as you get near the bottom, look out for a sign on your left saying something like *waste recycling*,' he said.

Lou heaved five big bags of rubbish into her car boot and set off, following Phil's verbal directions. The last time she had been to a dump, admittedly years ago, had been straightforward – drive in, dump, drive off. It appeared times had changed, though, for facing her now were different containers with large signage: *household, garden, plastic, glass, electrical.*

'Bugger!' she said. She had been planning to just throw everything in one place but there was a fierce-looking commandant on duty presently having a stand-up row with a bloke who was trying to put bub-blewrap in with the cardboard. It was quite a faff in the end, but eventually Lou's rubbish was sorted and dis-tributed to the relevant places and so she set off back home for the second load. She had overstuffed the bags and one of them split as she was hoisting it into the boot, allowing a big jar of old faded beetroot to smash and splash on the drive. There had to be an easier way than this, she thought. Huffing, she cleared up the beetroot, unknotted all the bags, pulled all the cardboard out, then set off back to the dump in a car that smelled hideously of vinegar. She got there just in time to see the gates close in front of her.

Oh, gr-eat, said Lou to herself. *What do I do now?*

The answer to that question was literally just around the corner for, as she was waiting for the traffic-lights to turn green at the junction, there to her right was a bright yellow skip full of planks of wood and carpets and a huge plastic plant that was more Triffid than the Japanese Fig it purported to be. There was a name and number sten-cilled on the side, which she quickly jotted down on her hand. *Tom Broom.* It had a nice purging sound to it.

Chapter 7

Tuesday had all the promise of being a day-to-get-to-the-end-of-as-quickly-as-possible. Not only did Lou have the prospect of trailing after her mother in the supermarket, but someone from HR at work had asked if she could spare them an extra afternoon because one of the other job-share accounts women was off with some dreaded lurgy and the other had been signed off with stress. Cold, windy and rainy, it was the sort of day on which you switched off the alarm, turned over and went straight back to sleep – if you didn't have a pesky conscience.

But her first job of the day would be to order a skip. Something about the name 'Tom Broom' made her smile; there was a solid, honest quality to it. Then again, with her track record for judging personalities, Tom Broom was most likely a cross-dressing serial killer with a particular hatred of short, auburn-haired women with Yorkshire accents.

Nevertheless, she rang his number and a deep-voiced man answered the phone to take down her details. She hadn't a clue skips came in different sizes until he asked her if she wanted a two-, three-, four- or five-ton one.

Two-ton sounded huge and plenty big enough to take a few bin bags, surely. So she ordered a mini-skip to be delivered the following Tuesday. Payment on delivery – £70. Blimey, it was true then. Where there was muck there *was* brass!

She suspected her mother might need something the same size to box up all the things she bought for Victorianna's 'hamper from home'.

'I thought American supermarkets were teeming with goods!' said Lou, as Renee picked up a tin of anchovies in some farty oil.

'Oh Elouise,' was all her mother said, in a very fatigued tone, and added some special offer basic toilet rolls to her trolley.

'She'll not want those, surely,' said Lou. 'She'll want super-dooper-softy-wofty-six-ply-woodland-scented—'

'They're for me,' Renee interrupted.

Her mother's shopping items were nearly all 'super-value' items. Renee could quite easily afford the branded goods for herself but chose not to. She preferred to raise the crucifix of her being-on-a-pension-status against the demon of luxury spending at every available opportunity, even though she was comfortably off and would be forever, at the rate she spent money. Unless she went mad, ran off to Las Vegas for a year and blew all her savings on Cristal champagne and high-class gigolos. But that was hardly likely. As with many of that generation, raised in frugal, waste-not environments, Renee was terrified of running out of money – although she never quibbled about what she paid for those stupid hampers that her youngest daughter asked for, Lou noted.

As they were wheeling their trolleys out of the supermarket door, Lou stopped herself just in time from
suggesting they go and grab a pot of tea and a big cream
cake in the café. She had long since been aware that the
world was divided into those who saw food only as a
necessary fuel and those who relished it with passion and
pleasure. Renee and Victorianna were of the former
group. Renee would have sooner had a triple-heart
bypass without anaesthetic on the booze aisle floor than
partake of a custard slice. How sad that some people
would never get turned on from watching Marco Pierre
White going berserk with olive oil, Lou often thought.
So, instead of cake-scoffing, she dropped her mother off
at her house to go and bubblewrap all her jars and boxes
and put them in an enormously heavy box for
Victorianna and Wee Willie Winkie whilst Lou went
home to butter a quick sandwich and then go off for a
thrilling afternoon in the Accounts department at work.
Not.

Nicola was in a foul mood because she was under stress
with half her staff being off ill. She was out of her depth
running that department and she knew it, and so her
defence mechanisms were permanently set to projecting
her inadequacies onto other people – one thing she *could*
manage with great skill.

Nicola Pawson had acquired, through a mixture of
flattery and flirting and goodness knows what other
means, friends in high places in the company and basked
luxuriously in her association with Rogering Roger
Knutsford. She was a master in the art of 'impression
management'. Anyone with the slightest potential to be

useful to her found her to be a smart, fresh-faced young woman with a prettily symmetrical ready smile (close-lipped, obviously; open-lipped and they'd have run a mile). They could never have guessed at the hollowness that lay behind her pale eyes.

People were either wary of her or sucked up to her – both of which inflated the sense of her own power. A power that masked her own inabilities and a history of being one of life's inadequates. It wasn't nurture that had made her so – Nicola Pawson was simply born without the emotional repertoire to enjoy connections with other people. From her earliest days at school, all that had really mattered to her was playing the game of controlling others. She struck out at those less able than herself, trained her inner laser on other people's weaknesses, tried to bring down anyone popular or likeable. But yet she secretly envied those with values she was too weak to adopt. By the time she had reached adult life, her manipulative skills had reached a near-genius level of sophistication and her greatest pleasure was creating fear and discord. She was, in psychiatric terminology, a borderline psychopathic bully. And in general conversational parlance – a right nasty little cow.

But two people stopped Nicola from reigning supreme in her present position. The first was Karen, who was more amused by her than anything. Especially that put-on exaggerated accent of hers that would have made the Queen sound like a navvy. Karen unashamedly relished the fact that Nicola so obviously envied her private education, beautifully polished vowels and her double-barrelled surname. The second – Lou

Winter – would have been totally gobsmacked to learn
that she got to Nicola so much.

Lou and Karen were true professionals; always punc-
tual, always smart, and they knew their financial onions.
They were warm and well-liked and respected, and
people in the company affectionately labelled them
'Little and Large in Accounts', bracketing them together
as a double act. Neither woman gave Nicola a crack to
seep her poison into, since showing how much they
detested 'Metal Nicky' would only have given her something to kick against – and one thing Lou had learned
from Phil was how empowering a show of indifference –
real, or assumed – could be. Lou wore the indifference
like a suit of armour at work and could never have begun
to imagine the chaos that it set off in Nicola's head.

But simpler, gentler people like Zoe and Stan were
ready meals for sharks like Nicola. She knew they would
never report her for her treatment of them. They would
never make a fuss, knowing that such action would only
make things worse for them and bring them to Roger
Knutsford's attention in the worst kind of way. Plus
Nicola saw to it that anything they might have to report
would sound very petty and totally unreasonable. She
had a clever way of putting her own warp on things so
that her story and the opposing one were almost alike,
but her version was infinitely more articulate and believ-
able. *But Stan is always late, you can ask anyone in the
department. I have asked him on a few occasions if he would be
happier going part-time, as I think it would be so much better
for his health, but he's always adamantly refused.* Even Stan's
wife Emily had looked a little sceptical on occasion
when he'd gone home and offloaded his daily woes. She,

like most other people, couldn't understand why anyone would go out of their way to torment another living creature just because they could. And Stan knew that if he couldn't make a loving partner believe him 100 per cent, he wasn't going to have a lot of success with the far more impersonal HR department.

And boy, was Nicola in the mood for taking her frustrations out on someone that day! Rogering Roger was taking one of the newly appointed designers out for a 'business lunch.' Her name was Jo MacLean and she was a serious contender for position of Teacher's Pet. Tall and willowy with perfect red lips, her flawless complexion, long swishy brown hair and vulnerable doe eyes poked annoyingly at those dark insecure places within Nicola. It was no coincidence that Zoe, with her own flawless complexion and long dark hair, was first in line for Nicola's vented spleen.

Nicola leaned over Zoe's desk and, with a disarming closed-mouth smile, whispered, 'Can I have a word?'

'Yeah, course,' said Zoe, already nervous at Nicola's tone, which didn't exactly intimate that she was going to be giving her an 18 per cent pay rise.

'Roger isn't happy,' said Nicola. Three words only, yet she managed to imbue them with a menace that threw Zoe immediately into a state of distress.

'What do you mean?'

'Isn't it obvious?'

Yes, it appeared to be obvious. There was only one interpretation Zoe could think of for her words. She'd just bought a car and was saving up for a house with her boyfriend. She couldn't afford to lose her job.

'With me? Why? What have I done?'

'I haven't got time to talk now. Later,' said Nicola.

'Nicola, please, what do you mean? You can't just say that and then leave it.'

'I said not now,' said Nicola, and swept off leaving Zoe close to tears. She might have been young, but she knew that big companies could get rid of anyone if they felt like it. And how good would that look on her CV, that she'd been sacked from her last position? Zoe came from a hardworking family with good, strong values. Clean, scrupulous fighters were always hampered in such battles by their morals.

Stan saw Nicola edge close to his desk and the hairs on the back of his neck sprang up. He couldn't understand why she made him feel like this. He was an older, working man – a grandfather, for goodness sake – and she was a mere girl by comparison. But logic didn't come into it. Nicola effectively held his life in her hands and he knew she knew that. He couldn't afford to leave this job before his sixty-fifth birthday because it would affect his pension and, ergo, his future security. It never crossed Stan's mind that this was a bullying campaign. He thought bullying ended at the school gates.

'Can I have a look at what you're doing, Stan?' she said. Her voice was quiet, with a girlish lilt that belied her intentions.

'Here you go.'

She made him feel like a five year old in front of the headmistress. His work had always been immaculate, but Nicola made him doubt his abilities and once or twice recently, he'd checked his figures to find he really had made mistakes.

'Ooh, I don't think that's quite right, do you? How can an eight and a six make sixteen?'

'Let me see that.'

She handed back the print-out with a long sigh. Dammit – he had made an error. Was it her micro-managing that was stressing him out enough to make mistakes, or was it his mistakes that were making her micro-manage him? He didn't know any more. He just wanted out of this bloody place before it killed him. He was snapping at Emily because he couldn't relax when he eventually did get home. His mind was already preparing for the bus being late the next day and another confrontation with his boss – another day of being made to feel like a foolish child. But even if he did report her, what could he say? *I'm sure she taps her watch when I go to the toilet?*

'Roger's concerned . . .' she said, trailing dramatically off.

'What about? Me?'

Nicola leaned in conspiratorially. 'I know you're just killing time until your retirement . . .'

'Excuse me, but I'm not—'

'Don't raise your voice, Stan. I'm trying to help.'

'Sorry.' *Was* I raising my voice? he asked himself.

'As I was saying, Roger's been picking up on all the mistakes.' She said *all* as if he were churning out one every thirty seconds. 'He's concerned. I'd be careful.'

She drifted off back to her desk leaving him with an increased heart-rate. The effect made her feel good, in control. It was fun and it distracted her from thinking about what crap Roger Knutsford was spouting to Miss Jo 'Long Legs' MacLean.

Neither Zoe nor Stan looked up when Lou came in. Their heads were down, concentrating hard on the work they were doing – checking everything time and time again and then fretting that the checking was taking up too much time.

Lou felt so sorry for them. She would have bet the contents of her purse that Nicola had been on their backs again. It wasn't fair and she wished she could do something. But standing up for her colleagues might only make things worse. Of course, if this had been school, Lou would have had Nicola by the scruff of the neck like she'd had her then nemesis – Shirley Hamster – on numerous occasions for bullying the younger kids. But that Lou was long gone. This Lou sat at her desk and got on with her work quietly and expediently, and didn't rail against the social order.

She couldn't have known that some primitive sense in Nicola was alert to the dormant strength which still lay within her. The irony was that Lou felt the weakest of them all, especially at the moment. Never had her name been so apt. Inside, she felt as cold and dead as Winter itself.

Chapter 8

The night before the skip arrived, Lou totted up ten bin-liners-full of throwaways, not counting an old carpet that she had had to cut up into strips with a Stanley knife. She had asked Phil to help her lift it downstairs in one piece but he had looked at her in total horror and said, 'I'm not knackering up my back lifting that thing. Why don't you just leave it where it is for now?'

Lou found that was no longer an option. Her initial plan might have been merely to clear out a few drawers and cupboards, but knowing there was so much space taken up by the useless and the broken had seriously begun to irritate her and, once she had started, she found she couldn't stop. The clear areas just showed up the cluttered areas more by comparison. How could she have lived for so long with so much rubbish and not seen it? Plus she hadn't had as much enjoyment from getting her teeth into something since she and Deb had planned *Casa Nostra*, despite the fact that all her nails were broken.

'Well, if that is how you want to spend your leisure time, Lou, you go right ahead,' said Phil, watching her heave bulging bin-bags downstairs. 'But all I want to do when I get home from a hard day's work is sit down, have my tea and read the paper.' He omitted to mention that he had spent most of that day sitting down, drinking tea and reading the paper.

The skip wagon reversed down her drive at nine o'clock the next morning and out of the cabin jumped a man and a shire horse. Well, he was certainly as big as a shire horse anyway and he stole Lou's heart instantly – ran away with it and refused to give it back.

The dog bounced over to her, sensing that in her he would have a warm reception, and dropped into the play position, his great furry head on his paws, his huge dark eyes looking up pleadingly at her for attention.

'Clooney, you big tart, come back here!' said the skip man gruffly.

Lou bent and ruffled the huge German Shepherd's head and when he opened his mouth to pant, it looked as if he was smiling.

'Clooney, what a great name,' said Lou, taking in the skip man for the first time. He was a wardrobe in overalls with dark hair that flopped at the front over a pair of very smiley bright grey eyes. He wasn't her type, though. Lou had never really gone for big men. It was too impractical for a five-foot-one woman to smooch with anyone over five foot seven on a dance floor without her neck being half-broken, and without them looking like a pair of total prats. Marco Pierre White excepted, Lou's tastes had always been for the smoother, average-heighted blokes. That said, Lou's inner checklists, for some unknown reason, were telling her that this was a man who was making her pupils dilate.

'He gets all the women. I wish I had his knack,' said

the man, unloosening the giant hooks on the skip.

'Shall I pay you by cheque or cash?' asked Lou as Clooney nosed her hand for a stroke.

'Either's fine,' said Skipman. 'But, let's say, cash is always slightly better.'

'No worries,' said Lou, who guessed he would say as much and had the money ready in her jeans pocket. 'Although these days with all the fake fivers about, I wonder!' she laughed.

They both instinctively looked down at the money she was holding out towards him.

'Not that these are fake,' she said quickly. 'I didn't mean . . . They're all real . . . I think anyway. I wouldn't know how to check. Oh, help!'

Skipman threw back his head and let loose a deep, gravelly laugh.

'I'd set the dog on you if they were, but I don't think he'd be much of a threat.'

Clooney was growling softly, looking very much as if he were trying to scratch an itch on his nose and not quite hitting the spot. He overbalanced with the effort, looking clumsily adorable.

'Give us a call when you've filled it,' he said. 'Level to the top, please – no piling on.'

'Saturday would be great,' said Lou without hesitation.

'Sure?' asked Skipman, helping Clooney out with a good old scratch.

'I'll have it filled by then,' said Lou decisively. 'And can you deliver another one as soon as you can after that, please?'

'I can deliver it Sunday, if you want. I'm a seven-day-a-week man!'

'Perfect.'

'You're going to be a busy lady, I see, filling my skips in between printing out some more fake fivers to pay me with.'

My skips. So this must be Tom Broom himself then. He had a very curvy smile. Nice teeth. Natural.

Lou laughed. 'Precisely. Not enough hours in the day for us forgers.'

'Well, see you Saturday then.' He hoisted Clooney into the cab and held up his hand in a masculine wave.

But Lou was already at work, hurling black binliners into the mini-skip and looking brightly forward to a whole afternoon of filling it with many more.

Chapter 9

Two days later, the small Accounts department surprised Lou with a big fresh cream cake bearing the number 100 in wax candle numbers accompanied by a rendition of the 'Happy birthday to you, you were born in a zoo' version of the song.

'Very funny,' laughed Lou and divided the cake between them. Nicola wasn't there. She had taken an extended lunchbreak to go shopping for Sheffield's best designer gear. She and Celia would have got on like a house on fire.

Karen gave her two envelopes, one of which was her card, which had *must not be read until tomorrow* written all over it, but the other she ordered Lou to open up there and then.

'This is to say Happy Birthday from us all and to thank you for your support in our continuing fight against evil,' said Karen.

'Not a letter bomb, is it?' asked Lou tentatively.

'Do you think if we had a letter bomb we would have given it to you and not *her*?' said Zoe.

It wasn't a letter bomb. It was a voucher for a colour

and restyle at Anthony Fawkes, the trendiest hair salon in Barnsley.

'We've fixed it for ten o'clock tomorrow. If you can't make it, ring them now and say so, but it's with Carlo,' said Karen. 'He's an Italian. A drop-dead gorgeous Italian, as well. I couldn't resist booking him.'

Karen knew all about Lou's penchant for things Italian. A sexy Latino man running his fingers through her colleague's hair would give her the best start to her day.

'I'll be there, I'm not doing anything else,' said Lou. 'And can I just say, that's a fantastic present. Thanks, guys. I'm touched.'

'We all wanted to get you something special,' said Karen, without any of her customary joking.

Lou looked at the smiling crescent of people surrounding her and she suddenly felt very emotional, which led to Zoe having to give Lou one of her tissues for once, and Karen put her arm around her and gave her a big sisterly squeeze. She thought that Lou was worth a lot more than a hairdo and, if ever her numbers came up on the lottery, Lou was near the top of her list of 'people to treat big time'. She would force her friend on a grand tour of Italy so she could visit all those wonderful things and places she dreamed of: the Sistine Chapel and the Trevi Fountain in Rome, the Ponte Vecchio in Florence, the Grand Canal of Venice, the Amalfi coastline, the streets of Sorrento, the ruins of Pompeii . . . Lou's eyes would light up when they talked of things Italian, and yet the only place she ever seemed to holiday was Benidorm.

Karen had the distinct impression that something was

very wrong in Lou's world, despite her jolly exterior. Karen was a very intuitive woman and she would have put money on the fact that at some point or other, Lou's husband had had an affair, and Lou had never really got over it. Amazing how women could sniff another woman's knobhead from a mile off, but alas, the gift rarely extended to their own.

'I'm having my hair done tomorrow,' said Lou to Phil that night over their customary Friday curry. He grinned.

'That's good, because I've got a little birthday surprise for you myself.'

'What?'

'Nope, not telling!'

'Oh come on, you can't not tell me. Tell me!'

'Nope,' he teased. 'It wouldn't be a surprise if I told you, would it?'

'Oh please, please, please, please, please.'

'Well, all I'm saying is, be ready for half-past seven in your gladrags and don't have anything to eat before.'

Lou gave a small gasp. 'Are we going out?' She wanted to make doubly sure after last year, when she had got all dolled up only for Phil to turn up with a giant pizza.

'Might be,' said Phil. Lou's face lit up like November the fifth.

It takes so little to please her, thought Phil. Half of him smiled at that; half of him thought that sometimes it was like being married to a puppet. Therein lay the irony of having a surrendered wife.

The next morning, Phil gave her a big sloppy card and a

big sloppy kiss and tapped his nose on the way out of the door.

'Remember what I told you. Seven-thirty!' he said to his wife, who was beaming like a little child who was first in the Santa's grotto queue.

Lou had a birthday call from her mother, who reminded her of the arranged Sunday lunch as the usual birthday treat.

'I've sent your card – have you got it?' she said. 'I didn't post your present; it's here waiting for you. It wasn't cheap so I didn't want to risk it getting lost.'

'Oh Mum,' said Lou. 'Yes, the card came yesterday and yes, it's lovely, and you didn't have to buy me anything.'

There were quite a few cards to open from work colleagues and her old friend Anna and her old Auntie Peggy in Cork who had put ten euros in it. Victorianna sent an ecard, on time for once. It had some American critter she could never remember the name of, getting a picnic out of a hamper. Gentle hint or what? There was a beautiful and expensive 'best friend' card from Michelle with a flowing verse and a *Sorry I've been such a miserable cow, I really will make it up to you*, handwritten message. Lou smiled at the intricate little flower cartoons Michelle had drawn on the inside. It must have taken her ages to do! If Lou could have had one birthday wish granted it would be that Mish would sort herself out and once again be that nice, smiley, considerate person she had met in the cookery class. She was still in there somewhere, Lou was convinced of it.

There was nothing from Deb, although Lou didn't really think there would be. Really.

★

Lou got dressed and walked down into town. It was a dry day, devoid of April showers and full of the promise of bright sunshine, both outside in the sky and inside in her spirit. The hard physical graft of yesterday had left her tired and she slept a deep healthy restful sleep. This morning she felt energized and raring to go.

The hair salon was very white and very chrome and Lou felt immediately stupid by pushing the pull door, then pulling the other push door, before finally and correctly pulling the pull door and entering.

The receptionist was a very tall girl, spaghetti-thin with hips that a child would never get through in a million years. She smiled in a far friendlier way than Lou would have expected in such a pricey establishment and said, 'Do you know, everyone does that. I don't know why they don't get doors that swing both ways.'

She gowned Lou up and led her to a chair which was pumped up so her legs dangled, and then the Angel Gabriel appeared behind her and started weaving his hands into her hair.

'Hi, I'm Carlo,' said a voice rich in bolognese sauce.

He was front cover magazine-stunning with dark colouring, a pencil-line of black beard and spiky, platinum hair that shouldn't have worked, but did to great effect. He had lips that were pink and looked very soft and kissable. To boys or girls or both, she couldn't tell. Maybe he swung both ways like the doors should have done. He was far too young to fancy, but she could easily appreciate his gorgeousness. For a split second she imagined that she was his mother. What would that feel like? To look at a boy as beautiful as this and know he was your son? It threw her a little because she hadn't had thoughts like that for a long time.

'So, what are we doing for you today?'

Sending me to sleep if you carry on doing that much longer, thought Lou, as he played with her hair and studied her in the mirror.

'I don't know, to be honest. What do you think? I've had this style – well, forever . . .'

Carlo stared at her reflection in the mirror, and then obviously inspired, he reached for a colour chart. After a lot of page-turning his eyes locked on a loop of dyed hair.

'What do you think?' he said.

Lou gulped.

'Trust me,' said the Italian Angel Gabriel.

Two hours later, Lou was watching as Carlo snipped at her hair in much the same wildly extravagant way that she used to when playing hairdressers with her dolls. Lou watched him wide-eyed with horror in the mirror, remembering all too well those end results. Her mother went nuts at the sight of Bald Tiny Tears.

'Relax!' said Carlo. 'You will look fan-tas-tico!'

Her eyes strayed to the detached snippings by the base of the chair. Clumped up together they looked like Dougal from *The Magic Roundabout*.

Carlo spun her around so she couldn't see the finishing touches he was making. He fluffed, he sprayed, and when he twisted her back to face the mirror, Lou's eyes widened like a startled owl's. Then her lips curved into a smile.

'I can't believe it. You've made my hair actually look longer!'

'It was too heavy before – you really needed those layers and a good cut. I know you wanted to keep your length but it was pretty scraggy for the bottom four inches. And it's much lighter up top so you can achieve some volume now. What do you think of the colour? Not so frightening now it's dry, huh?'

Lou examined the effect of the chilli-pepper orange heavily highlighting the front of her auburn waves, with just delicate touches of it at the sides. She felt trendier and looked younger than she had done in years. Why on earth had she ever stopped having her hair done? She used to love the feeling that was skipping around inside her now, that only a hairdresser could give.

'I absolutely love it!' said Lou.

'It brings out the colour of your eyes,' drawled Carlo sexily. 'My, they're so green. *Mamma mia!*'

Sod being his mother, now she wanted to snog him. That voice! He could have been reciting a shopping list and she would have started dribbling. She wanted to dip some focaccia in him and eat him all up.

Her hair was heavily sliced at the front and flicked round onto her face, with choppy layers at the back. He'd even managed to sex up her blunt fringe. It made her want to go out and buy a new outfit. Sod it, it was her birthday – she *would* go out and buy a new outfit.

She handed over her gift voucher to the reception desk and gave Carlo a heavy tip. The fact that they didn't try to coerce her into buying a cabinet full of essential hair products that she would have caved in and bought, knowing she would probably never use them, made her doubly keen to book a follow-up appointment. Obviously with Carlo.

Lou had a pleasant mosey around town then and bought a very brave orange top and some bronzy copper jewellery, and a thrilling glossy lipstick that was guaranteed to stay on through dinner, drinks and a world war. It was a bright day but nippy, and so the treat of a hot coffee and a scone in the Edwardian Tea Rooms seemed very much in order. The scone was the size of a basketball and she slathered butter thickly on slices of it. That would keep her going until her romantic meal for two. Actually, it would probably keep her going until next January. She felt a buzz of excitement vibrate down her veins at the thought of the evening to come. It had been so long since she had gone out with Phil; she was looking forward to the ritual of dressing up in her new clothes and the delicious anticipation of the eating venue. *Please make him take me to an Italian*, she dared to ask the cosmos.

The skip was still there when she got home, but by the time the kettle had boiled there was the beep-beep-beep of something very large reversing into the drive.

'Hi there,' called Lou, emerging from the front door as Tom Broom jumped down from the cab and started unrolling a huge net. She looked around the truck. 'No dog?'

'He's in the cabin. He can be a bit of a pest. Not everyone likes seeing a hulking great beast bounding towards them. Or the dog either,' he joked.

'Oh.' She couldn't hide her disappointment.

'What? You want him out?'

'Well, if it's no trouble,' said Lou.

'No trouble to me,' said Tom and seconds later,

Clooney was bounding towards Lou with his tail wagging a force-twelve draught.

'Shall we see if we can get you a biscuit?' said Lou.

Clooney woofed and turned excited circles.

'He can understand "biscuit", just to warn you,' said Tom with a lazy grin, and as he hooked up the skip, Lou went into the kitchen, closely followed by Clooney, where she gave him some of the dog biscuits she had just bought for him that morning in the pet shop.

She so missed having a dog. They'd had a German Shepherd cross called Murphy at home. Her dad had been dead only weeks when Murphy's back legs collapsed. She carried him to the vet's down the road where they kindly told her she had to let him go and she cuddled her dog whilst they gently put him to sleep, then she howled like a banshee when they took him away in a blanket. She scattered his ashes in the same place where they'd scattered her dad's and prayed that they would find each other in heaven. She dreamed of them together a lot: walking in the park, her dad throwing a tennis ball and Murphy chasing after it over the early-morning grass.

Phil was dreadfully allergic to all animals with fur, so a 'proper' pet was out of the question.

'Still want another skip tomorrow?' Tom Broom enquired, helping Clooney back up into the truck.

'Yes, please,' said Lou.

'About ten o'clock? Or will you still be in bed then?'

'Don't worry, I'll be up.'

'How's the forgery business? Still making the fake fivers?'

'It's going very well, thank you,' she said, feeling her cheeks warm up.

Tom did that big deep laugh again. It was a lovely sound, borderline-boom, like a big friendly giant in a panto. She noticed the wrinkles that gathered around his eyes, then quickly reprimanded herself; she had no business looking at wrinkles gathering around other men's eyes. She was a married woman, and her husband was taking her out tonight. Was this new hair-do of hers turning her into a sex maniac, eyeing up two different men in the space of a couple of hours? Both sharing that sexy Mediterranean look.

'Nice colour, by the way.'

'Sorry?'

'Hair. You've have it done since last time. Looks nice. It suits you.'

Then Tom Broom climbed up into the driver's seat and was gone before Lou could register that, before today, she couldn't remember the last time a man had complimented her appearance.

Chapter 10

A long soak in a deep bath would have been a nice birthday treat, but the less said about that the better. Lou gave her quarter-finished building site of a luxury bathroom a hard, frustrated look, shook her head and went into the ensuite for a shower before she could get so wound up that she risked spoiling what had been, so far, a lovely day. Bloody Keith Featherstone! A name to make a saint swear.

Phil refused to get involved in Lou's dispute with the builder. She'd wanted the fancy bathroom so she could sort it out. He reckoned she should cut loose from the man and organize another firm – it wasn't as if she'd paid Featherstone in advance or anything stupid like that. Phil was quite happy with the shower in their large ensuite anyway. He couldn't see the point of wasting time lying about in water full of the filth you'd just soaked off. He told Lou to use her feminine charms. Builders always responded to a bit of eye-fluttering and a nice cleavage. Well, lazy useless unreliable bloody Keith Featherstone hadn't.

Lou had a blissful half-hour after her shower reading a

Midnight Moon romance, a big cup of coffee in her hand, and nibbling on a couple of the Godiva truffles that had been put through the letter box, courtesy of Des and Celia Winter-Brown. (That Lou had missed their visit was a big fat added bonus to the day.) No ordinary 'Brown' surname for Celia – she had insisted they both adopt a double-barrel after their wedding vows. How she and Deb had laughed at Celia's fancy signature with its cascading loops, like Elizabeth I did on her death warrants. God, she so wanted to pick up that phone now and dial Deb's number.

Lou took a lovely long time getting ready for her birthday surprise. She wondered what sort of restaurant Phil was taking her to. Anything would do, but an Italian really would just add the cherry onto today's cake. There was little to beat the relaxed romantic ambience of an Italian bistro.

When Phil arrived home at half-past six, he had a strange sneezing fit in the kitchen that nearly made him drop the bags he was carrying.

'Have there been any animals in here, Lou?' he said.

'Don't be silly,' said Lou. *Whoops.*

'I have presents, I have champagne,' he announced. Champagne was pushing it a bit. It was very brutal Cava relabelled *Vintage P.M Autos*. He would give a bottle to every new owner of a Phil Winter car, along with a *P.M. Autos* keyring and a pen. After a glass, who could tell it from the proper stuff anyway?

He had two presents for Lou, one in a white plastic carrier and the other in a gold gift bag.

'Here you go, babe. You know I'm no good at wrapping.'

Well, blokes weren't, were they, agreed Lou silently, not that it mattered to her. She opened the white bag to find another of his amazing electrical appliance purchases.

'Oh, an omelette-maker! Great – thanks, love,' she said, overdoing the enthusiasm a tad to override the guilt she felt because she had already earmarked it for the charity bag. Phil seemed very keen for her to open the other present. Smiling, Lou reached in and pulled out something frothy and black on a plastic hanger. She held it up to the light, not that there was all that much to hold up. It was a minuscule nightie in something scratchy with holes in strategic places. It came complete with a set of panties with a frilly slit where the crotch should have been. Phil's hands came from behind and twiddled Lou's nipples as if trying to tune into *The Archers*.

'I thought we could have some fun with it when we get home later.'

'We'll see.' Lou smiled a paper-thin smile whilst behind it she was trying to blot out all sorts of mixed thoughts. Why couldn't it have been something sweet and sexy, not this tacky thing? Then again, this meant that he still fancied her, didn't it? Surely that was a good sign? She really was Ungrateful Wife of the Year.

Phil slapped her bottom, hard enough to propel Lou forwards a couple of steps.

'What colour's that supposed to be on your head?' he laughed, before heading off to the ensuite for his shower.

At half-past seven that evening, the taxi pipped its arrival outside.

Lou slipped on her jacket and followed Phil outside into the spring-chilly night. She felt great in her new outfit and make-up, and Phil looked extra-handsome in his dark green suit. It was his best and she took that as a sign that he was really going to push the boat out for her tonight. It made her feel *safe* and in turn, *safe* made her feel happy. She was going to have a wonderful evening, she just knew she was.

There were people already in the car so Lou turned back.

'False alarm, Phil, it's not ours,' she said.

'Yes, it is,' said Phil.

'Can't be. It's got people inside – look.'

'Little birthday surprise.'

'Birthday surprise?'

'Yes, love. I asked Fat Jack and Maureen to join us,' Phil said, talking through a rictus smile in case the people in the taxi were watching their approach.

'You. Are. Joking,' said Lou in much the same way. It was like a private ventriloquist's convention.

'I thought it would feel more like a party with another couple. This is all for you, Lou, please don't spoil it for me.'

'Don't give me that. You're going to talk business, aren't you, and leave me with Boring Maureen all night? It'll be just like last flaming Christmas all over again,' said Lou, still gritting her teeth.

'Lou, what do you take me for?'

She didn't answer that one.

Fat Jack and Phil moved forwards into the restaurant, their identical smiles flashing superiority at the

Chinese waiter, one an older, brasher version of the other. The ladies followed an almost dutiful five paces behind.

Jack seemed more colourful and dynamic than ever but Maureen seemed to have aged a few years in the few months since Christmas. Her customary 'teak sideboard' hair shade hadn't been touched up and the greys and whites ran wild in her short tight perm. A long twisty hair was sprouting unchecked out of the large mole on her neck which Lou tried not to stare at. Maureen looked as thin as a baby bird, hollow-cheeked and pale – almost as if she was fading away to ultimate transparency.

Fat Jack ordered a Chinese banquet for five (the greedy sod), and scampi and chips for Maureen who didn't eat foreign food – and just as Lou had predicted, Jack and Phil talked cars, with the occasional foray into what Barnsley FC should do to have any chance of winning the FA Cup next season, and then onto the fascinating subject of Jack's new koi carp fishpond, complete with waterfall, sauna and internet café (or at least that's where the bragging was heading). Halfway through her crispy duck and hoi sin sauce, Lou gave up trying to catch Phil's attention, she gave up trying to start up a conversation with monosyllabic Maureen and she gave up believing that this evening had anything to do with her birthday, or her. Stupid Lou.

Lou ate her food and drank her wine and watched the hands of the wall clock lazily circle. Maureen had eaten hardly anything, but had been drinking wine unnoticed in the background at a surprising rate, then she had a double Tia Maria instead of banana fritters as well. It was a wonder she wasn't on her back by the time the bill arrived.

Lou just couldn't wait for someone to ring a taxi to take them all home.

'Have you rung for a cab?' she asked Phil.

'Er, we thought we'd just nip to the club down the road for a couple,' said Phil as he helped her on with her coat. 'Birthday drink?' he added hopefully.

'Oh, you remember it's my birthday, do you?' said Lou quietly but crossly.

'We'll have our own little birthday party when we get home.' Phil grinned and gave her a suggestive wink. He was saved from Lou's response because attention turned to Fat Jack, who had just fallen over his chair from the effect of all the brandies.

The club was slightly more depressing on the inside than the rough brick exterior suggested, which was a feat in itself, but it did serve the best pint in the area, apparently, and that was a far more important factor to local men than any fancy furnishings. It had also been designed with a very long bar, to accommodate more 'leaners' and the comfortable women's seats were deliberately positioned a small taxi ride away from it. All that was missing was a barbed-wire fence down the middle with a serving hatch.

Phil brought Lou and Maureen two double vodkas and Cokes each, then he rejoined Jack at the bar. Lou sipped at one of them and her eyes flitted around the flaked paintwork, the cobwebs snagged on the Artex and the black and white picture of some mouldy ex-club Chairman given pride of place on the wall. The pressure to engage with Maureen all night had tired her brain out and she just wanted to go home and have a bath. Then she remembered she didn't have a bath.

She and Maureen had socialized four times before and yet she had heard Maureen say little more than, 'Please,' 'Thank you', 'Hello,' 'Goodbye,' 'Nice place,' and, 'Just going to the toilet.' Oh, not forgetting her famous, 'Those mince pies were nice. Did you bake them yourself?' at Christmas. Boy, she had really let her hair down that night. So no one was more surprised than Lou when Maureen suddenly started to talk.

'I'm a grandmother, did you know?' she said with a wistful, slurring pride.

'Congratulations,' said Lou. She knew their only son, Peter, lived out in Australia, although not much more about him than that. 'When did that happen then?'

'Five years ago today,' said Maureen. She really did know how to entertain, did Maureen.

'Well, slightly belated congratulations then,' said Lou. 'Boy or girl?'

'Girl,' Maureen sniffed. She opened the locket around her neck with trembling fingers to show Lou two blurry pictures, one of a baby and a blonde toddler on the other side. 'This is my Charlotte,' she announced, gulping on the name.

'Aw, she's bonny,' said Lou truthfully. 'You must be feeling as if you want to just hop on a plane and go out there. Have you any plans to?'

Maureen shook her head. Then Lou realized she couldn't speak because there were great big fat drops of salty tears dropping down her face and making beads on her little tweed skirt.

'Maureen, are you OK?' asked Lou.

'Jack wouldn't ever go and see Peter now, so I've never seen my granddaughter,' Maureen said at last. Lou fished in her bag for a tissue, which Maureen utilized completely.

'Scared of flying, is he?' said Lou.

'No,' said Maureen.

'I see,' said Lou, thinking that was the end of that conversation. Still, it was a record for Maureen. Then Maureen reached over, took a long swig from her drink and started up again.

'Our Pete always wanted to travel but Jack was all on for forcing him into the business. He said if Pete didn't stop his fancy ideas then that would be it, he could fuck off and not come back. Pete told him he was quite happy to do that and not come back and went out of the door with just a bag on his shoulder. That was the last time I saw my son.'

The tears drop-dropped. Maureen's eyes glazed over as she was dragged back to that happy Christmas scene of her family being smashed up in front of her eyes. She felt Pete's kiss again on her cheek, heard his sweet young voice saying, 'Bye, Mam, I'll ring you soon.' She heard Jack telling her that she could fuck off as well if she wasn't going to back him up.

Maureen pulled herself forwards out of the raw pain and started foraging amongst the jumble of bingo pens and cigarettes in her bag for her own packet of paper hankies. Lou still had her eyebrows raised from hearing Maureen swear like that. None of these words seemed to be coming from her lips, but those of another woman, one buried deep inside her. Lou watched the older woman blow her nose and take a long, shuddering breath, looking momentarily elegant as she presented her fine-boned profile to Lou. Phil had told her that Maureen had once been Miss South Yorkshire, something Lou had scoffed at until now, looking side-on at the remnants of a much-faded beauty.

'Pete was never interested in cars. He was a lad that used to take himself off into the countryside and draw. That's what he's doing now – graphic art in Sydney – and he loves it. He's done really well for himself, despite his father telling him over the years that "he'd come to nothing, painting all the bloody time."' Maureen laughed a little manically.

'All those years I stuck with Jack to keep the family together, turning a blind eye to his women – and for what, because it all collapsed anyway. All those bloody years wasted.'

'Jack had other women?' said Lou. As if on cue, Fat Jack laughed loud and crudely at the bar, his great blubbery belly years past the effort of being sucked in, and Lou wondered what Maureen had ever seen in him – never mind what anyone else had seen in him. Then again, there were always women who could put up with anything for a man with a fat wallet who wanted a bit on the side, as she well knew.

'He could always get women, love,' said Maureen, looking at him also but seeing a different Jack – a younger, slimmer Jack with sharp suits and smooth patter.

'It nearly killed me the first time I found out about it, but I didn't want him to leave me so I just let him get on with it. There was Peter to think of, you see. He was only a bairn and where would we have gone? I didn't work because Jack wanted me at home and I wasn't talking to my family by then. I couldn't have given Pete the comforts Jack could supply. We'd have ended up in a hostel, and what life is that for a lad?' Maureen gave a bitter laugh. 'Course, his flings always ended because he just wanted the thrill of the chase. His tarts weren't exactly the type to have his tea on the table for him every night, but it never got any easier, seeing him drown himself in his best after-shave and then lie to you that he was off out for a pint with a business contact.'

Lou felt quite sick and very guilty. To her shame she'd presumed Maureen had always been a limp lettuce. She had never even considered that once she might have been someone whole and pretty and confident, who had been whittled away by small cruelties over the years. But then *this* Maureen at the side of her, crying softly into a glass of vodka, would never have attracted someone as strong and forceful as the young Jack. Once upon a time, it seemed, there had been a sparky beauty queen and a dynamic go-getter who had butted together perfectly, but then the power balance had somehow tipped and kept on tipping until they had evolved into little more than parasite and host. Jack the lad and Miss South Yorkshire were long gone, leaving two strangers behind.

'Pete's last words to his dad were that he thought more about his koi carp than us. He told me when he got settled he'd send for me and I'd to go over there.'

Maureen dabbed at the tears that flowed slow, fat and consistently down her cheeks.

'And did he ever send for you?' asked Lou softly.

Maureen nodded. 'Aye, he sent for me, lass.'

'Why didn't you go?' *And leave that revolting bastard.*

'Jack said I'd to make a choice. Him or Peter. I couldn't have both.'

'No!' said Lou incredulously, although she didn't know why that surprised her. There was meanness behind Jack's eyes, for all his loud matey laughing and back-slapping camaraderie.

'There were always choices with Jack – him or my sister, him or Peter, him or my friend Bren, and, fool that I am, I picked Jack every time because I loved him and I couldn't bear to lose him. He doesn't know I've got this picture of Charlotte. Don't tell him, Lou, will you? He won't let me contact our Pete again and it's the only thing I've got of her.'

Let?

Lou's body stiffened and she gave the corpulent, jocular Jack a hard stare. How on earth did a woman get into a state where a man was 'letting' her? And putting her in the position of making her choose between those she loved and him.

Maureen's thin hand fell onto Lou's and she said in a way that sounded more like a warning than a statement, 'It wasn't all his fault. I didn't stop it happening.'

'*Why* didn't you?' Lou asked. She wanted to go much further and demand: *Why didn't you stand up and fight your corner? Why didn't you leave him? Why didn't you go to your son and start a new life? Why did you let go of all you had been?*

Maureen looked up at Lou with eyes that had nothing behind them but tears and alcohol.

'I just left it too late,' she said.

★

'Come on, you drunken old mare!' said Jack, bursting into their conversation, laughing and pulling Maureen to her feet, a little too roughly for Lou's liking. Behind him, a droopy-eyed Phil looked as if he was about to say something similar to Lou, but the withering look she cast him put paid to that.

Lou followed the man in the massive sheepskin coat and the woman in the little mouse-grey fur jacket out to the taxi, and a thought flickered into her drink-fuzzy brain – but was just out of reach to be caught and examined. It hid instead in a quiet place in her head and would pay another visit, for longer next time.

Back at home, Phil was waiting for Lou with two glasses and the chilled bottle of fake champagne when she came out of the cloakroom toilet. She was annoyed, he could tell, but Lou was so easy to play. She was incapable of staying pissed off with him for any longer than five minutes. She'd be upstairs and in that little black number being fiddled about with in no time after a few flattering choice words, that much he would have staked his life on.

'Fancy trying out your birthday present?' he said, swivelling his hips, knowing her smile was on its way out and just needed a little coaxing to the surface.

'You want an omelette at this time of night?' Lou answered glibly.

Phil swaggered over to her and pressed his groin against her, crooning seductively, 'Don't be silly, babe, you know exactly what I mean.'

But Lou surprised him by stepping out of the closing cage of his arms.

'Not tonight, thank you, Phil,' she said wearily, and then she turned away from him and headed up the stairs towards the much-needed comfort of her old pair of pink impenetrable flannelette pyjamas.

Chapter 11

For as long as he could remember in his marriage, the smell of bacon wafting up the stairs had been Phil's gentle Sunday-morning alarm. Ironically, it was his senses in shock from the defiance in custom that now sparked him awake. He relieved himself, slipped on his robe and moccasins and padded downstairs to the kitchen to find out what was going on. There he found Lou, sitting on the floor like a desert island in a sea of books taken down from the giant antique bookcase they had against the wall in there. There was evidence that she had intended his breakfast at least – the pans were on the hob and the eggs and bacon out on the work surface, but her present absorption had assumed importance over tending to his needs, which would have been extra grounds for sulking, had she been responsive enough to notice.

'What are you doing?' he asked.

His voice jolted her momentarily from her concentration, although trance seemed a more appropriate word.

'Clearing the bookshelves,' she said, returning to some big black file she was reading.

'Never!'

When she didn't engage, the effect on him was tanta-mount to a smack. He knew only too well the power of indifference. It was his own personal favourite weapon. Not that he was worried she wouldn't be back to her old Lou self in no time. OK, she was still annoyed about last night so she was having a womanly moment, but Lou knew he was a businessman first and foremost, and last night he and Jack had got a lot of important talking done. Anyway, it wasn't as if it had been her twenty-first or her fortieth; it was only an ordinary birthday, for God's sake. Thirty-six wasn't exactly an 'open up the Dom Perignon' landmark.

'Er, I thought instead of the usual that we might try out your birthday present? The other one?' He was care-ful to say *we*.

'Yes, I'll sort it in a minute. I've run out of black pud-ding, though.'

It occurred to him that she wasn't listening.

'It's OK, I'll have peas instead,' he tested.

'No worries,' she replied.

Lou hadn't planned to clear out the books. She had gone down, automaton-style, to cook Phil's Sunday breakfast, but what she saw when she first opened the door was the last remaining vestige of disorder in the kitchen – the bookshelves. On the bottom shelf there was a stack of holiday brochures. She thumbed through them, and pic-tures of Venetian canals and pretty hotels taunted her from the pages. The hot Italian sun beamed out from the photographs and she could almost smell the coffee in the street café scenes. The next shelf up was full of her

Midnight Moon romance collection, telling stories of the sort of fiery passion that could only exist in works of fiction, and a box full of instruction manuals and guarantees for appliances, most of which she no longer had. On the other shelves were all her many cookery books and the files of recipes she had collected over many years. Her regular-as-clockwork routine was totally overridden by an undeniable compulsion to tackle this job first. It simply couldn't wait. Phil's breakfast, for once, could.

She stripped all of the books from the shelves and piled them up around her on the floor. She ripped out pages of the tried, tested and rejected recipes and started to refile those with a big fat tick into mains and desserts – so many lovely desserts. She had quite forgotten the *Casa Nostra* file was there amongst them. *Casa Nostra*. The name set off a flare in her head and in its temporary light she glimpsed all the associated memories lying there covered in dust. The premises they'd found to convert, the furnishings they had planned, the excitement when the bank manager agreed to the loan, and how they'd jumped up and down in his office hugging each other (and hugging him as well, Lou remembered, with both a cringe and a smile). *Casa Nostra* was just a working title. They hadn't ever found the name that would have been just *right*, but whatever it was going to be finally called, would be a coffee-house like no other. It was going to bring a little Italy to their corner of Yorkshire, with proper fortifying coffee to wash down the most extravagant, indulgent cakes in the world. They were going to name their fare after people like de Niro and Pacino and Sinatra – and Marco Pierre White, of course. It was to be the start of their empire that couldn't fail because they *knew* that, together, they were an indomitable force.

Deb's big rounded handwriting was scribbled everywhere.

Lou — what do you think of this for a pud of the week?

Lou — let's make it our aim to de-naff Black Forest Gâteau.

Lou — let's make the biggest pudding in the world and call it a Brando. What should it be I wonder?

Lou — followed this recipe to the letter and it tasted like shite.

They had been touching the dream, until the day when she had found Deb on the doorstep in a dreadful state and five minutes later, Lou's world had fallen apart. Her agony had been unbearable, but Deb's had been too.

Lou, I've got something awful to tell you . . .

It was a terrible responsibility to shoulder.

Phil's having an affair. I've seen them together.

Yet Deb nursed her through the heartbreak with patience and selflessness. Then Phil came back and made her choose. And Lou had chosen him.

Lou made Phil a smaller than usual fried breakfast and she hadn't used her new omelette-maker, he noted.

'One egg?' he questioned, struggling to keep the petulance out of his voice.

'We'll be at my mother's eating lunch in two and a half hours,' explained Lou.

Phil groaned. 'Oh, flaming Norah — I forgot about that. Can't I give it a miss?'

'You can if you want, but you'll have to make your own lunch,' came the reply.

'OK, I'll go,' said Phil, like a small child reluctantly being dragged by his mam to the supermarket. Phil loved

his food and would have been the size of a pregnant ele-
phant if he didn't burn it off with long runs. He had
noticed the creep of middle-age already around his
waistline recently and would have to add a few more
miles to his routine soon. Settling for a half-breakfast
wouldn't do him any harm for once, he decided.

'Er, I've been thinking about holidays,' he said, after
swallowing the last mouthful of egg. Lou wasn't on best-
friend terms with him yet, that was clear, so this just
might turn her round. 'Fancy going somewhere different
this year?'

Lou looked up from her lake of books.

'What, like Italy?' she said with a gulp, her heart
already revving up the thumps in anticipation.

'No, I don't fancy Italy,' said Phil.

'Why not Italy?' said Lou. She feared that 'somewhere
different' might mean a caravan in somewhere bland like
Blegthorpe-on-Sea.

'I don't like it.'

'Phil, you've never been!'

'Put it this way then: I *won't* like it.'

'Why?'

'It's full of Italians for a start.'

'Precisely,' said Lou. 'And fantastic Italian architec-
ture . . .'

'Boring churches, you mean.'

'The Colisseum isn't a church,' said Lou, fighting back
the exasperation that was spiralling up inside her.
'Neither is the Circus Maximus or the Forum or
Pompeii.' *Places she so wanted to see. Places Miss Ramsay
had brought to life for her in school Latin lessons.*

'I hated Latin at school,' said Phil. 'And I've seen

Hadrian's Wall. What a bloody thrilling day out that wasn't!'

'OK then,' said Lou, trying a tack tailored to his likes, 'what about the wonderful food and the beautiful wines?'

'I hate pizza and I'm not that bothered about wine.'

'Sunshine, Phil, Italy is bursting with sunshine!' Lou half-screamed. She knew she had him here. Phil worshipped at the altar of Apollo.

'Yeah, but it's Italian sun, it's different. I was thinking about Torremolinos. I've seen a five-star that you'd love, Lou.'

Lou knew she couldn't fight the illogical with logic. It was like raising Excalibur to slice fog. Strength of argument meant nothing – not that she was equipped to win any battle of wills with Phil. His voice faded to white noise in the background as he blah-blahed on about a holiday he had probably already booked. It would be, as usual, a very nice hotel, five-star, the one he wanted in the area he wanted. They always holidayed where and how Phil wanted. They always did everything the way Phil wanted, come to think about it. Lou slid the brochures with their promise of a different sun into a carrier bag to take out to the skip. There was no point in keeping them. She would only ever go there in her dreams.

At a quarter to ten, whilst Phil was engrossed in the sports pages of the *Sunday World* in the conservatory, the skip wagon reversed into their drive.

'Good morning,' said Lou breezily, coming out to meet it. It was such a crisp day, refreshingly chilly, and as bright and beautiful as the hymn. There were still one or two snowdrops lingering in the flower borders, but purple crocuses and daffodils with their trumpets as orange as fresh egg-yolks had pushed through for their turn in the limelight. 'And good morning to you, Clooney.'

Clooney started play-biting Lou's hand, until Tom shouted at him to stop.

'He's not hurting me,' said Lou, getting a dog biscuit out of her pocket.

'You're spoiling him,' said Tom. 'He'll not want to come home.'

'I'd have him in a shot,' said Lou.

Tom coughed. 'I was just wondering if you'd like to go . . .' He was talking at the same time as Lou added, 'But my husband is allergic to pet hair. Oh, I'm sorry, you were saying?'

'No, it's fine,' said Tom quickly, whilst giving the back of his neck a hard rub and muttering to himself: 'Oh well, that's that then. What a shame.'

'Oh, don't feel too sorry for him – he doesn't like dogs anyway. It hasn't exactly affected the quality of his life, not having a pet.'

Tom looked confused by what she had just said, but before Lou could retrack on the conversation, Clooney barked and distracted them. He'd found a rubber ball under the hedge.

'Drop it. It's not yours!' said Tom.

'It isn't anyone's. I don't know where it's come from,' said Lou, and held out her hand for Clooney to bring it to her. She played fetch with him on the lawn whilst Tom lowered the skip off his wagon.

'You're keen, I'll give you that,' said Tom, looking at the bags of rubbish piled by the wheelie-bin awaiting his arrival. 'Maybe you should have got one of the bigger-size skips.'

'The mini-skip will be fine. I can't have that much more stuff,' said Lou. 'I'll have filled this today so you could pick it up tomorrow if you can. Do you know,' she went on, 'I would never have imagined that clearing out a few old carpets and stuff could make me feel so . . .' She hunted for the word but couldn't find it, so gestured joy with enthusiastic hands instead.

'You're not the first to tell me that,' said Tom, nodding with understanding. 'Some say it's better than therapy. I might change my name to "Tom Broom, Waste Therapist" and charge double. Not that any price increase would matter too much to someone who prints her own money.'

Lou smiled a smile that mirrored his.

'I bet that was a nice little cracket in its time,' Tom commented, pointing to the small crude rectangular stool there amongst the pile of stuff which was covered with the palest coat of sparkly frost. 'A really handy piece to have around.'

'It was, and just the right size for sitting on or standing on to reach things, as I invariably have to,' said Lou with a little tut. 'I must confess I still feel a bit guilty throwing it away, but it's so battered now.'

'It still looks pretty solid to me, despite the knocks. It must feel like you are giving up an old friend,' said Tom, reaching for the stool and brushing at it with the heel of his hand. 'It's harder than it looks sometimes to let things go, even if they are old and useless. Things gather emotions to them so that people often feel they are throwing so much more away than an old vase that their granny gave them.' He smiled and Lou gulped. This big man standing in front of her in his overalls sounded almost as if he was reciting poetry. 'It's amazing how attached some people can get to old rubbish, but they've lived with it for so long it's become the norm. And throwing it away is too scary and doesn't feature as an option.'

A picture of Maureen drifted into her mind and Lou nodded.

'That's very true, Tom.'

His head gave a little jerk when she said his name. She hoped she wasn't being too presumptuous. Lou liked to use people's names where she could, and calling him 'Mr Broom' sounded stupid. As if he was her headmaster or something.

'Be careful you don't overdo it,' he said, with that little twinkle in his eye. 'Those bags look heavy.'

He had stubble this morning. She wondered fleetingly what it might feel like rubbing against her chin, or elsewhere. Enough of that, Lou Winter, she reprimanded herself. Still it was an interesting thought that left behind quite a quivery sensation in its wake.

She quickly got out the money from her back packet. It was embarrassingly warm, nearly steaming as it hit the cold air, and she hoped he wouldn't notice, but of course he did.

'Hot off the press, is it?' he said to her horror. She felt her cheeks heating up too, but attempted to laugh it off.

'Yes. Be careful, the ink's not quite dry yet.'

He grinned. Stubble and grins. Lou went even hotter.

'Anyway, thanks. Just give us a ring when you want it picked up. Come on, Clooney, we've got kids to take to the park.'

A bucket of water hit Lou's heart and extinguished the smiley feelings that were hopping about in there. Of course someone like him would be married with children, she said to herself. Why should that be such a shock to her? Anyway, what was any of it to do with her? What difference did it make? Why was she suddenly upset to learn that he was married with children? Lou didn't know. Her head was all over the place this morning. It was as if someone had stuck a big wooden spoon in it and was stirring around.

When Tom's wagon drove off Lou rolled up her sleeves to start, but the sight of that faithful old stool on the heap of rubbish brought a sudden rush of tears to her eyes.

Chapter 12

Lou kissed her mum on the cheek. Despite his grumbles, Phil was there behind her with an extravagant show of affection for his mother-in-law, encouraged by the warm, meaty smell coming from the steamy kitchen.

'You've had your hair done,' said Renee, looking at it from a few angles.

'Birthday treat from the people at work. Do you like it?' said Lou, preparing herself.

'It's a bit orange,' Renee replied.

Renee had bought Lou a jumper for her birthday. It was a very nice plain black top, slash neck with three-quarter sleeves and four pearl buttons off centre.

'Mum, that is really lovely,' said Lou. 'Thank you.'

'It wasn't a cheap one,' reiterated Renee.

'Mum, I know. It's classy, I like it.'

'It's very slimming, is black,' said Renee. 'I didn't know whether to get you a size smaller to give you some encouragement.'

Lou gulped her sherry. Her mother meant well, she told herself.

Renee Casserly served up a very nice pork lunch. Lou

noticed her portion was considerably smaller than Phil's but she didn't comment. It was, after all, very pleasant just to be sitting there whilst someone else did the cooking. She had been too cross last night to enjoy that particular pleasure in the Chinese restaurant.

Just after the washing up had been done, the phone rang.

'Hello,' said Renee, wincing as it rang again in her ear. She would never get the hang of these newfangled cordless things where you had to press a button to be connected.

'Oh hello, lovey.' Sunshine flooded her voice. Lou could name that caller in one. 'How many degrees? Ooh, that is warm, isn't it? It's very cool here, but sunny and dry . . . Ooh, smashing . . . Yes, I'm very well, thank you . . . Yes, I've packed it. I just have to get it to the post office.'

Aha, thought Lou, listening and filling in the gaps. The preliminaries dealt with, Victorianna had got down to the real business in hand. *When's my hamper coming, Mummy dahling?*

'. . . Tuesday, I hope. Elouise is here if you want to have a quick word . . .'

The life savings Lou would have put on the answer to that one being a yes were safe.

'Oh, I see. Well, never mind, another time if you're rushing . . . She sends her love.'

No, I bloody well don't, Lou thought loudly.

'Bye bye, dear . . . Yes, I love you too.' Renee put the phone down looking as if she'd just had a private audience with Daniel O'Donnell. 'That was Victorianna.'

'Really,' said Lou.

'She sends her love.'

No, she bloody well doesn't, thought Lou again.

'Will you give me a lift to the post office with that parcel for her on Tuesday? Everything's all wrapped up now,' said Renee, pointing to an enormous box in the corner.

'Course I— Flaming heck, Mum. That'll cost you a fortune. I don't know, she really is a . . . making you do this.' Lou omitted the word. She was having trouble finding one that summed up Princess Victorianna without resorting to expletives.

'She didn't make me, she asked. I could have said no. Oh Lou, why are you always so aggressive where Victorianna is concerned?' snapped Renee. 'What on earth did she ever do to deserve all that sniping?'

Mum, you really don't want to know the answer to that one, Lou said inwardly.

'You were so close when you were young as well,' said Renee, shaking her head in exasperation.

That wasn't quite the way Lou remembered it.

'Anyway, are you going to do it for her or do I have to get a taxi?'

'Yes, of course I will,' sighed Lou, adding to herself, *but I'm doing it for you, Mum, not Goldentits.*

When it was time to go, she woke up Phil who was snoring in the armchair. Fed and watered, he had dropped off stretched out on Renee's enormous leather recliner next to the radiator that was pumping out heat. When Renee shuffled off this mortal coil, he thought sleepily, he would have to make sure Lou got him that chair.

It occurred to Lou, as she walked out to the car, that she couldn't remember the last time anyone had said they loved her.

Chapter 13

'Hello, Keith Featherstone,' announced a voice thick with the smoke of twenty years of filterless fags.

'At last, Mr Featherstone! It's Mrs Winter,' said Lou, with half-shock, half-relief at finding herself speaking to his actual voice and not the gravelly answering-machine message.

'Ah, Mrs Winter, I am so sorry, everything's been mad. I was going to ring you later on today.'

Yeah, right. Lou steeled herself.

'Mr Featherstone, I really need you to finish this bathroom. It's been over six weeks now since you left it.' Lou dropped her voice so Phil wouldn't hear the next bit, as he would have gone totally bonkers. 'And I did pay you cash in advance so you'd treat this as a priority. As you promised you would.'

Lou felt sick saying it. Sometimes she was like a stupid daft puppy that trusted everyone and invariably got booted, although no one could have kicked her more over this whole bathroom business than she had kicked herself.

'You are totally right, Mrs Winter. I feel awful about it, and I will be along as soon as I can. I'll ring you this afternoon when we're a bit closer to completing this job that we're on with now.'

'I'll be at work. Have you got my mobile number?'

'I have indeed, Mrs Winter, and your home number just in case.'

'I must have this finished. It's not very fair of you.'

Crikey, talk about the hard-line tactics she had planned. She'd stamp her foot in a moment and that would really show him.

'I can't leave what I'm on at the moment, that's the problem. Old lady, you see, got broken into and her windows and doors are all totally smashed. You should see it, Mrs Winter. Terrible. I couldn't forgive myself if I didn't sort her out.'

'Oh dear,' said Lou, feeling humbled and a little like a child screaming for cake after just being told there were children starving in Africa.

'I'll be there as soon as this is finished, Mrs Winter. I promise.'

'OK, Mr Featherstone. As soon as you can then. Thank you.'

She could have sworn she heard sniggering before the line went dead.

Her phone bleeped the arrival of a text message as Lou pulled into the office car park. It was from Michelle.

LETS GO OUT FRIDAY TO CELEBRATE YOUR BIRTHDAY. SORRY HAVEN'T RUNG. MET G8 BLOKE. BEEN IN BED ALL W/END. WOW!! NEED TO TALK SOON XXX

Lou shook her head. She thought back to the one and only time she had agreed to go out with Michelle on a Friday night after a campaign of constant badgering.

Needless to say, Phil hadn't been very pleased about it, so Lou had underplayed the excitement she felt about getting dressed up and going for a rare girly night out on the town.

Once she had been released into the town, it took Lou about five minutes to discover that she wasn't an integral part of their evening at all. Her whole evening consisted of being dragged from pub to pub whilst Michelle trailed after various fanciable men and then, when she got an audience with one of her quarries, Lou was pushed off to entertain 'the mate'. At one point Lou spent an exhilarating half-hour with a drunk who had a bruise under his thumbnail in the shape of the Phantom Flan Flinger, so at least they had a talking point (well, in his case a slurring point). At the end of the evening, just when she thought her feet might drop off from shoe-pain, Lou was forced to stand for another three-quarters of an hour at a freezing taxi rank whilst her ears rang with the echoes of the weird and over-loud electro music that had been playing in the club. But before Lou could end her evening, she had to take an extremely drunk and sobbing Michelle home and make sure she was locked in safely and tucked up in bed with a pint and a half of water and two paracetamol in her stomach. Then, and only then, could she jump back into the waiting taxi to head across town to her own house. The taxi driver could barely steer for imagining how much his passenger was going to have to fork out for this fare. It would have been cheaper for Lou to charter the *QE2* home.

She had never really bonded with Phil's house but felt like throwing her arms around it and kissing it when the taxi pulled into its drive. It was worth every penny of the exorbitant fare just to take off her shoes in the porch. Going around town at seventeen in skyscraper stilettos with mates like Deb was brill, but doing it in her thirties, with someone like Michelle, had been excruciating.

Lou remembered trudging up the stairs, stripping off her clothes and leaving them in an uncharacteristic heap on the bathroom floor because she just wanted to go to bed and snuggle into Phil's back. However, he was sulking and shook her off. He continued to sulk until the following Wednesday. Not even a lamb roast and a chocolate brandy roulade, the size of a Californian Redwood trunk, could bring him round, although Lou thought her cooking magic had worked on the Monday because he had woken her up in the middle of the night by silently caressing her and they had made love. Lou gave herself wholly, glad this was the end of his drawn-out tantrum, but when he was satisfied, he had once more turned his back in bed and carried on ignoring her for another forty-eight hours. Boy, that had hurt.

When Michelle finally did ring her that weekend, it was to ask if Lou was up for another 'fun night out' as she laughingly put it. 'When the disciples partied in hell', was the phrase that crossed Lou's mind at the time. Lou used Phil as a convenient excuse, saying that he wasn't keen on her going out at nights. That exchange marked the start of the first big crack in their friendship as Michelle made a couple of snide comments about Lou being under the thumb, saying that she should stop letting herself be manipulated. Under pressure from Phil's punishing, cold attitude, Lou had snapped back that she was trying to hold her marriage together and chasing men around pubs wasn't the best way to go about it.

Michelle had burst into tears and said she had felt very depressed recently and wasn't thinking straight. It had the desired effect of making Lou feel like a right old cow and she'd dashed round to Michelle's house with a couple of strawberry tarts from the bakery and a bottle of wine. She hadn't seen then that Michelle could out-manipulate Phil when she wanted.

Maybe, once upon a time, Lou might have been under the illusion that Michelle's birthday invite was borne of selfless motives. But not now. She texted back: GLAD ABOUT THE MAN. TALK LATER. CANT DO NIGHTS SORRY XXX.

The reply came back almost instantaneously.

PLEASE PLEASE PLEASE XXX

Lou thought again of that interminable wait at the taxi rank to get home with her feet throbbing like an AC/DC track.

SORRY SORRY SORRY. LUNCH WOULD BE GOOD THOUGH XXX

The few lunches she and Michelle had together in the beginning were nice.

IF WE MUST text-sulked Michelle, although Lou knew it wouldn't happen. There weren't that many desirable men to stalk at noon in the Edwardian Tea Rooms over giant scones.

Lou walked into the office and her heart sank immediately on seeing that Karen's space was unoccupied. Stan wasn't in either and Zoe was gazing intently at her screen and looked as if she had been crying or was just about to. Nicola was sitting at her desk. She made a deliberate head-swivel towards the clock after spotting Lou. It was a move intended to needle because they both knew Lou was never late. But as usual, it didn't work.

'Where is everyone? It's like the *Marie Celeste* in here,' said Lou to Zoe when Nicola had marched off with a very important walk and a folder.

'Stan's wife phoned him in sick – migraine, apparently – and Karen's little boy is poorly so she's taken a day off,' said Zoe in a voice more cracked than Keith Featherstone's smoke-ravaged voice.

'Hell, girl, you should be at home with that throat!' said Lou.

'I rang in this morning but *she* said that if I didn't get in here then I'd be in trouble, what with everyone else being off.'

'Someone really should have a quiet word with HR She can't do this sort of thing.'

Although, as they all knew, there was no such thing as a quiet word or an 'off-the-record' chat with Human Resources. It was a department full of cans of worms and as soon as you opened your mouth in there, you turned into a tin-opener.

'Yes, but she can do it because she is doing it, isn't she, Lou?' croaked Zoe.

The skip was just being lifted by the truck when Lou arrived home. She spotted it from the end of the street and was all too aware that as soon as she had, her foot pressed down on the accelerator. She tore down the cul-de-sac like Nigel Mansell.

The big skip man acknowledged her with a nod, but to her disappointment it wasn't Tom. She had been really looking forward to seeing Clooney too. She had a bag of dog biscuits with his name on in the house – safely hidden away from Phil, obviously.

'No dog today?' she said lightly, despite the sensation of a cannonball in the pit of her stomach. 'I was really looking forward to seeing him. The German Shepherd,' she clarified.

'Clooney, you mean? He's the boss's dog. Only ever goes with him,' said the skip man.

'Oh, what a shame. That's the bloke who usually comes, is it? He's the boss?' Lou said with breezy innocence. 'I didn't realize he had anyone else working for him.'

'There's a few of us,' said the skip man, pulling at the net, which had snagged on some wood. 'There's me, Steve and "Part-Time Eddie", except those two are off at the mo' and Tom's not been working the last couple of days, which is why we're short handed and I'm having to do this so late on.'

'He's not ill, is he?' said Lou, poking a little further.

'No, he's not ill, but someone in his family is.'

'Not one of his children, I hope?' said Lou, slightly ashamed that she was being so nosy, but she was unable to stop herself all the same.

'Tom's kids?'

'Yes.'

'Tom ain't got any kids. I think it's his sister who's poorly.'

Tom ain't got any kids.

That little cloud nudged in her chest although she was then cross with herself for not having the forethought to say, 'Not his *wife* or his children, I hope?' If she had got it wrong about the children, he might not be married after all. He didn't wear a wedding ring, but then she didn't half the time – well, when Phil wasn't around anyway. Then again, what difference did it make if he was married with forty-five children or single, gay or celibate, for God's sake? She was married, and Tom Broom was a bloke who was nice and chatty because he had a business to run and he was probably extra nice and chatty to her because she was probably bankrolling his business from all the skips she was hiring. Anyway, even if he was straight and unattached, he wasn't exactly going to be interested in a dumpy little married woman coming up to the back end of her thirties with a bum so big it could be seen from orbit. Considering she wasn't interested, she was spending a lot of headspace on not being interested, she realized. What the hell was up with her?

Lou went inside and checked the phone when the skip man had gone. There had been no missed calls, which meant bloody Keith Featherstone hadn't rung her on the house phone either, because he certainly hadn't rung her on the mobile. But then, had she really believed that he would?

Chapter 14

Spring had to be Lou's favourite season for flowers. It was so pretty when the sun shone and woke up the buds. Her stocky hyacinths on the windowsill were releasing their pungent scent into the kitchen. Outside, the cherry blossom was thick on the tree branches, banks of daffs nodded to each other in the breeze and there was a blur of violet in the woods as early bluebells unlocked. But according to the weather forecast, Sunday was going to be the last day of good weather for a week at least, and so Lou was up early to make the most of it. She had decided that the garden was next in line for an overhaul.

She had rung for one of the larger skips midweek, dictating her order to an answering machine, and it hadn't been Tom who had delivered it either. By nine o'clock today, it was already half-full of the bonfire pile that had been waiting for a match for a year and a half. It was far too sodden to burn now and would have ended up smoking out the estate if she had tried. It was only since she had started this clutter-clearing that the sight of it had begun to annoy her. Every time she looked out of the kitchen window, she saw it staring at her, like the mountain from *Close Encounters*. She had the distinct feeling that if she didn't shift it before long, she would start recreating it everywhere in mashed potato.

She set to, sawing all the huge wooden tree branches into smaller pieces, then she wheelbarrowed them over to the skip. Phil hadn't ever shared the male obsession with arson, so goodness knows what he was thinking of in the first place, making the pile so big. It was as if he had been moving the problem rubbish from one place to another but never actually getting rid of it. Not surprisingly, the clutter-clearing article highlighted such action as a total waste of energy.

Lou wrestled with a garden chair possessed by a clingy weed behind a row of conifers with a force that suggested she was battling something else, but triumphing over a bulky bit of plastic could not quite take away the frustration and disappointment she was trying not to put a name to. Well, she might not be able to control who delivered her skips, but at least Lou could have the upper hand over the chair. A cameo of Nicola's face with its scary chrome canines popped into her head for no reason at all, which made the next tug a mightily aggressive one.

Phil teased back the curtain to see Lou pulling at something white from behind the line of firs. He knocked on the window, but she was too involved with the silly bloody nonsense to hear him. His stomach growled like a caged bear and, in his pyjama bottoms, his penis bobbed like a charmed snake. He could have done with some attention this morning and where was his wife? Out wrestling rubbish like a small Big Daddy – again. Slipping on his dressing-gown and moccasins, he went downstairs, padded across the slate-tiled kitchen floor, opened the back door and called out to Lou.

His shout coincided with her last heave and Lou, feeling as victorious as Boudicca, dropped the chair on the grass as if it were a dead Roman, before strolling back across the lawn to the house. Her hair was tied back in a girly ponytail but strands of it had fallen across her face, and she pushed back at them with the clean heel of her hand. Her arms and clothes were filthy. She was panting like an animal.

It must have been his imagination, but she looked leaner. Actually, he thought, she looked quite sexy. For Lou, these days, anyway.

'I'm awake,' he announced.

'Yes, I see you,' Lou replied breathlessly. It was back-breaking work but exhilarating. Letting her body work whilst her head was free to butterfly had an effect similar to sticking herself in a battery charger. The harder she worked, the more energized she felt, and it had the unexpected side-effect of revving up a libido she thought had been waiting for its last rites.

'Break for breakfast?' queried Phil, who really meant: Leave the sodding trees alone and get the Big George grill out.

'Yes, OK,' said Lou, stripping off her gloves.

Her lips are blood red, thought Phil. He steered Lou into the house with his hand on her bottom, not for a moment expecting what would happen next – for no sooner had they made it through the door when Lou turned around, they collided and then he couldn't believe what sparked between them, but he wasn't going to turn it down. He struggled her bra off and started rolling her nipples around in his hands, a quick grope before he moved in for the main event . . . but Lou, it seemed, had other ideas. He undid the belt on his robe and just as he was about to take her hand to guide it down to the bulge making a bid for freedom out of his pyjamas, Lou grabbed his hand first and made it do a bit of bidding of her own. He barely had to do anything before she was gasping out her orgasm, and judging from the noise she was making, it had a few seismic waves attached to it. Then, before Phil had a chance to protest, Lou pushed him onto a kitchen chair, sank between his legs and pleasured him in his absolute favourite way. It was over in seconds, his orgasmic scream borne out on a blasphemy of the highest order.

'Wow,' said Phil breathlessly, popping his spent equipment back under cover as Lou stood up and started dressing. If the truth be told, he had been getting a bit annoyed with all this skip and cleaning business, and had decided not to let her carry on with it any more, but if this morning was anything to go by, maybe he should, because advantages were starting to manifest themselves. The sight of the constant skips outside the front window was beginning to piss him off, but in saying that, he had really noticed changes in the house. It sounded daft, but every time a skip left, he could have sworn the house felt lighter.

'I think we could definitely do with some breakfast now,' Phil grinned. 'I'm starving.'

He gave her breast a squeeze, not noticing how Lou suddenly shrank from his touch. With her body now satiated, her brain was busy trying to analyze what had just happened. It wasn't love-making by any stretch; they hadn't kissed once during their activity. No, Lou Winter had just shamelessly used her husband to satisfy a basic need, and the worst of it was that anyone would have done. It didn't make Lou feel very good about herself to admit that, for a few seconds back there, she had been imagining someone else's hands all over her; big rough hands that knew exactly where to touch her, instead of Phil's clumsy pinging and tweaking. It was thinking about *him* that had both brought her to that wild point of no return and then caused her to feel so guilty afterwards.

She was thirty-six and this was her one and only experience of sex that had everything to do with selfless gratification and nothing with affection. Was this what men felt all the time? Was it this detachment that allowed them to pull up their trousers and disappear into the night without a backward glance, that let them cheat on their wives and then jump back into bed with them before the top note of the other woman's scent had faded on their shirts?

Her sex-life had never been all that adventurous, even in the college days. There had been two lovers before Phil, who had both been to the 'Climben ze on, Climben ze off' Swiss Finishing School of Copulation. She'd always imagined when she got married that she and her husband would start to build up a sexual repertoire, but that hadn't happened. She and Phil hadn't even made a dent in the index of the *Kama Sutra*. Adventurous sex had never been a priority in her marriage. Phil seemed to get more pleasure closing a car deal than he did in bed. In fact, sometimes it was as if the deal was the sex and the sex was the celebratory cigarette afterwards. 'Mr Missionary' got bored doing foreplay but then again, he had rather been led to believe that he did the business superbly well because of his wife's kind but misguided attempts to fake her pleasure. Lou found herself trapped in a web of her own making and, as such, had to put up with it because it was far too late to come clean. Actually, Lou could take or leave sex but Phil took a pleasure from her, usually on Sunday mornings, which she was happy to give. Her own sex-drive was low, and now that she was fast approaching middle-age, her libido was barely breathing. At least, she had thought that was a fair assessment of the case, until the injection of freak hormones that morning, of course. It seemed that what she had thought of as dead was merely dormant – her libido was less 'Corpse Bride' and more 'Sleeping Beauty'. There was nothing said about that in the clutter-clearing article!

While Phil was happily reading his usual spread of Sunday newspapers, Lou's phone announced the arrival of a text message. CAN U TALK? It was from Michelle. Now was as good a time as any for a chat. She couldn't put anything more in the skip now, it was filled to the max. Maybe she should have gone for the even bigger size!

'Hiya.' Michelle answered the phone sounding breathless but bright. 'Oh Lou, I've got loads to tell you.'

'I've rung you a few times in the week,' said Lou. 'Did you get the messages I left on your answering machine?'

'Yeah, sorry, Lou, but I've been out at aerobics – got to get rid of these flabby bits now I've got a fella. I did mean to call you back, honest. I don't know where the time goes.'

'Well, I'm listening now anyway,' said Lou, settling down in the lumpy armchair in the corner of the conservatory. She'd never liked it. It would have to go, she decided.

'It's official, I've got a boyfriend,' Michelle squeaked excitedly, in much the same way that she would have said 'I've won the lottery.' They were more or less the same thing to Michelle.

'Come on then, tell me the details.'

'His name's Craig, he's thirty-three . . .'

'Ooh, toyboy . . .'

'Only two years, so I'm not exactly cradle-snatching! Anyway, he's a mechanic, comes from Leeds, six foot, blond hair, although he's got it shaved in a number one, blue eyes, really really nice smile, unattached, no kids . . .'

Well, so far he sounded promising – suspiciously so.

'He's in between jobs at the moment. Shame, really, but the garage he was working in caught fire and the owner couldn't afford to rebuild it. It's killing him being on the dole because he hates not working. Anyway, he was married but he's separated. They're at that sorting out the financial stuff stage at the moment. He's sleeping on the couch.'

Ah, here we go, thought Lou. She knew it was too good to be true.

'Met him in the *White Hart* last weekend, then we went clubbing and I invited him back for a coffee, although by then I had no intention of putting the kettle on,' Michelle beamed. Lou knew she was beaming because the sunshine was oozing out from between Michelle's teeth, coursing down the telephone line and making Lou's ear warm.

'Anyway, we started snogging on the sofa like teenagers and then we just seemed to float up to bed, it was so weird. My clothes just seemed to fall off like they do on films. We spent the whole weekend at it, apart from him watching the match on Saturday afternoon and the sports highlights at night. I tell you he's got some stamina, it was fantastic. He even got up to make my breakfast. Well, tea and toast, that's all I had in the cupboard.'

'I hope you used protection,' said Lou, feeling like a bucket of cold water as soon as she had opened her mouth.

'We did the first time but he's allergic to rubber. Anyway, I'm on the pill. God, Lou, he is quite honestly the most gorgeous man I've ever met.'

'Have you heard from him since?' said Lou, trying hard to sound frothy and positive and not like the angel of doom.

'Course I have. I said to him, "Ring me when you get home and let me know the taxi arrived safe", and he did. Well, he phoned from his mate's house – he hasn't got a mobile.'

A bloke without a mobile?

'Taxi to Leeds? Crikey, that will have taken care of his week's dole money, won't it? He must be keen,' Lou said.

'It was my fault he missed the taxi home with his mates, so I gave him the money for it. And I know what you're going to say about that, but listen to this, he's coming over next Friday night and he's making me a meal here as a thank you, so really, it's a good job you can't do *evenings*, because I would have had to cancel anyway,' Michelle added pointedly.

'That's nice,' said Lou. It wasn't her place to turn into her mother and start fire-extinguishing Michelle's happiness. Who knows, he might be a genuine guy after all.

'He's gone down to London this week to see if he can get a job there with his mate. God, I hope he doesn't get it. That would be awful, wouldn't it? Just finding the most fantastic bloke ever and then he emigrates. I suppose if everything worked out, I could move down there, though . . .'

Clearly Michelle had already designed her wedding dress and picked their children's names.

'So, are you looking forward to him turning up on Friday then?' asked Lou.

'Of course,' said Michelle tightly. 'Why wouldn't I be? Why did you say it like that?'

'Like what?' said Lou. Heck, how had she said it?

'Sarcastic. That little phrase about him "turning up",' and she repeated Lou's words but gave them a waspish, mocking tone. 'You don't think he'll turn up, do you?'

'I hope he does,' said Lou.

'Hope? You hope?'

Lou obviously wasn't equipped for this conversation with Michelle. She wasn't in full military anti-landmine gear.

'Oh Mish, I really *really* want you to find someone nice, and what I'm trying to say is that I hope this guy turns out to be the one for you,' said Lou, trying her best to sound jolly and encouraging. 'I meant I hope he does turn up and you have a great time.'

'He *will* turn up!' Michelle was cross now. 'You know, Lou, I was dying to tell you, my *friend*, all about him but I just knew you'd have to try spoil it *as usual*. Remind me not to phone you again if I have any more good news, will you? Speak to you later. Maybe.'

With that, Michelle slammed the phone down, leaving Lou wondering once again why she always seemed to be on a different footing to the rest of the universe.

Chapter 15

The skip was lifted the next day whilst Lou was having a horrible rough Monday at work with office morale sinking a few more notches towards the centre of the earth. Karen had been sent off on a course, leaving Lou alone with Jaws and her amazing performing steel gob. Still, it made the Tuesday that followed it all the sweeter, not only to be away from the place but to be up early waiting for the next skip to arrive.

Lou got all her old garb on then twisted off her wedding ring, leaving it in its usual 'waiting place' in the spoon rest. She and Phil had chosen their rings together in a lovely old-fashioned shop down a back street in Leeds. His was a huge, heavy rose gold hoop, and he had chosen a similar one for her over her choice of a delicate plain band. It was far too wide for her little hand and totally impractical to wear and, since she had put on extra weight over the last year or so, it felt tight and uncomfortable when her fingers were warm. Not that she would admit that to Phil — for between the way he and her mother harped on about her bum, she sometimes felt she should pack in her job in Accounts and go and enroll on a Sumo Masters course. Plus it was her wedding ring, the precious piece of gold that Phil put on her finger when he pledged to love her for ever. It would be OK again when she lost a bit more weight, she knew, but for now she would content herself by sneaking it off when Phil wasn't around to let her finger sigh with relief.

The air was considerably nippy and damp, but that didn't stop her from slipping on her gardening gloves to tackle the five-foot nettles, the last leg of the garden clearance. Then what – the cellar or the loft? The cellar, she decided. She was in no way ready to clear out what lay in wait for her *up there*.

Phil pulled off his wedding ring and rubbed at his finger to try and reduce the slight indentation it made. Women customers always flashed a glance to that third finger, left hand. Its presence, or absence, helped to put a man in some context. To some that ring was a symbol of a solid, trustworthy soul but he could also instinctively spot the others who preferred to see that finger naked because it gave them a guilt-free opportunity to flirt down the final figure. Obviously, he made sure they were successful at doing that, but then again, he always left enough margins in his prices to be able to do that anyway. Everyone, without exception, loved a bargain.

Reading people was all part of the game and Phil was an expert at it. He could spot the blokes who would know what he was talking about by a 'fixed-head coupé' and the bullshitters who didn't know a V8 from an After Eight. He knew when a woman enjoyed being flattered that her legs were too long *surely* to fit in that teensy weensy little sports car, and when to dumb it down to being quietly, but charmingly civil.

That sunkissed little blonde number at the other side of the windowed wall in the scarlet suit, for instance, eyeing up the quality end of his car market, was definitely the rings off, full-throttle flirtation type. Popping his wedding band into his pocket, Phil prepared his smile before moving out of the office to show Bradley a real master at work.

Lou barely registered the arrival of the skip lorry; her head was so full of its own debris as she heaved on the devil foliage. She had been thinking about work and what an increasing nightmare it was for everyone who worked alongside her in the department. Zoe was a living ghost these days and Stan looked as if he had left his mind at home and just sent his body out to go through the motions. It wasn't only work that was clogging up Lou's head, though, for that Sunday sex episode with Phil was still circling her head like a deranged vulture; also she didn't know whether to ring up Michelle and apologize for coming across as Saint Elouise of Doom. Then again, could she deny Michelle the opportunity of ringing her after the weekend with a much savoured 'I told you so'?

It made her revisit those easy friendship days with Deb for the zillionth time recently. They'd only ever argued about one thing – the ratio of flour to egg in a Yorkshire Pudding. It hadn't exactly been pistols at dawn stuff, plus they'd been totally ratted on Zombies at the time.

'Hello.'

Lou snapped her head up and immediately swallowed.

It was *him*, complete with dog, which he was holding at the collar as Clooney whined and pawed to get to the nice lady who gave him biscuits.

'Oh hello,' she said, trying to do casual and failing dismally as her voice squeaked like a mouse which had woken up to find its head in a Persian cat's mouth. He really did have a lovely, lovely grin — slightly lopsided but his lips looked soft and generous and — STOP! She reined in her observations as she felt herself starting to colour. She quickly bent down to beckon Clooney, who broke free from Tom and bounced towards Lou with such enthusiasm that he knocked her completely backwards into the wet grass. Her embarrassment was only lessened by the fact that she had jeans on and not a skirt that would have given him a point blank-view of her big Marks & Spencer's stomach-holding-in knickers.

'Clooney, down!' boomed Tom with such command that the dog dropped immediately to the ground, his ears flat back against his head.

'Are you all right? He's bloody barmy that dog, sometimes,' Tom said, striding over to her.

'Yes, I'm fine,' said Lou, shrugging bravely. Fine apart from feeling a total twerp, that was.

Suddenly he was standing over her, bending, and his hands were under her armpits. *Oh no. Oh no no no no no!*

Most women have a fantasy about being lifted effortlessly up into a man's arms as if they were light as a size zero feather, and Lou Winter was no exception. However, she was all too aware that, were that scene to be played out in real life with her as female lead, Prince Charming would probably buckle over with the surprise weight of her, mutter a very unroyal expletive, completely knacker his back and then be in traction for six weeks. Tom Broom, however, was a strong bloke and

Lou found herself lifted easily to her feet without any snapping of spines, blasphemies or exclamations of pain on his behalf.

'Thank you,' said Lou, not really knowing where to look, and simultaneously displaying every nervous gesture that was possible – blinking, neck rubbing, hair fiddling, moving from one foot to the other, clearing her throat, turning into a living, breathing beetroot. At one point, she was almost Guinness Book of Records material.

'I'll leave him in the van in future,' said Tom, mildly mirroring a couple of Lou's gestures.

'No, no, it's not his fault. Please don't, I love to see him,' she pleaded. Her heart was racing like Zola Budd running to the chip shop.

They both looked at Clooney who was lying, nose down on the ground, great dark eyes flicking from one to the other in desperate appeal for forgiveness, although for what he hadn't a clue. He was only being friendly to the biscuit woman.

Lou's head was a blender full of mixed-up ingredients. She was feeling sorry for the dog, feeling embarrassed for herself, feeling God-knows-what at being air-lifted up from the ground by this man with hands the size of spades, a face that said *Made in Italy* and an unbreakable back.

'Have the other lads been looking after you then?'

'Sorry?'

'The other skip lads. Whilst I've not been here.'

'Oh y . . . yes,' stuttered Lou. 'They delivered and picked up on time and had nice manners. I can't ask for any more than that.'

'I suppose not. And did you palm them off with some more of your counterfeit money?'

'Absolutely. Fifteen-pound notes this time.'

'Ha! I shall make sure I check the tills when I get back.'

Good – they were suddenly back on a normal footing. Well, so long as she stayed on her clumsy feet they were anyway. Lou took a deep breath and prepared to put a mental Sherlock Holmes deerstalker on.

'They . . . er . . . said someone was ill in your family. I hope he . . . or she . . . is better now.'

'Well, she's not exactly ill. It's my sister – she's pregnant with her fourth kid.' Tom tutted fondly. 'She's been having a bit of a rough time, though. My brother-in-law is working away at the moment so he's not at home as much as either of them would like. I sometimes take the kids off her hands to give her a break – you know, whiz them off to the park for a game of footie and a push on the swings.'

'No children of your own then?' Wow, big brave Lou! She impressed herself.

'No.' Tom shook his head. 'Not that I know of, anyway. Me and the wife were never really that bothered.'

'Ah, I see.' So he was married then.

'. . . Then we split up just as I was starting to get interested. Being close to my sister's kids made me see just how great it would be to have my own. Ah well. *C'est la vie* – or *Così va il mondo*, as the Italians say.'

Lou tried to rope in the smile that threatened to spread right across her face and meet full circle at the back of her head. How ridiculous and childish was she? Her emotions were glued onto a runaway rollercoaster.

'You got any kids?' Tom asked.

'No,' said Lou. 'I can't, I'm afraid.'

'Oh bloody hell, I'm sorry,' said Tom. His hand twitched instinctively as if he might have wanted to give her a comforting touch, although it was overridden by the stronger forces of etiquette. 'Sorry for saying "bloody hell" then, by the way. Shouldn't swear in front of ladies.'

He needed rescuing himself now, Lou realized. He was the one in a knot this time. People never really knew what to say when an inability to conceive was admitted to.

'It's OK, I'm fine with it,' Lou said, switching on her totally-at-ease-with-the-subject face, which would have fooled all but the most discerning eye. Deb's, for instance.

Clooney gave a low woof to remind them of his presence.

'Can I give h-i-m a biscuit?' Lou whispered, in all innocence.

Clooney barked joyfully. He was forgiven. Otherwise, why would she have said 'biscuit'?

Tom Broom threw his head back and laughed. 'Y-e-s, you can give him a biscuit.'

The joke passed two feet over Lou's head as she took a lolloping Clooney off towards the biscuit cupboard. There was still a ghost of laughter playing around Tom's mouth when she returned the dog to him. She paid him for the skip, he held the notes up to the light to 'check for Tippex', then he gave her a cheery wave and a, 'See you soon, no doubt,' and drove off. Lou tried not to notice that her insides felt as if they were full of warm olive oil.

Chapter 16

Renee twisted the three gold bands around her finger. One a thin, old gold wedding ring, one beautifully studded with a full range of precious gems that Shaun had bought her to say he would love her for ever, the third an engagement ring with three emeralds and five diamonds. They had cost him a small fortune at the time, but they were exquisite pieces and the young jeweller who designed them went on to be a big name in the industry. Shaun couldn't possibly have known what an investment he'd made when he bought those rings. He had placed them on Renee's finger when his heart was full of the ambitions that charmed her down the aisle with him. Shaun's enlarged heart was always going to be the undoing of him.

When Elouise came along, Shaun decided he didn't want to be a man who worked all hours and never saw his wife nor his child, so he found the plâteau job that enabled him to provide well for his family but be home every evening to eat with them and enjoy them. No one could say that Shaun Casserly didn't provide for his family; they wanted for nothing. Well, none of the basics anyway. However, even Renee had been shocked to find out the true extent of his provisions for her, just in case they didn't make it to his pension together. The insurance policy he had in place would see her in good stead for the rest of her days, but it had all been much too late for Renee.

Elouise's birth had marked the death of all Renee's greater plans for their early married years: the monstrously huge house and three-acre garden, the flash car, the holidays cruising the Mediterranean . . . She wanted so much more than this three-bedroomed bungalow with a conservatory, even if it was big enough to swing a very large cat in. Material possessions made life's journey a happier, more comfortable affair. Love was, she found, a cheap firework that blinded with its flare before dying and leaving nothing of its original promise.

Renee treasured her rings, though, even more so since they went missing a few years ago. She had taken them off to get a manicure and couldn't for the life of her find them afterwards. She and Victorianna had looked everywhere but they'd simply vanished. She couldn't have imagined how much they meant to her until then, which somehow managed to assuage some of the guilt she felt at never missing Shaun as much as she should.

It was a big relief when Lou managed to find them, but oddly enough they had turned up in a place that Renee was sure she had searched quite thoroughly herself. It had all been a very odd business.

Chapter 17

Lou promised Phil she would make the car showroom accounts her priority the next morning, but instead she found herself in her old jogging bottoms and T-shirt, heading down the cellar steps with a roll of black bin-liners. She fully intended to clear out the cellar in the morning and then spend all afternoon doing the books – well, that was the original plan, anyway. However, five spare pillows, four packs of carpet tiles, three demi-johns, two chipboard tables – alas, no partridges nor pear trees – later, Lou knew there was no way she was going to break off her clutter-clearing in order to sit at a desk trying to put Phil's financial affairs in order.

The showroom accounts were a nightmare. Phil had so many little tax fiddles going on, most accountants would have gone blind or insane or both with it all, but at least they would have got paid whilst they were going doolally, which is more than Lou did. Occasionally he threw her the promise of 'making it up to her with a nice surprise', but the surprise in question never materialized. Unless one was to count the various new 'surprise' kitchen gadgets.

There were three big dry cellars under the house. One

was totally empty; Phil had been talking about turning it into a gym for the last six years. So far he had bought a small trampoline from Argos which was stuffed in a corner still in its wrapping, and an unpunched punch ball hung from a rafter. The middle cellar housed all the past years' account files, the artificial Christmas tree and all the decorations. Lou searched through the bags and found some broken baubles and anaemic tinsel, but annoyingly nothing to really get her rubbish-clearing teeth into.

Most of the junk was concentrated in the first cellar, where the many shelves were full of 'useful' items which it was thought good to have to hand. There were countless bags of screws and nails, light fittings, switch plates, paintbrushes with a bald patch resembling Phil's, a selection of torches that needed batteries and bulbs, rusty hammers, garden hoses that had been awaiting mending for longer than Lou could remember (and had been long replaced anyway) and lots of plugs that Phil had cut from defunct electrical appliances 'just in case'. There was a big box of his old videos covered with dust and verdigris: cowboy films, some B movie action titles she had never heard of, a couple of Chuck Norris's, and tucked away right at the bottom, wrapped in brown paper – *Breast Side Story* and *Titty Titty Gang Bang*. She carried them back upstairs in a binliner and threw them in the skip before breaking for a quick sandwich. Now that she had got stuck in, she knew there was no way she was going to do any accounts before the space was totally clear.

There was a stack of books on the shelves that she remembered Phil buying on a whim from a closing-down sale ages ago, but she had never yet seen him read anything but newspapers and car-focused periodicals, so she knew they wouldn't be missed. Lou read avidly, but these titles in her hand didn't appeal to her much. However, they were in far too good a condition to throw away, so they went into the cellar charity bag to join a candle-making kit and some white plastic garden tubs which Lou had bought on an impulse but never really liked.

She swept up shovelfuls of dust and cobwebs, trying to avoid the spiders. Phil would have screamed at the size of some of them, and though Lou didn't exactly want them within cuddling distance, she never killed them. A thought of her dad visited her, telling her what an important job they did in killing the big noisy germ-ridden flies who filled up their clogs on dung-heaps then went tapdancing on cakes. Her dad had been full of little stories like that to make her laugh. She'd hoped one day to tell them to her own children. Ah well, she shook that thought away before it took a grip.

Under the shelves she discovered with glee the antique airer she had bought the previous summer and totally forgotten about. She had sanded the few rough bits and waxed it when she had first got it home, but had been unable to find any pulleys to attach it to the ceiling beams, so she had stored it down the cellar until she had time to go on a more detailed hunt for them. The first time around, B&Q had sent her to Focus, Focus had sent her to Wickes, and Wickes had sent her back to B&Q.

The article said that if she was to mend any such broken items which had potential for use then she should strike whilst the iron was hot. *Utilize or bin it.* With that in mind, Lou made a mental note to go pulley-hunting at her earliest convenience.

Stored underneath the airer was a shirtbox full of photographs, and as she had just about finished and was ready for a cuppa, she took it upstairs and opened it up whilst she was waiting for the kettle to boil. She couldn't remember why she had kept them, for the few important photos she wanted to keep were in her 'treasure box' in her bedroom. Lou wasn't a great one for photographs; she had been quite content to carry the memories of various special days around in her head rather than look at second-rate snapshots of them which rarely succeeded in capturing any true essence of the moment.

Seating herself on the floor in the conservatory with a mug of strong instant coffee, she tipped the box out onto the rug to look at the stills of her past. Most were out of focus or long shots, or were just plain boring landscapes of once-nice days, now just unrecognizable vistas. Amongst them was a family shot of her wedding. Her mother was in dark blue with a hairdo that made her look like a minor member of the Royal Family. She was colour coordinating (by prior arrangement) with Phil's mum, also in navy. Lou had never really got to know Sheila Winter much, beyond the fact that she had indulged her offspring to nutter proportions, instilling in them the belief that they were beings more supreme than the Daleks and destined always to get everything they wanted. Maybe if Phil and Celia had had a few more tantrums which didn't work, it would have done them good, Lou had started to think recently. Sheila had retired to Devon and died suddenly three months after the wedding. The funeral had been an odd affair, peculiarly emotionless. Sheila's sisters, and even her twin brother, had seemed more interested in getting first pick of the after-service vol-au-vents than saying goodbye to one of their own, and weirdly, there had been a photographer there as they all got together so rarely and didn't want to spoil the opportunity for some family groupings. ('Can we have one with the corpse and immediate family?' 'Now let's have one of the corpse throwing her wreath?' Lou had thought blackly at the time.)

Phil had been understandably quiet, but was back to work the next day with a 'life goes on' comment at the door. Celia was mourning openly with dramatic wails and cries and getting lots of attention, but was out shopping the next day, 'to take her mind off things'. It was all so different to when her dad died. Lou hadn't stopped crying for months, and trying to slot herself back into normal life had been like feeding herself onto a motorway full of fast-moving lorries whilst riding a skateboard.

Feeling the pressure of tears build behind her eyes, she turned resolutely back to her wedding pictures, shuddering at the sight of Des and Celia bracketing her on the photograph: Celia, looking very designer-clad in a hat that was part-Royal Ascot, part-standard lampshade; Des, looking part-Bryan Ferry's younger brother, part-Nosferatu. Phil looked so lean and handsome with thick fair hair. He had always looked younger than his age, but with that air of supreme confidence that had attracted her so much. He wasn't smiling like everyone else on the photograph; in fact, he looked rather surprised. At one side of him was Victorianna, a younger, fresher, more glamorous version of Renee, and the minx was wearing a white dress. It had caused a bit of an incident on the day, as the old organist had started playing 'Here Comes the Bride' when she walked to her seat, which Victorianna would have loved, of course. The angle of Victorianna's arm disappearing behind Phil's back made it obvious that she had just nipped his bottom. And *that,* Lou remembered, was why this photograph was in the reject bag.

In the line-up, Lou was smiling, looking exceedingly pretty in a long plain ivory dress that pushed her in and out in all the right places. She had always had a shape – Phil hadn't complained then about her not being like a beanpole. In fact, if her memory served her right, he'd rather savoured her curves. Then there was Deb, her one and only bridesmaid, in a shade of scarlet, looking slim and blonde and gorgeous and more like a blood relative of Victorianna's than Lou did. That similarity had come in exceedingly handy during Operation Great Ring Rescue.

There were some holiday shots: a pinprick in the sea which she remembered as being a dolphin she spotted on their honeymoon in Benidorm; hideous family shots of Phil's horrible uncle with his pet brown cardigan who came to stay seven years ago and gave Lou the longest fortnight of her life; the façade of the Hotel Artemis in Corfu. It was the only holiday they'd had outside Benidorm in all the years they'd been together. Lou had wanted to go to Rome but Phil had 'surprised her' and booked Greece instead. They had gone there to celebrate their sixth wedding anniversary and Phil had gone missing after their celebratory meal. She found him emerging from an olive grove with a woman called

Wanda from Wakefield who was residing in the same
hotel. She was a brassy piece in her fifties, hair bleached
to inflammable straw and a mouth full of Stonehenge
teeth. He said he'd been helping her look for her husband Alf (who turned up the next day snoring away in a
fishing boat cuddling a bottle of Ouzo) and of course
Lou had believed him. It was only later, when Phil left
her for Susan Peach, that Lou wondered if he had, after
all, indulged his passion for mutton that night amongst
the fruit trees of Greece.

There was an old school photograph in the pile, her
last one, when she was sixteen. She couldn't remember
all the names of her classmates, but two faces stood out
from the rest. The pixie-faced Gaynor Froggatt, who was
to die in an alcohol-and-heroin haze six years later, and
Shirley Hamster who was so jealous of Lou's long hair
that she had once snipped some off during Latin. She
had been little prepared for Lou swinging around and
giving her a right hook that sent her flying backwards
over the chair and into the bookshelf behind. It had been
worth Renee's abject disgust, the headmistress's lecture
on ladylike behaviour and a week's detention translating
Catullus' love poetry, especially as she had rather enjoyed
doing it, as she recalled. Her dad had given her the
thumbs-up but only when her mother's back was turned.

Elouise Angeline Casserly. In those days she had stuck
her chin and her chest out wherever she walked; a girl
who was scared of nothing and primed to take on the
world. She was half-goddess, half-pit bull terrier. She
dived headfirst not only into life but also off the stage at
college discos, knowing that the rugby lads would always
catch her. She was a demon on the hockey pitch, blasted

aces out at tennis and was still dancing long after the die-
hards had dropped with exhaustion. She was
indestructible, spirited, marvellous. So what had turned
her into this little woman who wore minimiser bras and
was terrified that the wrong word or an extra inch on
her waist would spell the end of her marriage? Where
the bloody hell had Lou Casserly gone with her insane,
loopy, passionate, determined spirit – the woman who
was going to make her fortune opening up the best
coffee-house in the world with the best friend anyone
could ever have in the world?

Before thought, sense or reason could get in the way,
Lou levered herself up, letting the photographs tumble
from her lap, and reached for the telephone.

She could still remember the number. In saying that,
what guarantee was there that it would still be the same
one? And wasn't it a bit stupid, ringing during working
hours? But she dialled the number all the same and it
connected and burred five times before a dear, familiar
voice answered.

'Hello.'

'It's me – Lou . . . Casserly . . . Winter,' Lou said with
a cracked voice. 'Deb, is it possible? Can we meet?'

Chapter 18

'Debra Devine,' was how Deb had introduced herself to Lou many years ago on their first day at college. 'I know, I know, I sound like a crap nightclub singer or at best a porn star. Let's go and get a coffee and have a natter.'

Lou had laughed, following her to the college cafeteria where their friendship was born over cappuccino and biscotti. In a way it had ended over the same, she thought. She had missed that friendship so much these past three years. The ache of loss had never faded completely and, like arthritis, had flared up often, making its presence felt.

The two women arranged to meet at the weekend in *Café Joseph* just behind Barnsley Park. The phone conversation had been short and polite and consisted mainly of the social niceties of, 'How are you?' and, 'Lovely to hear from you.' Lou decided that there would be plenty of time for talking more freely when they met.

Needing a distraction, Lou reached for Phil's accounts. They really did need to be done – *cleared from her agenda.*

It was midnight by the time she had completed them, heaving a huge sigh of relief. Thank goodness she hadn't left them much longer. Even at the best of times, they were like unravelling a ball of wool that a barmy cat had tried to decimate.

Thursday and Friday were just ordinary days at work; they passed without incident. She had long since abandoned any hope of getting job satisfaction there, but since finding the old *Casa Nostra* file, it did make Lou realize she wanted more for herself than a part-time job in an accounts office.

She desperately tried to keep a cap on being excited about the imminent prospect of meeting Deb again after so long, but various thoughts tortured her. What if they had nothing to say to each other? What if Deb changed her mind and didn't turn up? It wasn't unlike the anticipation that preceded a blind date.

She was so preoccupied with the what-could-go-wrongs that she over-spiced Phil's curry on Friday night. He still ate it but wasn't best pleased and made a point of fanning his mouth and drinking copious amounts of water throughout his suffering.

There was no text message from Michelle, so Lou happily presumed that Craig the still-married-but-separated mechanic had turned up. A good man was just what Michelle needed, but was Michelle what the good man needed? Lou just wished her mixed-up friend would chill out a little and allow anyone she hooked up with to breathe occasionally, but it was impossible to tell her that without phones being slammed down or dramatic walkings-away occurring. These days, Michelle seemed determined to take everything Lou said to her as a lecture, and it was, quite frankly, becoming a nuisance to have to screen everything Lou intended to say for potential double meanings.

★

Lou arrived at *Café Joseph* ten minutes before time. The place really irked her. It couldn't make up its mind what it wanted to be, she thought – an ice-cream parlour, a cake-house, sandwich shop or a pretentious bistro – and as such, it did none of them very well.

She had just found a table next to a giant paper flower display when Deb arrived. Lou stood and waved tentatively with a nervous but excited smile that was half-afraid to show itself. Deb came over and they both missed the moment when an embrace would have been natural. They scraped their chairs back on the tiled floor and sat down opposite each other.

'Hello, Deb,' said Lou. 'It's really nice to see you.'

'Hello, Lou. How have you been?'

Lou opened her mouth to reply, 'Fine,' but nothing came out.

Deb looked just the same as always, give or take a very different hairstyle. It had been cropped when Lou had last seen her; now it was almost bum-length and made Lou realize just how very long they had been apart.

Lou suddenly felt ashamed, unable to put this right, unworthy even to be asking. It was such a terrible, terrible thing that she had done. How the hell had she ever let that happen? Lou couldn't speak; something roughly the size of Everest was blocking her throat and wouldn't be gulped away. Then, against all her best intentions, Lou started to cry. And the more she tried to stop it, the faster those tears oozed out of her ducts, as if they were being pumped out by a saltwater artery.

Deb immediately came around to her side of the table and hugged her.

'Give up, you daft tart. Now look what you've made me do! Everyone will think we're lesbians.'

Lou snorted with involuntary laughter, still crying even though she desperately wanted to stop. She couldn't bear it that she was drawing attention to herself, but Deb's perfume was the same as she always used to wear and it hurt her heart to smell it. Scents were very powerful at dragging Lou back to a past she couldn't otherwise access. She couldn't smell Aramis without being back on her dad's knee whilst he read *The Magic Faraway Tree*, putting on the voices of Moon-Face and the mad deaf bloke with all the saucepans.

A young fresh-faced waiter arrived to take their order and jiggled about behind them for a while, not knowing whether to melt off and come back again in a few minutes.

'Two coffees, please, and two of your biggest pieces of cheesecake if you have any,' said Deb, in her best Hyacinth Bouquet voice which made it sound as if big pieces of cheesecake were the norm for ladies of quality who lunch.

'I'm sorry,' Lou said, as Deb handed her a serviette. 'I wasn't prepared for this. I don't even know where to start saying what I feel.'

'Elouise Winter, if I had any negative feelings about us meeting again, I wouldn't have turned up. You don't know how many times I've wanted to pick up the phone and see what we could do to sort this out. I have a few sorrys of my own to say too, you know.'

'No, you don't.'

'Yes, I do.'

'I bet I look gorgeous now, don't I?' said Lou, tipping

her head up to let the last of the tears drain back from her eyes.

'Absolutely gorgeous. Besides, I've always liked pandas,' said Deb.

Lou smiled a red-eyed smile as she did a quick repair job on her face with her powder puff.

'How's your mum these days?' asked Deb, sitting back down again.

'Oh, she's . . . just the same. Still playing one-upmanship with her mate Vera, although Vera is up on points with a holiday to the Bahamas.'

'And Victorianna?'

On the sound of her name, they instinctively both held up their fingers in the sign of the cross and chuckled together.

'She is most definitely still the same. She gets us to send over parcels of English stuff. She's shacked up with this bloke who's stinking rich and looks older than God's dog.'

'There's a surprise!'

'Any man on the scene for you?' asked Lou.

'There's been a couple, but . . . well, one wasn't special enough and the other one thought *I* wasn't special enough,' said Deb. 'I'm having a rest from the unfairer sex for a while, and jolly nice it is too.'

'How's your mum then?'

'Oh, we lost her last year, Lou.'

Lou felt her eyes filling up again, especially when Deb carried on, 'It was a toughie, I have to admit. You know how lovely she was. I had my sister there but I wished I'd had you to talk to.' She held up a warning finger as Lou started wiping at her eyes with her serviette. 'Look, Lou, we can't change the past, but we're here now, so let's make each other a promise to not look back. Please, let's just go forward.'

They clutched hands over the table, just as the waiter arrived with their coffees. He had never actually seen any real-life lesbians before, and the image of these two good-looking mature women 'at it' would feature in a few of his future fantasies.

'He definitely thinks we're a couple,' said Deb, pointing at his back. 'I think we've turned him on. Pervy little bugger.'

Lou laughed. She realized then why she liked Karen so much. She was a good girl in her own right, but there were so many echoes of Deb in her.

'It's quite a varied menu here, isn't it?' said Deb with raised eyebrows as she read from the ornate leaflet propped up beside the cruet. 'What the frigging hell is Olivian Chicken?'

'Don't know, but it's offset by Simple Vegetables,' said Lou.

'How's Phil?' asked Deb, unconsciously making the small leap in subject-matter. 'More to the point, how are *you* and Phil?'

'Oh, we're fine,' said Lou, aware that they had temporarily strayed into Polite Land again, where they would only skim the surface of the subject. 'We're still together. He works six or seven days a week – he's still obsessed by cars.'

She didn't say she was happy, Deb noted.

'You ever . . . managed . . . did you have any . . .?'

'No, no children,' said Lou, saying 'the word'. 'It obviously wasn't to be.'

'You never went for IVF or anything?' Deb was amazed. She knew how much Lou had wanted a child of her own.

'It's pretty gruelling, is IVF, and I know that Phil just wouldn't do all the stuff it entails. We know he's OK, of course, because of his twins, so it's obviously me who has the problem. Anyway, I know he doesn't really want children, so there's not much point in me going to be prodded and poked, is there? I've come to terms with it. I'm fine, really,' said Lou.

Yeah right, thought Deb, changing to a lighter subject about their jobs. There would be plenty of time to catch up on what was really happening in Lou's life. It was so good to see her, she thought. She had a couple of extra lines around the eyes since their last meeting, but so what? She looked a hell of a lot nicer than the last time Deb had seen her, reduced to the image of the gaunt, walking dead. Deb noted her friend's still-lovely kind face and her curvy pink smile, but she wasn't as content-looking as Deb would have expected her to be. Not after all she went through to get that piece of crap back anyway. There was definitely something going on behind those cat-green eyes of Lou Casserly ... Winter.

'Are you still working in Sheffield?' Deb asked.

'Yes, I'm still stuck in Accounts. Great bunch of people, except for the office manageress who is a total witch, but it's a job. You?'

'Yes, still living just outside Maltstone, still running Mrs Serafinska's bakery, still the same bunch of Derby and Joaners working for me, plus an absolutely delicious eighteen-year-old student called Kurt. And yes, I'm still dreaming of opening up *Working Title Casa Nostra* and ruling the world.'

'Cheesecake,' interrupted the waiter, slightly disappointed that they just looked like two old friends having coffee now and there was no sign of any girl-on-girl action.

'Thank you,' said Deb, poking the hardened exterior of a dessert that was as fresh as one of her Uncle Brian's jokes. When the waiter had gone to another table she whispered over to Lou, 'We would never have served stuff like this in our establishment. This cheesecake is so old that I don't know whether to eat it or buy it a pension book cover.'

Lou smiled and speared a forkful of her portion. It was passable, although it had far too much sugar and not half enough lemon in it.

Deb had another look at the menu and put it down with a huff.

'The owner has been watching too much Marco Pierre White on the telly!'

'You still fantasizing about him?' said Lou with a grin.

'Of course,' said Deb. 'Aren't you?'

'Absolutely!'

'The only man we were ever likely to scrap over bedding.'

'Why didn't you go it alone and open up a coffee shop?' Lou asked Deb midchew.

'Didn't want to,' said Deb. 'Plus I don't think *I* could have. It was always a joint or neither thing.' She melted into a soft couch of nostalgia. 'It was fun planning it all, wasn't it? Mum was more excited than me, I think. Oh – and remember you snogging the bank manager?'

'I didn't snog him, I just hugged him.' Lou smiled. 'Do you know, I found the big file recently? Remember the "Brando" you were going to invent?'

'Oh yes, my Brando! I never did find anything good enough to bear the holy name. Talking of good enough, I've never yet been in a coffee shop where I didn't think we could do better, and I've been in lots of them. I'm stuck in a state of eternal research.'

'I know how you feel. It didn't die for me either.'

'Really?' said Deb, tilting her head. 'Because I'll tell you this, Lou babe, it certainly didn't die for me.'

Their eyes locked and each transmitted something to the other that wasn't quite formed yet. Psychic microbes made up of memory cuttings and the raw, thrilling emotions associated with them of what could have been. Lou felt a glimmer of excitement that she tried to stop reason and sense and thoughts of Phil and her mother spoiling. She looked at Deb who was feeling it too, she just knew it. *This is crazy! We've only just met again. Let's not get carried away. Let's be sensible!* But Lou's mental processes were in overdrive.

'So, where do we go from here?' she said. 'Are we going to see each other again or have I turned into a hideous old bag and you're sorry you came?'

'Yes, of course you have, darling,' said Deb. 'But let's meet up anyway.' She dropped her eyes and inspected her nails. 'Will you tell Phil? I presume he doesn't know you're here.'

'I haven't thought that far ahead.'

'You don't have to tell him anything, of course. He won't like it and it would only stir up trouble. '

'I'll pick my moment then tell him we bumped into

each other in town. I'll take it from there. He can't stop me having friends.'

But he can and he did, thought Deb. However, she stayed silent.

Lou paid the bill as Deb said that it was the least she could do after poisoning her with old cake on their reconciliation. Lou laughed and hugged her tightly before they got into their respective cars, much to the waiter's delight as he observed them through the window.

Lou watched her friend drive off with a thrill akin to having a secret affair. That was how Phil would definitely see it, anyway – a threat to his marriage, an illegal union. There was no way he would countenance her friendship revival with Deb. But equally there was no way Lou was going to stop seeing her now. She realized, as she climbed into the driver's seat, that she really hadn't thought this through at all. She couldn't live a lie and she couldn't tell her husband the truth about what she had done. So, what the hell *was* she going to do?

Chapter 19

Sometimes when Lou did a crossword and couldn't get the solution, she'd put it to the back of her mind and later, when she was least expecting it, the answer would deliver itself unbidden to the front, just like that. Maybe if she employed the same strategy now, her subconscious would chew on the problem she faced about how to bring her renewed friendship with Deb into the open, and then present her with exactly what she should do. So, after saying goodbye to Deb, she concentrated on getting those pulleys sorted out for her wooden airer and drove through the centre of town where there was a small privately owned timberyard. They wouldn't have them but they might know a man who did.

'You want to try the *Ironmongers Tub*,' said the ruddy-faced owner with Noddy Holder sideburns who looked more like a butcher than a woodman.

'Where's that?'

'Townend. Do you know where St William's Yard is?'

'Side of the old Tin Factory?' Lou tried.

'Good girl. That's the place. They'll fix you up. No bother.'

'Thanks,' said Lou, as much for him calling her a 'girl' as for the directions. It was a simple but rare treat these days.

Nothing much went on in the Townend, except for graffiti. Once it had been a lively quarter but the major commercial emphasis had shifted to the other end of town. The shop rents were cheap, which attracted transient cheap businesses that held little shopping appeal, and the lack of passing trade soon spelled their demise. After fifty years in business, the old Tin Factory had closed, though the building still stood. Well, just about – a good blow and it would fall over. Lou hadn't ever noticed an ironmonger anywhere around there, but then again, she had never had any cause to go to the back of the derelict factory.

She was surprised to find a large car park full of trucks, vans and cars there. A very old row of buildings faced her, suggesting, by the number of their doors, four shopfronts. The two on the right were unoccupied; the third, a decent-sized transport café with signage above the door reading *Ma's Café*, looked healthily occupied inside, and the end one was the ironmonger's – very Dickensian, with scrubbed small-paned windows and a swinging sign that read *Ironmongers T.U.B.*

Lou pushed the door open and a bell tinkled. She walked into an Aladdin's cave of floor-to-ceiling wooden shelves, drawers and huge apothecaries' cabinets that gave her the feeling she'd just broken through a time barrier into the past.

'Two ticks,' said a man's deep voice from the back.

A movement to her right caught her eye. The paws of a big dog on the floor there twitching in sleep. It looked like . . .

'Can I help you?'

The man who had called out to Lou came into the front of the shop. He was out of his skip-wagon context, which confused her for a brief moment.

'It's you!' exclaimed Lou with a surprised grin.

He didn't look as bulky in jeans and a denim shirt as he did in his skip overalls, but the small shop only served to emphasize his height and bigness. The pint of water in his hand looked like a half-pint glass; his shoulders looked as if they might jam in the doorway if he walked straight at it.

'I didn't recognize you with your clothes on,' she joked, although it sounded a lot funnier when Eric Morecambe said it.

'I think you're thinking of my twin, Tom,' the man said. 'Big handsome bloke, black hair? Runs the skips?'

Oh, pants. Was she going to make a total arse of herself in front of his whole family?

'Oh, I'm sorry,' said Lou, feeling herself go warm on the inside, a sure indicator she was going red on the outside. 'You're so alike.'

Best to get down to business quick. Then she could go home and drown herself. 'I'm looking for a couple of pulleys for a wooden airer,' she said, adopting a business like tone. 'I've been told you can knock me up with some.'

Tom's brother turned quickly away to look through some boxes. He appeared to be biting his lip. Did they all do that in their family – laugh at people, she wondered. If so, it must have been like growing up in a house full of Frank Carsons.

'Here we are,' said the brother, reaching up about

twelve foot and bringing down a box. Lou would have needed crampons and oxygen to get up that far.

'Crikey, that was quick,' she commented. 'I wouldn't have thought you would know where to find them in here.'

'A place for everything and everything in its place,' said the brother, tapping his nose as if letting her into a big secret which, of course, it had been until she had commenced her clutter-clearing exercise.

This man was the spitting image of Tom. She had known a few sets of twins in her time, but only one other set of truly identical ones. She had gone to junior school with Robert and Robin Ramskill. The teachers had asked their mother to send them to school with some identification as they were always pretending to be the other, so she had knitted them both jumpers with RR on them.

'You'll need a single pulley and a double one, if you want a workable system. I presume you want to pull it up and down and not just hang it up as a decoration.'

Lou nodded and Tom's twin brother got a piece of rope out from a drawer and fed it through the pulley wheel to show her how to set it up. It looked fairly straightforward with a little thought applied to it. He had big meaty hands, neat nails and no wedding ring either.

'I'll need a cleat as well,' said Lou, taking care not to make it sound anything like *clit* (thereby avoiding giving the Broom brothers an aneurysm).

'Call it three pounds fifty, please,' said the nameless brother.

'That all?' queried Lou, who had been expecting to pay at least a tenner.

'Pay more if you like but that's what they cost,' he

smiled. 'It's a pound for the single one, two pounds for the double. Which leaves fifty pee for the cleat.'

He mirrored her pronunciation of the word: 'cleeet'. The length of the vowels wouldn't have sounded out of place in a spaghetti western about Mexican bandits.

Lou flashed him a look but he was totally straight-faced. They were too similar and it crossed Lou's mind for a moment that he didn't have a brother at all, and this was actually Tom himself. But that would be taking a joke a bit far, wouldn't it?

She handed over a five-pound note which he held up to the light to inspect. Cheeky so and so, Lou bristled. She hated it when people did that. Usually cocky little blighters in supermarkets who wouldn't spot a fake Queen if she had eyebrows like Noel Gallagher. And though she and Tom might have shared the jokes about counterfeit money, she didn't know this bloke from Adam to take such a liberty.

'Is that Clooney?' asked Lou, receiving her change with a cool and collected 'Thank you'. She was more than disappointed that he was asleep. At least he wouldn't have found her so flaming hilarious.

'No, it's his brother from the litter,' said rude-man. 'My sister's kids have been playing with him all morning, so he's t-i-r-e-d out.'

He even has the same twinkle in his eye as Tom, thought Lou, although he was too familiar with strangers for her liking, and so when he disappeared to his back office to get a receipt book, she sneaked out. She'd had enough for the time being of people thinking she was a joke.

★

There were two calls waiting for Lou when she got home. One from Michelle saying it was just a quickie as Craig was in the bath, but yes, he was there and they were having a fantastic time. The other was from her mother saying that Victorianna was going to some dinner with Edward Wankystein and that the Deputy President of the United States was going to be there as well (big wow – *not*). Bloody Keith Featherstone still hadn't rung. She tried to put it to the back of her mind, which wasn't all that easy, but there wasn't going to be any chance of getting him until Monday now. She got on with preparing Phil's evening meal: cappuccino of pea soup, lamb fillet and treacle sponge with home-made custard. She needed him in a good mood for what she was about to tell him.

Chapter 20

'Hello there!' said Phil, flashing his perfectly white teeth at Miss Scarlet Suit. This was the second time she had been in the showroom this week. He never forgot a face. Or a pair of tits, especially not ones as perky as those. She reminded him of someone from his past that he couldn't quite place. An old girlfriend, somewhere along the line.

'You told me to keep popping in, if you remember,' the rather lovely punter said, refreshing his memory about the line he quoted her on her last visit. 'Stock changes daily?'

'Indeed it does,' said Phil. 'Have you any idea what you are looking for in particular? You weren't quite sure last time, as I remember. Has anything inspired you since?'

'Something older perhaps,' she said, looking up at him from under a sexy little fringe. 'Classy, though. I don't mind a few miles on the clock if I know it's going to be reliable.'

Cheeky little minx, he thought. Like he didn't know what she meant!

'Have you seen this one?' said Phil, leading the way over to a nice old Jag.

'Too big,' she said, rejecting it before he had even opened the door to thrill her with the walnut dash and the leather upholstery. Well, at least here was a bird who knew exactly what she didn't want, and that was always one stage closer to knowing what they did want.

'I want something sporty. I want something *me*. I want something—'

'Singular?' suggested Phil.

'Yes,' she said, as if pleasantly surprised that he knew such a word, and she was obviously very flattered that he'd applied it to her.

Phil mulled this over, and then suddenly snapped his fingers.

'I've got just the thing for you, although it's not in the showroom yet. A 1960s MG Roadster, British Racing Green, absolutely beautiful – and, here's the best bit – it's got less than forty thousand on the clock. It's a fantastic car – I'm expecting a rush when it's actually here in this window. It's even got the original green log book, and a full service history, of course.'

'Is it a hard top or soft?'

'Hard. You don't want a soft top in this climate.' He dismissed the British weather with one sweep of the hand. In saying that, had it been a soft top he would have said, 'You can squeeze out the last drop of the British sunshine with this little beauty.'

'Oh yeah, and what do you drive then?' she tested.

'Audi TT,' said Phil, adding, 'hardtop!' accompanied by his best lopsided grin.

'Nice. Not exactly a family car, though?'

Ooh, she really was pressing for info, he thought. Clever.

'No family,' he said, with the tiniest regretful sigh.

'So where's the MG now?'

'It's getting the full treatment, once-overed, valeted, polished, one hundred and thirty point check and generally getting touched up by expert hands. It really is absolutely stunning. One lady owner from new and that is no lie.' Well, one doddery old tart who drove a gorgeous little car like that at 15 m.p.h. to go to the post office once a week. How the hell she had managed to even clock up so much mileage was anyone's guess. She must have got lost a few times.

'How much are you looking at for it?'

'Not one hundred per cent sure at the moment, but it will be in the region of nine . . .'

She didn't flinch.

'. . . nine and a half maybe. Thousand,' he clarified, just in case she thought he meant hundreds. So far, he couldn't tell if she was a blonde inside the head as well as outside.

'Obviously. When will you have it in for me to look at?' she asked.

'Couple of weeks, maybe three. Tell you what, you leave me your number and the moment I have it in, you will be the first to know about it.'

If he did have it in, boy, she *would* have known about it as well, he thought lustfully. He smiled a soft, benign smile, which belied the groin-thrusting going on in his brain, and beckoned her into his office where she scribbled down her name on his desk pad.

'I'll give you my mobile number and my name is Miss Susan Shoesmith.'

She definitely emphasized the 'Miss', he was sure of it.

Sexy, sassy, spirited Susan Shoesmith, he said to himself, trying to trigger a memory that he knew was there. Who was she like?

'Don't forget me,' she winked. She had British Racing Green eyes.

'Forget you? Not a chance,' said Phil.

As if the day at work wasn't good enough, Phil opened the door to his favourite smell of all time, apart from the aroma of banknotes untouched by human taxman.

By the time he'd had a wee, there was a starter waiting on the table – a frothy pea soup and a little plait of warm white seeded bread and butter. He had only a tiny second helping because lamb fillet was to follow, in a rosemary and honey sauce with cider gravy poured over some divine buttery mashed spuds and asparagus spears.

Lou was having plain chicken fillet, mixed vegetables and no gravy. He wouldn't have liked to have swapped his for hers.

'What have I done to deserve this?' asked Phil, starting conversation after he had got to the end of the interesting bits in his newspaper.

'Nothing,' said Lou, shaking her head in a fine semblance of innocence. 'I fancied chicken and I know you aren't really keen, so I just picked up some lamb in the butcher's whilst I was there.'

'Been shopping then?'

'Yes, I just nipped into town to get some fresh air.'

'Accounts all up to date are they, love?' he enquired.

'Yes, of course. Treacle sponge?'

'I'm so full.'

Phil rubbed his stomach, hoping for a liberating burp.

It came and left a perfect space for pudding. 'Oh, go on then. Just a bit.'

He had a little portion then followed it up with a big one; after all, she had gone to all this trouble for him. More trouble than usual . . . now the big question was *why*.

Lou poured him a brandy and delivered it to him with a cigar and the matchbox. He watched her with suspicious eyes. He knew how much Lou hated lamb; he wasn't stupid, whatever she might think. Whether she realized it or not, she served it up when she felt desperate for his approval.

'So,' he said slowly, as he puffed up a glow on the cigar. 'What's all this about then, Lou?'

'What's what all about?' She wasn't giving him eye-contact and that told him volumes.

'Lamb? Treacle sponge? I know you, remember, so what are you building up to tell me?' He gave her one of his fixed smiles that wasn't reflected in his eyes. The one he saved for the VAT man.

'Well, actually there is something.' Lou started clearing up the plates.

'What?'

She was licking her lips; they were dry as autumn leaves.

'What?' he asked again, impatiently. It had better not be bad news about his accounts.

Lou took a deep breath and tried to begin.

'Phil . . .' This was stupid. Just say it, she urged herself. Why was it so difficult to say she'd met up with Deb again? She opened her mouth to speak. The sentences travelling from her brain ripped themselves apart and reformed in her voicebox.

'Phil, I want to throw away the armchair in the conservatory.'

He tutted. 'Is that it?'

'Yes. I . . . I just wanted to make sure you were OK with that.'

'You can throw it out, if you want. It's hell to sit on anyway.'

'We'll get one of those recliners, like my mother's.'

Phil nodded. He liked the sound of that.

'Right, well, that's that then,' she said, carrying on clearing.

Phil took a big swallow of brandy and studied her as she moved around the table. That wasn't it, though, was it, Lou? he thought. Her face might be all smiley but her body was screaming tension to him. If she had served him lamb because she wanted to get rid of an old chair, he was Johnny Depp. No, it was something much bigger. Now what was really going on in that little brain of hers?

Chapter 21

Lou started her Sunday morning as she meant to go on: leaping out of bed, ignoring her stomach's plea for breakfast and getting right down to the business of ridding the house of yet more rubbish. The anger Lou felt at her own weakness ironically generated enough adrenaline-driven strength for her to drag the massive conservatory chair out of the back door, into the drizzling rain, down the path and heave it into the skip without so much as stopping for a breath. At least venting some frustration on an ugly, awkward old chair distracted her from bashing her own head against the wall.

Talking of ugly old things . . . Lou snapped off a binbag from the roll. In her present mood, there were some things she wasn't going to shy away from any more. *Be sentimental by all means, but discriminating,* the article reminded Lou, as she sprinted up the stairs into the smallest spare room like a woman possessed of a demon with an aggressive penchant for spring-cleaning.

Phil's mother had bought them a ceramic vase as a wedding present, which stood on the chest of drawers there. Neither of them had ever liked it; it was so

hideous that it was an offence even to blind people, and
thoughts of taking it to the charity shop didn't even feature. She just wanted to blast it to smithereens so some
other poor sod wouldn't have to be tortured by the sight
of it. *Throw out everything ugly and broken*, the article went
on. *Your space should only be full of things pleasing to your eye
with pleasant emotional vibes giving out positive energy.*

'Right,' said Lou, geeing herself up. 'Lou Winter is *in
the building!*'

Grabbing the hideous vase, she dropped it into the
bin–bag. The carriage clock with the dodgy movement
joined it seconds later. The repro jug and wash-basin that
had been broken at some stage and glued together again,
shattered in the bag, as did a grotesque warped glass
ornament that had been there long before Lou moved in,
and a huge carved barometer that she looked at briefly
for probably the first time – it was reporting that it was
minus 6 degrees and snowing. In the larger spare room
there was a collection of brass ornaments that Celia had
palmed off on her and which Lou had always felt obliged
to gratefully display. She wiped them from the shelves
into the bag with one sweep of her arm – the brass
teapot, the windmill, the cat, the Aladdin's lamp, the
bell, another bell, another bell, the coffee pot, the bear,
the mouse whose tail was designed to hold rings, the
woman with the crinoline and especially the hook-nosed
pedlar who reminded her of Des.

Next, she ripped the loathed horse-brasses off the
wall. To follow were lucky pixies, castanets, maracas,
some coloured glass ball things encased in knitted string
which Renee had bought her as a present from
Plymouth, a cheap sketch of Haworth Parsonage she had

bought as a souvenir from a trip there once, and four boring pictures of seasonal flowers painted onto silk. They had been quite pricey, as she recalled, but she was way past the stage of caring. She knotted up the bag, only to unknot it again to put in another couple of pictures from the landing of lamenting Renaissance women. One crying over a dead duck and another over a bloke who supposedly wasn't coming back from the wars. They had a sad energy about them in their scenes of pain and loneliness and Lou needed no pictorial reminders of what those feelings were all about.

She heaved the sack downstairs like a pre-menstrual Father Christmas and swung it up onto the skip, where it made a series of satisfying smashes after she bashed it flat with a plank of wood. Her neck spasmed after that final exertion and she was forced to take a moment to rub some warmth into it to soothe the muscle.

She needed to sink her whole body up to the nostrils in a warm bath, big-time. She wished now she'd just kept the old seventies avocado bath suite that had been in the building-site room. At least then she could have filled the big ugly thing full of Radox and climbed into it and soaked herself until she was as wrinkled as a dried apricot. *Bloody Keith Featherstone.* His name brought a surge of frustration. What was she going to do about the whole Bloody Keith Featherstone business? Threatening him with legal action wouldn't get her anywhere because he would use that as an excuse never to darken her doorstep again, even if he had any intention of doing so. Plus, thanks to her operating on a basis of stupidly placed trust, there was no proof she had paid him any cash upfront, and he could simply deny everything. She had left another polite message on his voicemail during the week and was still waiting for him to return the call.

She settled for a steamy shower. Afterwards, still wrapped up in the towel, she found more things to be cleared in the mirrored bathroom cabinet. There were loads of free sample sachets she had been storing like a vain squirrel, not to mention bottles of body moisturizer that came unwanted in cosmetic compilations at Christmas along with their dreaded counterparts – the hand creams.

There was some four-year-old suntan lotion and Phil's old haemorrhoid ointment, which she picked up with cautious pincered fingers. Her mother said that people were putting it on their faces these days as it had skin-tightening qualities. Yuk.

She didn't wear pink eye-shadows or lipsticks any more and yet she had a cache of them in her make-up basket, along with an Abba-blue eye-shadow complete with glittery bits. The article had said that old make-up collected bacteria and should be thrown away after six months. Whoops, thought Lou, as she spotted the actual lipstick she had worn at her wedding. It was a lovely dark-wine red that had worked beautifully with the autumn shades of her hair. It had been a nice wedding day, although it could never have been perfect because her dad hadn't been there to give her away. She'd cried on her wedding morning because of that and spoiled her make-up, and Debs had to do it all over again for her.

The sun had shone, the wedding breakfast had been superb, and her groom was the most charming, loving, caring bloke in the world. Just like her dad. A Winter family future stretched before her like a fresh field of snow, inviting her and her man to stamp their unique pattern all over it. They would have a lovely house, a big garden, a son, a daughter, a big bounding puppy, a summer villa on a Tuscan hillside, a car lot, a restaurant and together they were all going to live happily ever after.

Lou put the lipstick in the bin bag.

She rang Tom's number to tell him that the skip was ready for collection and 'Eddie' told her that they could lift it that afternoon. Her hair wasn't even dry from the shower when she heard the wagon reversing, and when she went out to greet it she was more than happy to see a big dog's head framed in the passenger-side window.

'Hi,' called Lou, striding over sure-footedly, making a conscious effort to regain some of the elegance points she had lost last time. At least he was working, which meant his back hadn't had any delayed shock after lifting her from the ground. She had guiltily played that scene over and over in her mind, albeit heavily edited. Now it was about ten minutes longer, full of heaving bosoms (hers) and Italian accents (his) and there was a 'Midnight Moon' backdrop of Mediterranean night sky and wishing stars.

'Hi there,' called Tom, while Clooney came straight over to Lou for a fuss and, obviously, a biscuit.

Lou fed him whilst Tom slipped the hooks onto the skip.

Looking for a point of conversation she asked: 'Where does it all go?' indicating the rubbish.

'Well, it gets loaded into a massive ejector trailer and then goes off to a landfill site on the other side of Leeds.

We recycle what we can and do our bit for the environment. For instance, we get the occasional piece of old but good furniture and there are places that can redistribute that to people who need it. And if we get some decent tins of paint, we can pass them on to charities which use it. Sometimes we find old medicine and pills and take them back to pharmacies in case they fall into the wrong hands.'

'I did wonder what happened to it all,' said Lou. She hadn't really; she just wanted to chat to him. Still, once he started talking about it, she found it quite interesting.

'You can wake up now,' said Tom.

'No, really. I wanted to know.'

Tom narrowed his eyes at her in mock suspicion and said, 'I shall ask you some questions the next time I see you and test you.'

The next time I see you!

God, she was turning into Michelle, analyzing everything he said and the way he said it. Next thing, she'd be poking about in food looking for holy images, like Michelle had done in the past, and getting on the internet to hook up with lovers on Death Row.

'You must be nearly at the end though, surely?' said Tom.

'I thought I was,' laughed Lou, 'but I keep finding more nooks and crannies to go at. It's neverending once you start clearing stuff out. I just can't believe I've got so much that I don't need. Or want any more, come to that.'

'Did you get your airer fixed up?' he then enquired.

'Not yet, that's this afternoon's job. I got some pulleys from your shop. I didn't realize it was your place until your brother served me,' said Lou, her lips tightening as she thought of Tom's darker half. 'I made a bit of a twerp of myself actually. I thought he was you.'

Tom stopped dead, trying to loop the last hook onto the skip. 'He *was* me,' he said with a disbelieving little laugh. 'I haven't got a brother.'

'It was you?'

'Yes, of course! That's why I held your money up to check it – to see if it wasn't one of your counterfeits.' He grinned.

Lou sifted through her recollection of buying the pulleys and mentally slapped her forehead with the heel of her hand. It seemed so obvious in retrospect that he had been having her on. How would he know about the airer if he hadn't served her? She felt her brain blushing and the heat radiate out to the surface of her skin.

'I'm sorry,' said Tom. 'I thought you guessed. I wondered why you ran off when I went to get you a receipt.' He laughed heartily. 'Didn't you hear me say "you must be thinking of my big, handsome brother" or something like that?'

Is that Clooney? she had asked as well. *No, it's his brother.* God, she was so thick, she deserved to be laughed at. A stupid, silly woman, two prawns short of a cocktail, who was having stupid, silly daydreams about a man who took her rubbish away. The enlightenment hit Lou like a lump hammer, and then her imagination took it and ran with it and embroidered a Bayeux tapestry around it.

He had probably had a good laugh about her to all the skip lads. Maybe that's why different blokes kept delivering them, because he was sending them all up to have a look at her. *Clooney knocked her over and I nearly broke my*

*back lifting her up. And — you won't believe this bit — she actu-
ally took in all that crap about me having a twin, the silly fat
bag. I think she has the hots for me as well. Guess what, lads,
she's even got biscuits in for the dog!*

Lou felt momentarily sick, as if the six-million-watt
light bulb that had just switched on had drained her
system of stomach stabilizers. *When will you ever learn,
Lou?* said a weary inner voice. *When are you ever going to
realize that you are just one of life's stooges?* Jaws, Phil,
Renee, Victorianna, Michelle, Bloody Keith
Featherstone — they all thought she was a bit of a joke.
And now him — (drum roll) — Mr Funny Skipman and
his amazing performing brother. Why didn't she just get
out the red nose, stick it on her face and change her
name to Charlie Cairoli? Tom Broom laughing at her felt
worse than the rest of them put together.

Some little part of her that used to be Elouise
Angeline Casserly flared up inside her and defied Lou
Winter to spill those tears that were gathering behind her
big green eyes. Instead, it pushed up her chin and, with
reclaimed dignity, forced herself to make a semblance of
joining in with the hilarity and say, 'Silly me, yes, I see
my mistake now.' Which indeed she did.

It made her give Clooney a final pat on his great soft
head and say a courteous goodbye to Tom Broom. Then
it gave her the strength to walk calmly back to the sanc-
tity of her kitchen without giving into an all-escaping
run. There, it decided for her that there would be no
more skips or contact with Mr Tom 'Mick-Taker-
Extraordinaire-Egomaniac-I'm-So-Clever' Broom again.
She didn't need anyone else around who made her feel
inadequate; there were too many of those already. She

had thought he was different, but he wasn't. And she didn't need rubbish like him in her life.

Phil walked in at four o'clock to find Lou putting the finishing touches to the airer which she had just screwed into the kitchen ceiling beams. Lou knew her way around a toolbox, thanks to years of trailing after her DIY-mad dad and learning from him. He bought her a set of power tools at fifteen and set her projects to do. Her dad had made some beautiful things for the house in his cellar workshop and she would watch him, sitting on the little chair with the heart-shaped hole in the back that he had made for her. Her mother was grudgingly grateful – it was obvious she would rather have impressed the neighbours with some posh furniture van delivering what she wanted.

Phil could wire up a plug but was terrified of drilling holes in case he hit a water pipe or cut through a cable and gave himself a free perm. He watched her screwing some metal thing into the wall and wondered how she could be bothered. She still hadn't told him what all that buttering-up meal business was about yesterday, but he knew he wouldn't have to wait long to find out. Lou couldn't keep secrets. She would have been hopeless having an affair, not that Lou ever would have an affair, that was an impossibility. Lou would never do that to him. Lou was a lovely person, even if she did have a bit of an arse on her these days, unlike the trim Miss British Racing Green Eyes. He really would have to watch that. Phil was going places these days and it wasn't enough for him that Lou was nice inside; he needed her to look good on his arm. He didn't want people laughing at him, like they laughed at Fat Jack when he brought Maureen out of her coffin to socialize.

As Fat Jack said, whilst eyeing up a little scrubber who was trading in a Fiesta, 'When women start neglecting themselves, they deserve everything they get.' When a bloke's eye wanders, his missus should get the wake-up call to go and sort herself out. Jack himself had been unlucky on that front because Maureen had only got worse. Phil thought of that hairy mole on Maureen's neck and shuddered. It was so big he felt sure it had its own brain. It was obvious that Jack only stayed with her because she serviced him with cleaning and cooking, and he didn't want to fork out for a divorce. At least his Lou had cared about their marriage enough to fight for her man, and he'd had some very attentive sex and fantastic meals as a welcome-home-from-your-affair present. Fat Jack had got bugger all. Maureen hadn't even shaved off her beard.

The telephone rang as Phil was in the shower. Something stopped Lou from picking it up and she let the answering machine take it whilst she listened on the screener.

'Mrs Winter, it's me, Tom Broom. I wasn't sure if you said you wanted me to bring another skip or not earlier on when we were talking. If you do, can you call me? Thanks. Hope you had a nice weekend. Bye now.'

Hope you had a nice weekend, Lou mocked. He was obviously crawling now because he was scared he wouldn't get her business any more. And with good reason. Lou went to the cupboard and got out the dog biscuits which she thrust down to the bottom of the kitchen bin, in a simple but definitive act. No, Lou wouldn't call him back. She wasn't going to pay him for the privilege of being an object of ridicule. Especially when he didn't even know her first name!

Chapter 22

When Harrison's Waste Disposals turned up the following Saturday to drop off a new mini-skip, Lou realized she had no cash in the house and hurriedly wrote out a cheque to 'Tom Broom', which the skipman sourly gave her back. She contemplated the fact that she might have developed some Pavlovian response to skips, whereby as soon as she saw one she was obliged to make an absolute prat of herself.

She had found an alternative skip-hire company after searching through the *Yellow Pages*. Seeing Tom's name there in black and yellow had given her a nip of sadness. His absence had cheated her of a secret fantasy that had brought a harmless thrill to a life that she was increasingly recognizing as joyless, empty and boring. She hated that Tom Broom's brief cameo appearance had caused so much disruption. She had been content with her lot before he came on the scene with his bloody dog and his bloody skips. *Hadn't she?*

In the week that had passed, Lou's subconscious still hadn't presented her with the solution to the letting-Phil-know-about-Deb problem, after all; the whole thing was too mammoth for it to cope with. The only thing it had come up with was the thought that maybe she should talk to someone about it and get a fresh view on the subject. But who was there. Karen? Too young. Her mother? Do me a favour! That left Michelle.

Michelle hadn't been in touch since the text message saying that everything was hunky dory and she was loved up. Lou supposed she had been forgiven now and rang to leave a message on Michelle's answerphone. There was no way she would pick up because it was Saturday and she was probably halfway to her fortieth orgasm of the weekend with Craig. But Michelle surprised her by answering after three rings and sounding really glad to hear from her, apologizing as usual for not being in touch: busy, busy, gym, gym, sex with Craig, sex with Craig . . .

'So it's going well then?' said Lou carefully.

'Fandabidozy. He is gorgeous! He can't keep his hands off me!'

'That's great. Michelle, look, the reason I rang you—'

'Hang on, I must tell you this – we were going to pick up fish and chips last night and he said he thought he was falling for me. Can you believe it? I just melted.'

'Not there now, is he? I'm not interrupting, am I?'

'Lou, do you think I'd have answered the phone if he was?' she laughed, whilst making a clear point. 'No, he's going to a football match with his mates.' She sighed indulgently. 'It'll do him good, getting some fresh air. This house stinks of sex. I've had to buy in a bulk load of Shake 'n' Vac.'

'I want to ask you—'

'Mind you, he hardly got any when he was married, so he's just making up for lost time with a decent woman.'

'Michelle, can you help me on something—'

'You should hear some of the tricks his wife's done on him, the bloody bitch. I've told him he can move in here for a while but it's too far away from Leeds for him. Do you know what she did once? You won't believe this . . .'

Thus steamrollered, Lou gave up trying to interrupt and there followed a half-hour character assassination of Craig's wife. Lou heard it but didn't listen because five minutes into the monologue Michelle's voice became white noise.

The Deb and Phil thing was something she would have to sort out on her own, Lou thought, with a guilt-free yawn and a mind that was a million light years away from Craig and his incredibly talented penis.

Chapter 23

For three consecutive Saturdays now, Lou had been slipping out to meet Deb. It felt as if they had never been apart, except for one big difference. In the old days, there was nothing they couldn't talk about; now there were a couple of taboo subjects. Phil being the biggest. And as much as Lou would have liked to have exorcised the ghost of Tom Broom through a good gossip, it seemed a bit of a cheek to talk about a bloke she fancied – *had* fancied – with a friend she had once given up to save her marriage. There, she had finally admitted it to herself: she had fancied him. Not that it mattered now that he was totally gone from her life.

She and Deb had talked on the phone a few times during the week, on her mobile because she didn't want the number showing up on the house phone bill. She couldn't afford to rock the boat in any way, especially because she had the distinct feeling that Phil knew she was *up to something*. Some sixth sense within her was waving a bright red warning flag. Phil was as wily as a fox and nothing got past him.

In saying that, she *was* deceiving him. She had fibbed twice, saying she was shopping in Meadowhall when all the time she was drinking coffee and eating cake with Deb. That couldn't be right, could it? Lying to her husband went against everything Lou believed in. The pressure was starting to weigh heavily on her. God knows, she would never have been able to put up with the strain of having an affair. Not that there was anyone she fancied enough to have an affair with. Not since the only person recently to have made her heart beat faster had turned out to be a bit of a shit.

In Maltstone village garden centre café, Lou and Deb were just devouring two very nice slices of chocolate fudge cake. They hadn't gone back to *Café Joseph*. They didn't want to send the waiter into hormonal overdrive.

Talk flowed easily enough between them. Lou told Deb that she had ordeal-by-lunch-with-mother to look forward to on Tuesday, which would probably be light relief after another soul-destroying day in Accounts on Monday, but Deb seemed a little distracted.

'You OK?' Lou asked.

'Yes, of course. No, I'm not actually,' came the contradictory answer. Deb put down her fork and stared hard at Lou without saying anything.

'What's up?' said Lou, through her last mouthful.

'Lou, I've got something to ask you.' Deb was biting her bottom lip. She used to do that when she was nervous, Lou recalled.

'God, it sounds like you're going to propose. If you are, I have to tell you I'm married already.'

'Yes, to a total prick though,' said Deb without thinking. She took a sharp intake of breath; it was as if she was trying to suck the words back. 'Sorry. I didn't mean for that to come out.'

Lou let loose a bark of laughter. 'It's actually a big relief,' she said. 'I know you can't stand him and you really don't have to pretend that you do. You don't owe him anything.'

Except a boot in the knackers, thought Deb.

'Anyway, this isn't about *him*,' she carried on. Not dignifying *him* with a name. 'This is about you and me.'

'Go on.' Lou was all ears.

Deb opened her mouth to start, and then shut it again. She'd forgotten her well-rehearsed opening gambit. There was nothing for it but to plunge in headfirst.

'What?' urged Lou with amused curiosity.

'*Working Title Casa Nostra*,' blurted out Deb. 'I don't suppose you fancy giving it another go?'

'Yes,' said Lou immediately.

'Take your time, I know it's a big decision. I so want to do this but I understand that it would probably cause trouble between you and you know who . . . and there's a lot more at—' Her brain suddenly caught up with her ears. 'You're joking!'

'I've never been more serious in my whole life.'

'Bloody Norah!'

They stared at each other, hardly daring to breathe. Then they valved out to a childish bout of giggles.

'Deb, I am so glad you asked. I would never have dared, seeing it was my fault in the first place that we never went ahead,' said Lou.

'It wasn't your fault, it was . . .' *that cretinous balding twat's* '. . . well, it doesn't matter about faults. Maybe it wasn't the time for us back then. The older I get, the more I believe in fate and timings. Are you sure you want to?'

'I am totally, positively sure I'm sure. Ever since I found that file again I haven't been able to get it out of my head.'

'I could scream I'm so excited,' Deb said with a full-capacity smile.

'So where do we start?' asked Lou.

'Well, you're going to have to start by telling Phil about me,' said Deb. 'Otherwise it will be a bit hard to explain where all those millions sat in your bank account have come from, when the business takes off. I'll start by borrowing the *Casa Nostra* file from you and refreshing my memory on what the sodding hell I was planning to make a Brando out of.'

'I won't let you down this time, Deb. Whatever happens,' said Lou earnestly.

'I know,' said Deb, and she did know – although it was probably a good job that at that precise moment, neither of them knew just how much *would* happen.

Chapter 24

Lou opened her wardrobe doors and looked through the banks of clothes for her black skirt and red top. She was taking her mother out for her birthday lunch to a lovely Italian restaurant just outside Wakefield, but what should have been a simple clothes-choosing exercise turned out to have complications. The realization struck her like a slap: she really did have some awful clothes. Her eyes were tugged towards the burgundy suit she wore so often for work. Looking at it, head on, bulkily sitting on the hanger, she could see why Karen took the mick out of it so much. It looked short and thick and squat – was she really that shape? There was no way that it was going back in the wardrobe now that she had seen it through her recently acquired objective eye. Sliding it from the hanger, she dropped it quickly onto the floor before she could change her mind.

She checked the clock; she had a spare half-hour to make a start if she wanted to do what had suddenly landed in her mind and Lou did want to, very much. She could no longer tolerate *any* potential rubbish that she spotted, and she had spotted a lot in her wardrobe. *Do you wear 20 per cent of your wardrobe, 80 per cent of the time?*

the article had asked and she concluded that she probably did, looking at this junk hanging up.

Pushing up her sleeves, she started at the left, pulling out a loose black dress in which the whole Billy Smart family and some Bengal tigers could adequately have performed. *But it's comfortable and OK for lounging about the house in*, said a weak little inner voice. *Tough*, returned Lou, and replaced the empty hanger on the rail. It might have been a comfy purchase, but she looked like a gothic Mama Cass in it. 'And there's another for the rubbish pile,' she said to herself, seizing a faded pair of red track-suit bottoms that were big enough for Santa to change into after his Christmas dinner.

The blue suit was a bland necessity for work. The black one was her favourite but it had been a 'to slim into' purchase, and she never had. It wasn't made from a stretchy fabric nor did it feature the elastic waistband she so favoured these days. It really would have to go, along with all the other 'too smalls' that waited patiently but in vain for Lou to regain the figure she had twenty years ago. It was a very classy two-piece though, she thought. She tried it on again for old times' sake and found with some surprise that it slipped over the hips it usually snagged on. The jacket, which she had never been able to close across the bust, buttoned up beautifully now. Not only that, there was actually room when she rotated her shoulders and jutted out her chest in the exaggerated fashion of Barbara Windsor in *Carry on Camping*. Looking at herself in the mirror, she was pleasantly taken aback at the reflection. *I've lost weight! Flaming heck, when did that happen?* Either that or a benign fairy was coming in and stretching her clothes at night.

A loose pink shirt with white spots started a separate charity-shop pile. It had been one of her favourites until Phil pointed out that she looked like Mr Blobby in it and totally put her off wearing it. Next, it was goodbye to that size eight pair of grey check trousers, a lovely red dress and some sundresses, all size tens, which had been hanging up and taunting her that she was too fat to fit in them. Well, they wouldn't be there to taunt her any more! Next . . .

Within twenty minutes 75 per cent of Lou's wardrobe was crammed into four bin-bags, along with a fifth one full of old knickers, ancient bras, bobbly tights and unwanted shoes, including the ridiculous high heels that she had worn that night out with Michelle and couldn't think of without associations of pain, inner and outer, and a *Highway to Hell* soundtrack. The old black faithful skirt that Lou was originally going to wear for lunch was now in a charity bag, teamed up with the gathered red top, which she knew didn't make the best of her chest, but it hadn't bothered her that much, until now.

The remaining clothes in her wardrobe suddenly had room to breathe and the sight of the fresh space gave her that curiously light and uplifting feeling again. Plus, it would be quite fun to replenish her wardrobe, she thought. But from now on she was only going to buy clothes that looked and felt and fitted as well as the black suit. There were to be no big fat comfortable clothes that made her feel like an old frump or impossibly small clothes that made her feel bovine by comparison. She put her lovely black suit back on and looked forward, for once, to her mother's verdict.

★

Renee opened up the car door and climbed gracefully out. She had a smart little taupe suit on that made the best of her trim figure and slim legs, and she carried the matching light brown handbag that Lou had bought her for her birthday. Mother and daughter strolled into the Italian restaurant and were greeted by a round-faced but attractive waiter with a pronounced accent.

'Have you lost weight?' asked Renee, who had been studying Lou from the back as they walked to their table.

'Yes, I think I have,' Lou confirmed. 'It must be all that exertion filling my skips.'

'Haven't you gone on the scales to find out?' said Renee, who weighed herself every morning naked, after her ablutions and before her Bran Flakes.

'I don't have any scales,' said Lou.

'Well, you want to keep it up and before you know where you are you'll look nice again.'

'Thanks, Mum,' said Lou tightly.

Once seated, they studied the oversized menus over slimline tonics, ice and lime.

'Thank you for the flowers, they were beautiful, by the way,' said Renee.

'Good, glad you liked them,' said Lou, aware that her mother had shifted her scrutiny from the menu to her face.

'Your skin's looking nice,' she said at last. 'Have you been doing anything to it?'

'Just drinking a lot of water,' said Lou. Her skin had always been nice, though. She hadn't suffered any of the volcanic facial activity that had plagued, and continued to plague Victorianna despite her diet of healthy-this and healthy-that. Tee Hee.

'Nothing better than water for the skin,' said Renee.

'Filling the skips is a thirsty business,' Lou added, whilst thinking, Wow, two compliments on the trot. There's a first! Betcha there wouldn't be a third. She curled her fingers away before her mother noticed them. The life-improving qualities of intensive physical clutter-clearing didn't extend to cuticle-care and nail preservation.

'What are you going to have?' said Renee.

'I think I'll start off with garlic mushrooms.'

'Oh you're not, are you?' Renee screwed up her face, disapproving. 'You'll undo all that good work if you eat a big plateful of butter.'

Lou snarled inwardly. 'What would you like me to have, Mum?' she said with a fixed grin.

'Have what you like,' sniffed Renee. 'I'm only trying to encourage you.'

'I'll have the tiger-prawn salad,' said Lou. She just prayed the prawns' last meal had been garlic mushrooms.

'What about for main?' asked Renee eventually, after she had decided on the salmon.

'Lard pie and chips,' Lou answered with flat petulance.

'Don't be ridiculous, Elouise,' said her mother, as if she were nine and had just asked for a gerbil.

Lou ordered chicken in a mushroom and white wine sauce. She forewent the gastronomic pleasures that *Café Ronaldo's* garlic bread would have given her, knowing she wouldn't enjoy it all that much with her mother watching her every mouthful.

'Have you heard from Victorianna?' asked Lou, after the waiter had taken their order.

'Yes, she rang very early this morning and her card is

on its way, apparently. Their post takes ages,' said Renee, waving away the whole American postal system with one sweep of her small, thin hand. 'I don't know – they can send men up to the moon, but they can't get a birthday card here on time. Typical!'

'Has she sent you a present?' Lou enquired sweetly.

'She's put some money in the card for me to get what I want,' replied Renee, adjusting the serviette on her lap so she wouldn't have to look Lou in the eye. 'Vera's going to visit her son in Germany for her birthday, did I say? Her son's paying for her to go out there.' Renee couldn't help the almost indiscernible sigh that came out with it and despite all her criticisms and pettiness, Lou felt a sudden all-engulfing wave of sympathy and love for her mother. Victorianna really was one-way traffic. She must have known how much their mother wanted to go out there and how it hurt her that she had not once been asked.

'You should tell Victorianna to invite you over,' she said.

'I can't *tell* her to invite me, Elouise,' Renee snapped.

No, thought Lou, with a plan already sparking into life in her head. But I can.

Later that evening, Lou was snuggled up in a bed with fresh, cosy sheets on it, which felt extra comforting as the wind howled outside and rain lashed against the window. Phil had tried to initiate sex, but she had said she was too tired. He hinted at doing 'other things' instead, but she hinted back that she was too tired for those as well. He punished her with his back and no kiss goodnight, which didn't bother her half as much as it was intended to.

She had just drifted off to the shallows of sleep when she was woken up by a rude shake.

'Lou, Lou, what's that noise?' Phil was hissing.

'Wha . . .'

'*Shhhhh!* . . . Listen.'

Lou did as instructed. She was just about to say she couldn't hear a thing when her ears caught a scratching noise.

'There's someone trying to get in the back door,' whispered Phil. 'Did you put the alarm on?'

'Yes, of course I did. Go and see who it is,' Lou whispered back.

'There's no way I'm going downstairs,' said Phil gallantly.

'Look out of the window then!'

'No, they might see me. Where's your mobile? Mine's downstairs on charge.'

'So is mine.'

'Oh, bloody marvellous!'

'Shhh,' said Lou, straining to hear. Threaded amongst the whistles of the wind was a definite whimpering. Whatever it was, it was animal not human, and sounded in pain too. She hopped out of bed.

'Where are you going?' said Phil.

'To look out of the window,' replied Lou. She nudged the curtain open and peered down, but the rain was hitting the glass at full pelt and her view was distorted.

There it was again, a clear yelp.

'That's not a burglar, it's a dog,' said Lou, slipping on her dressing-gown and heading for the stairs. Phil jumped out of bed and followed her tentatively downstairs to the kitchen. As Lou typed in the code to turn off the alarm, Phil made a clattering grab in the drawer for a bread-knife.

Despite his expectations, there was no spooky silhouette of a mass murderer framed in the glass of the back door. Phil stood behind Lou, serrated-edged weapon at the ready, as she unlocked the door as far as the chain would allow. There on the doorstep was a very soggy and bedraggled German Shepherd.

'Chuck this at the bloody thing,' said Phil, handing her a pan. 'SHOO!'

Lou huffed loudly and slipped the chain off.

'Fucking hell, don't let it in!' Phil yelled as she then flung open the door and Clooney shivered into the kitchen.

'It's the skip man's dog,' said Lou, grabbing a towel from the top of the ironing basket and bending to his side. He was shaking, trembling, his ears flat against his head.

'Well, what's he doing here? Market bloody research?' demanded Phil, watching incredulously as she made soothing noises and attempted to rub the dog dry.

'How do I know, Phil? He's obviously remembered the house.'

'How can a dog remember a house?'

'In case you haven't noticed, my name's Lou Winter not Barbara Woodhouse.'

Clooney sneezed and then Phil sneezed.

Lou couldn't resist. 'You're allergic to each other,' she smiled wryly.

'It's not funny. Get it out of here,' said Phil crossly, making a move to grab the dog's collar but thinking better of it when his hand got within three foot of the dog's jaws.

'You are joking!' said Lou, fighting the mischievous urge to say, *I wouldn't send a dog out on a night like this!* 'You can't let him back out in this weather, poor thing.'

'Well, you can't keep him here, can you?' said Phil, who could feel his nose beginning to fill up with mucus.

'Pass me the phone,' said Lou. 'I'll ring the skip man. He'll be frantic.'

'He's not going to be at work now, is he? It's . . .' Phil looked at the clock on the oven . . . 'half-past pissing one!'

'Well, I don't know where he lives, Phil, so leaving a message is the only thing I can do!'

Lou could remember Tom Broom's number, but thought it wiser to go through the pretence of looking it up in the telephone directory. As expected, an answering machine clicked on.

'Hello, Mr Broom,' began Lou efficiently after the announcement and the long beep. 'It's Mrs Winter, number one, The Faringdales, Hoodley. It's one-thirty on Wednesday morning and I've got your dog here. He's OK but very wet. I'm going to bed him down here for the night—'

'Oh no, you're fucking not, Lou! You fucking aren't bedding that scruffy, smelly, hairy bastard thing!' screamed Phil in the background.

Lou ignored him and carried on, '. . . So there's no need to worry. He seems fine. Anyway, that's it, end of message, bye for now. Oh, and here's my number . . .'

She put down the phone and turned to defuse Phil, who sneezed again dramatically enough to be right up there with any passing Oscar nominees.

'He can sleep in here,' she said calmly, trying not to

inflame the situation by pointing out what a big girl's blouse Phil was being. 'I'll disinfect the place tomorrow. You won't know he's ever been here.'

Phil's brain recalled him sneezing like this before in the kitchen. *Have you had a dog in here? And she had answered, 'Don't be ridiculous!'*

'He's been here before, hasn't he?'

'I brought him in for a biscuit once, that's all,' said Lou.

'Where are you going now?' asked Phil as Lou marched out of the kitchen, leaving him alone with the Hound of the Baskervilles. The vicious-looking thing was enormous, and his head was on a level with Phil's balls. Phil did a quick exit and trailed behind Lou as she went to the top of the stairs and pulled down the loft ladder.

'There's a sleeping bag up here,' said Lou.

'*My* sleeping bag? The one I use for camping?' Phil yelled.

'Use? Phil, the last time you went camping was before you met me,' reminded Lou. 'These days, your idea of roughing it on holiday would be only one Michelin star and no malt in the mini-bar.'

Phil opened his mouth but no counter-argument came bounding out so he hung redundantly around the bottom of the steps whilst she climbed up.

Lou switched on the loft light and saw that the sleeping bag was right by her feet. It smelled a bit, having been stored in the forgotten air up there, but it was dry and would adequately fulfil the purpose of a temporary dog bed.

She hadn't been up to the loft for over two years now, into this final resting-place for things she didn't want to think about. As soon as she saw the shadowy shapes up there again she knew that there were ghosts here she must exorcise. She needed to finally move on – and to be able to do that, she needed a hell of a lot of bin-bags and yet another empty skip. For now, though, there was a distressed dog to sort out.

'You're cooking chicken at this time of night?' shrieked Phil, watching open-mouthed in disbelief as Lou cut up fillets and poured some rice to boil in a saucepan. 'Want me to toss it up a chuffing side salad as well?'

'Phil, just go to bed,' said Lou wearily, resisting the urge to point out that he was already being a big enough tosser as it was. His sniffling and swearing were starting to annoy her. He could be such a wimp sometimes. Quite often actually, when she thought about it.

Phil had another aggressive sneezing fit which made up his mind for him. This was his house, after all.

'No, no, I'm sorry, it's not staying here. It can go in the garage.'

'No, he can't,' said Lou quietly but firmly.

'Yes, it can, Lou!'

'No, he can't!'

She matched him for intensity if not volume, but she was aware that she had now strayed into the sort of argument that she always lost, the type where strength of will was involved. Then she would end up bloody and hurt as Phil fought his corner with low blows about her weight, thinner women, letting herself go.

His voice spiralled to a scream.

'I'm not letting you keep that animal in my house and that's that!'

Let?

It was that word again.

Lou's mind wagged her own words back at her.

'How on earth did a woman get into a state where a man was "letting" her do things?'

LET?

Like a long-dormant volcano stirring into life, Lou's inner magma suddenly started to rise and spit. She couldn't have stopped its course to the surface if she'd tried.

'Oh, by the way, I meant to tell you, I bumped into Deb,' she said with calm defiance. 'And we had a coffee together. A few coffees together, actually. And it's very possible I may be going into business with her, same plan as before. Our coffee-house, do you remember?'

'What?' said Phil, wondering for a moment if he was asleep and having a bad dream. Either that or he was experiencing a psychotic flashback as a result of taking some speed back in the eighties.

'I said I bumped into Deb . . .'

'I heard you the first time. Well, I'd give up any plans of seeing *her* again or—'

Lou spun on him. 'Or what?'

'Eh?'

'Or what, Phil?' Lou snapped. She was looking at him in a way that reminded him of when they were courting; in those days, she had a fire that he had loved to poke into even more flames. It was only when he realized that the blaze was getting away from his control that he'd put it out. Phil suddenly remembered who British Racing Green Eyes reminded him of.

He chain-sneezed.

'Oh, I'm going back to bed,' he said grumpily. He'd give her a fight any night of the week and win it because he knew exactly what to say to make his wife start sobbing into a hankie and saying her sorrys, but presently he was debilitated by itching eyes and a nose full of snot. He thudded heavily back upstairs, his head bursting.

Lou wrapped up her loudly ticking travel alarm clock in a tea towel and put it under the sleeping bag for Clooney. Her dad had done that for Murphy on his first few puppy nights at home, to give him the comfort of a simulated fellow heartbeat. How had she ever once thought that Phil was like her dad, Lou wondered, sitting by Clooney's side and stroking his damp quiet head as she waited for his supper to finish cooking.

Upstairs, Phil was lying awake and thinking, So that's what she's been up to − meeting that bitch Deb again. Not only that, but she had been *lying* about having dogs in their house − *his* house, actually − when she knew he was allergic to the fucking horrible flea-ridden things. And she had started refusing him sex. And she'd burned his curry. *Who does my wife think she is?*

There was only room for one dominant person in their marriage. It was in danger of losing the equilibrium it needed to survive, so Lou Winter, he decided, needed bringing back into line. And Phil Winter knew the very best way to make that happen.

Chapter 25

Phil washed, dressed and went down to the kitchen for a quick pre-work coffee, totally forgetting about the presence of Scooby Doo. On seeing it, he spasmed backwards, sending himself careering into the table and chairs. Scruffy smelly bastard hound asleep on his best sleeping bag!

He shouted up to Lou, who was just putting on some make-up. She hadn't got to bed until nearly three o'clock and it was only seven o'clock now. There were black circles under her eyes that needed attention. Thank goodness it was Wednesday and she wasn't at work today.

'Get rid of this dog quick, Lou!' Phil said.

Clooney opened up one eye, viewed him briefly and closed it again. This small action totally infuriated Phil. How dare the bloody thing look at him like that! In his own kitchen as well. Who did it think it was? The Duke of Sodding Edinburgh?

He grabbed his jacket and shouted upstairs again. 'I'll get my breakfast at work.'

He knew that would irk her, denying her the chance of cooking his bacon. He had almost skirted around the *thing* to go out of the back door when Clooney's lips pulled over his ferocious-looking teeth to do a yawn. He emitted a strange, unholy noise that made Phil's bowels momentarily jerk.

'Sweet Baby Jesus on a bike!' he said, tearing off to the front door instead, and stamping out muttering and swearing loudly to himself.

In contrast, when Lou came downstairs, Clooney was up on his feet, tail wagging and the most pleased to see her that she could remember anyone ever being in recent times. She let him out of the back door where he did a dutiful wee, then he was back inside again for the attention of Lou and a warm towel. It was still lashing down outside and she dreaded to think what state he would have been in, left outside all night – and he would have been, if she hadn't stood up to Phil in a way that had surprised even her. Then again, it was always easier to stand up for someone else – she'd always battled with Shirley Hamster that bit harder for bullying the little kids – the real test was standing up for yourself. Thanks to her not backing down for once, though, Clooney was warm and dry and breakfasting happily on more chicken and rice.

Lou was washing up when there was a firm knock at the door and, through the patterned glass there, she saw a big shape with black hair. Abandoning his meal, Clooney started whining and howling and getting very excited – and that was all the evidence Lou needed to know that it wasn't the postman.

She had a quick panic about how she must look with her puffy, tired eyes. Making a quick adjustment to her hair in the kitchen mirror, Lou hastily checked that the zip on her jeans was in the 'up' position, then mentally slapped herself. What was she doing? What did she care what he thought of her? Just let the man get his dog and then he could be out of her life again. Straightening her back, she went to open the door. But for all her outward composure, her heart was thumping a loud betrayal in her chest.

Clooney barged past her to get to Tom, who bent down and scrubbed him with his hand and said affectionate man-to-dog things like, 'Hello, lad, how ya doing? Hello, boy.'

'Come in out of the rain,' said Lou, cursing herself but standing aside so he could enter. That damned politeness-override reflex again.

He walked in and tried to wipe his boots on the mat whilst Clooney fussed around him making pathetic 'missed you' whines. Tom Broom looked totally knackered. He had circles around his eyes that matched her own.

'Thanks so much for taking him in,' he said to Lou. 'I didn't get your message till I got into the office this morning. I've been out all night looking for him. A mastiff went for him on a job down in Ketherwood last night and chased him off.'

'Ketherwood? That must be at least two miles away!' said Lou. No wonder Tom was worried. They ate dogs in Ketherwood.

'How he got here I'll never know,' said Tom, giving his adoring friend an extra hard scratch.

'Would you like a coffee?' asked Lou graciously.

'Am I holding you up? You off to work?'

It would be unforgiveable, really, to pretend that all this had caused her a lot of trouble when it hadn't, apart from having to listen to Phil's tantrum. But hang on – this guy needed bringing down a peg or two.

'No, I took a day off,' she said stoically, lying through her teeth.

'Because of this? Oh, I'm so sorry!'

'No, it's perfectly all right. I couldn't have left him, now could I?' she smiled so sweetly that the sugar almost crystallized on her lips. 'Please sit down, have a coffee.'

He sat down meekly at the table, Clooney at his side, head resting on his master's knee. Lou got two cups and filled them from the hissing, spitting percolator.

'White or black?' she asked.

'White, please. No sugar.'

'Ah, me too,' she said with a nice-lady-hostess laugh that rang a very false note.

The cup looked tiny in his large hand.

'Thanks, I needed that,' he said after a big glug. The rain was dripping off his hair. His jacket was so saturated that Lou just couldn't stop herself from asking, 'Look, why don't you take your clothes off for a minute and get dry.'

Oh nuts!

'Outer clothes, I mean. Your coat! Obviously not all of your clothes. That would be ridiculous . . . being naked . . . in my kitchen,' Lou struggled, momentarily losing her upper hand.

'Thanks,' he said. He was doing that grin thing again as he slid off his coat and hung it over the radiator. She wished she hadn't said anything now. Even her rescuing his dog didn't stop him from thinking she was a living breathing joke.

Tom drained his cup and she poured him another

immediately. She would show him that she was a generous, benevolent being, far superior to someone who got
their kicks making fun of others. Her hospitality would
make him ashamed of trying to take the rise out of such
a nice spiritually-generous person with his 'I've-got-a-
twin-no-I-haven't' puerile game.

'I hope it didn't cause any problems for you last night,'
said Tom. 'I remember you saying your husband was
allergic to dogs.'

'No, he was fine about it,' said Lou with a fixed smile.

Tom didn't say that he had heard Phil's little voice-over
on her answering machine message, nor did he reveal that,
as he was driving up The Faringdales estate, he was just in
time to see a man slamming the door to number 1 and
stomping over to his car issuing expletives to the cosmos.
Tom had driven on and parked around the corner for five
minutes until he was sure the immaculately groomed man
had gone, for he had the distinct feeling they wouldn't get
on. It was pretty obvious that Clooney's arrival at Lou's
house had caused her hassle that she wouldn't admit to
him. Plus, he wanted to get her on her own after what he
had just seen parked outside her house.

'I think I owe you an apology,' said Tom.

'Really, Clooney was absolutely no trouble at all.
Don't even think—'

'I didn't mean about that,' said Tom, putting his cup
down on the table.

'Oh? Why would you think you owe me an apology
then?' asked Lou, her eyebrows raised to a perfectly
innocent height.

'Because you've got a full Harrison's skip parked on
your drive.'

Farts! She had forgotten about that.

'I wasn't sure if I'd upset you with all that twin business. When I saw you'd defected to the enemy, it was obvious that I had.'

'I don't know what you mean,' flustered Lou, convincing no one.

'I *knew* there was something wrong when you walked out of the shop without waiting for that receipt,' he said, 'even though the last time I saw you and you said there wasn't, I just *knew* it. And then, when I didn't hear from you about any more skips . . .'

'Another coffee?' offered Lou, who couldn't think of anything else to say.

'Thank you,' said Tom, and then added softly, as she was pouring it, 'I'm really sorry if you thought my joke went too far. I wasn't laughing at you, not in a nasty way . . .'

'Forget about it,' said Lou, suddenly feeling a little silly.

'I take up far more than my fair share of the world as it is – it wouldn't be environmentally friendly of me to have a twin!'

'Yes, of course not.' *Yes, of course not?*

'No twin, there's just me and my sister Sammy. Well, my half-sister.'

'Really, it's fine.'

'The shop is all mine as well as the skips. That's what the T.U.B. stands for – Tom Broom, although everyone's called the place the *Ironmonger's Tub* since I put the sign up.' He looked genuinely contrite.

'So . . . what's the U initial stand for then?'

'I could tell you, but then I'd have to shoot you.'

'Oh, why's that?'

'It's one of those embarrassing names you just don't want to admit to,' Tom smiled, scratching at the back of his head in a nervous gesture.

'Can't be all that bad,' said Lou.

'If you promise not to laugh, I might just tell you,' said Tom.

Lou crossed her heart.

He took a deep breath and then said, 'Umberto.'

It wasn't that funny but Lou laughed anyway because a) promising not to laugh automatically made her want to laugh and b) her insides felt like a pressure cooker that had wanted to burst open since he walked in with his big soggy coat on and tired eyes.

'See, I told you that you'd laugh,' said Tom with mock indignation.

'I'm sorry, I'm only laughing because I'm not supposed to. It's a nice name. Where does it come from? Do you have someone in the family called that?'

He leaned in conspiratorially. He has such a nice face, she thought. There was a bump on his nose and a slightly cauliflowered ear that old rugby games must have been responsible for. He was rough where she liked smooth, dark where she liked fair, big where she liked slight, not her type at all. So why was there a warmth spreading inside her chest?

'My grandmother was Italian,' he began. 'She came over here when she met my grandfather.'

Gulp, you're a quarter Italian! thought Lou.

'And when she was sixteen, my mum went across to Italy to stay with the family for a holiday and met a guy called . . .' He urged Lou to fill in the gap with a roll of his hands.

'Umberto?'

'Precisely. Need I say more? Signor Umberto Baci.'

'Baci, that's a nice name.'

'It means "kisses" in Italian.'

Blimey, that was a bit of a conversation stopper. Lou swallowed. He was looking right at her, unblinking, his eyes grey as steel. *Jesus! Half-Italian. More than half. Double blimey.*

'So . . .' Lou gulped, 'do you like pasta?' *Oh no – what a crap question!*

'*Sì, signorina!*' he said in an exaggerated accent.

Their gentle laughs linked and Lou topped up their cups with coffee, yet again. She nearly dropped the pot because her hands had gone all shaky.

'Do . . . do you speak any of the language?'

'Indeed I do,' said Tom. 'Do you?'

'I did a year at college, but that was way back. I've been meaning to take another class for ages,' said Lou, thinking, Another thing I let go of when I shouldn't have.

'You should. You could order your skips in Italian then. Can I have a skip tomorrow, Mr Broom? *Posso avere un cassonetto per domani, Signor Broom?*'

'Yes, I will,' Lou smiled. 'It's a beautiful language – so expressive.' *Il mio tesoro, ti amo.* Lou had a flash of being in bed with a big sweating man whispering passionate Roman endearments in her ear. She hoped her head wasn't transparent.

'Mum was never on the scene much so our grandparents brought us up and *Nonna* used to only speak Italian to us when we were together so she could force us to learn it. Sammy speaks it to the kids and we've been over to visit the relatives a few times in Puglia, so we keep it nice and fresh.'

'Lucky you. I've never been to Italy,' said Lou with a heavy sigh.

'You should go,' said Tom, 'it's beautiful. Obviously it has its rough places, but the parts that are beautiful are really *bellisimi*.'

'I should die if I didn't go to Venice before I die,' said Lou. 'But my husband is more of a Spain man.' Of course, Spain was beautiful too, but Phil wasn't interested in any of the real Spain. He wanted to be surrounded by English speakers, hot sunshine, cold San Miguels and lots of cheap British food and entertainment in the bars whilst he was drinking those San Miguels.

'You should have a change,' said Tom.

'Yes,' said Lou, somewhat wistfully, but somehow she couldn't see Phil snogging her in a gondola. Once he found out how much they cost to hire, that would be the end of that. As for flicking a coin over his shoulder into the Trevi fountain to guarantee they'd return – *Don't be so sodding silly! I'd look a right fool. Besides, I don't bloody want to come back!* She could hear him saying it now. She shook him out of her head. She didn't want to think about Phil at the moment.

'Your mum never married Umberto then?' Lou asked.

'Ah well, it seems that naughty Umberto was already married. A couple of years later, Mum played out exactly the same scene on a skiing trip to Norway with a guy called Sigi, which is why my sister is all blonde and dainty. We were brought up between my grandparents and my Uncle Tommy and Auntie Bella – they couldn't have kids of their own. It was such a shame, they tried for years and then there was my mum who only had to walk past someone and she was up the spout.'

Lou nodded understandingly. 'Yes, that's often the way of it.'

'Am I going on too much?' Tom asked suddenly, taking his signal from Clooney, who had removed himself to the sleeping bag where he flopped down with a bored grunt.

'No, not at all,' said Lou, who was thinking that it wouldn't matter if he was expounding on the history of plastic injection moulding, it was just ashamedly nice to be near him.

'Uncle Tommy built up the ironmongery business and ran a skip and cement sideline and when he died, he left it all to my sister Sammy and me. I bought her shares so now it's all mine. She's happy to help me out part-time, we work it around the kids.' He smiled fondly. 'She's a good girl, is Sammy, she's just finding that carrying this one is harder than all the others put together. They were so easy.' He stopped, remembering what she had told him about her inability to have children and quietly cursing himself for his insensitivity. He drank some coffee.

'Do you get much trade in the shop?' enquired Lou, guessing exactly why he had closed up that line of conversation.

'Loads,' said Tom, happy for the turn of subject-matter. 'You wouldn't believe how far people will travel to have a poke around. Whatever anyone wants, however obscure, I guarantee to get it for them. I love that whole detective part of it.' He twiddled the ends of an imaginary Hercule Poirot moustache. 'I have a store on the internet too. My sister runs that side of things for me, as she can do it from home so it's handy for her, but me – I like being surrounded by all that stuff far too much to give it up. I always did, even as a kid. I worked with my Uncle Tommy any chance I got. I recently sold off the cement side because we have too much work on as it is, but I like getting out in the skip wagon and meeting nice people . . .' Tom coughed, embarrassed. 'Anyway, this is all about me. What do you do for a living?'

'I'm a part-time accounts clerk,' said Lou, aware that it was a conversation-stopper also, but not half as interesting as Tom's had been with his Italian kisses. If she'd had a pound for everyone who had said, 'Ooh, an accounts clerk? That's interesting, do tell me more,' she wouldn't have a single pound. At least now, she had a pleasant conversational codicil to offer.

'But I'm in the process of setting up a business with my friend Debra,' Lou went on. 'We're both qualified chefs, you see. We wanted to set up a business a few years ago but plans got altered,' which was putting it mildly, she said to herself, 'so . . . better late than never, we've started looking for premises with a view to launching ourselves upon an unsuspecting public.'

Tom was leaning forward with wide-eyed interest. 'A restaurant business? Wow! What sort of food?'

'By a startling coincidence, an Italian coffee-house, specializing in proper coffee and incredible cakes. There are plenty of over-priced conveyor-belt services out there but not a lot of quality and value for money going on.'

'I love cakes. Can you tell?' said Tom, jiggling his tum which looked pretty solid to Lou. She found herself wondering if he had a little line of hair stretching down from his navel. A small silence hung between them before Tom broke it with a loud tut.

'Harrison's Waste, eh?' he said, shaking his head accusingly. 'I don't know. You give someone superior service and look what they do to you.'

'Defecate to the enemy, like you said,' said Lou.

At Lou's unconscious misuse of her native language, Tom's grin appeared again. It was lopsided and wide, but she saw it for what it was, gentle and teasing and totally devoid of any malice. She had misread him over the twin business.

'More coffee?' she asked, guiltily avoiding his gaze.

'Thanks, but no. I'll be running to the loo all day if I have any more.' Disappointingly he got slowly to his feet and stretched, banging his hand on the beam above.

'Oh, your airer's up, I see,' he pointed.

'Yes, tell your brother thanks,' she said.

He smiled and turned to get his still-damp and steaming coat off the radiator.

'Look, thanks again for taking care of Clooney. Can I . . . I don't know . . . buy you lunch or something to say thanks?'

Lou smiled regretfully. *Damn.* 'Thank you, um, but I don't think that would really be appropriate.'

He interjected, 'Yes, of course, I understand. You don't have to explain. It was just lunch. I shouldn't have . . . I wouldn't . . .'

'Oh, of course! I didn't think that you meant anything else,' Lou interrupted back, over-anxious to make sure he didn't think that she thought that he might fancy her, which he didn't anyway, clearly. It was just one of those polite offers that was said in the hope it would be refused, that was obvious — like saying to Des and Celia or Fat Jack and Maureen that they 'simply must come and spend Christmas with us.' Ugh! Tom would have run a mile if she'd not played the game and said, '*Ooh yes, lunch would be lovely.*' Which it would have been, actually.

Tom stood in the doorway and looked down at her.

'Well, I'd like to say thanks, other than just saying "thanks" if you know what I mean. What can I do for you?'

Don't answer that, Lou Winter, she said to herself with a bit of a sneaky giggle. Her imagination jerked hard at its rein. She thought for a moment, sensibly though. There *was* one thing she needed.

'Tell you what,' she said tentatively. 'If you don't mind — if it's not too much of a cheek after my betrayal . . .'

Tom urged her to answer with beckoning hands.

'OK,' said Lou, taking a big breath. 'That skip outside will be getting picked up anytime now, so . . . I'd like one of your mini-skips, please.'

'I'll get Eddie to drop one off for you this afternoon,' said Tom.

'I don't need it until Saturday morning.'

'It's no trouble. Actually, it's better for me if he does it this afternoon, Saturday morning is going to be quite busy for us.'

'Oh, OK then. That's great, thank you.'

'Obviously there will be no charge,' said Tom.

'No! I didn't mean for free!' Lou protested.

'You don't think I'd take any money off you after what you did for Clooney, do you? Oh no.'

'No, really, I—'

'NO! I said no charge,' he insisted, quelling her argument with a big arresting palm. It was quite nice; him being so masterful made her feel all little and girly. Why didn't Phil make her feel like that when he was reciting the rules?

'Just ring and tell me when you want me to pick it back up.'

'As near to four o'clock on Saturday afternoon as you can, please,' she said.

'OK then,' said Tom, wondering why the precision, but not wanting to be intrusive.

Clooney jumped to his feet as Tom opened the back door. He went down the two steep steps to ground level and turned to Lou. He was still taller than she was.

'And look, I'm sorry if I went too far with the twin joke. I really am.'

'You must have thought I was a real bimbo,' admitted Lou quietly.

'God, no, Lou. I think you're—' He stopped and started again, but the pause told her that it wasn't the original intended ending to his sentence. 'You're not someone I'd feel happy about upsetting, that's all. Thanks again.'

He went, he turned back, he waved. Lou waved back, she came inside, closed the door, and slid down it. *Lou.* He had called her Lou.

Chapter 26

'Can I ask you a question?' said Lou at work the next day when she was halfway through her yogurt.

'Ask away,' replied Karen, wolfing down a piece of lemon meringue pie, which was so dire she couldn't wait to get to the end of it.

'When you were still married to your husband . . .'

'Lou, come on, are you trying to make me throw up?'

'No, really. Please this is important. When you were with him,' she began again, 'in the early days, when you were happy before . . . well, did you ever look at anyone else?'

Karen, who had been expecting a frivolous conversation, put down her fork. 'As in other men, you mean?' she asked.

'Yes,' said Lou, trying to make the whole conversation sound hypothetical. Something she realized must have failed dismally as a wide and wicked grin threatened to split Karen's face in two.

'Why, Lou, have you got a *friend* that this has happened to?'

'No, I've got my reasons for asking and they aren't anything like you think. So, did you?'

The tone of Lou's voice made Karen suspend the teasing. It was pretty obvious why she was asking, whatever she might have said. The only mystery was the 'who', but Lou was a pretty private person and if she was going to tell her more, she would do so in her own time.

Karen leaned on the table and looked back under the dust-sheets at her life with Chris, the father of her babies, who had run off with her best friend's mother. Of course he realized he had made a big mistake, when the thrill of varicose veins ran thin, and wanted to come home. But Karen was a girl with a strong sense of self-worth. She had told him *no* in no uncertain terms, and indicated somewhere very warm where he could go forth and multiply instead. She allowed herself a rare mental trawl back through the carnage his affair had caused. In saying that, he was back in the kids' lives and was shaping up to be quite a good dad, but he would never be allowed back in hers. He'd killed that chance the moment he let his zip be opened by someone else's teeth, but boy had it taken some strength to tell him that. It did, when you loved someone as much as she had loved him. So *had* she ever looked at anyone else when they were in that love-you-forever place?

'Well,' Karen began slowly, 'Chris had a friend – James. I used to think he was nice, really good-looking and so funny.'

'But did he make your heart go faster when you were in the same room as him?'

'No, not really,' said Karen, thinking back to how it was. 'He was a lovely man – your typical tall, dark and handsome catch. I actually fixed him up with one of my other friends – although it didn't last, which was a shame. I could *appreciate* him, but I didn't want anyone else but Chris in those days.'

There. That was Lou's answer. It wasn't normal behaviour, looking at other men when she was in love with the one she had. So she needed to get a grip.

'Although,' Karen clicked her fingers in recognition of something Lou had said about her heart beating faster, 'before Chris, I was going out with this guy called Creighton. We were OK together, you know. He was incredibly good at cricket. Boring bastard game, though, I never went to watch him. Then along came this Ryan chap who had come over from South Africa to spend the summer playing for the town side. Looked like a young Michael Caine.' Karen smiled as long-forgotten memories made themselves known with a warm 'hi'. 'We started talking and I realized I quite fancied him. In fact, the more I saw him the more I liked him, until I couldn't get him out of my head. I started going to the cricket matches but only to see him because just being around him made me . . . glow.' She sighed. 'My life seemed to be on hold during the week. I couldn't wait for Saturdays when I knew I'd see him again. Nothing happened between us, not even a kiss, but he switched on feelings in me that I'd never felt for Creighton, never felt for anyone before. I didn't think I was missing anything until I met Ryan. I suppose he made me realize I wanted more than I had, whereas with Chris I felt totally satisfied. When I had him, I felt I had everything. Does that answer your question, Lou?'

'I'm not sure,' said Lou, trying to apply what Karen was telling her to her own situation.

'Some people just can't help themselves chasing that

bit of excitement, however good they have it. Like Chris – he was always looking for greener grass. But me, I'm the faithful type, as you know, Lou,' continued Karen. 'I wouldn't have even looked at anyone else, had I been as happy with Creighton as I thought I was.'

This was, and wasn't, what Lou wanted to hear.

'Hello, is that Sue?' asked Phil, knowing full well it was.

'Yes, it is. Who is this, please?' she said efficiently.

'This is Phil Winter about the green MG.'

'Well, hello,' she said, like a female Leslie Philips, warmth flooding her voice.

'It's coming in Saturday morning. Would you like to see it?'

'Saturday morning? Let me just look at my diary.'

Of course she will, thought Phil.

'Yes, what time do you open?'

'Well, to the public, nine a.m., but I could give you a private showing at eight,' said Phil. 'It won't be on my shop floor long, I warn you. She's an absolute beauty. You'd look well together.'

'OK, I'll be there,' she chirped.

'Come to the side door, to the right of the building as you're looking at it head on.'

'Knock three times and say a password?' she giggled.

'Absolutely,' said Phil lightly. Resisting the urge to joke as to what the password could be. 'Shag-me-sense-less-big-boy', for instance.

'So, see you Saturday first thing then.'

'Look forward to it, Sue,' smiled Phil, deliberately using her name. Women liked that.

Softly softly, he thought as he put down the phone. Softly softly.

Later that afternoon, Lou found Zoe in the toilets re-applying her eye make-up.

'You OK?' she asked.

'Sort of,' said Zoe with a very wobbly voice. 'No, I'm not, actually. I hate that bitch, Lou. I'm going to smack her right in the gob someday soon. How can she get away with bullying people like she does?'

'You should learn to ignore her. You do realize she feeds off you getting all upset?' Lou said gently.

'But why, Lou? Why would you want to go around upsetting people to make yourself feel good?' asked Zoe, shaking her head. Judging people by their own standards was the disadvantage nice people would always have.

'I don't know, love, it could be any number of reasons. Sometimes when people aren't in control of some areas of their lives, they find something else they can control to make themselves feel on top of things.' Lou thought of herself, wrestling with that chair on the day she was angry at herself for not telling Phil about Deb.

'I think it's simpler than that: I think she's just a psycho.'

Lou laughed and gave her a comforting squeeze. 'The best way to deal with her is not to let her have any inkling at all that you are bothered by her petty behaviour,' she said encouragingly.

'But that will make her do it more, until she can see that I *am* bothered, surely?' sighed Zoe.

'You know, the more she taunts you, the more of *her* energy and *her* headspace she is spending on you. Rise

above it, lovey, have a sense of worth. Think of it as the
more she tries to bring you down, the more important a
threat you are to her.'

'I am going to have her,' snarled Zoe, subconsciously
curling up her fist.

'Trust me, that would be a very hollow victory,' said
Lou, pulling Zoe round to face her, square on. 'Promise
me you won't do that. It would get you sacked instantly
and cause trouble for you if you tried to get another job.
Not to mention the fact that she might or might not
press charges. Then she *would* have fun and games, mentally torturing you.'

'But it would feel good, wouldn't it, for those few seconds?' grinned Zoe, savouring the thought of her fist
crunching into all that metal.

'No, because then she would have won. You'd
instantly turn into the bad guy. Trust me, in real life you
wouldn't feel half as good after doing it as you might
think.' Lou wished someone had given her this advice,
before she lamped Phil's other woman in the middle of a
crowded Boots in Barnsley town centre.

Tom was as good as his word – Eddie had delivered the
skip as promised. As yet, it sat there waiting, hungry
for the things from the loft, although wouldn't it be
nice if she could use it to put Nicola in instead and
save everyone in the office from her sadism, Lou
mused as she left the cloakroom. She pictured her
trapped in the skip, unable to get out, possibly
anchored to the sides by her magnetized gnashers.
Then creepy Des and Celia could join her, and
Victorianna, and Carl Ball, who used to chase Lou

mercilessly at school with daddy-long-legs, and big Shirley Hamster with her scissors, and Martine McCrum up the road, who told her that Santa had died in tragic circumstances, thus ruining her seventh Christmas. And Susan Peach with her startled-poodle perm and skinny open legs. *And Michelle, and Renee, and Phil!* her mind screamed. The shock of those last three additions brought her game to an abrupt end.

That lunchtime, and after work, Lou went clothes shopping and was surprised to find that she had dropped a whole dress size. The changing-room mirror experience was as horrific as usual, but in a gentler *Dracula AD 72* way, as opposed to a more frightening *Texas Chainsaw Massacre* way. She'd gone slightly mad in celebrating her new size and bought far more than she intended to. Now, hot and exhausted, Lou opened the front door to 1 The Faringdales, tapped in the code to turn off the burglar alarm and dumped all the carrier bags on the table.

She pulled out a couple of size fourteen skirts, one stone, one chocolate; both long and flattering with fish-tail hems that made her waist look smaller than it was, and a really nice leaf-green crossover top that she felt very elegant in and which suited her colouring down to the ground. To accompany it she had invested in a jacket, scarf and pendant, all in very brave colours for her and a break from all-forgiving black.

According to the article's laws of clutter-clearing, for every thing she brought into the house, she should throw some other thing away. The house was looking pretty minimalist these days by comparison to how it used to look, but visualizing all the people in the skip had given her an idea. Apart from the loft, there was one place she hadn't yet visited for cleansing.

Lou got a coffee and went into the office where she kept her big Filofax. She turned to the address pages, which were a mass of scribbles, Tippex and alterations, and ripped them all out. Then she took some fresh blank sheets and started to copy some, but not all, of the names back in. Her current doctor, dentist and electrician, the man who mended vacuum cleaners and Anthony Fawkes the hairdresser were musts. But there were addresses of friends from so far back in time she probably wouldn't recognize them if she bumped into them in the street, and if she did, they'd probably have nothing to say to each other. Not any more, anyway. There was a bunch of people with whom she had exchanged Christmas cards for years, but contact in between Decembers had long ceased. At first the cards had been chatty and newsy, and then over the years they were reduced to a signature or a short message, if she was lucky. Then the round robins started – long, rambling impersonal typed CVs of how wonderfully the Fartington Family were doing at their badminton and gymkhanas, and how they could only manage the fourteen skiing holidays that year.

The cards were sent out of habit now and no longer out of a genuine desire to keep in touch. Her Great-Auntie Peggy was an obvious exception. Her old scratchy writing always made Lou smile, even though she hadn't seen her since she was a child and probably would never see her again. Likewise she enjoyed writing her Christmas letter to lovely Anna Brightside, with whom Lou had once worked and in whose gentle company she had positively basked. Lou put both Peggy and Anna's addresses back into her book, but her old friend Sarah's Christmas cards had become almost a game of one-upmanship. Gone were the funny quips and gushing catch-ups, now it was all how many medals the children had won for junior nuclear physics, how many millions her brilliant Ph.D husband was pulling in, how much work they'd done on the (manor) house, how many times they'd been to Mars in their his-and-hers Porsches and how they simply must get together that year – as they had been going to do for the last fourteen. Lou had found herself responding with the same tarted-up codswallop: how great her job was, how successful her husband was, how happy she was . . . Lou didn't write Sarah's name on the new pages.

Two coffees later, her address book was decidedly lighter. Maybe the deleted entries would send her Christmas cards this year, but she was sure that when they weren't reciprocated she would be deleted from their lists too. She knew it would cause a momentary sadness because somewhere in the dark caves of their hearts existed the ghosts of the people they once were, clinging onto the friendships they once had. It was time to let go though, and only the people who were relevant to the Lou she was now would be part of her life from here on – people who meant something to her and to whom she meant something. Lou knew the time had definitely come to fill the last skip.

Chapter 27

Phil hadn't really taken all that nonsense seriously about Lou starting up the coffee-house business. Where would she get the money for it? Because he certainly wasn't going to lend it to her and she had no money of her own, and the bank would laugh her out of the building. Surely for a posh café to be successful, it would have to be in a town-centre location where the rent would be extortionate.

Lou might have been clever at doing a few accounts, but that wasn't going to be enough. She and that other silly bitch wouldn't survive five minutes baking fancy buns in a gritty Northern town! However, he found himself on the horns of a dilemma. He didn't dignify it by mentioning it again, although he was pretty cool and monosyllabic towards her, but he needed her on-side because he'd invited Des and Celia plus brats around for Sunday dinner. He'd got a lovely Audi in and Des was interested but wavering like a total old woman. A nice piece of lamb cooked the Lou way could just tip the balance in his favour. Still, for the lying and wet dog episode and meeting that Deb again business, his wife needed to know he wasn't happy by a long chalk.

He made sure that Lou knew he'd got up an hour earlier than normal that Saturday morning and that she saw
him putting on a shirt for work that he only ever wore for
best. He made a point of humming merrily because he
never hummed and that was bound to raise her suspicions.

'Just in case you try to get hold of me later, I'd better
warn you that my mobile might be off for a while,' he
threw behind him as he headed out, filling the air with
his expensive 'going out' after-shave and not his usual
daytime one. 'I've got an important business meeting.'
Phil could hear the cogs cranking up in her brain already.

Lou parked up at the supermarket but her head was back
at the house, watching Phil go through his morning routine. The differences were subtle ones, but they were
definitely there. Of course she had noticed the best shirt
and the after-shave and the time, as she was meant to.
And he never turned off his mobile; it was on vibrate if
he didn't want to be disturbed. Did he want her to think
he was up to mischief? To throw her off-balance for
seeing Deb again? Or was he really up to something? She
knew she must keep it all in perspective. *No*. He would-
n't have another affair – not after last time.

Sue Shoesmith was there waiting when Phil got to the
showroom. Slipping off his wedding ring, he stuck it in
the glovebox before getting out of his Audi.

'Oh no – am I late for you?' He made a big show of
looking at his watch, although he knew he was on time.
The *for you* was a sweet personal touch, he thought.

'No, I'm just keen,' said British Racing Green-eyed
Sue with a glossy red smile.

'Come on in before you get cold,' he said, even though it was a May-mild morning.

He went through his routine of disabling the alarm, switching on the lights and putting on the coffee percolator. As she waited, he could see she was champing at the bit to view the car. Opening the door to the showroom, he led her through with an extravagant courteous flourish.

He had to admit, the MG did look bonny. He'd only had a cursory look at it the previous night when it came in and he'd left Bradley to give it a valet. Sue gasped open-mouthed and Phil knew he had sold it. She walked around it, her eyes like saucers.

'It's absolutely gorgeous,' she breathed.

'Told you,' he said.

'Can I get in it?'

Phil opened the door and she climbed in elegantly. Nice legs. Very nice, in fact. She was rehearsing how it would be to drive it, checking the pedals, adjusting the rearview mirror, fondling the steering wheel.

'Can I take it for a test run?' she asked.

'I'd have to come with you,' he replied almost apologetically.

'Oh, of course,' she said smokily.

'Quick coffee before we head off?'

'That would be lovely.'

She didn't get out of the car as gracefully as she got in. He got a lovely flash of her thighs and some stocking lace. They both knew that was deliberate.

After Lou had unloaded the food shopping from her Saturday-morning supermarket trip she changed into her scruffy clothes. Despite telling herself to keep Phil's little *game* in perspective, she had spent the last two hours' worth of headspace ripping apart that little domestic scene this morning like Quincy did with a corpse, laying all the viscera out to see what it meant, or what it could mean. Finally she had managed to convince herself that Phil wouldn't be playing Happy Families with Des and Celia on Sunday if his head was being turned by another woman, so in a perverse way she was glad they were coming. She would make it extra jolly and push out all the stops: homemade broth to start with, meat and five veg, Yorkshire puddings with thick homemade onion gravy and a chocolate and cream tarte to follow. He was just trying to unsettle her for talking to Deb again and letting Clooney into the house. He would be far more secretive if he were having a frisson, not flash it in front of her face. Silly woman – she was just being paranoid.

Sue put her foot on the accelerator and the car zipped forward.

'Wow, powerful, isn't she?'

'Oh yes. Quick as a cat, but the control is all yours – we're both in your hands,' said Phil graciously.

Sue gave a throaty laugh. 'Well, in that case, I may just be ready to slip it up a gear and see what happens,' she said with obvious double-meaning.

Phil responded with a shy cough and a comment about the nifty gear system. Not too much, too quick, he thought. Slowlee slowlee catchee monkee. Women always tried a bit harder when they couldn't have what they wanted on demand.

*

Armed with her binliners, Lou pulled down the loft ladder and with a fortifying deep breath inside her, she climbed up the steps. She switched on the light, and the low-wattage bulb cast a dull glow over the stored items. It was so quiet and still up there under the eaves; it was as if everything wanted to remain there undisturbed in the shadows, to be left alone in peace. But the things up here didn't rest in peace, did they, said Lou to herself. Their energies were far from dead and threatened her with their old seductive promises of how life should be but never would be. Lou went back downstairs for a 100-watt bulb.

After the paperwork was completed and the monies transferred, Phil presented Sue with a *P.M Autos* fob bearing her new keys and a bottle of Moët that he had just sent the new lad Dennis to the nearby supermarket for – no cheap fizz for this customer. She was flushed with excitement from her new acquisition, especially because she could take it home there and then. Here was a woman who didn't like to wait for things, thought Phil.

'There's a full tank of fuel for you and a set of new car mats,' he winked in a 'You are *so* special – I don't do this for everyone' kind of way.

'And if I have any problems with anything, can I call you . . . personally?' she asked, her eyes not blinking as they locked with his.

'I would expect you to,' he said, smiling and softly stroking the bonnet of the car as if it were a woman's skin. He could sense her brain purring. 'What a very special lady. And the car's not bad either.'

'Aw!' she said, taken aback with delight at his compliment.

'You take good care of yourself,' he said, feigning bashfulness as if he had just gone too far and was knocking down to first gear again. 'Drive carefully, but enjoy her. Life's too short not to have any thrills.'

'You're a man after my own heart,' she said.

And after your knockers and after what lies at the top of those stockings as well, he added to himself.

Sue British Racing Green Eyes climbed into the driver's seat and started up the engine. She beeped the horn and waved goodbye to him out of the window with a long elegant arm. She'd call, of course, on some pretext or other. He gave it three days.

Chapter 28

Lou looked around in dismay at the amount of Phil's rubbish: electric razors that he had long since replaced with all-singing all-dancing ones, three ancient portable TVs, lamps and other odd bachelor bits that she remembered transporting to the loft when she first moved in. It was hard work carrying them downstairs and she was soon looking like a Dickensian chimney-sweep child. Her hair was stiff with dust and she doubted she'd ever get the grime out from under the few remaining nails she had left. The thought of a good long soak brought with it the far more unpleasant one of Bloody Keith Featherstone, and she wondered if she should just write off the money and go and get someone else to finish the job. At least that way he would be cleared out of her head. Then again, she had paid him a *lot* of money. And why should he get it for doing absolutely nothing? The issue consigned itself back to the 'to do' tray in her head. Again.

She had a small break for lunch – a nice long glass of clean sparkling mineral water and a thick egg and spring onion sandwich to fortify her for the task ahead. Her stomach had obviously shrunk recently because the sandwich filled her adequately, but her hand reached automatically for the biscuit barrel anyway. The chocolate digestive had just touched her lips when she realized she didn't really want it — it was just habit. She was clearing out the house but still filling herself up with rubbish. Lou threw it away and headed, once again, up the stairs.

Back up in the loft, Lou found a box full of souvenirs from school containing a purse that an old penfriend had sent her from Australia, made from a kangaroo scrotum. There were exercise books and paintings and her handwriting-practice jotter in pencil and scratchy ink, *I hate Shirley Hamster* in her best copperplate on the cover. Then there was her school diary with a photograph of herself aged eight stuck on the first page. She flicked through it and found the story of when Dad took her to the zoo and she heard a bear trump, which made Lou laugh out loud to read again. She remembered it so well, still. She could even recall that when her dad had paid the entrance fee she was given a fold-up map, blue on the front with a big black and white zebra's head and they'd had a bag of vinegary chips sitting on a bench. She had bought her mum and her baby sister a Wade Whimsie each as a souvenir of her very lovely day. For a moment it felt as if that young Lou was a separate entity from herself, one blissfully unaware of anything but the pleasures of childhood, who didn't know that her father's heart would start to fail in a few years and that he would be taken away from her for ever. The little girl in the photo had no inkling that she wouldn't have his love to lean on when she would most need it, when she discovered that all men weren't like the benchmark he had provided. Lou wanted to reach back into her past and cuddle that little girl, and tell her she would survive when pain crashed into her life like a juggernaut at full speed. She looked so little to have all that future hurt to face.

There was a broken cuckoo clock that her dad had bought her from Germany. Victorianna had pulled it from the wall during one of her tantrums – although Lou had then propelled her little sister out of the back door by her blonde pigtails and thrown her headfirst in their dad's compost heap. Lou put the clock into the bin-bag, then immediately brought it out again. She couldn't let it go – it would be like saying goodby e to her dad all over again – yet hadn't she kept it unlooked-at for years? Lou smiled tearfully. She took some time and thought it through until a clear voice of reason, made both from the words of the article and her own commonsense, directed her what to do. She didn't need the corpse of a broken clock when she had the living memory of walking into her bedroom and seeing it hanging there on her wall for her. Her mother had gone mad because no one could sleep through its cuckooing in the night, but Dad had said it was staying and eventually they all got used to Klaus the cuckoo. She wasn't betraying her father by throwing away the clock; she wasn't letting *him* go by letting *it* go. Lou didn't care how ridiculous it was, but she kissed the broken old clock and said, 'Goodbye, Klaus,' before she bravely put it back in the bin-bag.

Next came a suitcase containing old summer holiday clothes that she remembered from their Corfu trip: her ethnic wraparound skirt and bright T-shirts and Phil's sandals that they'd both laughed about because they were flat boat-like things that they could have sailed home in, had the plane been indefinitely delayed. There was a pair of his red shorts that looked so narrow in the waist, ticket stubs from the excursions they'd taken, seashells from the beach. It was the last time she could remember feeling truly content with Phil – getting off the plane into the hot Greek sunshine, discovering the little bay where they snorkelled with the fishes, eating meze in a taverna surrounded by lemon trees and she feeding the local stray cats with tins of pilchards.

Lou didn't need the clutter-clearing article to tell her she had kept this case in order to hold onto a fortnight of time, a time when she was lovable. She couldn't go back to those days, however many reminders she had kept of what life had been like before she and Phil had started drifting apart, before Phil had his affair with Susan Peach. She manoeuvred the bulky case down the loft ladder then took it straight out to the skip. That was the easy bit over and done with.

Lou knew only too well what lay in the hoard of boxes and carrier bags in the binliners which were coated with nearly two years of dust. Handbags and shoes that she had bought when Phil had left her, purchases made in the hope of stemming the crater-sized hole in her heart – a five-second fix with every thirty quid spent. There were hundreds of pounds' worth of goods there – never used or worn, each one immediately sullied by the reason she had bought it and each one a reminder of that awful build-up to Christmas when her eyes just wouldn't stay dry. She had been a sad island in a sea of jolly festive merriment, drunks with daft hats on and excited children crowding in shops. Hell had nothing on that year, trudging around stores doing obligatory Christmas shopping, desperately craving the arrival of cold, dull January whilst soul-piercing brass bands threatened to break down the crumbling wall which was keeping the tears back in public places. Everywhere she went, carols pumped out around her with their lyrics of love and joy. 'Simply Ha-av-ing a Wonderful Christmas Time' tortured her in every shop. She had made a mental promise that year that if she ever met Paul McCartney, she would ram that record right up his rectum.

The well-used clutter-clearing article sat in her pocket but it had been long absorbed into her psyche. She knew her struggle to let these purchases go was all to do with feeling obliged to make use of them. They were emotionally blackmailing her with their price tags, making her feel guilty for wasting so much money. *You can't get rid of us, we cost too much.* Things had controlled her, she now realized. They were trying to force their way into her life with all their negative connotations. Well, she didn't want them. Pretty as they were, they made her feel sad to look at them.

As she carried them downstairs she knew the Heart Foundation women were going to have a field day, but it gave her some comfort to know that items bought in such a deeply sad way would have their energies reversed. People would re-buy them in happier circumstances and the charity would profit. It was a win-win situation, really. Taking them down to the garage, she put them straight into her car boot for drop-off first thing on Monday morning before work.

Downstairs the phone rang, but Lou ignored it. There

was just the one corner left in the loft to clear and she needed to do this now, with no interruptions. Steeling herself, she took a deep breath and pulled off the dust-sheet which covered the items beneath. There they were, the pieces of cot, never constructed, the carrier bags of soft baby clothes, still in their packs, nappies that moths had started to nibble, a baby intercom, sheets and blan-kets, a mobile of cotton-woolly lambs that would never hang above a sleeping baby, but it was the bag of tiny white socks that sent her crumpling to the floor. And yet people said you couldn't grieve for what you never had.

Just after they married, Phil suddenly announced that he didn't want children, and no amount of pleading with him would change his mind. Then two years later, he just as suddenly announced that if she still wanted to try for that baby, then they would. Lou threw her pills away with a happy flourish, but whatever time of month they did it, the longed-for baby never arrived.

She started fantasizing about Phil and his twins rec-onciling and visiting. She imagined going shopping for sweets and treats for them and even planned how she would decorate two of the bedrooms for them to stay in, but that dream had died the day they met them in Meadowhall.

'Chuffing hell, it's Sharon and the kids,' Phil had said with abject horror.

A passing glance at the blonde woman told Lou she was indeed every bit as pretty as Phil's sighing recollec-tion of her (whenever he wanted to stir up Lou's insecurities) made her out to be. It was the children, however, who stole her attention. They were beautiful: honey-haired with huge chocolate-brown eyes and thick dark lashes. How could any father not have wanted them? But Phil's extreme reaction made it perfectly clear that Lou would even be denied a stepmother-ship. She never mentioned to him the grief that followed, when she couldn't get their little faces out of her head. She would lie in bed in the dark and transpose herself and Phil into a Santa-queue scene with their own little boy and girl. But that was when she still had a heart full of hope that they might have children of their own, a hope that died a little more with the bleed of each passing month.

Then, not long after he returned home from his affair with Susan Peach, Lou's periods stopped. Not only that but her nipples ached and she felt decidedly queasy. Lou didn't need to do a pregnancy test – it was obvious she had caught on. Of course it would have been wise to wait and not buy stuff yet, but stocking up on a few odd things wouldn't hurt, surely? And buying them forced her pregnancy to be real. She had a true taste of happiness arriving at the hospital for her first scan. There had been a shop there and she had bought those little socks, knowing she was shortly going to see on the screen the little feet that would one day wear them.

The doctor at the hospital had been kind. Her scan, and the following urine sample, said there was no baby. He explained that in rare cases, the body can cruelly mimic the signs of pregnancy to this degree.

'A phantom?' Renee had said. 'I thought only Labradors had those!'

'Pull yourself together, love,' Phil had said, when she told him that night through tears that there was no baby growing inside her. He tried not to sound as relieved as he felt when he clumsily comforted her with the words, 'You can't miss what you never had.'

But Lou knew that you could.

Lou couldn't bring herself to pass these baby things onto the charity shop. They stank of rank energy and bad luck, not the best inheritance for a fresh new baby – a baby that would always belong to someone else. She knew now that saving these things had not helped to keep her dreams of being a mother alive; they had done exactly the opposite, serving only to remind her of what she would never be.

As Lou piled them all into the skip she knew she was saying that final goodbye. It felt as if she had ripped part of her heart out and put that into the skip too.

Back upstairs, she swept the naked loft, barely able to see what she was doing as her eyes started to leak years of stagnant pain. As it became too much to hold back, she let the brush fall and sank to her knees, howling from some primal place within her which held the mother-lode of her agony. The tears cut clean paths through the dirt on her face and the saltwater stole into her mouth. Letting go of that dream life, cutting it loose from her and watching it sail off into the sky like a precious party balloon, made her feel empty and lost – and so very, very alone.

At four o'clock exactly, Tom reversed the skip wagon up the drive. She wasn't there to greet him so he left Clooney in the cab. As soon as he saw what was in the skip, he understood completely why she wanted it cleared away that day, and he could only guess what it must have been like for her to let those things go. He felt her sadness acutely on this day – the same day when his sister Sammy had brought her new little daughter into the world.

He didn't usually knock when picking up from customers. He had no reason to now but he rapped hard on Lou's door. He had the weirdest feeling she was *in*, and, inappropriate as it might have been, he so much wanted to see that she was all right. No, more than that, he wanted to put his arms around her and hold her.

Chapter 29

When Lou was little, she used to have terrible migraines — dark headaches and vomiting that almost turned her inside out. But the day after, she would awake with a buzzing euphoria; a sense of calmness and inner peace that was almost worth the previous night's pain. Apparently it was a common symptom. And was not at all dissimilar to how she felt that morning after the final skip had gone.

Lou had been up and dressed before Phil woke up to the smoky aroma of his breakfast. He gave off a sullen air which hinted that things were most definitely not back to normal between them. Less was more in the arena of mind games, which was why he also resisted his Sunday-morning sexual pass at his wife. A break in routine should get her thinking . . . His toxic seed had obviously started to germinate, it seemed, because she had been in a very troubled place yesterday. When he came in from work, she looked as if she had been crying for hours. Her eyes were swollen and she hardly said two words all evening. She'd blamed it on all the dust up in the loft, but he knew better.

*

Of course, Lou *had* heard Tom knock the previous day, when he came to take the skip away, and she knew that he had waited a considerably long time before finally climbing into his cab. Even then he drove off slowly, looking up at the windows, as if he expected to see a curtain twitch. There was no way she would have let him see her in that state – scruffy and swollen and ugly from crying and *raw* – but much more than that, she had been feeling far too vulnerable to be anywhere near Tom Broom. The merest hint of sympathy would have opened up the floodgates to a dam of grief, and goodness knows what she would have said or done.

It had drained her to lose so many emotional possessions at once. They had anchored her firmly to places in the past where she was comfortable – with *the devil she knew*. Taking them away cut her adrift, to a place where the waters were dark, scary and unknown.

At first she panicked when Tom's wagon started up to transport them to where she would never be able to see them again and she almost ran after him to tell him that she was taking them back. Nonetheless she took a deep breath, closed her mind against the urge and finally let them go. They were just things that had no magic to make the past return even if he had doubled-back. The facts were clear: there was no loving father waiting in the wings to make everything better; she couldn't wipe away Phil's infidelity; she would never hold her own baby in her arms. *Deal with it, Lou, and move on,* said the voice within her, firm but supportive for once. It was time to stop waiting for hopeless dreams to come true. Time to take control of her own destiny and start looking forward instead of back.

She had slept the solid, dreamless sleep of the exhausted and now, in the morning, life felt *fresher*. Like her address book, it was no longer full of crossings-out with names still visible under the lines. Life was suddenly before her as a whole new space to fill with *Casa Nostra* and Deb and a new, stronger phase in her marriage, free from the long shadow of Phil's affair dulling everything. She had to put that fact to the forefront of her mind – their marriage *had* survived Susan Peach and, however shaky it might sometimes appear, it was still standing, which meant its foundations were strong. Phil was a controlling man – true – and he'd made a mistake once, but there were much worse husbands out there. He didn't abuse substances and he abhorred men who used physical violence on women. He was spoiled that was all – and that had been partly her fault for letting him get his own way so much. But he was generous and hardworking, and *her husband*, after all; the man she'd been pledged to *till death do us part*. In saying that, she was glad that Phil hadn't pushed her to make love that morning.

The aroma of meat wafted towards Phil's receptive nostrils as Lou opened the oven door to baste it. Then it hit him that it wasn't the smell he was expecting.

'That's beef!' he said.

And the Sherlock Holmes Award for Outstanding Deduction goes to Phil Winter of Barnsley, thought Lou.

'I told you to get lamb! I'm trying to butter up Des to buy a twenty-seven-grand car, for God's sake!'

'Phil, I don't like lamb and I presume I'm going to be

eating too. Or would you prefer me just to scoff a Ryvita at the table whilst you five tuck in? Besides which, I don't know whether Celia likes lamb but I *do* know she likes beef.'

'Everybody in the world likes lamb but you, Lou,' he growled sullenly. 'You're just weird.'

'It'll be every bit as nice. Better even,' said Lou. 'Trust me.'

Phil knew it would be. He could always trust Lou – about anything. Lou would never let him down. It wasn't a quality Phil particularly envied, though. One should always maintain a hidden weapon with which to surprise.

'This is gorgeous beef,' said Des, swirling it around the onion gravy before delivering it to his mouth where it melted wondrously on his tongue.

'I like my beef more pink,' commented Celia, although she hadn't exactly left much by way of protest.

'Me too,' said Phil in agreement. 'I think Lou's over-cooked it slightly.'

'No, Lou hasn't,' clipped Lou sweetly. 'Lou just hasn't *under*cooked it. I like it heated all the way through, myself. Plus I don't like the idea of giving children pink meat.'

'More wine?' said Phil, slightly taken aback by her verbal parry. Was this the start of the *Change*, he wondered. It would go some way to explaining all this clearing-up bollocks and that impromptu sex they'd had in the kitchen. He hoped she wouldn't start growing facial hair, like Maureen. Fat Jack must wake up in the mornings and wonder if he'd married Geoff Capes.

Celia initially refused a slice of the chocolate tarte when Lou put it on the table, although her eyes stood out like ping-pong balls with obvious desire for it. She patted her concave stomach and said something about already being half a micro ounce overweight.

'Oh I don't know, it would be nice to have something to get hold of,' said Des, his eyes darting involuntarily to Lou. It was only a flicker, but one noted by both Lou and Celia.

Oh well, that explains a few things, thought Lou with a raise of her eyebrows, even if it didn't excuse it.

'Yes, but you can have too much to get hold of,' said Phil, also flicking his eyes at Lou and making sure she caught his meaning.

'I think Lou has lost a little weight, am I right?' said Des. 'On a diet?'

'Lou's on the rotation diet,' said Phil. 'Every time I turn my back, she eats something.'

He howled at his own joke and was joined by the children, although they were really laughing at Uncle Phil laughing.

Lou experienced a pang of humiliation that quickly changed to anger.

'Hark at Twiggy!' she said, and watched Phil's lips contract. She had never come back at him with a spiky riposte. She had always taken the joke like a dutiful comedian's stooge.

'Well, maybe I'll have just a little pudding,' said Celia, popping the bubble of tension that was puffing up like a giant man-eating vol-au-vent. 'It does look delicious.'

She nibbled her slice daintily. Too daintily, thought Lou. She ate the same way that Victorianna used to eat, craving the food in front of her but knowing if she didn't put the brakes on hard she would be diving into it head-first, only to have to rush up to the toilet to stick her fingers down her throat. Well, putting away a few puds might not be ideal, but Lou had always thought it was a damn sight more healthy than making your body go through all that laxative, deprivation and regurgitating nonsense.

Scheherazade, who had not inherited her mother's aversion to calories, stuck her finger into the remaining cake, scooped out a digitful and transferred it lascivi-ously to her mouth. Lou waited in vain for either parent or Phil to reprimand her because she had never felt it was her place to say anything when the children were bouncing on the furniture or nosing around in her drawers and cupboards upstairs. Her anger would stew inside but never find its way out, because she was too damn polite for her own good – see Bloody Keith Featherstone for more evidence of that one. But Lou Winter was indeed going through a Change (if not *the* Change) and she was thinking at that moment that Scheherazade and Hero might not be her children, but this was her house, and that beautiful chocolate tarte was her creation and she wasn't going to stand by and see it desecrated.

Scheherazade's finger came out again and Lou whisked the tarte away before it made contact.

'Now would anyone like me to cut them an extra piece? Scheherazade?' asked Lou.

'Yes,' said Scheherazade.

'Yes what?'

Celia's eyes snapped up.

'Er . . . yes, please,' said Scheherazade.

'Right,' said Lou with a knife in her hand and a knife in her smile. 'I'll give you this piece that you've just stuck your finger into, shall I?'

Scheherazade took the plate, which Lou didn't relinquish until she got a stunned 'thank you'. The withering effect rippled through everyone at the table. They continued to eat in silence with only the tinkle of cutlery on crockery to break it.

Phil stole a glance at Lou but she was pouring some cream and seemed quite oblivious to the fact that she was acting menopausal.

'Gorgeous, that tarte,' said Des, spraying crumbs as he spoke.

'If you like it, darling, I'll get the recipe,' said Celia.

'Sorry,' said Lou, tapping the side of her nose. 'Trade secret.'

'For God's sake, Lou, it's only a bit of cake,' said Phil, attempting to laugh off his annoyance. She'd better not cock up this sale for him with her crazy oestrogen levels. What the hell was up with her? Was she going to go bright red and start sweating in a minute?

'I'm sure Colonel Sanders had plenty of people saying, "For God's sake, Harland, it's only a chicken!" Good job for him that he didn't give his recipe out to everyone who asked, wasn't it?'

Goodness knows how she had remembered what he was called. It was one of those odd trivial facts that brains store away, patiently waiting for its moment to shine.

'Hardly the same, is it?' said Phil with a crooked little smile. He was back on terra firma with a chance to show off his clever razor-like wit. 'A multi-million-pound industry versus one woman and a few buns.'

'Everyone has to start somewhere. Who knows, I might have overtaken him in profits if I'd started my business when I was originally going to,' returned Lou.

'What's this?' said Des, jumping in with interest. He was a financial adviser and the word 'business' always stirred his brain into whirrings.

'I'm opening up a coffee-house,' said Lou. 'With my friend Debra.'

'Debra?' said Celia with a sniff. 'Isn't that the person who nearly broke up your marriage?'

'No,' Lou said flatly. 'That was Phil.'

Phil went beetroot. Even Lou was a bit taken aback by her audacity on that one. Standing up for herself had once been second nature. When had it become so difficult? The room temperature dropped like the track on a white-knuckle ride.

'Go and play, children,' said Celia.

'Can we go upstairs?' asked Hero, shovelling the last of the tarte into his mouth.

'Yes, of course,' said Celia, at exactly the moment when Lou said,

'No, you can't.'

'Jesus Christ!' Phil snarled quietly between his teeth.

Ignoring him, Lou got up from the table holding out her hands to the children. 'Come on, there are lots of DVDs in the lounge you can watch, or there's a Connect Four in the cupboard so take your pick, kids, but please, don't go poking around upstairs. It isn't polite.'

Des, Celia and Phil cross-fired glances at each other

but were too stunned to say anything. This wasn't Lou. This was a Doppelgänger from Planet Crank.

The children grumpily found a DVD they were vaguely interested in but were won over when Lou said they could lounge on the floor with all the cushions from the sofa and some pop and the tin of Quality Street. They were only allowed to perch on the pristine leather furniture at home and marble tiles weren't conducive to floor-sprawling.

Phil was about to whisk Lou aside and ask her what the hell she was up to when he realized that, now the kids were out of the way, they could get down to business. He'd deal with her later, after he had sold Des the car.

Lou went dutifully into the kitchen as Phil started up a conversation he would quickly steer round to the Audi. Sure that she was out of earshot, Celia advised her brother to get in some Oil of Evening Primrose quick for his wife. Either that or an Exorcist.

Lou filled up the dishwasher with what she had carried through. As she straightened up to go and get the rest she turned to find herself face-to-chest with Des and his dirty plate. He was so close to her that they could have auditioned for *Dirty Dancing*. Lou's hand came out and slowly but surely she pushed him back.

'Steady on there, Des,' she said as frothily as a soufflé, but with her volume button twisted all the way up to number ten. 'Don't they have personal space on your planet?'

Celia snarled loudly from the conservatory. 'Des! Here – now!'

She might as well have said, 'Heel!' for the effect it

had on him. He slunk back to the dining table like a kicked dog.

Interesting, thought Lou. So Celia was aware of his quirk. Maybe that's why she bought all those designer shoes and handbags. Maybe she too was clinging on to something she felt was slipping away and was trying to comfort herself. Although in her case, Lou would have definitely preferred the slingbacks to the man.

Tension hung over the table like a hydrogen-filled Zeppelin flying low on Bonfire Night. Phil annoyed with Lou, Celia annoyed with Des.

'So,' said Phil, attempting to direct the conversation back where he needed it to go. 'Has he told you about the car, Ceel?'

'Yes, he has,' she said, attempting to smile and look normal as Phil started his sales spiel.

Lou poured four coffees and dispensed home-made truffles made with crème de menthe. She's gone to a lot of effort, thought Phil, deciding that gave her a few brownie points. Though not enough to get her totally out of the woods. This afternoon's performance only went to prove he needed to take even firmer action.

'Fantastic machine.' Phil passed the box of cigars over to Des before choosing one himself. Celia lit up a cigarette. 'Previous owner only drove it in dry weather. Two years old and less than six thousand on the clock. Goes like shit off a shiny shovel. You name it and that baby's got it.'

'I'll get you an ashtray,' said Lou, scurrying off meekly – like her old subservient self, they were all relieved to note.

'So – are you going for it then, Des? I'll cut you a deal that only family can give you.'

He addressed his brother-in-law but looked at his sister. Maybe Des trying to grope Lou in the kitchen would have put him nicely in Celia's debt. Buying a big fancy black car for her to swank about in might just get Des out of the mire.

'Oh, I don't know,' said Des with a regretful shake of the head. 'I've seen a gorgeous silver BMW in *Buckley's*.'

'It's a lot easier to keep clean than black,' said Celia, who had set her heart on a car with the blue and white BMW button. It was far more prestigious in her book than a series of hooped rings.

Phil knew instinctively that they'd already made up their minds before they came today and had taken advantage of his hospitality. Even worse, they were buying from 'Mr New-Kid-on-the-Block' Jack Buckley, his sworn business rival. Well, if they weren't buying then they might as well piss off until December, he thought. Des was as entertaining as syphilis and Celia was only interested in being bigger and better than them. Oh! He must remember to tell Lou that he'd invited them for Christmas dinner. His classic car business would be nearly up and running by then, and he and Fat Jack could apply double pressure on Des to invest, greased further by copious amounts of brandy and Lou's turkey and trimmings. Oh yes, and he must tell her Fat Jack and Maureen were coming as well.

'I've got a surprise for Christmas dinner this year,' said Phil, five minutes after waving off Des and Celia with an outward smile and an inward, 'Thank Christ.'

'Christmas? But that's half a year away yet!'

'It'll be on us before we know it. I want to get plans in place.'

'Well, if you're already thinking about it, how about going out for the big meal this year? Apparently the Queens Hotel do a fantastic one. And they've started taking bookings, I see, in the *Chronicle*.'

'Er, even better than that, I thought . . . a traditional family Christmas!' said Phil, making it sound like she'd just won the star prize on a gameshow.

Lou looked at him blankly.

'At home,' he went on, and stood there expectantly as if he was waiting for her to shout, 'Whoopee!' and start leaping around with joy.

Lou let out a long breath. It wasn't hard to see where this one was going.

'I thought we could have the kids around at Christmas. I know that would be nice for you, Lou – kids and Christmas and all that.'

Manipulating git, thought Lou, but listened on.

'And obviously Des and Ceel.'

'Obviously,' said Lou. She knew what was coming next. Phil wasn't as opaque as he thought he was.

'And your mother. We can't leave her out.'

'No. Absolutely.'

'And . . . Fat Jack and Maureen. I noticed you got on like a house on fire with her last time. Chatting away together for ages, you were.'

He made a move to hug her and no doubt then would have gone on to paint a jolly picture of a house full of dear friends and family engaging in Christmas merriment and gleeful children sitting opening gifts under a glittering Christmas tree. There would be a gentle snowstorm outside and Perry Como scoffing mince pies at the door complete with a group of carol singers and chestnuts roasting on the open fire. Lou could have quite happily roasted Phil's nuts on an open fire.

She put up a hand to stop his affectionate advance.

'So let me get this straight. Instead of a six-course meal made by someone else in a lovely hotel, with no washing-up to do afterwards, I get to slave away making a dinner for nine with no one to help me cook it or clean up?'

'We'll all muck in.'

'No one ever helps me, Phil. Celia has never got up off her backside to rinse a cup in all the time I've known her and Des only comes in the kitchen to push his luck.'

'He's harmless . . .'

'He's a creep!'

'I promise, I'll help you. It's important to me, Lou. This new joint venture with Fat Jack is my . . . our future. It'll be up and running in a few months.'

'What about what's important to *me*? What's in it for *me*, Phil?' asked Lou stiffly.

Phil stared at her open-mouthed. He was having a little trouble today equating the mild-mannered Lou with this lippy cow who was making his life so much hard work.

'What's in it for you?' he barked. 'Why are you suddenly so "me, me, me", Lou?'

'Maybe I've suddenly remembered there is a "me" worth considering. Everyone else seems to have forgotten!' said Lou, sweeping past him, grabbing the first coat her hand fell on and striding out into the afternoon.

Aware that his jaw was hanging somewhere by his knees, Phil snapped it shut.

Let her have her tantrum, he thought. By Christmas she would be nice and compliant again. His game was well underway now and pretty soon he knew that she would be agreeing to anything he suggested.

Chapter 30

As soon as Lou had got to the lip of the estate, the heavens opened and big splashy rain started to fall. The thin jacket she'd picked up afforded little shelter from it, although Lou hardly noticed because her brain was too busy churning over the events of that hideous afternoon. Why was she painted as the bad guy just for saying 'Don't destroy my furniture, children,' and, 'No, I'm not giving you my recipe,' and, 'Don't come so close to me, you ghoulish sleazebag,' and, 'Colonel Sanders and I were born equal'? Wasn't she allowed to have an opinion? Was she put on earth merely to put up with Phil's snidey comments about her weight and Des's CS gas breath on the back of her neck?

She was automatically heading in the direction of Michelle's house. She needed face-to-face female company and a cup of tea. She wanted to clear it all from her chest about Des and Celia and Phil and Deb and Tom and Jaws with someone not connected to any of them. Lou just wanted to talk. And, more importantly, she wanted for once to be listened to.

Michelle lived in a small end-terraced house over half an hour's walk away. It was shabby by comparison with all the others in the row, with their new windows, matching white uPVC doors and nice crisp curtains, but Michelle hadn't displayed much inclination to improve the house since she bought it. *Your home is a mirror that reflects what is going on in your life.* Looking at the neglected, grubby façade, Lou thought that there was more than a hint of truth in that. She was saturated by the time she got there. The rain was dripping from her hair, her nose and it had even got into her shoes.

Lou knocked on the mustardy painted door. It was the colour of a very bad bowel movement and it opened immediately.

'You were quick— oh!' said Michelle, holding a thin baby-pink satin dressing-gown shut across her obviously naked body. Her hair was sticking up like barbed wire. She had clearly been expecting someone else. 'Sorry, I thought you were Craig. He's just nipped out for some fags,' she said, smiling a little awkwardly. 'He'll be back in a minute,' she added, careful not to ask what had brought Lou unannounced to her door in case the answer took longer than thirty seconds and there were tears involved as she suspected there might be.

'I was just wondering if you were free, but obviously not,' said Lou.

'No, sorry, I'm not really,' said Michelle, her eyes darting over Lou's head for Craig. She thought it was a bit off of Lou, calling around unannounced, so she felt justified in not inviting her in.

'It's fine,' said Lou with a smile. 'I shouldn't have come without a phone call first anyway.'

'I'm sorry, Lou. Craig and me . . . we only see each other at weekends so every moment is precious.'

'Oh, it's OK, please don't worry,' smiled Lou. Her escapee tears were camouflaged by the rain.

'Look, I'll ring you as soon as he's gone,' Michelle said.

'OK,' said Lou.

'See you then. Sorry.' The door was already shutting; slowly, but closing all the same.

Lou turned back down the street, passing a tall, hollow-eyed, scruffy-looking bloke with facial piercings and some weird blue tattooed writing on his neck. He was opening up a packet of Embassy and dropped the wrapping on the ground. As he passed Lou he gave her a thorough look up and down which left her feeling slightly tainted. Surely that was never him – *the most gorgeous man she'd ever seen.*

Lou's feet hurt slopping around in her shoes. The rain was relentless and she didn't even have her purse to get a taxi. Going back to Michelle and interrupting her shenanigans with Creepy Craig to ask for a brolly or the loan of a fiver obviously wasn't an option, so she faced a long, hard and wet walk home. Today, Lou could have been forgiven for believing that everything, even the elements, had conspired against her.

Chapter 31

For once, Phil was wrong. Sue Shoesmith left it a full seven days before she contacted him with a text, and just a few hours before he would have given in and rung her himself. Obviously it was better that she took the initiative; it proved she was keen – not that he had any doubt on that one.

HI MR AUDI TT. CAR IS GRRREAT THANKS. SLIGHT PROBLEM THOUGH. CAN I BRING IT IN AND SHOW YOU?

He texted back. WHEN? YOU NAME THE TIME.

The response was immediate.

CAN DO THIS AFTERNOON. 5?

5 OK. I WONT TURN THE COFFEE OFF he responded.

STRONG, BLACK 1 SUGAR. X came the quick reply. Christ, she must have had a texting speed of 300 wpm, he thought. A fast bird, in all senses of the word.

I REMEMBER. God, he was as smooth as his own Columbian Roast. And he would have bet his life-savings there was nothing wrong with the car.

'Salad?' said Deb, recoiling with horror.

'Yep, salad and a sparkling mineral water please,' re-iterated Lou to the Maltstone Garden Centre café waitress,

who promptly disappeared with an order for that and
Deb's lasagne.

'Don't tell me you're going all healthy on me,' said
Deb. 'Especially as we're planning to open up the artery
clogging-capital of the world!'

Lou laughed. 'Don't be daft, I just feel like a nice crisp
leafy salad. Anyway, it's not that angelic – it's got cheese
and tortilla chips in it.'

'Seriously though, Lou, you have lost weight since we
met up again,' said Deb. 'Actually, you're looking pretty
sex-on-a-stick.'

'Give over,' Lou hooted.

'No, really. I did mean to say it before, but I know
your mother is always on about your figure and I didn't
want you to think I'd joined the "let's monitor Lou's
weight" club. Have you been dieting?'

'Deb, I think I've started a fresh diet every day for the last
three years and failed every one. I've lost this just by clearing out some rubbish from the house and getting physical
filling skips and drinking lots of water. Ironic, isn't it, that
I lose it when I'm not even thinking about losing it?'

'Well, you look lovely,' said Deb, quickly adding, 'not
that you didn't before.'

'I certainly feel different,' Lou admitted. 'I'm sleeping
a lot better and I am much more energized. I'm enjoying the feeling so much, I'm not going to go back to my
old ways of comfort eating.'

'Well, good for you,' said Deb steadily and meaning it,
but not asking why she would need to comfort eat at all
if things were OK in the Winter household.

'But I do love my puddings,' said Lou with a child-like
grin.

'Well, I hope you're having one today,' said Deb. 'I'm not eating a big Rocky Road whilst you sit there chewing a baton of cucumber.'

'Don't you worry,' said Lou. 'The day I stop enjoying desserts will be the day I ask you to shoot me. I'm not turning into Victorianna, trust me.'

'On that horrible thought, back to business,' said Deb, shuddering as she sank her breadstick into some creamy chilli dip. 'The biggest problem we have is premises. It's holding everything else up, unless we want to move it out of town to somewhere like Wakefield.'

They both shook their heads. They wanted *Casa Nostra* to be born in Barnsley, for sentimental home-town reasons.

'I've totally drawn a blank with the estate agents, apart from the old kebab shop on Pitterly Lane.'

'Hardly central, unless you're a druggie,' said Lou. 'No, thanks.'

'Precisely.'

'So we wait.'

'For a miracle.'

'Either that or a fairy godmother.'

And funnily enough the fairy godmother appeared that very afternoon in the form of a six-foot-six skip man with an ironmongery, an imaginary twin brother and a large German Shepherd dog.

As Deb was paying the bill, Lou rang home on her mobile to listen to any answering-machine messages. She had left Keith Featherstone a polite but barbed message that she would take this matter further if she had no response by lunchtime. There was one message to collect and it wasn't from Keith Featherstone – nor Michelle, who hadn't rung as promised.

Hello, this is Tom Broom. I hope you're OK. I just won-dered . . . I know you said you were looking for some premises for your coffee shop . . . well, I might be able to help. Can you ring me when you get this message? Thanks, bye.

Lou stabbed in the number without delay. It would be just her luck that it would switch onto his answering machine, but to her surprise and delight, she heard a deep and far-from-automated, 'Hello.'

'Oh hi, it's Lou.'

Silence. An embarrassing silence – he'd obviously for-gotten her already.

'Er, Lou Winter,' she clarified. 'One, the Faringdales.'

'Yes, sorry, I know who you are. The line just went a bit fuzzy then,' he explained.

'Oh, shall I call you back?'

'No,' he said, sounding amused. 'I'm in the wagon.'

'Oh, don't crash because of me!'

'Don't worry, I'm sitting having a sandwich. I'm not driving at the moment, but the signal isn't great here.'

'Oh, OK, then, so . . . you were saying?'

'Look, I'll be back at the *Tub* in about twenty min-utes – can you meet me there?'

'Yes, yes,' said Lou, a little taken aback. He said some-thing else, but the signal was lost and the line went dead.

'Can you come with me somewhere?' she asked as Deb caught her up in the foyer of the café.

'Yes, of course. I've nothing planned for the rest of the day. Why, where are you taking me?'

'Well, that was my skip man and he says he might be able to help us with our premises problem.'

'Lead the way immediately,' said Deb, taking her arm.

'So would you like to tell me a) why *your* skip man is looking for premises for us, b) why you refer to him as *your* skip man and c) who *is* your mysterious *skip man*?' Deb was grinning as she put on her seat belt.

So Lou began at the beginning, and as she drove, told her friend everything about the article and clearing out the drawer at work. Then about going home and clearing the kitchen, then the whole house and the kerfuffle at the tip and spotting Tom Broom's name on a skip. She didn't say that she found herself thinking about Tom Broom too much and sometimes fantasized about snogging him.

'What's he look like?' said Deb.

'You'd love him,' said Lou. 'He's just your type.'

'Ooh,' said Deb, whose type was tall, wide men. She was almost six foot herself so the bigger the better.

'Hair?' she enquired.

'Black with grey flecks.'

'Eyes?'

'Two.'

'Colour, you daft cow!'

'Grey.'

'Aha – that was a test question. How come you know what colour his eyes are?' said Deb, pointing an amused and accusing finger at Lou.

'It's the first thing you notice about him,' said Lou matter-of-factly.

'Something you're not telling me, Lou Winter?' asked Deb.

'Nope,' said Lou. 'I don't look at other men in that way.'

Lou might not have any control about who her heart picked out for her to fancy, but she had the choice of what to do about it. Doing nothing meant no one got destroyed, which was invariably what happened when someone had an affair.

Lou led Deb into the ironmongery and there she watched her best friend's eyes round in approval as they took in Tom Broom and his big solid body. She also watched how warmly Tom looked at Deb as he shook her hand. They were two single, lovely, tall, good-looking people, so of course they were going to be attracted to each other. But Lou was human and that fact did not prevent a little stab of disappointment inside her. Clooney, however, was all hers. He was whining a warm welcome for her and turning excited circles.

'Haven't seen you for a while, have I, buddy?' said Lou, giving him a good old pet.

'Come on,' said Tom. 'I'll take you both for a coffee.'

Tom led them next door to the grotty transport café where Lou and Deb sat on a torn plastic-covered bench whilst he went to the counter to get the tea.

'How come it's so busy?' murmured Deb, leaning into Lou. 'It's a total dump.'

They were surrounded by big burly men eating belt-buster all-day breakfasts and drinking from enormous mugs. The air was full of grease and cheap bacon. Nothing matched, the crockery was jumble-sale oddments in all shapes and colours, the ceiling purple and the walls a shade of yellow that was reminiscent of a bad cold. A tinny radio provided entertainment for the hard-faced buxom woman behind the counter, wearing an apron that read *Nigella Bites but I Eat You Whole.*

Tom returned with a tray. He was obviously a valued customer since he managed to get three unchipped mugs – a spotty one, a striped one and one advertising Bovril.

'Shall I be Mother?' he asked, setting them out.

Shit. Shit. Shit. What a thing to say after what he'd seen in that skip. God, he could have kicked himself.

'So?' said Deb. 'Lou here tells me you might have something very exciting to tell us.'

'Well,' began Tom, looking at Lou, 'the reason I didn't say anything before was that I didn't want to insult you, so please hear me out.'

Lou and Deb nodded.

'The premises I was talking about?' said Tom.

'Yes?' they both said eagerly.

'You're in it now. *May's Café.* Although the Y fell off the sign so people know it as . . . er . . . "Ma's"' He stumbled on the word. *Why was it, the more he tried to avoid a subject, the more it seemed to raise its head?* He let the information sink in for a minute and watched their faces drop, as he knew they would.

'It's not really . . .' began Deb diplomatically.

'Let me finish, please,' said Tom. 'May is giving up the lease. This place is full from first thing in the morning to last thing at night – see, there's loads of parking space for lorries. The factory is getting knocked down and will be made into a shopping area with luxury flats to the side. It's been bought by a private investor, some American bloke who wants to start work very shortly and complete in record time so he's employed half of Poland to get it done. I've seen the plans and it looks pretty good. Obviously, until it's finished you'd be taking a risk on the sort of establishment you want to open until you build up some clientèle because this area, at the moment, isn't exactly renowned for passing street trade. The upside of that is the lease is nice and cheap. And you could take over the business as it is for now and convert it as and when. It does a cracking trade.'

Deb and Lou looked hard at each other, trying to read what the other was thinking. Total mass confusion, they both decided.

'What's the landlord like then?' Lou asked.

'He's a great bloke. Fantastic. He owns my lease too,' said Tom fondly. 'Really fair, very trustworthy – big, good-looking kid.'

'How do we get in touch with him to get the figures?' said Deb.

'Just ask him,' said Tom.

'Where can we find him?' said Lou.

Tom leaned over the table and whispered conspiratorially, 'He's sitting opposite you with a mug of the world's most disgusting tea in his hand.' He tutted at Lou. 'Haven't you learned anything yet?'

'You!' said Lou. 'I should have guessed. I'm surprised you didn't say it was owned by good-looking twins.'

'I thought about it,' said Tom. That grin appeared again, spreading across his lips and lighting up his eyes.

'Big, good-looking kid! In your dreams,' said Deb, with a head-shaking smile, and then turning to Lou she said quite breathlessly, 'We need to talk.'

'I'm going to have to leave you ladies, anyway. I've got

skips coming out of my ears today,' said Tom, throwing the tea down his throat and cringing afterwards. 'Think about it. The development will bring a lot of business back to this end of town. I'm not trying to offload the lease onto you. It's such a well-established business, I know I wouldn't have a problem letting it.'

'We'll let you know as soon as we can,' said Lou.

'Right,' said Tom, getting to his feet. 'I won't advertise the lease until I hear from you. You have first refusal, I give you my word. Bye, Debra, it was nice to meet you and I hope to see you again.'

'Bye,' said Deb sweetly. 'It was nice to meet you too, Tom.'

'See you again, too.' He winked at Lou, and he was away.

Deb left it a respectable three seconds before gossiping about him.

'So that was your Tom Broom then.'

'He's not *my* Tom Broom,' said Lou. Oh, how she wished she could split herself in two and one half of her could lay claim to him, whilst the grounded half did its duty to her marriage vows.

'So, what do you think of him?' she asked, trying to sound detached.

'Very nice,' said Deb with emphasis. 'However, we'll dissect the lovely Mr Broom later. For now, Lou, let's talk shop. Literally.'

Chapter 32

'I can't understand it,' said Sue Shoesmith. 'There was a clanking noise I wanted to talk to you about and now it's gone.'

Amazing that, thought Phil.

'It may be homesick,' he joked, handing her a cup of coffee. 'Black, one sugar, just as the lady ordered.'

'Thank you,' she said with a delighted little smile because he had remembered.

'Please sit down.' He pulled out a chair for her. And when she shivered slightly, 'Are you cold? Shall I put the heater on for you?'

He was such a gentleman.

'No, no, I'm fine,' said Sue. 'Don't let me hold you back from going home, though. It is Saturday night, after all.'

Phil dropped an almost inaudible sigh.

'Nothing for me to rush home for,' he said, casting his eyes down to the floor. Time for a quick change of subject and then see how she managed to steer him back to this for further investigation of his home-life.

'Anyway, how's the car been?'

'Fantastic. I've seen a lot of heads turn my way recently.'

'I'm sure you'd see that whatever you drive,' said Phil, smiling widely with full-on eye-contact.

'Aw, thank you, that's so sweet. Anyway, an Audi TT is far more impressive than my little car, isn't it?'

'They're nice cars, yes,' said Phil, opening up a biscuit tin and taking a few out to arrange on a plate. God, he was good. 'These are mine and only mine. You're so lucky even to view them, never mind that I'm asking you if you want to share them.' Make her feel special, thought Phil. *Share* was a good word.

She picked a chocolate Viennese from the plate he held in front of her like an attentive waiter playing for a big tip.

'You were saying you drive an Audi because you don't have any children to consider?' she continued.

Ooh, quick work, thought Phil. Well done!

'No, no kids. My wife was never really interested. We talked about it before we were married but she changed her mind afterwards.'

'Oh no!' said Sue with a 'what-a-total-bitch' expression.

'You married with kids?' asked Phil softly.

'No. Never met Mr Right,' said Sue. 'Met a few Mr Wrongs and a Mr Complete Tosspot, but not Mr Right. Are you still married then?'

Phil nodded slowly. 'Yes, sort of. What I mean is that we're joined at the name, but we lead separate lives these days. It's not what a relationship should be, not in my book anyway.'

Sue nodded in agreement.

'Gawd – listen to me.' Phil laughed a little too hard. 'You'll be waiting for the "my wife doesn't understand me" line in minute.'

Nice double bluff.

'No, not at all,' said his captive audience.

'She . . . sorry, I shouldn't be saying this, but you know men, we don't talk things over like you girls do and stuff gets stored up inside us.'

Sue leaned forward supportively. 'No, please, go on. I'm a great listener.'

Phil took a deep, dramatic breath. 'She – my wife – had an affair a few years ago. It nearly killed me, to be honest. Of course I don't entirely blame her. I work too hard and thought I could make my absences all right with a few nice bits of jewellery.' A man who could admit his faults to a woman was irresistible, and as negatives went, these came across as pretty positive ones. 'Anyway, she came back but really we both knew there was nothing left to save. She lives at one end of the house and I live at the other.'

Expert touch, implying both separate bedrooms and a massive house.

'We're strangers. I don't even wear my wedding ring any more.' He presented his hand as evidence. 'She's a lovely person, but I feel' (pat of heart) 'nothing.' Never diss the ex. Those women's magazines of Lou's always pointed that out as a sign to look for in a total bastard. He read them on the toilet – they were like lessons in women's psychology and came in very handy.

'Oh, that's so sad,' said Sue with great feeling.

'I made up my mind that by Christmas we'll have the

house sold and be well on the way to divorcing. It won't do either of us any good to draw it out longer than that. A New Year and a fresh start.'

Sue's hand fell on top of his and she squeezed it.

'Look, I'm a legal secretary. If you need any help with that side of things, I would be only too glad to point you in the right direction. Not that I'm touting for business.'

'Thank you,' said Phil, looking very vulnerable. 'You're just great and I'm glad our paths crossed. Can I . . .' He shook his head as if battling with himself.

'Yes?' Sue's pupils were like open black caves.

'I was going to say, can I take you out for a drink sometime? But I'm aware I'm still married and I don't want you to feel awkward,' said Phil. Then, 'No, forget it, it was a silly idea. Damn it, Phil – what are you thinking of!'

'No, no, I'd love to meet up with you again,' said Sue keenly.

Phil made his eyes light up. 'Really? Oh wow – that would be just great!' he beamed.

She stood to go. 'You have my number.'

'I do indeed.'

He led her to the door and there he placed a kiss on her cheek, like an awkward teenager would, letting her see the boy inside the man.

'Goodbye, Phil Winter, you nice man, you,' she said, and her smile was sparkling.

'Goodbye, Miss British Racing Green Eyes.'

'Wow! What a lovely thing to say!' she said, as breathlessly as Marilyn Monroe singing 'Happy Birthday Mr President'.

He watched her float to the car. What simple machines women were. They could run for miles on a mere promise.

Chapter 33

Lou parked near *Café Joseph* on the following Tuesday. The food, as they had experienced, wasn't the best around, but it was a convenient location for Deb who was in that end of Barnsley for a meeting, and as she had limited time to spare that day, it seemed the most sensible place to convene.

Lou had ordered for her, as instructed, to save even more time. Just as the waiter, Mr Teenage Hormones himself, was coming over with two lattes, Deb threw herself as heavily as someone so slim could, onto the chair opposite Lou.

'God, I'm glad to be here!' she exclaimed.

'Tough morning?'

'No, just glad to be here. With you. Talking about you-know-what.'

The waiter flashed her a glance. What was 'you-know-what', he wondered. Perhaps they were going to have one of those marriage ceremonies. Which one would wear the frock? They both looked pretty feminine to him, although the red-head looked different to the last time he had seen her. Sexier somehow, more straight-backed. She'd looked as if she had 10-ton shoulderpads on before.

'So, we've both had a few days to think it through. What do you say?' asked Deb.

Lou took a deep breath. 'I think we should go for it.'

'Me too.'

'I can't believe it, Deb.'

'I can't believe it either, Lou.'

They both clapped their hands in glee.

'I've been thinking about the décor,' said Lou. 'There's no reason why we can't go with the theme we picked last time. If we strip it out totally but put in those American diner sorts of benches, it would work for phase one – the continuation of the transport café – and we wouldn't have to alter it when the coffee-shop takes over as the main business.'

Deb tried to visualize it. She had always really liked that whole 'milk bar' retro concept.

'It was a belting idea the first time round, Lou, and it still is,' she said. 'So we need to see Tom, get some measurements, costs for the lease and builders' quotes.'

'Then we see the bank,' said Lou, trying to stop herself from screaming with excitement. 'I'll present our case to them exactly like last time. They seemed to think we'd done a pretty good job. I've managed to find lots of American diner-type pictures on the internet to inspire us even more, plus I've still got stuff from last time in the file. I think we could get away with local joiners rather than anything specialist, though, so we'll need to get them in to look at the place a.s.a.p.'

'Then we find a name for it,' said Deb. For sensitive reasons, *Ma's Café* wasn't fair on Lou.

The sandwiches arrived. The service was quick here, which was another bonus.

'Have you told Phil?' asked Deb tentatively.

'I've told him I'm going into business with you,' said Lou.

'What was his reaction?'

Lou's shrug was her answer. 'Not that I'm bothered,' she went on, shaking her head. 'It's not going to stop me that he thinks I'm making a mistake. That's just his chauvinistic side saying only men can succeed in business. It's all right for me to act as his accountant free of charge, though – but I can't be bothered arguing that point with him.'

'Things OK between you two?' asked Deb tactfully, ripping the fatty rind from the slices of sandwich beef.

'Yes of course,' said Lou, with a smile that didn't quite do the job. 'He's still a bit annoyed about the weekend before last. I think he blames me for Des not buying that car, even though it was quite obvious he'd decided on that before he walked through the door. I told off the kids and stirred up trouble between him and Celia when I pushed Des away from me in the kitchen. Any closer and we would have fused.'

'You didn't stir up trouble,' said Deb furiously. 'He shouldn't keep coming on to you.'

'Well, that's it, he's never really come *on* to me,' said Lou.

'He's not thick, Lou. He obviously gets off on being so close to the boundary without actually doing anything. It's a power thing. Weirdo.'

'From Celia's reaction that day, I'm almost sure it's something she's seen before.'

'I'll bet! By him not overtly doing anything, women feel as if they're overreacting by kicking up a fuss, so he gets away with it,' Deb said, abandoning the fatty beef totally and just eating the honey bread and salad, which was admittedly very nice. *Honey bread*. She popped that down on her mental notepad.

'I don't know how I managed to upset everyone so much that day. It wasn't as if I'd loaded up a Tommy gun and shot them all.'

'You should have,' said Deb. 'You did good standing up for yourself for once.'

'He needed a short sharp shock, didn't he? Do you think?' asked Lou, looking for affirmation.

'He needed a big sodding kick in the bollocks,' shrieked Deb. 'Phil should have said or, even better *done* something about Des a long time ago. It's a shame you aren't married to someone who would have sorted him out.'

Lou melted into a little private fantasy where Tom pulled Des off her and catapulted him across the room.

'Like Tom,' said Deb, as if Lou's skull was projecting images out.

Lou's spine stiffened. 'Tom?' she echoed, as if that was the furthest thought from her mind.

'Yes, Tom. He's a strong lad, isn't he? Looks the protective type,' said Deb dreamily.

'Yes, I suppose he does,' said Lou, avoiding Deb's eyes. 'Hadn't really thought of him like that, though.'

'And whilst we're on that subject, we'd better ring him and arrange a meeting. Can I leave you with that?' said Deb. 'It will be lovely to see him again. He's nice, really nice.'

Lou sipped her coffee. She was sure Deb fancied Tom, but she didn't ask if that was the case. She didn't want to hear the answer.

'Er, is that Tom?' asked Lou, knowing that it was.

'Hello, Lou, how are you?'

How silly was it to feel as if her stomach had just been hit by a big glass of vodka, just to hear him say her name.

'I'm fine, thank you. And you?'

'Yes, I'm good.'

'Great. Smashing,' said Lou nervously.

'Lovely.'

Talking to him was almost as bad as being on the phone with Wayne Jessop when they were fifteen and she knew he had rung her up to ask her out. It took five agonizing minutes of these niceties before he actually spurted, 'Jawannagooart wi'me?'

'Tom, the reason I rang was, we are really interested in the lease, so if it's OK by you, can we meet you again and talk over some facts and figures?'

'Yes, of course,' said Tom. 'I wish you could have been there today to see the customers queuing out of the door – and that's with May and her crappy bacon. God knows what business would be like with some decent grub.'

'Why is she giving it up, if it's so successful?' asked Lou.

'She's going over to live with her daughters in Australia.'

'Oh! I hope she's not taking her clientèle with her,' said Lou, smiling.

'I can't guarantee that. But if it does happen, I'll

refund you three months' rent.' He sounded as if he was smiling too. 'So, time and place then,' he continued. 'Er . . . maybe it would be best if you were to come to my house. I've got all the paperwork there and the plans. Oh, by the way, there's a small flat above the caff. It's not occupied and I haven't a clue what state it's in. When I say small, I mean *small*. May just uses it for storage. It hasn't got a separate entrance and that's why it's never been rented out.'

Come to my house?

'Well, I'm sure it would come in handy for storage,' said Lou.

'How about Friday at, say, six?' said Tom.

'Yes, well, Deb and I will both be home from work by then. I'm sure I can speak for her and say that will be fine.' COME TO MY HOUSE?

'OK, then.'

'Right, well, it's a pleasure to do business with you, Mr Broom.'

'And with you, Mrs Winter.'

'So we'll see you on Friday about six then,' said Lou.

'Friday at six it is . . .'

'Bye then!' Lou flipped shut her mobile thinking she had handled that very well and in a businesslike fashion without any major gaffes. Just as she put it in her bag, it rang and the screen said that it was Tom.

'Hello again,' he said. He was grinning, she could tell. What on earth had she done now to make him laugh?

'Hello.'

'Don't you want my address?'

Whoops, thought Lou.

'Unless you've been stalking me and know it already?'

Lou laughed and gulped at the same time. Of course she'd once looked him up in the telephone directory to see where he lived, but his home address hadn't been there, only the business one.

Lou quickly scribbled the dictated address – *The Eaves, Oxworth* – it sounded very grand. She suddenly felt like Anne in *The Famous Five*. This was all starting to feel like an adventure.

Chapter 34

Lou's head was bursting with ideas for *Ma's Café*. She kept having to break off preparing the evening meal just to write things down in her notebook. Phil came in at seven o'clock. He called, 'Hi,' peering over her shoulder to see what he had to look forward to gastronomically, and went upstairs to change out of his suit. It was his normal routine – with one notable exception. This was the third night in a row that he had kept his mobile with him and not put it on charge in the kitchen.

Now why would he not leave it lying around? a voice in her head questioned. Lou tried to ignore it. She didn't want to go down that analytical road to Nightmare Land again. After Phil's affair there was a time when anything he did out of the ordinary was ripped apart in her head: not finishing a meal, buying new underpants, chewing a different brand of gum – anything. She had found herself in that mad place where women sniffed shirts, checked cars for unfamiliar-looking hairs and stayed awake at night to see if he divulged secrets out loud as he dreamed. She had found nothing definite to substantiate the claims her paranoia was making, but still she couldn't eat, couldn't sleep, couldn't think straight.

It was emotionally exhausting, being a nutter. Phil said she was cracking up, and if her behaviour didn't stop he might as well go and do what he was being accused of. That scared her enough to fight hard against her neuroses. Each day of those inner battles was a living hell. Her mind tore her to shreds with questions. No, she would never go back to those days of obsessive suspicion again. Phil was not having an affair. End of.

But the question of the phone kept poking at her long after Phil had eaten his meal and gone to bed, and swept up in that thought path was his strange behaviour of late – the constant humming, the change of after-shave. Try as she might, it would not be ignored and pushed down. It kept springing up like a really annoying jack-in-the-box that demanded to be heard.

The prosecuting case was flimsy to say the least but she needed to think straight. It was Phil's way of punishing her about the Des and Celia afternoon, not forgetting her friendship with Deb. The clue was in the timing, her mind reasoned. He was trying to drag her attention back to him and away from the coffee shop. Despite his little pokes at her insecurities in the past three years he hadn't been with anyone else, she was as sure as she could be of that. But, however hard she had tried to fool herself that she trusted him as much after the affair as before it, that was really a lie she told them both. Trust was as fragile as Humpty Dumpty's shell. But she could never let him know that she didn't wholly trust him. He had said that there would be no point in going on with the marriage if there was no trust and that she would have to believe him when he said that he would never do that to her again – and that was that. But a vow in the end is just

words – a self-imposed boundary of nothing more substantial than ribbon. And, as such, Lou never quite lost
the fear that another Susan Peach was around the corner,
waiting to seduce her husband away. Maybe that day was
here now and Phil would level at her that she had
brought it all on herself with her café ideas and being
rude to his family.

Sitting there with a coffee and her recipe book at the
dining-table, Lou gave herself a slap. She was being
ridiculous, torturing herself with thoughts like these; not
to mention teetering on the edge of a dangerous abyss.
She should go about her daily business and allow Phil to
think he was teaching her his 'lesson'. She would let his
game run its course, then it would all blow over and they
could get back to normal. There would be no perfume
hunts or checkings of pockets because there was no other
woman. Even Phil wouldn't be that cruel.

Chapter 35

Phil's phone buzzed in his pocket, just as Lou had waved goodbye to him on Friday morning. It made his penis tingle as he read the sauce that appeared on the screen. The texts had started off very friendly and benign. HELLO, HOW ARE YOU? HAVING A GOOD DAY? But soon innuendo had started to creep in. ISNT IT COLD 2DAY? he had sent. And the reply came: I AM PRETTY HOT MYSELF. Still all harmless stuff, though.

Yes, a good soup was all the better for a simmer, as Lou would say; and didn't he know it. Bring it to the boil straightaway and you spoil it.

There was a small bag waiting for Lou on her desk when she walked into work. She opened it to find a box of matches. She didn't understand, then she saw Karen smirking – and then she *did* understand.

Lou bounded over and hugged her.

'Well, I didn't want to say anything before in case I hated it or it didn't work out,' said Karen. 'But yes, I'm on the course and, Lou, I have to say I'm really enjoying it. Thank you for forcing me to join. Now take those home and burn that bloody burgundy suit!'

Lou's face was all smiles – her mouth, her eyes, even her nose was trying to curve up its corners.

'Did you ask HR about funding you?'

'Don't be daft,' said Karen with a snort. 'I wasn't going to give them the satisfaction of turning me down. No, I can manage and Mum and Dad and my big brother Nigel, they've all chipped in for the course fees. It's manageable. Chris is going to take the children when I need to study. So . . .' she rattled the bag. 'Do as you agreed, Skinny.'

'I think "Skinny" is pushing it a bit,' Lou smiled, but enjoyed the novelty of being called it all the same. 'Anyway, I already put my burgundy suit in a skip,' she told Karen, 'so I can't set fire to it.'

By then everyone was clustering around Karen's desk to see what the fuss was all about. Stan gave her a big kiss and Zoe gave her a hug and said she wished she'd known, then they could have bought a 'good luck' cake.

'Never too late for that one,' laughed Karen, but they had a round of coffees and chocolate from the machine as an interim measure.

As they stood around, Nicola came in with a, 'What's this? What's going on?'

'Just a private meeting,' sniffed Karen, who could actually look down physically from a great height at her, as well as metaphorically.

'I'm sure Roger will be thrilled to know he's paying wages to people so they can hold their own private meetings in work time,' said Nicola with malevolence as she swanned off back to her desk.

'How does she walk with that spike stuck up her arse?' said Karen quietly to Lou.

Stan and Zoe melted timidly back to their desks.

'Lou, have you finished the return I left with you yesterday?' Nicola called over, knowing there was no way
she could have. Not unless she was Superwoman.

But with accounts, Lou *was* Superwoman and so
could reply with all honesty, 'Yes, it's on your desk.'

Karen smiled a 'fuck you' smile in support of Lou.
Nicola saw it and started to grow a blotchy neck, which
usually meant that she was going to try extra hard to be
foul. But Lou was extra impenetrable today. She knew
one of her feet was firmly out of this office and in their
coffee-house, and the other would soon follow. And later
on that day she was seeing Tom, which was a pretty good
excuse to smile in the face of even the worst adversity.

Lou picked up Deb after work from the bakery and they
headed out of the village and into the lovely countryside
on the scenic top road out of Barnsley, heading towards
the outskirts of Oxworth, where Tom lived.

'Any idea where you're going?' Deb enquired.

'Sort of,' said Lou. 'Look out for a sign for a small
estate called "The Horseshoe".'

'You mean, that estate called "The Horseshoe" that
we passed about half a mile back?'

'Oh poop, did we?' Lou did a five-point turn by a
five-bar gate and drove back to the signpost. 'OK.
Apparently, we turn immediately right here, then left at
a pub called the Salt Pot, then there's a long leafy lane
but we take the first right again up a drive.'

'Bloody hell,' said Deb, when they had turned onto
said leafy lane. 'That *is* nice.'

In front of them was an old double-fronted Victorian

villa with gables, set like a neat diamond in the mount of a very lovely garden with high hedges and deep borders of summer flowers that were just coming into colourful bud.

They pulled up at the side of Tom's car – a four-by-four big, manly vehicle that Lou could sense Tom in, rattling over rough terrain with his trusty hound at his side. He came to the door and waved a welcome.

'Hello again,' said Deb, striding out in her confident way towards him and kissing him politely on the cheek, setting a rather daunting precedent for Lou. What the hell was she going to do now? Should she follow suit? That decision was taken from her as Tom bent down to Lou, giving her a peck on her cheek too. It got her all flustered and instead of, 'Hello,' she said, 'Thanks.'

Deb hooted and unwittingly rescued her by saying, 'Oh no, I thought she was sober, so I let her drive. Big mistake, obviously.'

Tom laughed and led them inside with a large shepherding hand that touched Deb's back slightly as he guided them forwards, Lou noticed with a pang of envy.

A wide hallway greeted them, black and white tiles on the floor, fresh white walls and a beautiful chunky staircase in dark woods. There was a huge stained-glass window where the stairs turned, featuring a sun setting over the sea, which was flooding the hallway with lovely late-spring evening light. It was not at all like the cluttered man-zone Lou had imagined after seeing his shop.

'This is beautiful,' said Deb, rotating to take it all in.

'It's been a bit of a labour of love,' said Tom, 'but at least I've done all the knocking-down bits and am now at the putting-up stage. I've plenty to go at still, though – as you'll see in a minute.'

They followed him into a large echoey room, where the tang of sawdust suggested that the floors had been recently sanded. The walls were bare and re-plastered in patches. Apart from the huge table and chairs obviously in permanent residence there it was a blank canvas ready to create a beautiful dining room.

Tom brought a pot of pre-prepared coffee through and a big tin of biscuits.

Very nice biscuits, and obviously a new tin bought especially, although being a bloke he didn't put them on a plate, which made Lou smile a little. There was no false ceremony with this guy – but he was all man. She couldn't imagine him screaming at spiders or sneezing because an animal had looked in his direction, like Phil. Which reminded her. 'Where's Clooney?' she asked.

'My twin's got him,' said Tom, with a cheeky grin. 'OK, before you clout me, he's with my sister. He's too distracting, so he's out playing with the kids. I'm going to pick him up after we've finished doing what we have to do.'

'So to business . . .' said Deb, starting their meeting by using a pink wafer as a gavel.

An hour later, after Tom had shown them the plans of the place, gone through a copy of May's lease line by line to show there were no hidden clauses, discussed terms and payment and presented May's surprisingly neat set of accounts for Lou to cast her expert eye over, Lou and Deb were even more happy with their lot. Tom was being overly kind on the rent, Lou thought, but he seemed happy enough with the arrangement and had no objections with the fancy plans for what they wanted to do with the place – if the bank let them borrow the money, of course. If it didn't, the two women had discovered that they had enough saved capital between them to go for it, albeit with fewer, less fancy plans initially. Then they would need to meet again at his solicitors and sign papers. He advised the ladies to go and have a formal word with May if they wanted to check out his suitability as a landlord. Deb would, of course, and told Tom so. There were very few people she trusted on face value, however nice a profile they presented.

They were getting ready to leave when they heard Tom's outside door open and slam shut and a jolly female voice shouted out an echoey, 'Hello!' down the hallway, followed by the sound of paws skittering and heels clicking on the tiled floor.

Tom leaped up but he was too late to stop the owner of the voice coming into the dining room, carrying a car seat, with Clooney bounding behind her, fussing between Tom and Lou and giving Deb a quick hello sniff in between.

'Sorry, am I interrupting?' said a petite lady with short white-blonde loose curls. She took in both the women with a friendly smile: the small one with the lovely red hair and shiny green eyes, and the other long and leggy and golden-haired.

Tom looked instantly jumpy.

'No, don't worry, we were just going,' said Deb, curious as to who this was.

Right on cue Tom said, 'This is my sister, Samantha.' He scratched the back of his head nervously. 'Sam, this is Debra and Lou, who are going to take over May's lease.'

Sam said a formal hello whilst deriding her brother for calling her by her 'Sunday name'. 'Sorry, I didn't realize you had company. I had to pop out for some nappies and I thought I'd kill two birds with one stone and bring Clooney back so you wouldn't have to come and fetch him. Plus I thought Lucy might like to see her big Uncle Tom.' She twisted the car seat around and there, nestled inside a cosy pink blanket, was a tiny baby with a golden quiff of hair. Tom looked helplessly at Lou, Deb looked helplessly at Lou, whilst Sammy looked at the three stiff statues that now faced her in utter confusion. Her brother was the most awkward of them all.

Realizing that she was the only one of them that could rescue this, Lou gulped hard and came forward, bending to let the baby's hand grip her finger.

'She's absolutely beautiful,' she said breathlessly.

'Want to hold her?' said Sam proudly, wondering why her brother was doing all those weird gurning faces at her behind the woman's back.

'Yes, please,' replied Lou softly. Sam unstrapped her new daughter and handed her over to Lou, who cupped her hand under the baby's wobbly neck. She had butter-soft skin, smelled of baby powder and milk and was rooting for more on Lou's shoulder.

Lou had never held a newborn before. She could not have imagined how delicate they were; their hands, their nails, the thin legs, the tiny socks. Again the socks triggered the passage of tears to her eyes and she had to work hard to get them to sink back. Lou knew, though, that she could no longer go through life getting upset if she was within cuddling distance of a baby. The world was full of other people's sweet-smelling babies. She jollied herself up and handed back the armful of pink softness to Tom's sister who bent to the car seat to nestle her daughter back into her snug blanket.

'We must be getting back,' said Deb, grabbing Lou by the elbow and steering her towards the door, expecting the worst if they didn't get out of there soon. 'Goodbye, Sam, it was nice to meet you. Bye, Tom. I'll go and see May tomorrow.' And she gave him another peck.

Tom bent to kiss Lou and his lips fell softly near her ear.

'I'm so sorry . . .' he whispered before Lou interrupted him.

'Please don't say anything to your sister. I'd want the world to see my baby too if I was in her shoes.'

'We'll see ourselves out,' said Deb and waved quickly.

Once outside, Lou sucked in two big lungfuls of fresh air.

'You OK?' Deb asked.

'Course I am,' said Lou, over-brightly.

'Yeah, and I'm Kylie Minogue,' said Deb. 'Shall I drive?'

'Please,' said Lou with a grateful smile.

Phil couldn't remember the last time he'd had to turn off the burglar alarm and switch on the lights when he came in from work. The house felt cold, although the central heating had switched itself on automatically over an hour ago. There was no welcoming smell of his Friday-night curry cooking, no background noise from a CD or the TV, no Lou busying about setting the table. He usually went for a run on Friday – and this early arrival was part of his mind-bending routine alteration, the effect of which had been totally spoiled because she wasn't here to witness it. So where the fuck was she?

A text message buzzed again in his pocket. He would have to slow down on those. Then again, if Lou couldn't be bothered being a proper wife, who could blame him?

HOPE YOU ARE DOING SOMETHING NICE THIS WEEKEND X it read.

YOU 2 typed Phil in return. Then he erased it and stabbed in something far less harmless. FREE FOR LUNCH ON SUNDAY? XX. Sod it, he thought. The time had come to slam his foot right down on the accelerator.

Chapter 36

Lou woke up at 3 a.m. after Phil shouted out something in a dream. She could have sworn he said, 'Sue,' but her rational mind told her she must have imagined it. Still, it didn't exactly help getting back to sleep.

Rather than lie there, thinking too much, Lou decided to get up, re-track through a version of her usual pre-bed routine and see if that helped her find a sleepy place. It would be just after ten o'clock at night in Florida, she worked out. She could ring Victorianna and get her little 'mum-visiting' plan working. But in the present emotional climate that didn't necessarily seem like a good idea, because she had too much going on in her head to open up another project at the moment. Instead, she went downstairs for a hot chocolate and read a few pages of the latest novel by her favourite Midnight Moon writer – Bea Pollen, who was a local lass made good. It was such a shame those lovely, kind, thoughtful, *available* men she wrote about didn't exist in real life. Not in Barnsley anyway.

Upstairs, Phil cocked open an eye and allowed himself a moment of smugness before snuggling his head back down in the pillow.

★

Saturday was uneventful. Deb was doing an extra shift in the bakery, so Lou took Renee food shopping and then out for lunch where she ate quiche which came with a surprise side order of chips – a choice which her mother didn't even bother to comment upon. That alone said that Renee wasn't herself at all. Her friend Vera was in Germany at the moment with her son and, despite their keeping-up-with-the-Joneses relationship, Renee seemed to be missing her very much. Plus it hammered home the fact that she wasn't afforded the same courtesy by her own so-called nearest and dearest.

Lou wished she had just phoned Victorianna in the night and got it over with, but she wasn't sure she was ready for that one just yet. Her sister was a dirty fighter and there were a lot of things unsaid between them. When Lou tried to blackmail her with revelations, she was worried that Victorianna might fight back with some revelations of her own.

Phil seemed distracted that evening. He kept disappearing to the loo.

'You want to get your prostrate checked out. That's the eighth time you've gone in the last hour,' Lou said with an attempt at a light little laugh.

'I think you'll find it's prostate,' said Phil coolly on the way out again, 'but there's absolutely nothing wrong with mine.'

It was a blatant act of, 'Look at me, I'm up to something.' Especially as every time he came back to the sofa, he seemed to be trying to cover up a smile, which funnily enough he was. Sue was pretty prolific on the text front and she was most definitely hot for him. And that crack about how many times he had left the room told him that Lou was on his case. Perfect.

Lou expected her husband to initiate full sex the next morning. This was the longest period they had ever gone without it. She felt him shift in bed and braced herself, but to her surprise he swung his legs outwards and a few seconds later she heard him rather noisily opening drawers and wardrobe doors, looking for his clothes.

'Where are you going?' she asked.

'I'm off to work,' he said, as if he had just been asked the most stupid question in the world.

'Today?' said Lou.

'I often work on Sundays, as you well know,' said Phil.

'Yes, but you usually tell me. You never said you were working today.' She was aware that that sounded a bit wheedling and reeled herself in.

'Well, I'm saying it now,' he said with a very chilly smile. 'It's not an issue, is it?'

'No, of course not. Will you be back for lunch or shall I cook a later dinner instead?' Lou said, more steadily now.

Phil jiggled into his jockey shorts, aware she was scrutinizing his every move, analyzing each thread he was wearing.

'Late dinner, I think,' he said. He put on a good shirt and his expensive going-out after-shave again.

'Any particular reason why you're working today?' asked Lou, watching him knot his tie very precisely.

'I've got a couple of big sales hopefully and I don't want Bradley to cock them up. Don't get up, I'll send out for a bacon butty.'

He was as horny as hell. It was hard work, all this self-denial, but he knew without any doubt that, in life as well as business, one often had to speculate to accumulate.

Lou lay in bed, thoughts tumbling around in her head like jigsaw pieces that wouldn't fit together, whichever combination she tried them in. Phil was not playing his normal sulking game; it had gone beyond that. Her mind asked the dreaded question, *What if there actually is someone else? Another Susan?*

Sue Peach had been a rough-looking tart with a Halloween perm, but all Lou could focus on was how cocktail-stick thin she'd been. It had to be the absence of flesh on her bones that had attracted her husband because she certainly wasn't beautiful, or classy, or Brain of Britain. But Lou had never once asked him for a definitive answer. She had been so grateful to find him there on the welcome mat, days before what was looking to be the worst Christmas of her life, that she had just dragged him over the threshold, made him dinner and then taken him to bed. She'd been pretty thin herself by that stage – most likely why he stayed. He'd had it pretty easy, now she thought about it. The gaping wound to her own heart, though, had never been looked at properly, nor stitched up and treated gently with after-care. She had just stuck a quick plaster on it and hoped for the best. So was it any wonder it had never healed and continued to bleed?

She picked up the phone and rang Michelle.

'Oh hi, Lou. God, I'm so sorry, I meant to ring you

but I'm not even going to tell you how busy I've been,' said Michelle immediately.

Lou forgave her everything instantly just for being there and sounding pleased to hear from her.

'How's things?' asked Michelle, but then before Lou could answer she jumped in with, 'You just can't believe how great Craig is – *at everything*. He is simply the best. I was telling Ali about him and she thinks he sounds great too.'

'Ali?' asked Lou, aware that the name had been dropped into the conversation like a little pebble to see how far the ripples went. She shouldn't have been surprised, though, because it wasn't the first time this had happened.

'Oh, haven't I told you about Ali? She's fab. She's new at work. I've been given the job of "baby sitting" her. She's been round here to the house a few times – you know how it is – if you've got to work closely with someone it's good to socialize and get to know them better.'

Lou didn't really know about that. She had got on quite well with work colleagues without ever feeling the need to get plastered with them on tequila slammers in her own living room and bond with them over a bargain bucket of takeaway chicken, although Michelle wasn't known for doing things by halves. *Ali* must be another of her temporary friends. Each 'friend' took an intense but brief starring role in Michelle's life, only for a period of obsessive bitching to ensue and eventually a consignment to oblivion. Michelle never tended to hang onto these 'friends' for very long. They were about as transient as a snowflake in a tumble drier.

'Ali and I have had a great laugh since the first moment we sat together. You know, the other night she came around and I said, "Ali, I feel like I've known you for ages," and Ali said the same to me. Anyway, Craig won't be here this weekend, it's his mum's sixtieth birthday and she's having a do so Ali and I are going around town on Friday. I'd ask you to come with us but I know you don't do nights,' and with that she sniffed, making the point.

Despite all the activity going on in Lou's head she suddenly wanted to giggle. An old picture flared up in her head of Shirley Hamster at school parading 'prize friend' Julie Ogden past her one day in a misguided effort to make her jealous. It had been laughable then when they were thirteen; now it was bordering on pathetic.

'Well, I hope you have a good time,' said Lou, trying to sound serious.

'We will, don't you worry,' said Michelle with petty conviction. 'I have to celebrate my promotion.'

'What promotion?' said Lou.

'I've gone up a grade. I'm deputy supervisor now. That's why I've been given Ali to train up.'

'Oh well, congratulations then,' said Lou, feeling a sharp stab of disappointment that she hadn't been allowed to share some good news with Michelle for a change. She was being punished for some reason or other, that was clear.

'Anyway, I'll have to go soon because Ali said she might pop round so we can go shopping for something to wear next week. Ali's the same size as me so next week we're going to get a bottle of wine in before we go out and have a girly trying-on session.'

Lou and Deb used to get a bottle of wine in before going out when they were at college. Although swapping clothes was hardly an option.

'I've got a scarf that will probably fit you if we hem it up!' Deb had once said, looking her up and down after flinging open her wardrobe doors, and they'd laughed until they'd nearly wet themselves. She had never questioned whether what she shared with Deb was friendship, as she did so often these days with Michelle. She wasn't sure if she understood what relationships meant any more.

Phil pulled into the pub car park in the vacant space next to the natty green Roadster. As he got out of his car, Sue got out of hers and they gave each other a peck on the cheek that lingered a little longer than an ordinary kiss of greeting should.

'Busy morning?' asked Sue, daring to link his arm as they walked into the part of the pub signposted *Maltstone Arms Bistro*.

'Yes, very productive. I sold a beautiful Mercedes sports. And you?'

'I've been to church, of course,' Sue replied, raising her eyebrows innocently.

'I believe you, sister,' laughed Phil, holding the door open for her.

They walked past a long table laid for thirteen with *Goodbye, we'll miss you* balloons, and Phil made a joke about the Last Supper happening which made Sue giggle. Her eyes had that misted, happy look that told him she was wriggling on his line like a doomed worm. He felt a minute prick of guilt, but then told himself that, after all, she was safe. He had no intention of having an affair with her, and if she misread the signs, he wasn't to blame. In time, she would consider it all a mere learning curve.

They had starters and main course. Sue had a coffee, whilst he had a syrup sponge and custard. She smiled benignly at him, as he lifted the complimentary plate of chocolate mints and urged her to have another.

'I am really enjoying your company,' said Sue, with the sort of sigh Snow White did at the wishing well.

'Me too. It's lovely to have some good food, nice surroundings and last, but not least, the company of a beautiful woman to share it all with.'

She put her hand on his.

The Last Supper party started to file in. They looked old enough to have been at the original event, he thought, apart from the young good-looking bloke at the back with a fit girlfriend and . . . he couldn't believe it! Judas 'Debra' Iscariot herself! Even after all this time he would recognize her anywhere, although for one fleeting moment he thought it was Lou's sister. He shifted his stare to the hand placed on his, momentarily freezing with panic. But it was too late now; he knew he had been seen – *in flagrante delicto*. Hang on, said his brain, this couldn't have been better if you'd planned it. It was history repeating itself – *another pub, another Sue* – although admittedly his tongue had been down his companion's throat on that last occasion, and her hand had been busier than a hyperactive ferret down his trousers. And what had the outcome been? Pretty damn satisfactory, actually. Debra had scuttled off to tell Lou, thereby unwittingly saving his marriage and ending their friendship. And he bet it was all going to happen just exactly the same way again.

Aware that Deb's eyes were burning holes in his cheek, he lifted Sue's hand to his lips, making it obvious to his observer that this was no innocent contact. He kissed the top of her hand then gave the space between her fingers a quick suggestive lick, and when Sue pulled her hand away, shrieking with outraged delight, he made a move to gather up his coat and Sue followed. Still not letting Deb know that he had seen her, he guided Sue out, his hand low down on her hip, hovering near her bottom, pushing the point of intimacy home, as if it hadn't been already.

If looks could kill, he knew he would have been deader than a dead dodo in Deadland. How much more perfect could this be?

Phil was very chirpy when he got home that night. He read the Sunday papers and ate Lou's pork Sunday dinner with four veg and crisp Yorkshire puddings so light he had to weight them down with a pint of sweet onion gravy, then he had a huge portion of syrup sponge that made the *Maltstone Arms*' version taste like a pan-scrubber.

'Fantastic that, love,' he said with an approving burp. 'You have to be the best cook in the world.'

Lou smiled, not realizing he was setting her up for a fall.

'You'll never guess what happened today – something really weird. A woman came into the showroom and she was the spitting image of you when you were younger. It was uncanny,' Phil said, staring forward as if she had just manifested herself in front of him. 'I couldn't believe it. She could have been your twin ten years ago. Lovely, she was. Just like you used to be before you put on all that . . . well, like you were, shall we say?'

He watched the gulp in her throat and then she disappeared quickly into the kitchen and did something noisy with the dishwasher. *Bullseye!*

Phil plunged the spoon into the golden pudding with the pale golden custard sitting in the sunshine-yellow china bowl with the gold rim. Just for a moment, he knew how Midas felt.

Chapter 37

Marina Marklew had worked at *Serafinska's Bakery* for nearly forty years. She was a woman who didn't like fuss, which is why her idea of a perfect leaving do was a nice quiet Sunday lunch with her husband and the lovely bunch of people she worked with. That is what she wanted and that is what Mrs Serafinska had arranged for her. And because she was such a sweet old thing and would be sorely missed after she retired, Deb didn't walk straight out of the pub when she saw her best friend's husband pawing some woman she didn't recognize, nor did she leap up to confront him. She soldiered on, taking her seat and eating food for which she had no appetite, forcing smiles and a semblance of enjoyment even though her whole afternoon had been ruined as soon as it began. Yet another reason to hate that slimy little toad Phil Winter.

When Deb got home she immediately opened up a bottle of Merlot, poured herself a big glass and sat at her kitchen table, where she dropped her head into her hands and tried to work out what to do for the best. Exactly as she did three years ago? she asked herself, when she saw Phil snogging that cheap tramp scrawny barmaid with the electrocuted perm over a grotty pub dining-table – not to mention observing the manual activity going on beneath it. Back then, she had decided instantly on the course of action she had to take. Lou needed to be told! What woman wouldn't want to know that her husband was making a total fool of her? Especially with someone as tacky as that.

Thoughts of how it might alter the plans for their business venture had been way at the bottom of Deb's list. Lou's welfare was her only concern. She had not taken the time to envisage the possible fallout from such noble intentions.

Back then, it took Lou less than a minute to change from the smiling woman who answered the door of number 1, The Faringdales into a wounded animal fighting for her life. One minute she was ushering Deb inside, the next she was tearing through Phil's wardrobe, scavenging for any clue that could help her understand *why*.

Deb was still in the house when Phil came in from work – cocky as a dog with two dicks. But he knew the game was up as soon as he saw the scene of devastation that confronted him. Lou asked Deb to leave them to it, but it was obvious to her that the cowardly sod wouldn't want to listen to the barrage of questions to which his betrayed wife so badly needed the answers. Deb was right, of course. Phil just grabbed a case and ran for the hills.

Deb moved in and stayed with Lou, hearing her crying in the middle of the night, watching her get thinner and more hollow-eyed with every day that passed. When she wasn't crying she was relentlessly slicing her brain to bits with questions: how old was this barmaid, what colour was her hair, how thin was she, what was the expression on Phil's face like when he looked at her, did he look as if he was in love with her – until Deb wasn't so sure she had done the right thing any more.

Then, just before Christmas, three and a half years ago, Deb turned up at Lou's house to find her totally revitalized. And the reason for Lou Winter's rebirth? Phil had suddenly arrived back home, with his suitcase. Full of dirty washing, no doubt.

'What did he say for you to let him back?' Deb had asked on the doorstep.

'I don't want to even talk about it,' Lou had replied. 'I just want to start again as from now.'

'So you've let him off totally? Please tell me at least he's said he's sorry?' asked Deb with hard disbelief. She knew that Phil was listening from upstairs and she wanted him to hear this, so she didn't hold back. 'Lou, please think! He's done this to you once, he will hurt you again, he will cheat again – you'll never be able to trust him. I never did like the balding, greasy git.'

Balding, she knew, would really piss him off. Phil did hear, and he made Lou choose because of it. The deal was simple: if she stayed friends with Deb then he was off – permanently. Their marriage couldn't repair itself with Deb hanging around like a malicious pair of scissors, waiting in the background, ever-sharpening and insulting him. So Lou chose him, because Phil Bastard Winter had spent years chipping away at her self-worth with his rasping little comments about her looks and her weight and her abilities until she had only weak scraps of herself left that couldn't deal with the hurt of him leaving her for someone else.

Yes, Deb had been upset, but when you love someone you have to think about them and what they want – even if you *know* you know better. It was Lou's life, not hers. Deb loved her friend so much she hated the idea of her being in pain. So what on earth was she going to do this time?

Lou applied a big dollop of Touche Éclat to the black circles under her eyes. If she was awake, she thought too much; if she was asleep, she dreamed too much. It was a lose-lose situation.

'Are you all right? You look absolutely pants,' said Karen, when she got into work the next day, which made Lou think that the extra time in front of the mirror had not been worth it.

'I didn't sleep very well,' she explained.

'I'll get you a coffee from the super-dooper machine,' said Karen. 'With extra phlegm.'

'Lovely,' said Lou, sticking on a smile and licking some moisture back into her lips.

Nicola kept a low profile that day and everyone else seemed in a good mood. Karen was telling them all that she had hooked up with a single dad on her accountancy course – Charlie – who was 'ancient' (thirty-three), and two inches smaller than her but a great laugh, and 'awfully kind'. She said it wasn't serious, but her eyes were too dreamy to carry off that lie. After Chris she was understandably scared, although she would have denied that. But Lou was older and could sniff out the truth. She hoped Karen could have some fun with Charlie. It was well overdue for her.

That weekend, Stan had five numbers up on the lottery and, though he hadn't won enough to stick two fingers up at Metal Nicky and flounce out of the door a year early, it was enough to finance a nice sunshiney holiday for him and Emily for their Ruby wedding anniversary at Christmas. And Zoe's man was making her extra twinkly at the moment and not even Nicola's miserable face could dampen her spirits. Love was like a suit of armour, thought Lou; when clad in it, you could face anything. The trouble was, when it left, it not only took the suit back, but charged you the top layer of your skin too.

But the heaviest thunderstorms often follow the brightest sunshine, and so it was, later that same day, the dark cloud that was Nicola started to announce itself. Stan had accidentally deleted something he shouldn't have onscreen, which wouldn't have taken all that long to fix but, oh no, 'The Walking Scrapyard' had to make him look small and stupid in front of everyone. And where had Zoe put those promotional gift vouchers? Zoe couldn't remember putting them anywhere at all.

'If you've taken them, you know they're all traceable, so don't even think about spending them,' said Nicola with affected concern.

At the implication of theft, Zoe's eyes lifted and she looked at Nicola in the same dead black way a Rottweiler did before finally tearing in. It was like a slow-motion action replay, except the action hadn't happened yet. Lou saw Zoe's hand start to rise and she moved in like a cheetah, grabbed Zoe's arm, linked it and marshalled her out of the office, saying, 'We're going for a coffee.'

Let Jaws report her to HR for that if she dared.

Down in the canteen, Zoe's anger had softened into tearful frustrated rage.

'She accused me of stealing – you heard her! As if!' said Zoe, while Lou put something very white and creamy in front of her that, for once, seemed to be behaving itself in the cup. 'I would have hit her, Lou. And I wouldn't have cared!'

'Yes, I know,' said Lou.

Zoe tore open a sugar sachet and sprinkled it into her crappuccino, or whatever that particular strange coffee was called. Her hands were shaking so much, the table top got most of it.

'I'm going to tell you something now,' said Lou. 'About a friend of mine. It's private, so I'd rather you didn't spread it around. But I think . . . I hope it might help you.'

Zoe doubted anything could take away her regret at not twatting the blotchy-necked cow with the James Bond villain gob, but she had great respect for Lou so she nodded and Lou began.

'Just over three years ago, my friend's husband had an affair,' said Lou. She saw the look of confusion on Zoe's face and answered it. 'I know it's not quite the same, but I think you'll see the relevance in a minute. He went back to her but my friend's hatred for the other woman just wouldn't go away and she was totally convinced that the only way for her to get any sense of relief at all was to find this other woman and smack her right in the mouth. Anyway, one day, my friend saw this other woman in Boots, buying condoms of all things . . .' Lou gave a dry little laugh. 'She knew it was definitely *her* because she had called into the pub where she worked once to see what she looked like. My friend called out her name, the woman turned round, she went white and my friend said that, had she left at that moment, she would have been satisfied with that look on the woman's face. But she didn't leave; she pulled back her hand and slapped the other woman as hard as she could. Suddenly there were people swarming everywhere and all of them giving my friend the filthiest looks, calling for the security man. My friend ran out of the shop in a blind panic then, leaving the woman lying on the floor wailing and crying with a big crowd cooing over this poor innocent soul who had just been attacked by a nutter. In that moment, my friend knew that she had just thrown away her biggest advantage – her dignity. In short, she had given her power away.'

Lou gulped hard. Telling this story was harder than she anticipated. Her emotions were still very much knotted into the memories. 'My friend couldn't sleep for days afterwards, wondering whether the police were going to appear at her door, or if she was going to open up a newspaper or a magazine and see her name plastered over the front page as a loopy woman going mad in the centre of town. She said it was torture, one of the worst experiences of her life. She never regretted anything so much as losing control that day. Her life was hell and her self-respect gone. She hasn't been back in Boots since.'

Lou exhaled slowly, trying to rid herself of the spectre of that time.

'Did the woman end up having your friend arrested?' asked Zoe softly.

'No, although she might as well have done. I don't think my friend could have suffered more if she had. In a silly sort of way it would have been a relief, and then at least she could have faced it head on rather than be mentally tortured about what might be waiting in the wings for her. Then my friend heard that the woman had moved to Spain with her family, and finally – and that was months and months after – she started to let herself believe that it might just be over.'

Lou squeezed Zoe's hand. 'Zoe, sweetheart, get another job, walk away, bash a wall, but take it from me, hang on to your dignity. Nicola would love it if you slapped her. She would have the perfect excuse then to sack you. You wouldn't feel victorious – all you would feel is shame and anger that in the end she *did* have the power to make you snap, after all. Trust me on this. I know.'

Zoe looked at Lou's lovely face with her kind green eyes and gave her a big hug. She was young but she wasn't stupid. She knew perfectly who Lou's 'friend' was.

'Hang on in there, Zoe, please,' said Lou as they went back up the stairs to their office. 'This situation can't go on for much longer; someone will come along and change things. I'm one hundred per cent sure of it.'

Chapter 38

Lou pulled into the car park and looked at the grotty exterior of *Ma's Café* and she smiled because she could feel her dream stepping out of her imagination and becoming flesh. She felt a surge of excitement, visualizing the large black and white sign with the name of their café on it, whatever that would be, supplanting the yellow and brown one with the missing letters, and a throng of people coming especially for their cakes and coffee. This was so long overdue. She had never allowed herself to picture what would have happened if she and Deb had not abandoned their plans because to do that she would also need to imagine that her marriage had ended. She couldn't have had both the café and Phil then.

He had seemed normal enough the previous day, though he was still hiding away his phone and smiling too much for Lou's liking, which was actually starting to annoy her more than it upset her. How long had he been this pathetic, she found herself asking at one point, when he seemed to be humming a tune that fitted the lyrics: 'I know something you don't know.' When did he become someone who had to torture, to control, to hurt? Or had he always been like that, and she was just wising up to it?

So far though, Lou was coping, holding it all together. Thinking about *Ma's* concentrated her mind on things she wanted to think about, rather than those she didn't, and the obvious timing of Phil's behaviour, coming just after she announced she was going ahead with her café plans, only galvanized her sheer bloody-mindedness. She would show him that this time, he wasn't going to manipulate her into dumping her dream.

She was, however, worried that the time for ultimatums was looming and she wasn't sure what she would do if he tried to pin her down to '*Debra Devine or me.*' One thing was for sure: whatever happened, she would not let Deb down again. So, didn't that indirectly answer it for her?

Deb was taking that week off work and her Mini was already parked up when Lou got there. In the car, Lou checked her face in the flip-down mirror for lipstick on her teeth, just in case she should bump into any interesting males with smiley faces and big dogs. The mirror threw a drawn and tired reflection back at her. She pinched some colour into her cheeks and pasted on a smile. The last thing she wanted was for Deb to think that everything in the garden wasn't rosy, for it was more or less at this stage last time when their plans collapsed.

They were going to have a look at the flat above the business. Lou went into the café and May, wearing a *Gordon Ramsay My F***ing Arse* apron, waved her upstairs with a half-buttered bap.

Deb was waiting at the top of the stairs for her, smiling broadly.

'Welcome to our empire HQ,' she said with a flourish as she led Lou into a small dingy room with a few bits of furniture dotted around.

'Crikey, you couldn't swing a blind bat in here,' said Lou, looking around. Deb smiled but didn't correct her; she was used to Lou's mangling of the English language. It was one of those daft things about Lou that she had missed in the past three years. At that moment Deb so wanted to give Lou a big hug, but she feared if she did, she would start crying and pour everything out about what that bald-headed husband of hers was doing again.

The flat was clean, give or take a layer of dust and a neglected musty smell. However, the lime-green walls and purple ceilings were a bit violent on the eye. Especially when complemented by a burgundy alcove where the carcass of a double bed stood snugly between wall and window. A tiny little bathroom leading off had a seventies chocolate suite and the same burgundy walls, while the galley kitchen with its ancient appliances was the black side of navy blue.

'Where the hell did this paint come from?' said Lou. She wouldn't have thought it possible to fit so much bad taste into such a small space.

'It'll probably be in vogue in a couple of years when everyone gets sick of the neutral look,' laughed Deb.

'Don't put your life savings on it, love. I thought May used this place for storage. I was expecting to see boxes everywhere.'

'Apparently her nephew had it for a while at Easter so she emptied it for him. I think painting it was his way of paying rent.'

'Dear God, I hope he's not at art school,' said Lou,

shielding her eyes from the sunshine reflecting off the lime-green gloss. 'It would make a smashing little office, though,' she added.

There were two chairs and a small dining-table already covered with Deb's homework. She had brought a basket with tea and coffee and cups, as had Lou.

'Great minds,' said Lou, and even though she smiled, Deb thought she looked weary. She wondered if she knew about Phil already. Perversely, she both hoped she did and hoped she didn't, for obvious reasons.

'You all right today?' asked Lou. 'You look a little tired.'

Deb wanted to laugh: Lou asking if *she* was all right. 'Start of a headache, that's all,' she said. 'Must be down to all this excitement. Exclusive premises *and* a penthouse flat thrown in – who wouldn't be overwrought?'

'I have tablets,' said Lou, fishing in her handbag.

'Thanks,' said Deb, who doubted that three tons of Semtex, never mind a couple of Ibuprofen, would shift what was making her brain throb.

A cup of coffee and a shared Twix later, Deb was showing off the list of builders she had rung for quotes and some who had contacted her, having heard about the venture on some mysterious builders' grapevine.

'I'm seeing three lots this afternoon and taking them around the café,' Deb went on. 'I told them it's urgent and that I want the figures back as soon as. I reckon we'd need to shut up the café for maybe four to six weeks. But what do you think about this . . .' She leaned forward. 'We offer a free belt-buster breakfast to the regulars when we re-open.'

Lou nodded enthusiastically.

'I was thinking the same myself. Look . . .' She foraged in her bag and brought out her notepad, then presented a page to Deb on which she had scribbled her idea for a voucher to be given out to the regulars before the café closed, to be redeemed when they opened again as *Working Title Casa Nostra*.

'They're numbered as well, so we can keep a tally and guard against anyone just going out and photocopying them.'

Deb nodded. In work matters they were so much in tune. Shame they didn't think alike where other stuff was concerned. Phil and his over-active penis, for instance.

'Anyway, want to hang around and see some big hunky builders with me?' asked Deb. 'I've got this man coming around at one,' she said, handing Lou a letter of introduction from a builder. 'They were keen, I'll give them that. I rang them back and they seemed very hungry for the big stuff. And they guarantee to deliver on time.'

Lou studied the letter.

'I was going to check out the kitchen equipment,' she mused. She and Deb had been organized and written out a who-does-what list. 'However, I'd love to be around to meet this guy with you. Deb, I just need to nip home and change. Would you do me a very great favour when I come back?'

And as Lou told her what that favour was, Deb's first genuine smile in the last forty-eight hours spread over her pretty face.

Chapter 39

Deb led the builder around the café, which was busy with drivers and noisy with the sizzle of fried food and Abba songs blaring from the radio.

'As you can see,' Deb said with increased volume to make herself heard, 'we picked this place because of its tremendously popular location. You are familiar with our chain of coffee-houses in America, of course?'

The builder nodded and mumbled, 'Oh yes, certainly.'

'It's quite a phenomenon, how quickly it's grown,' said Deb, trying to rein in the giggle and keep it strictly within the parameters of a professional smile. The builder had taken all his notes and measurements and now she was leading him upstairs to the flat. She gestured, inviting him to sit at the table.

'I apologize for the surroundings. It's a little bit different to our base in New York.' She gave a tinkly laugh. 'Five million square metres of office space and its own helipad.'

The builder raised a bushy set of eyebrows. Well, one continuous caterpillar one that seemed to do a Mexican wave across his forehead.

'In the eighteen months since our chain has been

established in the States, the number of outlets has increased twenty-seven per cent more than McDonald's, Pizza Hut, Wendy's and KFC did in their first five years. That's quite some growth, I'm sure you'll agree.'

Deb stood proudly back waiting for the builder to absorb this and be amazed. He hadn't a clue how huge that was but made a series of impressed wheezes, accordion-like grunts and whistley intakes of breath. For a moment there he became a sort of South Yorkshire beat-box.

'This is why we have decided to come to England. It may seem like an odd place to base our first UK opening, but our Chairman has ancestral connections with this part of the country. Plus, as you may or may not know, an American conglomerate, which has integral business dealings with our chain back home, is buying up the land around here. Phase one involves two hundred new refurbs planned for this year alone, and we are looking for a team of builders who we can *one thousand per cent* rely on – possibly even to go on and cover our European phase which we intend to start within six months of *Casa Nostra* GB-One opening, i.e. this one.'

The builder's eyes were dilating. They were almost imitating cartoon eyeballs where pupils clicked up as jackpot pound signs. Deb could hear his heart palpitations from across the table.

'We have very good reputation for hour work,' said the builder, with a misplaced couple of aitches. 'No job too big hor too small for us, but reliability and satisfaction always guaranteed.'

'Perfect!' said Deb, clapping her hands together and giving the air of someone who has been totally sold. 'Of course our newly appointed Head of Ops is the one who will ultimately decide, which is why I am going to introduce you to her now. She has absolute authority in this matter. I asked her if she would mind meeting us here at quarter-to.' Deb checked her watch. It was quarter to on the dot.

Right on cue, Lou teetered into the room in her beautiful black suit, hair swept up into an elegant French pleat, seamed stockings and her tallest going-out heels.

Deb came forward with a reverent smile.

'Ah, Mrs Winter, I think we've found our man. Mrs Winter, meet Mr Keith Featherstone, Mr Featherstone, meet Mrs Elouise Winter, National Head of Global Operations for Casa Nostra International PLC.'

Fifteen minutes later, down in *Ma's Café*, Lou wiped away her tears with a serviette. Deb's head was in her hands and she was sobbing. That was the scene that met Tom as he pushed open the door.

He slid on the vinyl seat next to Deb and looked across the table at Lou, who was quite aware that, despite the beautiful clothes and coiffure, she must look an absolute sight.

Tom looked from one to the other.

'What's the matter?' he asked softly. 'Are you both OK? Are you laughing or crying, the pair of you? Come on, what have you been up to?'

Deb tried to tell him but dissolved into hysteria. Lou tried to take over and did the same thing.

'I'll get a round in,' said Tom with a big sloppy grin.

By the time he had returned with a tray, Lou and Deb had calmed down just enough to relate the story to him.

Neither of them could remember laughing like that since . . . well, not since they were together three years ago.

'I have never seen the colour drain out of a man's face so quickly!' said Deb. 'It was absolutely priceless.'

'What did he do when he saw you, Lou?' said Tom, caressing the cup with his thumb and making Lou shiver slightly. She could feel the heat of his leg very close to hers under the table.

'He did this,' and Deb made a strange gurgling sound. 'I thought he was going to choke!'

'I've never heard as much bull in my life,' said Lou. 'How many square metres of office space do we have in New York again?' She pressed at her cheek muscles which ached from a use they hadn't had in a long time.

'God knows, I was making it all up as I went along. Oh, you should have seen my friend here, Tom,' said Deb. 'She glared at him with her big green eyes and said, "I know Mr Featherstone's work *very* well, Miss Devine. We'll be in touch with our decision." Then she said, "Thank you," which sounded like "You are dismissed", and he scuttled out like a crab with his rear end on fire. I swear there were icicles on the window when she opened her mouth. Ice Maiden or what!'

The girls crumbled into laughter again, both glad for it. Both with so much on their minds where laughter had no place.

Tom smiled gently. 'But you're happy the way things are going so far?' he asked.

'Oh yes,' said Deb. She checked her watch. 'Anyway, in fifteen minutes I've got another builder coming in, so I'd better sort out my face.'

'Who is it?' asked Tom. 'If you don't mind me asking.'

'Don't mind you asking at all. Vernon Knowczynski and sons, apparently.'

Tom obviously recognized the name from the nod of approval he gave. 'He's a good, hardworking bloke, is Vernon Knowczynski. If you want my opinion, you would go a long way to beat him. He's fast, he's reliable and he'll cut you a good deal. Especially for cash.'

At this he secretly winked over the table to Lou, whose heart did an Olga Korbut-type leap and kicked itself out of sync for a couple of beats. 'The whole family are builders, lots of Polish cousins. Even his granny mixes the cement,' he went on.

'Wow!' said Lou, amazed.

'Lou! He's having you on,' said Deb, nudging him.

'I'd kick you under the table but my legs aren't long enough,' said Lou, shaking her head in despair at herself. She of all people should know what he was like by now, but she had long since dispensed with the idea that he was trying to make a fool out of her. He was teasing her. She liked the words 'Tom' and 'tease' bracketed together. She kept dabbing under her eye with her fingertip. She'd put so much power-eyeliner on, it was bound to have smudged to the max after laughing at Keith Featherstone and his smacked-backside face.

They all stood to go. Oh hell, now Tom would see her walking on those impossible heels, which were like stilts. She'd had to take them off to go up and down the stairs or she'd have broken her neck. She couldn't bear falling over again in front of him. This time she had a skirt on and would probably ladder her hold-ups as well as show him what she had had for dinner. Were her seams straight? They were probably helter-skeltered around her legs. She deliberately hung back and let Tom and Deb walks out in front of her.

'Want a lift to your car?' grinned Deb, nodding towards her shoes.

'I can give you a piggyback?' said Tom.

'No, get lost the pair of you,' said Lou, shooing them away.

'We won't watch you walk across the car park — promise,' chuckled Deb, and waved before she followed Tom into the ironmongery.

When Lou reached the Townend roundabout, she realized she had left her notebook in the psychedelic flat. Doing did a full circle, she came back into the car park, braking in a spot just opposite Tom's shop. The door was ajar, and through the aperture she could see Tom standing, concentrating on something, staring in front of him as if into thin air. Unseen, she allowed herself the luxury of watching him, his big powerful profile, his large gentle face, his wild, wavy black hair through which her fingers itched to weave themselves. Then Lou saw Deb move into his arms and she froze.

Her heart was thumping in panic as she watched Deb bury her head into Tom's shoulder. She could, at her height, whereas Lou could only have buried her head into his navel. They looked so good together — *so right*. Deb was leaning on him and he was cuddling her, stroking his hand down her back. Now he was holding her at arm's length and talking softly to her, about what Lou didn't know — she obviously couldn't hear and her limbs were too numb to drop the window down. Then

Tom cupped Deb's face in his hands and said something else. Tenderly, lovingly. Or was he kissing her? She couldn't tell.

Lou ripped her eyes away and started up the car. Her sight was blurred. She blinked it clear. Her whole body seemed to be one big heartbeat. There was a pulse in her temple that would pump out a migraine if she didn't get away.

She should be happy for them, she liked Tom and Deb so much, but it still hurt – in just the same way that it did when she saw Liam Barlow snogging Donna Platts at the school disco. He'd looked like a young Oliver Reed and his name was written all over her jotter in her I-Spy secret pen that only showed up in the dark. Donna was her best friend at fifteen. They weren't doing anything wrong – Donna didn't know how much Lou fancied Liam because she had always shrugged away any suggestion that she did. Just like Deb didn't know how much she fancied Tom because she couldn't admit it to her.

Not even Lou knew how deeply those feelings for Tom had taken root until she saw him holding her best friend the way she wanted to be held by him.

Lou Casserly hadn't crumbled at the school disco, despite that pain in her chest. She had taken a deep breath, stoked up her smile and got on with being happy for Donna. Lou Winter would just have to try and do the same for Debra.

When Lou got home there was a message on the answering machine. It was Bloody Keith Featherstone in his poshest voice.

'*Erm, Mrs Winter, this is Keith Featherstone. Would it be*

convenient for us to call tomorrow morning at eight o'clock to start work hon your bathroom? I really must hapologize for the hinconvenience to you and the delay. Hobviously there will be a significant reduction in the price due to the hinconvenience, which I will refund to you. Could you ring me back when it's convenient, please? I know you have my number but I'll leave it hanyway . . .'

Lou started to key the digits into the phone, then she put it down again before it could connect. This time she had the upper hand with Keith Featherstone and she was going to savour it for a little longer. This time there would be no Deb or fancy title or power suit or 'killer heels' to hide behind. This time it was just Keith Featherstone and Lou Winter. *High Noon.* She dialled again.

'Oh, Mrs Winter, hI'm so glad you returned my call.'

'I got your message, Mr Featherstone. Yes, it would be convenient for you to call tomorrow at eight. At last,' she added pointedly.

'Like I say, I do hapologize for all this delay,' said Keith Featherstone with a nervous laugh, 'HI've been so busy . . .'

'I've been very busy myself and I just want this work done, Mr Featherstone, if you don't mind,' said Lou with icy politeness. 'And done quickly after all this "inconvenience".' He seemed to like that word, so maybe it would strike the happropriate chord. 'Is that understood?'

Bloody hell, that was *me* talking, thought Lou.

'Yes, certainly, Mrs Winter. My lads will be there at eight prompt.'

'Thank you and goodbye, Mr Featherstone.'

Lou put the phone down first. Those with the power always made the break first. Result. Lou was shaking — but smiling too. She was really proud of herself for that. She clasped her hands together and passed a quick Thank You to the Great Man upstairs for giving her the opportunity to have that moment. She felt absolutely empowered, so much so that she could have tackled Victorianna. She looked at the clock — her sister would be at work, pandering to the rich and famous with spray tans and fake toenails. *Damn* — because, with all this adrenaline flooding her system, Lou was ready to burn it off in her transatlantic direction.

Chapter 40

The evening passed in a blur. Lou was determined to hold onto and use this feeling of power inside her which came from a recipe made up of post-Keith-Featherstone-confrontation and some crazy chemical that had been shooting around her system ever since she saw Tom and Deb cuddling in the doorway. It felt not unlike something Dr Jekyll might have thrown together in his laboratory. She needed to keep it on a slow simmer to hang on to the flavour – and only bring it to the boil at 3 a.m.

Phil misinterpreted his wife's distraction. He thought he knew Lou like the back of his hand and so concluded that she was in psychological hell – wondering why he was hiding his phone and behaving slightly oddly, but nothing that she would be able to put her finger on. He gave it another two weeks, then it would be a feast of blow jobs and lamb dinners, and life would settle down to being blissful again. Marriage was all about keeping an even power balance. There was only room for one partner with the upper hand in a relationship. He had a good marriage — it was worth his efforts to save it. And the end always justified the means in these matters. This was his last noble thought of the day as he drifted into the welcoming waters of sleep.

Lou watched the clock's hands crawl towards the allotted time. With every click of the second hand she felt her resolve threaten to slip away, but cling on she did because she had never felt as ready as she did tonight. This show-down was long overdue.

In an unsuccessful attempt to divert her thoughts, Lou watched a foreign film with subtitles on the TV. It was about some woman getting it together with a toy boy and having fantastic sex everywhere. It was fiction, obviously, because in real life she would be terrified to undress and expose her lumps and bumpy cellulite to someone she considered so perfect. She would insist on the lights out and him wearing big gloves. The thought of ever having sex with anyone but Phil in the future was both new and terrifying. Her thoughts slid towards what a first encounter might be like with Tom. He'd throw up! He'd take one look at those little red spider veins on the inside of her knees, or feel her soft cushiony tummy, and leap out of the window screaming. *But what if he didn't? What if he savoured you like a delicious main course* . . . She shook the thoughts away before they got too graphic. She was not available, Tom Broom was not available and besides, it didn't seem right fantasizing about grappling with your best friend's boyfriend. She should put some distance between herself and Tom and Deb for a few days to sort out her head and clear it of all impure thoughts. There was time to think about that later, though. Now she needed to concentrate on her sister.

At three o'clock exactly, Lou picked up the phone and dialled the dreaded number. Her heart was thumping like a bass drum laying down the rhythm for a Judas Priest-style version of 'I Do Like To Be Beside the Seaside'. Boom boom boom. Any minute now, it was going to do a John McVicar – break out of her chest and go on the run with one of her lungs.

There was an echoey foreign dialling tone and then that voice – that affected, jolly-hockey-sticks public-school accent of a woman who had graduated from a Barnsley comp with one O level in French (distinction for oral though).

'It's me,' said Lou.

There was a telling pause before Victorianna said with tight politeness, 'Oh hello, Lou, how are you? What do you want?'

Victorianna had already done her maths (or *math* as she would say) and worked out what time it was in England. She knew her sister wasn't ringing her for a bog standard 'how are you?' chit-chat.

Lou took a big gulp of air. 'I think you should invite Mum out there to visit.'

Silence again. Then Victorianna did one of those incredulous laughs that would shatter crystal. 'Lou, I'll invite my mother out when *I* see fit. Not when *you* tell me to.'

'I think you should invite Mum out there to visit,' Lou said again. Coolly, calmly, with conviction.

'Your record appears to have stuck, Lou. And, excuse

me, what are you on? Who the hell are you to tell me what to do anyway? Have you been drinking?' Victorianna was growing more and more incensed. Her posh accent was losing its grip on the Klosters slope slightly.

'How long is it since you've seen her, Victorianna? How long have you been having her racing around buying parcel stuff for you? Do you ever think about paying her for it all? Do you ever ring her when you don't want something? Isn't it the least you could do? Have you any idea how much she's missing you?' The adrenaline factory within Lou had recruited extra staff and they were working flat out to complete this urgent order.

Victorianna did a laugh of the 'I don't believe I'm putting up with this' variety. 'Who on earth do you think you are?' she said. 'I've had an incredibly long day doing complicated nail art on a bitch of a client who made me re-do her left hand three times and this I don't need!'

'Listen to me, Victorianna. I think you should invite—' but as Lou started on her spiel, the line went dead.

Lou growled and stabbed in last-number redial. The dialling tone changed to a chirpy American answering message read aloud by Victorianna and Willy Wonka in unison.

'*Hi, this is Edward and Torah; we're not at home right now . . .*'

Lou snarled.

'*. . . but please leave us a message and we'll gladly call you back when we are able. Bye now!*'

'If you don't pick up this phone, you little cow,' said

Lou with all the control of Ben Hur over his chariot horses, 'I will tell the good old British police and your precious Edward exactly how you financed your trip to the US of fecking A.'

When fighting Victorianna, it was best to dredge up a few Anglo-Saxon-cum-Irish roots, thought Lou. It worked, for the phone was snatched up at the other end.

'What are you talking about?' Victorianna demanded waspishly.

'I know all about it, Vic. Now get two tickets over to the States for your mother and her friend Vera. They're spending a couple of weeks in your chuffing big house with you and your amazing hospitality. You owe her that, at the very least.'

'I haven't a fucking clue what you're on about,' said Victorianna through her clenched new dentalwork. The posh accent had now left Klosters and was heading on public transport for Cleethorpes.

'Oh, I think you do,' said Lou, sensing the panic behind the aggression. For the second time today she was actually enjoying the feeling of power over someone. No wonder people relished it so much. She found herself playing with Victorianna – like a cat with an incredibly foul mouse.

'I'm not listening to any more of this! Go to bed, Lou, or take a sedative. You obviously need one.'

'Put the phone down on me again and just watch the damage I do,' said Lou, hardening her voice to steel. 'Allow me to explain. I opened a letter that arrived for you after you'd flown off. First-class ticket, was it? You could have afforded it, for what you got pawning your own mother's rings.'

'What?' said Victorianna, but a tell-tale tremor had appeared in her voice.

'I. Opened. The. Letter. From. The. Pawn. Shop,' said Lou slowly, as if she was an idiot, which Victorianna wasn't. On the contrary – she was a clever cow and a self-centred, nasty little thief as well.

Victorianna made a few pahs and huffs on the other end of the phone, but she didn't slam it down again, which told Lou volumes.

'Let me refresh your memory, shall I?' Lou went on, as calm as a still lake on a breeze-free night. She inspected her nails the way power-bitches did on the television whilst they spoke. All she needed was some shoulder-pads and she could have got the lead in *Dynasty*. 'After you left to go and live over there, a letter arrived from the pawn shop wanting to know if you had any intentions of buying back your goods, because otherwise they would be sent on for polishing and re-sale. I rang them but they wouldn't deal with anyone but the ticket-holder. Of course, I always wondered if you had anything to do with Mum's missing rings. Have you any idea how many times she turned the house upside down looking for them? It had to be you. All those manicure treatments you did for her, taking off her rings whilst you waxed and massaged her old fingers and painted her nails for her. Weren't you the perfect daughter?'

'You're barmy, you,' spat Victorianna.

'I rang them back, you know, pretended to be you and said I'd lost my ticket and what was I to do? They told me I had to pick up a form from them, take it to a solicitors with some ID and swear an affidavit that I was who I said I was, then they would release the goods.'

Lou let this sink in. Actually whilst she was saying it all aloud, she was amazed at how complicated it sounded. In retrospect, it seemed like something James Bond would have found daunting. But then, James Bond didn't do missions for his mum.

What Victorianna didn't know was that luck was on Lou's side when she found a passport that Victorianna had said she had lost (because the photograph wasn't too flattering) and had since replaced, so she had the form of ID the pawnbrokers and the solicitors requested. The problem was, Lou didn't look enough like Victorianna to pass for her. Deb did, though. It was Deb who stood in a solicitor's office for her and risked prosecution as she swore that she was Victorianna Eugenie Casserly in order that Lou could go into the pawn shop and pay a small fortune for the envelope containing her mother's rings. Then Lou had to hide them at Renee's and stage a grand search through the house, for them to miraculously turn up under the dresser in the dining room. Thank goodness there had been no comeback from legal quarters and her mother had seemed to swallow the charade.

Victorianna was quiet whilst her few brain cells not earmarked for sex and money matters whirred into long-overdue action.

'You pretended to be me?' said Victorianna, not quite believing that any firm of solicitors could mistake a little plump dark-haired blimp for tall, willowy beach-blonde her. Who had she got as lawyers – Stevie, Wonder & Wonder?

Lou didn't see the need to put her right and drop Deb in the mess. Plus, knowledge was power and she wasn't giving any away to her sister, so she simply said, 'Yep!'

Thinking anyone could mix up the two of them in the looks department would probably make her spontaneously combust, thought Lou with an inner snigger.

Victorianna's brain couldn't solve this one and she knew she was outsmarted – so she did what people like Victorianna do in this situation and, as Lou had anticipated, picked up anything resembling a weapon and prepared to use it.

'I know what all this is about,' she spat. 'You're pissed because of what happened between me and Phil, aren't you? This is your little revenge. So how many years has it taken you to think this one up?'

Lou steeled herself. This was the part of the conversation she had been dreading. Now, more than ever, she had to stand firm.

'Nothing happened between you and Phil, Victorianna,' she said, hoping it was true.

Victorianna laughed. 'No, you're right, it didn't. I'm not a total bitch, whatever you might think.'

Lou breathed a sigh of relief and felt slightly sick. For so long now, she had wondered . . .

When she and Phil had started courting, Victorianna was an extraordinarily pretty teenager – a bomb of hormones and untested sexuality. Putting a teenage brain in a body like that was like putting a child in charge of a Ferrari.

She flirted with Phil shamelessly. She so enjoyed the effect her teasing had on him. Even more did she enjoy the effect her teasing him had on Lou. Victorianna didn't want him because she had no use for him. He wasn't rich enough by half – and she didn't want to end up in Barnsley! It was enough for her to know she could have had him at any time; she didn't need to prove more than that.

'He'd have been off with me at the first opportunity if I had wanted him,' said Victorianna with relish. 'I drove him crazy. I made him hard just by running my tongue over my lips. I bet you any money he used to think of me when he was using you as a waste-bin.'

Lou closed her eyes against the mental image of Phil fidgeting in his trousers when he was around her precocious sister. She needed to keep strong now because Victorianna was starting to recover her ground.

'You always hated that I could have taken him away at any time, didn't you, big sis?'

Lou laughed. 'You've been listening to "Jolene" too much,' she said, hanging on to her bravado for grim death. She pictured Victorianna on the other end of the phone, swaying like a cobra, her neck swelling out in full attack mode as she tried to target the exact location of Lou's main artery. So Lou located her inner mongoose. 'I think you'll find he was flattered, that's all, and it doesn't take much to do that to a man,' she said smoothly.

'Yeah, right. Well, you keep telling yourself that's the way it was if it makes you happy. You should be delighted I moved over here. Out of your way. Out of Phil's way.'

'On stolen money.' Lou dragged it back to the point in question. 'On money you got from taking the rings your father gave to your mother.'

'But hang on a mo, *big sister*, you've just told me you're guilty of fraud! Swearing on oath that you were me in front of a solicitor? Tut tut now!'

'Very true,' said Lou, still sounding calm, and glad

Victorianna couldn't hear her knees knocking. 'But I'm willing to take the risk if you are, *little sister*. You do your worst, Victorianna, and I. Will. Do. Mine. Let's see who comes off better in the newspaper articles, shall we? Will you still go hob-nobbing with family-value-loving Vice Presidents when it comes out that you stole off your own mam?'

Lou sounded chilling even to herself, but then she was always a formidable force on the playground level. Ask Shirley Hamster.

Victorianna articulated her defeat succinctly. 'Fuck off!' she said, and the phone at the Florida mansion end slammed down.

Lou didn't need to ring back this time. She breathed in a long, slow breath and put the receiver back on the cradle. Sister or no sister, she knew they would never speak again. Victorianna was as good as in one of Tom's skips, as far as Lou was concerned. They had nothing in common but blood and genes, which did not forge a relationship, in Lou's sense of the word, any more.

Lou went to bed, and slept the sleep of the victorious, not waking once to hear Phil's nocturnal mumblings.

Chapter 41

Lou let in the builders as the clock in the hallway struck eight. She made them tea, showed them upstairs and then went to work in the small office downstairs. She had an idea she wanted to mull over about breakfasts in the café. At nine-thirty she called the bank to make an appointment to see the business manager the following week and sent Deb a text message to say she had done so.

Deb replied with: FANTASTIC. RU OK?

Lou affirmed that she was OK and very busy. She didn't want to meet or talk to her best friend for a few days because she was scared Deb was going to tell her that she'd just had fantastic sex with Tom. Of course Lou was OK. Never better.

In the afternoon, Lou called in at her mother's on the pretext of 'just passing'. Renee had the grin of a Cheshire cat with a coathanger stuck in its mouth.

'You'll never guess who I had on the phone this morning,' she said, putting the kettle on. 'Victorianna. And do you know why she rang?'

'Mum, I can't guess, just tell me,' said Lou with wide-eyed innocence.

'She has invited me and Vera over for the whole of September!' Her smile was fixed on with Superglue. It remained there while she brewed the tea and got out the cups.

'What, to America? You *and* Vera? What's come over her?'

Renee tutted. 'Don't start, Lou. She was only waiting until her house was finished, she said. She wanted me to see it complete. She's sending me two return tickets. I've just come off the phone to Vera and she can't wait either. We're going into Leeds next week to start clothes shopping.'

'Well, I'm stunned,' said Lou – and she was. Boy, Victorianna must have been really shaken up to act that fast.

'I knew she would invite me in her own time,' beamed Renee.

'I've got some good news too,' said Lou, thinking there was no more ideal moment than this to introduce her forthcoming business venture. 'I'm opening up a coffee shop with my friend Deb.'

The glue on Renee's smile gave out. 'Deb? Not *that* Deb, surely? When did she come back on the scene?'

'A few weeks now,' said Lou, with a sigh. Why didn't she ever learn?

Renee shuddered. 'And what's Phil said about all this?'

'What do you mean?' said Lou, wishing she had never brought it up.

'Well,' said Renee, not even trying to hide her disapproval, 'she almost wrecked your marriage. Not exactly the sort of person I'd want in my life once, never mind again.'

Lou shook her head in disbelief. She should have

known her mother was duty-bound to criticize and spoil anything she personally didn't approve of.

'Why on earth does everyone think Deb "wrecked my marriage"? Didn't the fact that Phil was having an affair have anything to do with it at all?'

'You've just said yourself that everyone thought she'd wrecked your marriage. We can't all be wrong, can we?' said Renee with a sniff.

Lou huffed in frustration at her mother's logic.

'Well, anyway, we've got premises and we're going ahead with it,' said Lou, finishing off her story, even though her enthusiasm to tell it had totally withered.

'And what about your job?' said Renee.

'I shall leave it, of course.'

'But it's a good steady job! You pulled out of these plans once before, remember. You must have realized then that it was a stupid idea. Honestly, Elouise – have some sense.'

Lou felt like a punctured balloon, but Renee hadn't noticed. She had turned and gone into the kitchen, her words hanging behind her in the air, like a trail of fumes from the aeroplane that would take her and Vera to her younger daughter's wonderfully fancy house and approved-of life in America.

'Don't suppose you know any good butchers, country girl?' Lou asked Karen in the office the next day.

'Are you kidding?' said Karen.

'I never joke about sausages,' said Lou with a straight face.

'My dad's got a farm shop and my brother's the butcher there,' said Karen. 'Why?'

'Come for a coffee to the canteen,' said Lou. Nicola was out doing something mysterious in the Manchester office. She would be in an even fouler mood when she got back because everyone hated going to 'Operations Manchester' – or 'The Black Pudding Hole of Calcutta' as it was universally known.

The German coffee machine for once delivered something quite impressive with a heavy layer of cream on the top, although Lou wouldn't be purchasing a machine like it. She had already sourced a fantastic all-singing, all-dancing Italian one.

And so, over a very nice *delicissimo* each, Lou told Karen all about the coffee shop that was presently a transport café and how they needed to find a supplier of good bacon, fresh eggs and fab sausages for some nice big breakfasts until that side of the business died out gracefully, to be replaced by coffees and puddings.

'God, Lou, I'll miss you like hell,' said Karen with her jaw hanging open.

'I shall miss you too,' said Lou with genuine feeling.

'I suppose if my dad and my brother come up to scratch, we'll be able to keep in touch,' Karen said hopefully.

'Of course. Is it good stuff in your shop?' asked Lou with a smile.

'Well, I didn't exactly grow up to be an undernourished midget from eating it, did I? No offence for the midget comment, by the way.'

Lou laughed.

'I tell you what, I'll ring Dad and get him to drop off some sausages and bacon for you to test. Then he can give me a lift home. Ha!' said Karen, reaching for her mobile and thinking that was a very good double-whammy plan indeed.

That night, Lou and Phil sat down to a dinner of breakfast, which threw him slightly, although it was lovely stuff and he commented favourably on the sausages especially, before earmarking the rest of the bacon for his breakfast the next morning. It was a perfect consumer test, although Lou thought it wise not to tell her husband that he had just been chief guinea pig for the café fare. Oh, and apparently they were going to Torremolinos for a fortnight at the end of June, Phil announced over his Devil's Food Cake dessert. Lou couldn't muster up so much as a, 'Wow.'

Chapter 42

Lou had booked the next day off work because she needed to see Deb with café plans. She could tell her the news that she had found a good farm shop. She only hoped Deb had no news of her own to announce about her and Tom.

Lou let in the builders again, made them tea, reiterated the invitation to help themselves to more and left them a key, hoping they wouldn't go upstairs and start snooping through her knicker drawer, as Karen laughingly said they were bound to. Then she set off for *Ma's Café*.

Deb was already there, her car parked cosily next to Tom's, which seemed pretty symbolic. Lou sighed. *Best get this over with.* She just wanted to hear it from Deb's lips that she and Tom had become an item and then everything would be out in the open and she would have to get on and deal with it.

Deb was coming out of the café as Lou was about to go in. She was looking a bit shifty, Lou thought.

'Oh hi,' said Deb, going back inside with her and closing the door. 'You're early.'

'Hi,' said Lou. 'Well, the house is full of builders. I didn't fancy hanging around.'

'Lou . . .'

Here it comes, thought Lou.

'I've got something to tell you,' said Deb hesitantly. 'I really hope you don't mind. Tom and I—'

Then the door behind Lou opened and Tom himself walked in. As stiffly as a Woodentop, he said, 'Hi there, Lou, I've just seen your car. Thought I'd come over.' But he didn't bend to kiss her hello. He seemed as out of place with her as Deb did. Were they so scared to tell her they were together? If so – why? Had he somehow guessed she had kissing fantasies about him?

'Er . . . have you told her?' said Tom to Deb, clearing his throat.

'Lou, come upstairs a minute will you, please,' Deb sighed.

Lou followed them silently up the stairs. It was like being led to a place of slaughter. Still, it would all be over in five minutes, and then she could say things like, 'Fantastic!' and, 'Brilliant!' and, 'Good for you two!'

Tom opened the door and the light hit Lou immediately. The flat was totally white-washed.

'Lou – Tom and I . . . we painted the flat. I just went ahead and made the decision. I know you'd have said yes, but I'm sorry I didn't ask. I paid for the paint. It's only cheap and cheerful stuff . . .'

'That's all?' said Lou incredulously. 'You painted the flat? Why on earth would I mind? It looks fab!'

'But I just did it, without even thinking to ask you! I never even thought. It's the principle . . .'

'Is that it? That's what you have to tell me?' Lou felt

like laughing hysterically and was really having to stop herself doing so.

'Yes,' said Deb cautiously. 'Why – what did you think I was going to say?' She hoped Lou hadn't found out about her knowing about Phil. But then again, how could she? Unless Phil had told her, and he was hardly likely to do that, now was he? Or was he? Maybe he had some sick, twisted plan. This subterfuge was doing Deb's head in.

'It looks great, Deb, and course I don't mind, you daft bat. You always used to paint when you needed to think in the olden days. Remember painting your room at college, just before Finals, because that flaming horrible grey made it look like the inside of a submarine and you couldn't concentrate?'

Deb smiled a, 'Yes, you're right,' smile. She still painted when she needed to think.

They'd had such fun at college – dreaming of the day when they would open up their own coffee-house. The day that was just around the corner for them now. Or was it? Would Phil wreck their plans a second time? And there was Lou standing with a grin as wide as a slice of watermelon, looking forward to so much and not having a clue what was going on behind her back. It broke Deb's heart.

Even while painting the whole flat, with all that time to think and talk out loud, Deb still hadn't worked out what to do for the best. Except that this time, she was going to hold them up and be strong for the pair of them if she had to. She had been as guilty as Phil last time in forcing Lou into a corner, bullying her nearly as much as he did to take action against him –

something she had come to realize over these past three years.

'Well, if you'll excuse me, I have to go on official skip business,' said Tom.

'Yes, OK, Tom,' said Deb.

'Bye, Lou,' said Tom. 'I'm so glad I'm not in your bad books for aiding and abetting Debra.'

'Don't be silly, it looks great,' said Lou.

'Bye,' he said to her again, and appeared to look at Lou for far longer than the simple word demanded.

'He's looking at me funny,' said Lou, when his heavy tread had reached the bottom of the staircase.

'You're imagining things,' said Deb, deciding to mention to Tom later to stop staring at Lou in such an over-concerned way. Did he want her to smell a rat? She put the kettle on and made them both an instant coffee and they went to sit at the solid old dining-table.

'So, he helped you do all this then?' said Lou, determined to get to the bottom of all that cuddly stuff between them and bring it into the open. Deb still hadn't said anything, and Tom hadn't given her friend more than a friendly wave on his way out. They couldn't have looked less like a couple now. It was all very odd.

'Yes, when he had some spare time in the evenings,' said Deb. 'By the way, the builder's quote came in. I'll get it out in a mo. How's Thingy doing with your bathroom?'

'Very well,' said Lou. 'Shame, really – he's a good worker, just unreliable. But I won't tell him that until he's finished and refunded me some money. I don't want to tell him he hasn't won the multi-billion-pound contract just yet.'

'Good girl,' said Deb.

Oh sod it, thought Lou. It was time to stop pussy-footing. 'So, tell me about you and Tom,' she said. 'Are you together?'

Deb whirled around. 'Together *in what way?*'

'"Together" together.'

'Good God, Lou, whatever gave you that idea?'

'I saw you cosying up in his ironmongery,' said Lou.

Deb hooted with laughter and shook her head. 'When?'

'The day Keith Featherstone came around here. I'd forgotten something and came back for it, and I saw you together.'

'Lou, you've got that so totally wrong. I was . . .'

. . . crying on his shoulder over what to do about you and that cheating-louse husband of yours . . . Deb had to think fast on her feet now. '. . . panicking, I suppose, Lou. It hit me that we were actually going to do this at last, and I came over a little emotional, which as you know is not like me at all.'

No, it wasn't like Deb at all, which is why Lou didn't quite believe her. 'Oh, well I thought you and Tom had got it together,' she said, 'and if that was the case, I wondered why you weren't telling me.'

'Don't be daft. There's nothing *to* tell on that front.'

'It's not daft. You both get on really well.'

'Lou,' said Deb softly, 'the reason I get on with Tom so well is because I don't fancy him one bit. He's lovely – a great bloke, in fact – but he's not for me, and I'm not for him either. He's fitted into my life very quickly as a friend. That's all.'

'Deb, there's more, isn't there? I think I know what you're scared to say.'

'What?' said Deb, her heart starting to thump faster.

'It was at this stage that I backed out last time. It's bound to be on your mind. But whatever happens, I swear to you, Deb, I won't back out. I promise. Not this time.'

Phew, thought Deb. She had only to nod an admission that Lou had hit the nail on the head and that would be the end to the matter.

'I know,' said Deb, and gave her an extra-tight hug. That stupid idiot Phil — did he know what he had in Lou? She hoped he didn't and he drove her away to find someone who deserved her. Someone, Deb thought, like Tom Broom.

Chapter 43

Lou was in bed by the time Phil came home that night. His curry was cremated and his rice dried to desiccated coconut in the pan on the hob. Not that he was hungry. He stank of the garlic-heavy meal he'd already had and Sue's smoky perfume.

It was getting harder and harder to stop at the kissing stage with her, but luckily the 'I'm married and I don't think it's right to make this relationship any more physical than it is *blah blah blah*' line seemed to get her off his back.

He was more than a bit pissed off that Lou wasn't sitting on the stairs worrying and awaiting his return like a fretting Cocker Spaniel. He checked his mobile. There was a missed call from her over two hours ago, but she hadn't left a message.

He didn't shower – just crawled into bed, hoping Lou would sniff out her rival bitch on his skin in the morning.

Lou awoke early the next morning to lots of snoring and an overwhelming aroma of second-hand garlic that hadn't come from the curry she had made for him. She wondered if Phil had eaten an extra smelly tea just to make her wonder where he had been the previous night – and with whom. He really was going to monumental efforts this time to get his own way. But further questions on the subject of the mysterious movements of her husband were stemmed by the excitement of a catalogue of flavoured coffees arriving in the post.

She had just settled down to read it when the phone rang.

'Hiya, Lou,' said Michelle. She sounded cross and huffy.

'You're up early,' said Lou.

'Well, I got to bed early, didn't I?' said Michelle grumpily.

'Wasn't it your big night out with *Ali*?' Lou gave the name an amused emphasis. She had a good idea from Michelle's tone that Ali might have toppled off her pedestal already.

'Huh, don't talk to me about Ali,' said Michelle.

'OK, I won't,' said Lou.

'What a bitch,' said Michelle. 'As soon as we were out she hardly spoke to me. She was too busy chasing people around town. "Ooh look, there's Gary", "Ooh look, there's Conrad", 'Ooh look, there's some other ugly boring geek I fancy",' said Michelle, doing a bitter impression of her temporary best friend. Or rather *ex*-best friend.

'Oh dear,' said Lou, while the words 'shoe' and 'other foot' gravitated to her brain.

'I tell you, I'd had enough by nine. I might as well not have been there. I think she spoke to me twice and she was on pints whilst I was on halves, cheeky cow. I was ready for off, but she wanted to go clubbing. By half-past ten she was so pissed I had to half-carry her to the taxi place and you know what the queues are like at that time with all the bingo crowd coming out as well. It was freezing, my feet were killing me and she was crying about Christ-knows-what. I stuck her in a taxi and then the driver said, "Oy, you're not leaving me with her", and so I had to go home with her and pay for the taxi because she was like a big, stupid, floppy doll. I stuck her in bed in the recovery position and then I had to wait there for another hour until I could get another taxi. I was so angry I couldn't sleep. I tell you, never again.'

Lou bit down hard on her lip. She tried to make sympathetic noises but, as usual, Michelle wasn't really listening to her, only using her as a sounding board.

'I'll have to go, Lou, someone's at the door,' she said mid-sentence and put down the phone. As usual she hadn't even asked how Lou was.

Phil came downstairs rubbing his eyes. Lou stiffened.

'Thanks for leaving me out a dried curry last night,' he said.

'I can reconstitute it for breakfast, if you wish,' she said coldly.

'No, it's all right, thanks. Anyway I ate out.' He waited for her reaction. She twitched slightly, but his radar still picked it up. 'And thanks for waking me, by the way,' he prodded, just to annoy her even more.

'You told me you weren't going in until lunchtime today, didn't you?' There was an edge in her voice he didn't like.

'Did I?' said Phil, all too aware that he had. 'And what if I'd changed my mind?'

'You'd have set your alarm, as always.'

'Humph.'

'Bacon and eggs then?' said Lou.

'Yes, that would be wonderful, love,' said Phil. Switch to being nice now – keep the ground like quicksand under her feet.

As Lou griddled the bacon, she let her mind float away from this house and Phil, to a fantasy house where she was cooking for a nameless figure with black unruly hair who treasured and wanted and loved her to distraction. She delivered Phil's breakfast to him automaton-style and missed his compliment on the perfect-looking egg, so lost was she in her fantasy.

As Phil chewed on the last of his toast he said, 'Isn't that your daft mate coming up my path? She's got a sore eye, by the look of it.'

He didn't 100 per cent blame whoever gave that to her. If he had to spend longer than five minutes in her presence he'd probably thump her himself – and he abhorred bullies who hurt women. But no bird over thirty-five should be going around in mini-skirts and cowboy boots, especially with legs like bleached knitting needles. She was barking! Silly cow fell in love with a multiple murderer on Death Row and would have wired her life savings across to his sister, had Lou not stopped her. Then there was that time she made a total arse of herself sending pictures to the *Barnsley Chronicle* of the image of Roy Orbison that she'd found in a pork pie. These were not the actions of a woman who was the full shilling.

'What did you say?' said Lou, coming out of the kitchen to see.

The front doorbell rang.

Phil grabbed his jacket, sensing a heavy female session with tears and tissues and 'all men are bastards' philosophies. He escaped out of the back door to the car. At that moment, his showroom seemed even more attractive than it usually did.

Lou opened the front door to see Michelle sobbing and looking as if she'd done ten rounds with a pre-menstrual Mike Tyson.

'What the heck happened to you?' said Lou, marshalling Michelle gently inside away from the fat summer raindrops and into the dry warmth of her kitchen.

'Craig . . .' she managed in between big snorty tears.

'Craig did this to you?' Lou was horrified, although not really surprised. He had looked a total thug when she passed him in the street.

'Nooo, Craig's . . .' more snot, more tears '. . . wife!'

Lou was even less surprised.

'Remember when we were talking this morning and I had to go because there was someone at the door?'

'Yes, I remember,' said Lou, guiding Michelle's hand towards a box of tissues.

'Well, I opened it and there was this woman – really hard-faced, ugly, fat, horrible thing.'

Well, she would be, thought Lou. Michelle would hardly admit to Craig's wife being a Claudia Schiffer lookalike.

'Anyway, she says, "Are you Michelle?" and I say, "Yes", and she says, "I believe you're seeing my husband?" and I say, "Craig?" and she says, "Yes" and then she just punches me right in the face. "Keep away from

my husband, you cow, or I'll fucking kill you next time".
Then she gets back into this old car and drives off. There
were kids in the back, Lou. Two little kids strapped in
baby seats. He never said he had kids!'

'It must have crossed your mind, surely, that something wasn't quite right?' said Lou.

'Why should it? I trusted him!' said Michelle, wanting
more sympathy than this.

'Well, you didn't have any phone numbers for him, for
a start, and he was still living at home with his wife,
wasn't he? Didn't you think that was a bit odd?'

Michelle dissolved into a fresh cascade of tears. 'How
could he do this to me?'

'How could he do that to *her*?' said Lou fiercely.

'I don't give a shit about her!' spat Michelle. 'I'm
going down to the police station in a minute to report
her for assault.'

'Don't you think she's had enough crap?' snapped
Lou. 'If she has got two small kids and a husband who is
playing about, no wonder she's in a state. He most likely
would have blamed you for leading him astray and the
wronged woman will nearly always pin it on the other
woman rather than her own man.'

'Whose side are you on, Lou?' said Michelle.

Lou looked hard at Michelle. 'Well, if I'm honest,
anybody's but Craig's,' she said. She wasn't in the mood
for her usual 'There, there.' Besides which, all that tea
and sympathy hadn't done Michelle any good in the long
run. All Lou had ever done was patch her up with PG
Tips and digestive biscuits and watch her go out and
make the same mistakes over and over again. She should-
n't have to pussyfoot around a true friend.

'You can't really be taking *her* side! Look at what she's done to my face!' Michelle half-screamed through her staccato sobs.

'She shouldn't have hit you, no, but I can understand where she was coming from,' said Lou.

Maybe one of Susan Peach's friends had told her the same thing after Lou had decked her in Boots. Maybe that's why she had never heard any more about it. She hadn't considered that possibility until now.

'How can you say that?'

'She doesn't deserve to be arrested.'

'Why not? Because your husband had an affair and you ended up hitting the other woman?' snarled Michelle, before Lou sternly cut her off.

'This isn't about me, Michelle. I'm trying to help you here. Draw a line under Craig now and move on. Learn the lesson!'

'But I love him!' More sobs.

'How can you love someone who treats people so badly? He's hurt his wife, his children and you, because he can't see past his own needs. He's an animal. You're well out of it, surely you can see that now.'

Michelle pulled a mobile phone out of her pocket. 'No, I'm ringing the police and I'm ringing them now.'

A vision came to Lou's mind of a woman in pain lashing out like a wild animal to cling onto her man. She grabbed the phone from Michelle's hand, snapped it shut and put it firmly down on the table.

'Oh no, not in my house you're not!'

Lou's words hung in the air.

Michelle was trapped in shock for a few seconds, then

she rose to her feet and grabbed the phone back, stuffing it deep in her hip pocket.

'Well, I see where your priorities are,' she said, snuffling loudly. 'Call yourself a friend? Well, fuck you, Lou Winter. Just because your man pissed about doesn't make you patron saint of married women, although I suppose the fact he had plenty of money and a big house didn't have anything to do with you taking him back. Anyway, you can stick your friendship, if you can call it that.' And with that, Michelle flounced to the kitchen door and slammed it behind her.

Lou replayed Michelle's parting speech to herself – a strangely objective operation for someone as emotional as her. When she had fully processed it, she concluded that these weren't the words of someone upset by a few home truths, they were the tip of a surprisingly deep resentment and jealousy that had no place in friendship. Her whole relationship with Michelle passed before her eyes: the honeymoon weeks, where they laughed and conversed and bonded, and after that all the self-pity and slammed-down phones, false judgements, recriminations and long, boring conversations in which Michelle starred as the tragic misunderstood heroine. Lou realized then that she had been waiting for the 'real Michelle' of the first few weeks to come out to play again – but the 'real Michelle' was the one who had just exited her house. The first Michelle had been the illusion, and Lou had merely been one of those temporary 'friends' who happened to have a little more patience than the others.

Lou allowed herself to savour these thoughts, standing there leaning on the radiator with her eyes closed.

Whatever she had with Michelle was not friendship in the Deb sense of the word, but it didn't matter now. When Michelle slammed that door, it had locked behind her. The relief, for Lou, was almost tangible.

Chapter 44

To Lou's horror and delight it was Mr Clarke who received them into his inner sanctum on the following Tuesday, the same business manager who had interviewed them for their first attempt at *Casa Nostra*. Lou took as much care now as she did then in presenting their financial case to him, dropping the proposals off beforehand so he had a chance to go through them. This time, they had some capital so didn't need to borrow as much as before. Deb had savings and Lou, unbeknown to Phil, had a nest egg tucked away too. She'd started squirrelling funds away for the *Casa Nostra* project years ago and, though it fell through, she'd never stopped adding to the account. After Phil's affair, it became a security blanket – just in case history repeated itself and she found herself needing a new place to live. She'd actually felt deceitful in keeping it secret from him. Something, however, had always stopped her from telling him about her private stash and she was glad of that now.

Mr Clarke gave a nervous laugh as he recalled Lou leaping over the desk to kiss him when he had agreed to the bank lending them the money to finance their project three years ago.

'I hope you're going to stay in control this time when I deliver the good news,' Mr Clarke said.

'*When* – not *if*?' said Lou, hardly daring to breathe.

'You're giving us the money?' said Deb.

And as he nodded, Lou leashed in the desire to let history repeat itself and settled for a vigorous handshake instead.

Mr Clarke had to admit to being somewhat disappointed.

The next stop was the solicitors to sign the lease and then Deb ran off to work, leaving Lou to pay Tom a cheque and start the fun business of ordering equipment.

This was it. Debra Devine and Lou Winter were in business.

'Tom, I can't pay you the rent,' said Lou, with the chequebook held limply in her hand.

Tom came round to her side of the table, already loosening his belt.

'Then I'll have to exact what you owe in other ways. Get on the bed, Elouise, and take all your clothes off . . .'

There was a loud knock on the flat door which shook Lou out of her daydream and almost gave her a heart-attack. Tom walked in to find her quite red-faced.

'I've just seen you come up. Wow, you look hot!' he said.

Had he really said that or was she still dreaming?

'Are you all right? Shall I open a window for you?' he went on. *Oh, that sort of hot. Stupid woman.*

Lou put her hands over her cheeks. 'Oh, er, just excited,' she said. *You can say that again*, echoed her ovaries. 'We've just been to the bank — we got the finance!'

'Fantastic!' Tom beamed. 'We'll have to celebrate.'

'We signed the lease and I just came back to write you a cheque for the rent.'

'Lord, there's no rush for that,' said Tom.

He seemed to have substituted his grinning thing for that intense caring look that a parent gives to a small child on his first day at school. His grey eyes were soft and intently trained on her face.

'What's the matter?' said Lou. Had she smudged her make-up? Did she have something green and leafy in her teeth?

'No, there's nothing,' said Tom, giving himself a mental kick up the backside. 'I was, er, just thinking that maybe you could both pop around to the house and we'll crack open a bottle of champagne.' That invitation was as much a surprise to Tom as it was to Lou. He hadn't been thinking anything of the sort, not consciously anyway.

'That sounds nice,' said Lou.

'Good. Right, well, I'm a boring bloke with no social life, so you pick any evening and come round and I'll cook something. Italian?'

'Wow, super nice,' said Lou. 'We're pretty boring too, so I think any night will be good for us as well.'

'Tomorrow then?' said Tom.

'Fine by me. I'm sure it's clear for Deb too.' She knew it was because they had arranged to go to the pictures, but this seemed a much more unmissable event.

'OK,' said Tom quickly. He needed to get away and stand in front of a mirror and practise how to look at nice people whose husbands, he knew, were having an affair.

Phil was virtually beating Sue Shoesmith off with a stick. It was all very nice to be so sexually desired but he didn't really want to have an affair again – and affairs, to him, were anything more than snogging. The last time had been a big mistake. Susan Peach was a sleazy barmaid who paid him some attention when Lou was neglecting him for her stupid café idea. He had never meant to let it get that far. He was flattered, and the idea of going out for an innocent meal with someone who looked at him with such adoring eyes wasn't doing Lou any harm when she didn't know about it. However, when Susan had unzipped his trousers under the dining table and started *doing things*, there was no way he was going to stop her. After that, he figured he might as well be hung for a sheep as a lamb, and as Lou was virtually ignoring him, he had the perfect excuse for his behaviour, should he need to explain himself. Anyway, he doubted it would ever come to that, seeing as he hadn't been found out the other two times he'd done the dirty behind his wife's back. So wasn't it just bad luck that in the grotty, back-of-beyond place he had picked to take Susan Peach for a meal and a grope, there was her best friend Deb with a group of her cronies. It was very hard to pass it off as a harmless drink in a quiet corner with a business associate, when his tongue was trying to tie knots in Susan's tonsils and her fingers were wriggling about in his flies.

He had expected Deb to call into the office and rant and rave at him. What he didn't expect in a million years was for her to go marching round to Lou to tell her everything. He didn't like to recall Lou's face that day when he walked in from work. She looked as though she'd had all her stuffing taken out. It had been far easier to pack a bag and run away than sit there amongst all that devastation.

He was in the wrong — what more was there to say? What good would analyzing it all have done either of them? *Hit and run.*

He went round to Susan's place and she took all the immediate guilt and pressure away from him with some very energetic sex, but three weeks later, her tiny dank flat, a constant stream of Australian soaps on the TV, a diet of takeaways, oven chips and Walls Balls and constant references to the divorce proceedings she presumed he was now going to initiate, were driving him stark staring mental.

In the end, Phil had gritted his teeth and turned up at the house, hoping that Lou would be so upset at the prospect of spending Christmas alone that she would let him in to talk. He wasn't looking forward to all those questions and tears, but if it got him home again without too much muck-racking he reckoned it would be worth it. He had a suitcase full of dirty clothes and a bag of prepared excuses about why he had left her, which amazingly he had never had to use. She just pulled him back into the house and never mentioned it. If he'd known how easy it was going to be, he'd have been back a fortnight sooner.

Now he just wanted life to return to how it was before all that stupid skip business starting kicking off. No Deb on the scene, no talk about stupid cafés and businesses and less of Lou's lip – then they could get back to being happy again. He would do whatever it took to achieve that. Lou would thank him in the long run, when their marriage was better than ever.

He texted a suitable reply to Sue's steamy request to do various things to her with strawberries. There was no harm in it – they were just words that he didn't have any intention of backing up with actions. His resolve was firm. He wanted to live his life with the Lou who gave him sex on Sunday mornings and cooked him lamb dinners. He was happy with her.

Lou was very much on Deb's mind too. She had never got over the feeling that she could have tackled it so differently last time. She could have confronted *him* rather than lay everything on her friend. So what about this time – what could she do?

Despite promising Tom that she wouldn't interfere, and despite promising herself the same thing, she waved goodbye to Lou outside the solicitor's office and set off in the opposite direction from the bakery, towards the industrial estate where *P.M. Autos* was situated.

She parked around the corner, took a deep breath and marched into the showroom, straight past Bradley, with his oily welcoming smile that dropped like a brick when he saw that she was about to barge into Phil's office.

'Oy, missus, you can't go in there,' he called, in lumpy pursuit behind her.

'It's all right, Bradley,' said Phil with a calm smile. 'I'll deal with this lady.' He imbued the word 'lady' with all the qualities of 'trouble-making cow'.

'How can I help you, Debra? Coffee?' said Phil, coolly

pouring one for himself from his percolator. He had nothing to fear from his visitor.

'Of course I don't want a coffee and I think you know why I'm here,' snarled Deb.

Phil opened his hands in a gesture of supplication. 'I haven't the foggiest idea why you're here, Debra. I presume it's not to catch up on old times.'

'*Maltstone Arms*, weekend before last, you and a bimbo eating each other alive – *that's* why I'm here. I know you saw me, so let's cut the crap. Didn't you learn anything from last time? How much more shit are you going to put your wife through, eh?'

'What has my life got to do with you, Debra?'

He's calm, thought Deb. Too calm.

'Finish it, Phil, or . . .'

Phil's eyes rounded. 'Or?' he urged.

He wasn't smiling, was he? Deb looked at his twinkling blue eyes. Her brain did a few quick machinations and came up with a ridiculous but oddly plausible explanation. *It couldn't be possible. He wasn't that sick, was he?*

'My God, you *want* me to tell her you're having a fling, don't you?'

Phil affected shock. 'That's ridiculous. I think you'd better go,' he said. 'But I will tell you that I'm not finishing my "friendship"' – and the emphasis he put on the word made it sound anything but innocent – 'with *Sue.*'

'You evil bastard!' said Deb. 'You even picked someone with the same name. Was that stage-managed?'

She didn't resist as he ushered her out of his office.

Could this have gone any better? Phil gloated. He knew Deb wasn't physically capable of keeping this sort of information to herself. Last time had proved that much.

Deb walked to her car in total astonishment. There was nothing she could do to stop Lou getting hurt – really hurt. She couldn't tell Lou – then again, she couldn't *not* tell her. She would just have to carry on as if everything was normal and hope that this time, their business venture was Lou's salvation when the big crash came.

Chapter 45

Lou spent an exciting Wednesday ordering more equipment and distributing the flyers that she had designed to some of May's regulars. They were invitations to the grand opening in eight weeks – 1 August. By a wonderful coincidence, that was also Yorkshire Day.

May was closing up at the end of that week and the builders were coming at seven on Monday morning. And at number 1, The Faringdales, Keith Featherstone would have finished the bathroom by the time she got home. His men were presently grouting the wall tiles. They seemed decent enough guys. Lou felt slightly guilty that they still thought they were in the running for the café business, but she quickly overcame it. It was the builder's own fault that he hadn't got the contract, after all – not hers.

And since her dramatic exit from Lou's house, Michelle had bombarded Lou with text messages and phone calls, the full spectrum from whining to suicidal, from pleading to bitter. Lou deleted them without reading or hearing them and Tippexed her out of her diary. Michelle was out of her life.

*

Lou picked up Deb from the bakery to go to Tom's house. Mrs Serafinska had a lovely cottage next door to it and had let Deb wash and brush up in her bathroom rather than have to drive home and all the way back.

'You look nice,' said Lou. Deb had on a navy-blue dress and a matching long jacket, and wore impossibly high stilettos that she walked on with the same ease as Lou did in flats.

'You don't look so bad yourself,' said Deb, giving her a longer than usual hello hug. 'And you're getting even thinner.'

'Give over!'

Lou was wearing a lilac shirt and a complementing violet jacket which picked out the Irish-green of her eyes. And she *had* lost more weight recently. It wasn't just a physical thing, though, that she appeared lighter. It was as if she had been given a transfusion of helium and could float into the air at any minute. Deb didn't want to be around to see her plummet to the ground when the news about Phil's latest affair punctured her spirit. *God, what a mess*. Deb rallied herself.

'I'm going to make you a Brando, that'll fatten you up,' she said.

'Oh, so you've created it!'

'Nearly. I think I know where I'm going with it.'

'What's it going to be made out of?' asked Lou excitedly.

'Wait and see, my darling, wait and see . . .'

They pulled into Tom's drive in Lou's car. The lights were on in the house, glowing softly behind half-open blinds. It looked extremely cosy for a large house.

'We should have got a taxi,' said Deb, suddenly realizing that Lou couldn't drink much as she insisted on driving.

'It's OK,' said Lou. 'Remember, I'm supposed to be at the pictures watching Orlando Bloom. Turning up home drunk in a taxi might blow my cover story slightly.'

Tom greeted them at the door, in very nice jeans, a beautiful soft blue shirt and a loosely knotted tie that was lopsided. His hair was tousled and his face looked harassed.

'I can't believe I'm doing this,' he said. 'I've invited two professional cooks for dinner and I can barely boil an egg. How stupid am I? Let me take your coats.'

Clooney was trying to get to Lou, wrestling his canine excitement at seeing the biscuit woman against his recent training that forbade him to jump up. He settled for lots of tail-wagging and happy whining instead.

'Clooney, get out of the way,' laughed Tom. He was all fingers and thumbs, first dropping Deb's coat, then Lou's. Deb took control, telling him to bugger off back to what he was doing while she hung the coats over the ball on the staircase newel post. Clooney retired to his basket in the hallway with his teddy bear and shoe-shaped chew for now.

The ladies followed Tom into a very nice farmhouse kitchen with a big chunky wooden table in the middle. It had a recipe book open on it. Tom had put on an apron with the lettering emblazoned across the middle: *Abandon hope all ye who I enter.*

'Like the apron. Very saucy,' said Deb, with a wink.

'Oh, go away!' he said. 'You aren't supposed to see it.

And you aren't supposed to be in here either. I'm nervous enough as it is.'

'Is it one of May's?' Deb teased as he pushed them out of the kitchen.

'Yes. Now go in there and open some wine. The bottle is in there and so is the corkscrew.'

Lou and Deb went into the dining room, still holding the bottles of wine they had brought with them. There was a CD playing soft rock music and wall lights gave the room a gentle and friendly glow. Three place-settings had been laid at one end of the grand table. There were fresh flowers in the middle and bread-sticks – and the biggest pepper-mill Deb had ever seen. She lifted her eyebrows suggestively at Lou, whose laughter pealed through to Tom in the kitchen. He smiled in response. He bet it was something to do with his pepper-grinder.

'OK, ladies,' he said, coming into the room soon after with a huge bowl of pasta and a large garlic and tomato pizza bread. 'Please be seated.'

Lou and Deb sat opposite each other and left him at the head of the table.

'I never asked if you were vegetarian or liked seafood or anything, so I hope this is going to be all right,' said Tom. 'I kind of played safe.'

'I don't think there's anything I don't like,' said Deb. 'Ooh, whitebait,' she remembered. 'How can anyone eat whitebait?'

'What about you, Lou?' said Tom, breaking off some bread.

'Lamb,' said Lou, not needing to even think about that. 'I hate lamb.'

'Ugh, me too,' said Tom, shaking his head. 'Never have liked it. School-dinner lamb – I could retch thinking about it. Agnes Street Infants . . .' He shuddered at the memory and didn't continue.

'Exactly,' said Lou, with a smile of absolute concurrence. 'Lots of fat and mint sauce.'

'Offal as well,' said Tom. 'Brains and hearts. My Uncle Tommy loved them. I remember seeing them once boiling up in the pan, bobbing about . . .'

'Will you two shut up,' said Deb through a mouthful of breadstick. 'You're putting me off.'

'Sorry,' said Tom. 'Well, let's talk about you two making loads of money instead, although you can do that quite happily by yourself,' and he turned to Lou with his smiley grey eyes.

'What's this then?' asked Deb with sudden interest.

'Tom's got this idea that I make counterfeit money,' Lou told her, in mock exasperation.

'Well, feel free to print me a few fifties, Lou. Ooh – and talking of making money,' said Deb, reaching over for her bag, 'before I forget – here, this is for you,' and she handed Lou a telephone number on a Post-it note.

'Mrs Serafinska's number,' she explained. 'We were talking about you and your clutter-clearing. She'd like you to help her.'

'Help? In what way?'

'Clearing some clutter, perhaps?' Tom suggested with gentle sarcasm. 'It's only a guess, mind.'

Deb punished him with a good-humoured glare. 'I'm being serious. Lou, she's been widowed for over three years now and never cleared out Bernie's stuff.

She happened to say she wished she had professional help. *I* happened to say that I knew a professional who could help.'

Lou nearly spat out her wine. 'I'm not a professional!'

'Four days at one hundred and fifty quid a day says you are.'

Tom nearly spat out *his* wine.

'Come on, Lou,' Deb said. 'These professional-clutter clearers charge over a grand and a half just for a consultation. Take her through the same process you did.'

'Deb, I don't know . . .' Lou's brow was creased in doubt.

'She's a lovely woman. She's determined to get some help and she's prepared to pay. If you don't want the job, she'll go to someone who probably hasn't got half the experience you have for twice the price. Pleeease!'

Lou considered it. What harm would it do? And if Mrs Serafinska wasn't happy, then Lou wouldn't charge her.

'OK, I'll give her a ring. It might be fun to clear some stuff again – I've really missed doing it.'

'Hey, you can use my skips,' said Tom. 'But I'll take a cheque this time. That last batch of Queens had pierced noses.'

And they laughed and ate pasta and sweetcorn and asparagus and peppers and mushrooms and garlic bread and washed it down with nice crisp Chablis and grape juice for Lou. Then Tom popped open the champagne and they raised a glass to their culinary venture. And then they ate something sloppy which Tom said should have been a baked Alaska, except the ice cream had all melted. The meringue, however, had an interesting crunchy toffee taste, which seemed to perfectly complement the coffees and minty chocolates that followed.

'It was crap, wasn't it?' said Tom, as Lou helped him clear the plates.

'No, it was lovely, Tom,' said Lou, meaning it. This evening wasn't just about the food, it meant so much more. Her eyes were sparkling like the champagne in the glasses as she stared at Tom's big, wide back as he bent down at the dishwasher. No man had ever cooked her a meal before. Actually, no man had ever made her a cup of coffee before either. And no man had ever made her feel like this. (Except possibly Starsky — she'd had one mighty crush on him years ago.) Her head was full of ridiculous, wonderful feelings that were zapping and fizzing around inside her. They were the bolts of electricity she had dreamed of having for a man, whilst she was reading her *Jackie* magazine. She'd never had them though, not even for Phil, and had put them down to love-folklore until now. Yes, she had fallen in love with Phil, in a comfortable, coupley way, but her heart had never sparked like a night full of fireworks sending reverberations down to her toes just because she was near him, like it was doing now because she was near to Tom Broom and his blue shirt.

He straightened up. God, he was so big. God, he was so close.

'Here, let me have those,' he said, his large square hands reaching out for the plates. She passed them over carefully, taking great care not to accidentally touch him nor daring to look up at him, because if she did, he would have seen everything in her eyes she wished she were free to say.

Deb came into the kitchen.

'Hey, great loo, Tom. Huge bath, but I suppose you need one.'

'Are you trying to say I've got a big bottom?' joked Tom.

'Well, you've got a big everything else,' Lou joked, then realized what she'd said. Oh crap – that came out all wrong!

Tom raised his eyebrows and folded his arms. 'Oh, is that so? And how would you know that?'

'I meant big house, big . . . dog, big . . . car, big . . . hands . . . er, house.'

Double crap. She didn't mean to say hands either.

Tom didn't move, just continued to stare at her with amused annoyance.

Deb, who had taken care to have just enough wine to relax her, but not enough to say anything she shouldn't, was bent double in the corner with laughter.

'Oh, get stuffed the pair of you,' said Lou, turning away and noticing as she did so the time on the kitchen clock. It was later than she expected. Phil would be hopping about in the kitchen wondering why his dinner wasn't making itself.

'Oh damn, we'd better go,' she said, like Cinderella at the ball, but willing to risk the wrath of magic for a few more moments in a Prince's company.

Deb went into the hall and retrieved their coats. Tom helped Deb on with hers. Lou got into hers before he could offer.

'Tom, it was wonderful, thank you.' Deb threw her

arms around him, giving him a great big tipsy kiss and a tight hug.

'Thanks, Tom,' said Lou quietly but with a warm smile. 'It was nice. Really nice.'

He bent and kissed her cheek, but this time, as his lips left her, his arms enfolded her in an unexpected and tight squeeze. His scent filled her nostrils, the washing powder his shirt had been washed in, the lasting note of some musky violety after-shave, his skin . . . She staggered backwards when he let her go. Her brain was mush and in danger of seeping out of her ears. God knows what state she'd be in if he ever bonked her. Not that she'd ever find out.

Deb hugged her goodnight as the car pulled up at her 'bijou' flat, as the estate agent had described it — 'poky' as everyone else did.

'You smell of Tom,' said Deb.

'Are you sure you two don't fancy each other?' said Lou.

'Lou, I love you to death but you can be so thick at times,' said Deb, blowing her a half-drunken kiss.

Phil was tucking into beef chow mein, fried rice and prawn won tons on a tray and watching a football match on the monster TV in the lounge.

'I had to send out for this,' he said, pointing down at it.

'I told you I was going to the pictures,' said Lou.

'I didn't expect you to be this late,' said Phil, looking purposefully at the clock.

'Phil, it's half-past nine. Even Cinderella got two and a half hours more parole than this.'

He stabbed up the volume on the remote control to a childish degree.

The magical night out was over. Cinderella was back to the same old routine.

Chapter 46

'The machine appears to have a chest infection today,' said Karen, putting two pre-work cappuccinos down on the canteen table, each with a frothy head that would have put Don King's hairdo to shame.

'How on earth are we supposed to drink those?' said Lou.

'I think we have to wait until they die,' said Karen, pulling an envelope out of her bag. 'Guess what this is?'

'An envelope,' said Lou after considerable scrutiny. 'I have been wrong in the past about these things, though, so please feel free to correct me. Stationery was never my strong subject at school.'

'It's my notice,' said Karen.

Lou's mouth opened goldfish-wide to say something, but nothing came out.

'I know you're going to hand in yours soon – and I can't work without you,' Karen went on. 'I'd go mad.'

'But—'

'Listen to the rest,' said Karen, holding up a shushing hand. 'I've been thinking hard recently. I love this accounts course. It's put everything else in the shade. So, I'm giving up the flat, moving back in with Mum and

Dad on the farm so I've got twenty-four-seven child cover, and I'm going to college fulltime, starting as soon as they'll let me go. This is all your fault, Lou Winter. You'll have to make it up to me by buying my family's bacon or I'll be out on the streets with two starving children.'

'Crikey, you have been busy!' said Lou with a warm smile. 'My business partner's ringing your dad today to set up a meeting, and I am absolutely thrilled you're going for this all the way.' She gave the tall young woman a big squashy hug.

'It really wouldn't be the same without you here, Lou,' said Karen, a little sadly. 'Plus Stan will be gone by this time next year, Zoe's got an interview for another job and I'm just sick of coming in and the first sight I see is that mouth full of scrap metal.'

'Yes, I know,' said Lou understandingly, attempting the coffee and getting a noseful of bubbles and a handlebar moustache.

'You look very sparkly today, by the way,' said Karen, scrutinizing Lou. *Were you with your mystery man last night?*

'Do I?' said Lou. She had felt quite sparkly during the night after a very nice dream about her very nice evening. She hoped Karen wasn't a mindreader.

'I'm pretty sparkly too,' said Karen. 'Charlie and I aren't "just friends" any more. He's taking me to Paris when I finish here.' Coincidentally, her smile was as wide as the English Channel.

'Oh Karen, that's lovely,' said Lou with genuine delight. 'I just hope he makes you happy.'

'So far so good. I wish you could find someone nice,

Lou. Someone who made you feel like I do at this moment in time.' She looked at Lou with real tenderness.

'What on earth makes you think I'm not happy?' Lou asked, with a defensive little smile.

'Oh Lou,' was all Karen said by way of a reply. She stood up then and squeezed Lou's shoulder. 'Come on, let's get up to the flames of hell before Jaws sends her four horsemen down to fetch us.'

Zoe was waiting for them just outside the office door. She was all dressed up in a trendy blue top and a black skirt.

'I've got an interview at lunchtime,' she whispered. 'It's at a firm of solicitors round the corner. Stacks more money than here, too. I am dead excited.'

'Good for you, darling,' said Lou. 'You look lovely.'

'Hope so. This outfit cost loads. I just hope I can keep it clean until twelve. No coffee for me today – I'm taking no risks!'

The clock said that it was one minute to nine. Nicola gave them all a satanic glare at cutting it so fine. She knew they had done that to annoy her, so prepared to annoy them back. She stamped on Zoe's buoyant mood by telling her to add some toner to all the machines on the floor. Just about the messiest job she could saddle her with.

'But that's not my job!' cried Zoe with dismay. 'And I've got my new top on.'

'Isn't your appraisal happening soon?' said Nicola, impervious to the girl's watery eyes. The implication in her words was crystal clear.

Zoe slumped off to the stationery cupboard just as Stan bounded in at nine minutes past nine, so Nicola had someone else to vent her spleen on. He had barely got his coat off when she silently stalked towards him.

'Can I have a word, Stanley, please? In the glass bubble.'

Stan humbly followed her to the said meeting room where the walls were Perspex. There were no chairs in the bubble, just a table at standing height. It was a room intended for short meetings so that people wouldn't get too comfortable and nod off. Lou noticed how stooped Stan's shoulders were. He had always been so smart and straight-backed until Nicola's regime began. It wasn't right that she could strip away a man's dignity like that, Lou thought, as she observed Nicola's destructive persecution of him through narrowed eyes. She watched Stan plead an obvious case in vain as he wiped sweat from his beetroot face with his white handkerchief. It looked like a flag of surrender.

'I've got toner on my jumper,' said a quietly horrified Zoe, with tears flooding down her face – and at that moment, with Zoe's crying and Stan's sweating, something within Lou boiled up and over like milk in a pan.

When did I become the sort of person that doesn't make a stand? said Lou suddenly to herself. *When did I start watching the little guys get hurt and turn the other way?* For years now she had been increasingly pushed further back into the corner by various personalities, discouraged from making a fuss about anything that didn't sit quite right with her, cowed into accepting order imposed by other people. *And when did I stop protecting myself?* Shirley Hamster would have wiped the floor with Lou Winter.

She wasn't her father's daughter any more. Well, maybe it was time to be Shaun Casserly's girl again.

'I've had just about enough of this,' Lou said, striding out with purpose – like the young Lou Casserly did when she was going to sort Shirley Hamster at playtime. OK, maybe life had progressed a little from decking someone to sort things out, but there were other ways of opposing authority.

'Lou, where are you going?' called Karen.

'Somewhere I should have gone ages ago,' she threw over her shoulder.

As luck would have it, the Head of Human Resources, Bob Bowman, was looking down at a black sticky mess in a plastic cup which the Executive Floor's coffee-machine had just delivered to him.

'Mr Bowman, can I have a word,' said Lou confidently.

'Official or unofficial?' he said, immediately recognizing her as 'Little' in Accounts.

'Both,' she returned.

He checked his watch. 'Yes, I've got ten minutes now if you have. Coffee?'

'Not for me, thanks,' said Lou, following him into his office.

Bob Bowman threw himself into his big plush leather seat and invited Lou to sit at the other side of his desk.

'So what can I do for you . . . Lou, isn't it?'

'Lou Winter, yes,' she said. 'Well . . .' She took a big breath and blurted out: 'It's about the Accounts department. Something needs to be done about the management there. Zoe has to fill up the machines with toner and has ruined her new jumper, Stan is at the end of his tether about his buses, Karen's leaving . . .'

Lou's voice trailed off as she watched a glaze come over Bob Bowman's eyes. She couldn't blame him – a grand rhetorical speech this was not. Lou sighed and rubbed her forehead.

'I'm sorry, Mr Bowman, this must all sound very petty to you, but I'm a bit too old to stand by and watch people I like and admire be bullied like this on a daily basis without taking some sort of stand. You think when you leave school that you'll never encounter bullying again in life, but in the workplace a bully causes as much, if not more, misery.'

Bob Bowman pricked up his ears at the repeated use of the word 'bully', for it was a word he was particularly sensitive to at the moment. It had always had mild and childish connotations for him, until he saw first-hand the torment and the misery his granddaughter Natalie had recently endured at school. He sat forward in his seat.

'Go on,' he said. 'Start from the beginning. What's the problem?'

'It's Jaws – er – Nicola Pawson – *that's* the problem. Our office junior is half-terrified to come into work. She's presently filling machines up with toner and has just ruined her clothes.'

'That's the technician's job, not hers, surely?' said Bob Bowman, pulling his neck back in mild disbelief.

'Yes, you're right, but when you're threatened with a bad appraisal for not doing it, you do it, don't you? Or at least that's how it works in our department. Did you know that my fellow accounts clerk, Karen Harwood–

Court, will today be handing in her notice because no one here's done anything to advance her career? Roger Knutsford sends work down to her because she's far more competent than his own team on twice the salary, although no one has actually ever acknowledged this fact publicly. So she is going on somewhere that *has* recognized her abilities and *will* capitalize on them. And don't get me started on all the people who have come and quickly gone or been off with stress. I wonder sometimes if our department is invisible to the rest of the company.'

Bob Bowman was following her every word now. He stiffened at the name Roger Knutsford. He was part of the breed of industry executive 'King-Bees', like Piers Winstanley-Black and Laurence Stewart-Smith, who got all the kudos because they had an army of little people propping them up, covering for their mistakes, wiping their backsides. That lot couldn't fart without an assistant helping them out. It wouldn't be the first time he had had to sort out one of Knutsford's messes where he had recruited entirely unsuitable people. Amazingly enough, he never seemed to set on anyone who wasn't female, attractive and available.

'Then I come to Stan. You know Stan, of course.' Lou took a deep breath. She had to get this part right for Stan.

'Stan Mirfield? Yes, I know Stan. He's been here how long now?' Bob Bowman tried to work it out.

'One hundred and fifty years,' said Lou with a straight face.

Bob Bowman smiled. 'Yes, it must feel like that to him.'

'You know what a good worker he is, Mr Bowman.'

'He'll be retiring soon, won't he?'

'Less than a year,' said Lou. 'If he makes it.'

'Why on earth shouldn't he?' said Bob Bowman. 'He's not unwell, is he?'

'He lives in the country, he doesn't drive and his bus timetable was changed – so to get in at nine o'clock on the dot he has to run like a maniac. If he doesn't die of a heart-attack then Jaws – Nicola – will kill him with stress. It's not only ridiculous, it's bordering on sadistic, the way she treats him.'

'What time does he get in?' said Bob Bowman.

'I don't think he's ever been later than quarter past.'

'But every department has a flexi-time option. He could come in any time from eight until ten. Why isn't it exercised?'

'Jaws . . .' *poop* . . . 'Nicola says she has had a word with you and you denied him the right to flexi-time.'

'I certainly did not!' Bob Bowman was outraged. *Ooh – big mistake.*

'Stan puts more time in than any of us. He works through his lunch-hour, he stays late and yet that doesn't count, apparently.' Lou could feel her temper rising inside her. 'These are good people being tyrannized by a woman who has created a climate of misery and fear, and they can do nothing but leave or turn up for their daily humiliation. Oh, she's very clever – has her bullying down to a fine art so that no one dare complain without making themselves look ridiculous. Hasn't anyone ever looked at the staff turnover in any department Nicola Pawson has worked in? I tell you, it's like living in a George Orwell novel!'

Bob Bowman was still gnawing on being held to blame for such inflexibility, especially as he had fought tooth and nail to bring in flexi-time to attract back the good people that incompetent idiots like Roger Knutsford had driven away. Bob Bowman prided himself on *being* Mr Flexible, for God's sake.

He flicked on his intercom and spoke to his PA.

'Fiona, ask Stan Mirfield to come down here at ten-thirty, please. Then get Nicola Pawson here at eleven.'

Lou had a momentary panic. 'Please, Mr Bowman, Stan won't want to stir up any trouble. His life in the office is miserable enough as it is. Jaws will make it hell for him. I didn't come here to contribute to his stress levels.'

'No, she won't,' said Bob Bowman firmly. Stan Mirfield had slipped under his radar for some recent early-retirement packages he had created. Bob was going to make that up to him and more in the next hour, and clear it with the board later before they had an uprising.

'I know I risk being labelled an insurgent,' Lou said, not realizing she even knew the word and hoping, with her track record for making the English language 'her own', that she'd got it right. 'I also know there isn't such a thing as an "off-the-record" chat with HR, so I'm putting all my cards on the table to you, and then I'm leaving too. Now. Today. I've had enough.'

It was an impulsive decision but it felt right.

'There won't be any need for that,' said Bob Bowman softly.

'I don't want to work here any more, Mr Bowman,'

said Lou. 'I thank you for the wages you've paid me over the years but I don't want to be in a company any more that promotes bullies and tyrants and totally ignores the people who could really make a difference in a positive way.'

Bob Bowman nodded. 'I'll make sure there are changes. But I won't accept this as your notice. Please take some time to think . . .'

'No, I've made up my mind,' said Lou adamantly. In her mind, Nicola and her career in accounts had just been thrown in the skip and Tom was about to tow it far, far away to the landfill site at the other side of Leeds, and it would be the biggest relief to see it go.

Bob Bowman considered her determined little face. Blasted Roger Knutsford again! He'd be the first to dance on that man's professional grave when his reign ended. And he'd do his own investigations on this Jaws . . . er, Nicola Pawson . . . woman – discreetly, of course. He hadn't had a lot to do with her but on the few occasions their paths had crossed he'd always found something a little 'off' about her.

'I'll make sure you aren't penalized for leaving without notice,' Bob Bowman said. He held out his hand to her and she shook it. 'But we could really do with people like you in this firm, Lou. Please think again.'

'You've got plenty of people like me in this firm already, Mr Bowman,' said Lou. 'Lots of good, hard-working people who deserve better.'

All eyes were on her as she strode into the office. Nicola slid straight over, smiling like a crocodile with a mantrap hidden in its mouth.

'A word in the bubble with you now please, if you don't mind.'

'No,' said Lou, and walked past her to Zoe. She gave her a tight hug and said in her ear, 'Make a joke about the jumper in your interview and they will love you. Good luck, love.'

Then Lou gave Stan a big hug and said secretly, 'Have a wonderful holiday and a wonderful retirement, and don't let the bastards grind you down.'

She gave an astounded Karen the biggest cuddle of all and said, 'It's been totally rubbish working with you. Go knock 'em dead, kid, and I'll see you soon about your dad's sausages.'

Then Lou Winter grabbed her coat and her bag and faced Nicola with eyes that glittered like chips of green ice. There was nothing behind those eyes for Nicola – no liking, no loathing, nothing. They barely acknowledged Nicola's nickel-gobbed existence – and that was the ultimate torment for the younger woman. She squared up to parry verbally with whatever Lou might say on her exit. Something beautifully bitchy, no doubt. Something – *anything* – that would bring them to confrontation point at long last. But Lou Winter said nothing. She merely walked out of the office with her head held at a dignified angle, uncrushed, undefeated – mistress of the unspoken word.

People in the whole building talked about it for months, long after Stan Mirfield left with a fantastically generous retirement package. What could 'Little' in Accounts possibly have done to have such a weird effect on Rogering Roger's bit? Office legend had it that Nicola turned into a sort of rabid combine-harvester and had to be restrained and tranquillized with WD40. And why was she moved so quickly over to a permanent place – in Operations Manchester?

Chapter 47

Fillet steak with all the trimmings, thought Phil with suspicion as Lou delivered his tea to the table. He didn't have to wait long to learn why a king's supper had been served up to him.

'I packed in my job today,' Lou said, just after he had taken his first mouthful.

He stared at her as if she had just escaped from a secure mental hospital and repeated her own words back to her flatly. 'You packed in your job.'

'Yes, with immediate effect,' she said.

'With immediate effect?' he echoed.

She was tempted to say that long place name in Wales to see if he repeated that too. That's how she used to treat Shirley Hamster when she tried to play the 'let's annoy Lou and repeat everything she says' game. '*Llanfairpwllgwyngyllgogerychwyrndrobwllllantysiliogogogoch.*' That never failed to shut her up.

'Now why would you do that?' asked Phil with calm annoyance. It wasn't that they needed the money from her job but it was another uncharacteristic display from this new Lou and, as such, it needed further investigation.

'Because I hated working there, that's why,' she said.

'And what are you going to live on now?'

That rankled her so she retaliated. 'I'll start charging you for your accounts work. If I put a bill in for all the back work, I could probably buy Microsoft.'

Phil needed this like a hole in the head, especially today. There had been a letter delivered in that morning's post from Sharon. The twins were going to be thirteen in a couple of weeks. They were getting expensive, she said, so she thought an extra payment of five hundred pounds on their birthdays and Christmas from now on wouldn't be unreasonable. Not each though, she added – which Phil thought was very fucking big of her! He'd spent ten minutes on the calculator working out how much extra that added to the overall bill. Then he came home to find that Lou wanted to parasite off him as well.

'The café will be up and running in eight weeks anyway, so I'm sure I'll have lots to do.'

Phil stopped chewing his meat, dropped his cutlery and rotated his finger in the air.

'Whoa, rewind – *café*? What do you mean, *café*?'

'What do you mean "what do you mean, *café*?". *My* café!' said Lou, totally bemused. 'I told you I was going into business with Deb.'

'Talk sense, Lou,' said Phil, laughing mirthlessly. 'You haven't got any money, you haven't got anywhere to put it—'

'Yes, we have. We've got finance and property and we open in August, all being well.'

Phil couldn't quite believe his ears. 'Hang on, when did all this happen?' he demanded.

'It's been happening since I first told you about it,' said Lou.

'You've done it all behind my back?'

'I have not!' said Lou indignantly. 'I did tell you. And if you remember, all you did was tell me that I obviously wasn't clever enough to run my own business, so I didn't bother you with any further details.'

'I don't believe I'm hearing this.' Phil pushed his plate across the table in a tantrum and it knocked over the salt pot. He got up slowly as if coming out of a trance.

'You're nuts, you are, Lou. You need to see a doctor.' He tapped his temple hard with his finger. 'Loop the fucking loop.'

'Where are you going?' said Lou. If Phil had left a steak, he was seriously annoyed.

He didn't answer her. Just grabbed his car keys and his jacket and slammed the door behind him on the way out.

After she had tidied up the table, Lou took herself off to her new bath to try and relax her nerves, which were still jangling from her altercation with Phil. The experience of sinking into a pool of bubbles wasn't half as wonderful as she had been imagining over the past months; it felt rather ordinary, to her disappointment. Nevertheless, she took a glass of wine with her and the cordless phone and checked the messages that were flashing up on the handset. Firstly she heard Keith Featherstone's humble-pie voice asking her if she was happy with the work, and saying that he hoped she had found the cash refund he had left hon the work-surface in a brown henvelope. Then he lightly enquired if she had made up her mind about the *Casa Nostra* quotation for phase one.

The second message was from Michelle. She was pretending to cover up tears and in a very controlled voice told Lou that she was a heartless bitch and she hoped Lou would have a nice life and this was the last message she would ever leave. The third message was Michelle who said that Lou was never to call her again and she hoped that she didn't have a nice life and this was the last message she would ever leave. Lou deleted all three messages without a second thought, and then she called Deb.

'Hi,' said Deb. 'What sort of a day have you had then?'

'Ooh, you know, ordinary. Packed in my job, stalked by crazed ex-friend, Phil's stormed out somewhere because he thought I was joking about opening the café and now he knows I'm not, Keith Featherstone's hounding me about the first phase of *Casa Nostra Europe Inc* . . .'

'Ho, so nothing to chat about then,' laughed Deb. 'You sound echoey, where are you?'

'In my new Keith Featherstone bath,' said Lou.

'I hope he's not in there with you,' said Deb, wondering where Phil had gone. Or rather – *who* he had gone to.

'Nobody could be that desperate to win my business!'

'Put yourself down again and I'll come over there and drown you in that new bath of yours,' said Deb crossly.

'Anyway, how are *you*?' enquired Lou.

'I'm fine. Never mind about me, tell me about the job. How come you're not working your notice?'

Lou told her.

'Well, you know what you need to do now,' said Deb. 'Ring Mrs Serafinska. Get onto it straight away. She was asking me this morning if I'd given you her number. We could do with that money to buy my fancy pink American Smeg fridge.'

'OK, I will,' said Lou.

'She's retired, so she'll be able to fit in to suit you. She only pokes her head into the shop because she's bored. Oh, by the way, I have a great recipe for some big soft cookies. They'd be fantastic with homemade ice cream.'

'Yum,' said Lou, who made beautiful homemade ice cream.

'Ring her, please,' implored Deb, who loved Mrs Serafinska like a favourite aunt.

'I promise,' said Lou, and as soon as she put down the phone to Deb, she did indeed call Gladys Serafinska and made arrangements to see her the very next day.

Chapter 48

Phil wasn't speaking to her the next morning. She wasn't surprised by that, but what did shock the living daylights out of her was that when he did come home in the wee small hours, he hadn't done his usual sulky trick of slamming doors and banging things to announce his arrival. Instead, her ears traced his unusually quiet footfalls up the stairs and into the spare bedroom, where he slept. He had never, ever slept in the spare room before and that buzzed around in her head like a very annoying wasp, threatening to sting her at its leisure.

Lou arrived at the bakery, gurned at Deb through the window and knocked on the adjacent cottage door with the pretty window-boxes full of June geraniums. She had never seen Gladys Serafinska but always imagined her to be a tiny little wisp with a foreign accent, not the great battleship that came to the door and said in a gravelly South Yorkshire accent, 'Come in, lass, before the rain starts yet again. Apparently it's going to belt down. Summer, eh?'

It was a typical cottage, low ceilings, beams, shiny brasses and wall-to-wall chintz and ornaments – so many ornaments that it must have been a nightmare to dust.

Lou sat on a big plump sofa whilst Mrs Serafinska wheeled in a little trolley set with china cups, a teapot, and biscuits made in the bakery.

'Debra said you'd help me,' said Mrs Serafinska.

'Mrs Serafinska . . .'

'Call me Gladys, please. For years I've told Debra to call me that, but she never does. "Mrs Serafinska" always makes me sound like an old headmistress.'

She seems nervous, thought Lou, watching her hand pour out the tea none too steadily.

'Gladys,' Lou smiled. 'I'll help you all I can but I do warn you, it might be harder than you think to let stuff go, so rather than me tell you what to do, how about we do it together?'

'Oh, would you?' said Gladys with a big gasp. 'You know, it's the silliest thing, but I think I'm scared.'

'You'll be fine,' said Lou, who knew exactly what she meant.

So, after their tea, Lou followed Gladys to a big room upstairs, off the main bedroom, decorated in darker gentleman's colours. The wardrobes were walnut and the furniture masculine.

'This is Bernie's dressing room. I made a start . . .' She pointed to some suits laid out on the floor. 'Sorry,' she went on, and sniffed as her eyes started to gush.

'Come on,' said Lou, leading her out of the room. 'Let's start with a drawer in the kitchen.'

Two drawers and an understairs cupboard later, it was clear that they would need to order a skip. Gladys Serafinska could never have imagined just how much junk she was hoarding, but she was thoroughly enjoying herself, warming up to the big project by clearing out all the kitchen detritus. Lou rang Tom's mobile. She could have rung the *Tub* but this way she was sure of speaking to him and not one of the lads.

'Hello there, Trouble,' said Tom merrily.

If he'd called her 'Cowface' she thought his voice would have had the same effect on her knees.

'I need a skip at the back of *Serafinska's Bakery* in Maltstone,' said Lou.

'You go ahead then, I'm not stopping you. Have a hop and a jump for me whilst you're at it,' said Tom, laughing down the phone.

'Very funny, Mr Broom. Now, if you wouldn't mind . . .'

'What size, Mrs Winter?'

She didn't like him calling her Mrs Winter.

'I think a mini will do, please.'

'I haven't got anything until tomorrow morning. Is that OK?'

'Harrison's have got them,' said Lou naughtily.

'I shall come around there and spank you in a minute, young lady.'

Lou gasped, not sure if she was horrified or thrilled and then deciding she was both – in a highwayman-bodice-ripping way. She pictured Tom in a frilly romantic shirt, tricorn hat, his big thighs in breeches . . . Her cheeks were burning so much she could have bar-becued a chicken on them.

'That's OK then, bye,' she said extremely quickly and dropped down the phone. Her head was sparking with pictures that wouldn't have been out of place in a porn film.

'Cup of tea?' called Gladys, doing a double-take at the sight of her flushed face.

'Lovely,' said Lou.

'Do you take sugar?'

'No, thanks,' said Lou, *but fourteen teaspoons of bromide, please*, she added to herself.

Lou got stuck in the traffic heading towards a demonstration the next morning and missed the skip arriving.

'What a beautiful dog that man had,' said Gladys Serafinska. Damn, thought Lou. Tom had delivered it himself. Although maybe it was better that she didn't see him for a couple of days. Her imagination had nearly blown the top of her head clean off last night. Then again, she had plenty of time to think, what with Phil not coming home from work until ten. At least he had phoned to tell her he'd be late, albeit in a perfunctory way. But he hadn't wanted anything to eat and had hardly said a word to her when he came in; he slept in the spare room again, which unsettled her.

'What are these?' Lou asked, pulling a bag out of a cupboard.

'Oh, er, just things I keep,' said Gladys quietly.

Lou spilled them out onto the floor to find children's books, pencils and crayons – all unused.

'Grandchildren?' said Lou.

'Not yet,' said Gladys sadly. 'We thought there would be once but it wasn't to be. I bought them, just in case, you know.'

Lou gave her hand a squeeze. 'You do realize that every time you open this cupboard and see these, it reminds you of what you don't have?' she said, then:

'Let's put them in the charity pile. Then when you do get grandchildren, you can enjoy going out and buying some more.'

Gladys was about to put up a protest, but she pulled it back. Lou was remarkable – and she was right, of course. Why on earth hadn't she given them away before? Had she hoped the presence of those things might force the cosmos to give her what she wanted?

Gladys disliked ornaments, but she had an excuse why each one couldn't be given away. This one was a present from a friend, this one was a present from a different friend, this one cost a lot of money . . . Lou cut her off, holding up a particularly revolting porcelain hound with lips worthy of Angelina Jolie.

'Gladys, do you like this dog?'

'Not really.'

'Then which pile do we put it on, because we are not putting it back on that shelf.'

'OK, the car-boot one.'

Gladys had always fancied doing a car-boot sale. Every month they held one in the pensioners' club. She would never have dreamed she could part with enough items to fill up a whole stall herself.

The room looked so much lighter by the end of the third day and Gladys felt the same way. Lou was the best tonic she'd had in years. She'd told everyone she knew about her and hoped the young woman wouldn't mind that she'd passed her telephone number around her friends.

Chapter 49

Phil did something he rarely did that Sunday morning, namely check the messages on the home answering machine. It seemed it was the only way to find out what his so-called wife was up to these days. He stared in abject disbelief at the phone as a shaky old voice said, *'Hello, this is Mrs Alice Wilkinson. Would you please give me a ring back on this number as I am interested in a consultation?'*

What the hell else was Lou doing now? Plastic pissing surgery? Not only had he to make his own Sunday breakfast but the papers hadn't arrived either. Lazy swine of a paper boy. And there wasn't anything resembling a joint or a fowl in the fridge. Where had Lou said she was going? 'Out' was all she said on her way – *out!* Then again, she was probably annoyed that he was getting in later and later at night and sleeping in the spare room, but it hadn't had the effect on her that he had hoped for. She should have been wringing her hands with worry, falling over herself to seduce his attentions back to her, but – bold as brass – she appeared to be playing him at his own game. There wasn't even any evidence that she'd made him a meal last night to come in to. There were no pans on the hob, nothing in the microwave, the oven was cold and the bin was empty.

He didn't want to sleep with Sue Shoesmith, but it was looking like he might have to go that far to prove his point. And Lou would have only herself to blame if he did.

Lou savoured the last of her buttery toast.

'Your bakery makes some cracking bread, Gladys,' she said.

'Thank you,' beamed Gladys. 'We haven't gone down the cheap route but we survive very well. Not everyone thinks of price before quality, thank goodness.'

'And long may those people reign,' smiled Lou. 'So, are you ready for the next round of clutter-clearing?'

'As I'll ever be!'

'Come on then, flower.'

They went upstairs into Gladys's dressing room – the penultimate step before the big one. Even at her age, Gladys had clothes hanging there she would never fit into again. The dress she wore to her Ruby Wedding celebration that she hadn't put on since and the gown she wore as a bridesmaid for her best friend's wedding over fifty years ago were the first to go on the charity shop pile and were quickly joined by more outdated separates and a Norma Desmond turban. Gladys started to panic.

'But look how much more room there is in your wardrobe now,' said Lou, accentuating the positive. 'Every single item in here now is something you use.' And Gladys had to concede that she was right.

Gladys had two drawers full of loose photographs that

she had been meaning to put in an album for years, but never had.

'I think I can get rid of a lot of these,' she said. She lifted one up and beamed at it. 'Not this one though. Look, this is my Bernie. Wasn't he lovely?'

Bernie was tall and straight with a big nose and a big smile. He wasn't classically handsome but the appeal was obvious in his cheery face.

'This is him and me at Blackpool, on our honeymoon. We had barely two pennies to rub together then.' She handed it over to give Lou a closer look. Bernie had his arm circled around a young, rounded, big-busted Gladys and they were both grinning blissfully at the camera. Gladys lifted another.

'And this is him and me just before our Golden Wedding on a cruise. That's the Rock of Gibraltar behind us.' The couple in the photo were standing just as closely together as on the previous picture, his arm was still circling her much-enlarged waist, and they were wearing those same smiles.

'You look happy,' said Lou quietly.

'Happy doesn't even touch it, sweetheart,' said Gladys. 'I loved him from the first moment I saw him, you know. Even though these scientists say that's not possible, let me tell you it is! We had such fun. We were always laughing together. Of course, like any married couple, we had our moments. But the making up was always very nice.'

She slid back into a particular memory that gave her joy, but it was a private moment and, from the look on her face, probably a saucy one too.

'He called me Parrot,' she confided with a chortle.

'On our first date I wore a hat with feathers on and the name just stuck.'

'Did you have a name for him?' asked Lou with a smile.

'Well I did, but I couldn't possibly tell you without you thinking I was a mucky old lady.'

Lou threw back her head and laughed.

'Look at him there,' said Gladys, handing Lou a picture of a much thinner and older man, drawn and pale in a dark blue suit. 'That was at our son's wedding – the last do he went to. Do you know, he made my heart beat just as fast on that day as it did when we were first courting. Oh, he did look good in a suit, even when the illness took hold and he got that thin. As we were posing for that picture he said to me, "Gladys, my love, I've never met a woman that was as bonny as you in my whole life". He said that to me, looking like this! He was such a gentleman; never treated me like anything less than a queen,' and she laughed and swept her hands over her large frame. A big wet tear landed on the photo, but it didn't come from Gladys's eye.

'Sorry,' mumbled Lou.

'Whatever's the matter, love?' said Gladys, coming to put her arm around the younger woman.

'Nothing,' swallowed Lou, quickly recovering. 'Come on, let's crack on with this room and finish it before I go.'

Sometimes other people's rubbish held more answers for you than your own, thought Lou.

Phil had bravely made himself a cheese sandwich and was eating it in the lounge. He was pleased to see that Lou was very quiet when she came in. Obviously she wasn't as unaffected by his antics as she pretended to be then. Good – his cold-shoulder treatment was working. He might not have to sleep with Sue Shoesmith, after all. He still didn't really want to. He just wanted to herd things back into line again, but it was taking a lot longer to do that this time.

'I'll make some pasta,' said Lou, going straight into the kitchen after she had taken off her jacket.

'That would be lovely, Lou,' he said, warmly delivering the words, just to add a bit of variety to the mix.

He had staged his phone quite specifically on the worktop after erasing all of Sue's saucy messages, but left a couple of tame ones there to set Lou thinking – if, as he imagined, he had driven her to take a sneaky peek at his in-box.

Just as she was supposed to, Lou spotted the phone immediately. She checked Phil's position and, assured he was settled in his armchair, reached for it. Then again, she knew he had left it there deliberately so there could only be something there that was meant to hurt her – some stupid faked message to make her believe there was another woman sniffing around him. So she put it back again. She poured some pasta in a pan and chopped vegetables for the sauce, her eyes drawn to that phone, however much she tried to resist its lure. *What if he hadn't left his phone there deliberately?* she started to think. *What if it was just a happy accident? Maybe this was a golden opportunity to stop the annoying questions in her head. Just one quick peek . . . go on! Find out once and for all if there really was another woman on the scene.* Her hand reached tentatively out.

With a heartbeat pounding in her head, Lou picked

up his phone and pressed the message in-box button. There were four messages from Sue BRGE. *A pet name. Another Sue.* She knew instinctively it must be the woman who came into the showroom looking like a younger Lou with her green eyes. Is that what the last two letters stood for – *Green Eyes*? Lou felt her stomach muscles clench as the smoke of her imagination started to solidify into fact. She checked behind her again; Phil was still reading the paper. Actually he wasn't, he was just holding it up in front of his face, shaking it periodically to make 'don't mind me, I'm still sitting here reading the newspaper' noises, his ear picking out the pronounced silence in the kitchen as a clear indication that Lou was looking at his messages.

HELLO THERE YOU said the first message.

THX 4 EVERYTHING said the second.

HAVE A G8 DAY said the third.

SENDING YOU A SMILE X said the fourth.

But Phil had not considered that Sue might send him a new message. The phone rumbled in Lou's hand, causing her almost to drop it in shock. She opened the new mail quickly before the tinkly alert went off and when she read it, it told her everything she needed to know.

Lou waited for the anaesthetic of shock to clear and then for her to be plunged into that dark hellish place. She waited for her hand to come to her mouth to stifle cries of panic, she waited for her eyes to be flooded with a damburst of tears, she waited for her legs to carry her at a pace into the lounge, she waited for her voice to demand answers as to why some woman was writing porn to her husband. But surprisingly, none of those things happened.

As she read the text, she realized her head had just caught up with a fact that her heart had apparently known for some time now: her marriage was dead. Yes, it had survived the affair with Susan Peach, but it had been mortally wounded in the battle and somewhere along the line, though she couldn't quite pinpoint the moment, it had taken its last breath. And still she had clung faithfully, devotedly, hopefully onto it, as she had clung onto so much dead but familiar rubbish.

Lou deleted the message, put the phone down exactly in the place she had found it and picked up a wooden spoon. She was strangely calm as she stirred up the smoked salmon, dill, avocado and cream and tossed it in with the cooked penne, the garlic, onions, green peppers, ground cracked black pepper and herb salt. Phil abandoned his half-eaten cheese sandwich for it and, though he didn't comment on how delicious it was, he feasted on second helpings. The glazed look on his wife's face had given him a healthy appetite. There was no pudding, but he was quite full anyway and in the mood for Stilton, port and a big fat celebratory cigar.

Lou was at the sink when he came in for a refill of port. She saw him in the reflection of the window. He was looking out into the garden, the cigar clenched in his teeth.

'I think I might get some koi carp for the pond,' he said, and Lou immediately knew when the crippled heart of her marriage had stopped beating. The little, fatal thought that had lain dormant since the night of her birthday, fluffed up its wings and flew slowly across the front of her mind, and she knew that the death certificate of their relationship would bear that date. She had seen it then, but not recognized it. She and Phil were Fat Jack and Maureen waiting to happen. Host and parasite. Two strangers.

Chapter 50

There were no tears as Lou lay alone in bed that night. Maybe her mind was in shock. Maybe she had cried so much in advance of this moment throughout the past three years that she did not need the comfort of fresh tears now. She slept soundly and dreamlessly, peacefully even.

The next morning, she was aware of Phil's cheerful getting ready for work routine as if she was watching and hearing everything through cottonwool. She even answered his cheery, 'Bye!' with an equally cheery one of her own. She set off for Gladys Serafinska's quite calmly and was totally in control as they shared tea and thickly buttered toast. Then they finally went up into Bernie's dressing room.

There were quite a few tears in store that day for Gladys, but none for Lou, who felt as if her emotions had gone into hibernation, until the climate was right for them to emerge again. Emotions had no place in what Lou had to do now – she needed her head for that, not her heart. The two women bagged up Bernie's beautiful suits ready to be taken to the charity shop. One of the bakery lads carried the heavy stuff downstairs, loaded it into his van and took it away to the Cancer Research shop. When it was all done and the empty space had been washed down and Gladys Serafinska had cried her last, she hugged Lou and pressed a thick wad of bank-notes into her hand. Lou felt guilty taking it and her expression obviously reflected this.

'You've earned every penny of this, lass,' said Gladys. 'I wouldn't have believed it if I hadn't gone through these last few days myself. It's been an experience and a half for me, a fantastic cleansing experience. I thought it would totally weaken me, but the opposite has happened. Do you know, I feel stronger than I have done for a long time. And I don't feel any further away from Bernie just for letting his things go, like I thought I would. I don't know why I didn't let them go before. He was the sort of man who would want someone to benefit from what he'd left; he wouldn't have wanted me to make a shrine for him. I feel so *light*. Me, light – imagine!' Her chins wobbled as she laughed. 'Thank you, Lou,' and she kissed her sweetly on the cheek.

'You really have been giving out my name,' said Lou, with a feeling akin to pride. 'I've had phone calls.'

'I hope you don't mind,' said Gladys. 'I think you're wonderful. Please contact Alice in particular; she could really do with your help.'

'I will, I promise,' said Lou, 'but first I need to do some more clearing out for myself.'

She knocked on the bakery door and Deb waved her over, holding up five fingers, then disappeared to get her bag and coat. Within five minutes, she had set the alarm and locked the door behind her.

'Hiya,' she said. 'Have you finished sorting out our Glad then?'

'I have,' said Lou. 'Got time for a quick drink?'

'Thought you'd never ask. Come on.'

They went across the road to the *Bonny Bunch of Bluebells*. It was a clean, if battered-looking place, with just a handful of after-work drinkers enjoying a slow pint.

'I'll get these,' said Lou, turning to the barman. 'A brandy, no ice thanks, and a—'

'Diet Coke,' said Deb, looking wide-eyed at Lou. 'Brandy? At this time?'

'Yes, I need one,' said Lou.

'I didn't know you drank brandy.'

'I don't.'

Deb noticed Lou's hand was shaking as she carried the brandy balloon to a darkened booth in the corner.

'Lou, what's up?'

'Phil's having an affair,' Lou said without emotion.

Deb sucked in her breath. In part she felt relief that the grubby little secret was out before she could be linked to it in any way this time. 'How do you know?' she asked softly.

'I've had my suspicions for a while, but yesterday Phil left his mobile out – deliberately, of course. There was nothing on it, just a few tame messages from some woman called Sue. But another message came up whilst I was holding it. I don't think he'd allowed for that to happen.'

'What did it say?' asked Deb tentatively.

Lou told her.

'The bastard!' was Deb's only comment. The message

had left no room for misinterpretation; there was nothing that could be rationalized away. Her instinct was to hug Lou, but her friend looked so stiff – brittle, even – as if she would shatter into a million pieces if Deb so much as touched her.

'What . . . what are you going to do?'

Lou took a swig of the brandy and her face squeezed up in disgust. Deb poured some of her Coke over it.

'That'll taste better, if you must drink it. Try that.'

Lou drank some; it was better, still not good though, but she needed that warm hit of alcohol because inside she felt frozen solid.

'You will come and stay with me for a bit,' said Deb.

'You've got one bedroom, Deb, and I think you did your fair share of babysitting last time.'

'I'm your friend,' said Deb gently, reaching out for Lou's hand. Lou gripped it tight but she showed no signs of being anything but in control.

'Yes, and you are the best friend I could possibly ever have, but . . .' She looked at Deb's kind, worried face and knew immediately what she was thinking. 'Don't worry, Deb, this time it's different. I know our marriage is over. There are things I need to do and I need to do them alone. It's the only way I'll get through this.'

'OK,' said Deb, touching Lou's cheek with soft fingers, like a mother preparing to let a child stand on its own two feet but still on full alert to catch it if it fell. 'I'm here if you want me.'

'I know. And I have our lovely café to look forward to. Last time I ran away from it instead of running towards it. I won't make that mistake again.'

★

Sue Shoesmith was crying.

'Phil, please don't finish this. I think I love you.'

Oh fuck, that's all I need, thought Phil. He gripped her hand even though his instinct was to make his excuses and leave. He supposed he owed her an extra five minutes. After all, she had been instrumental in the saving of his marriage.

'Sue,' he said tenderly. 'I can't do this any more. I am still a married man and it just doesn't feel right.'

'But you don't love her and you're going to get a divorce after Christmas.'

In your dreams, sister. This time next week I'll be stuffed full of lamb and loving. 'I'm not sure I can give you my best, and you deserve the best, darling.'

'I don't care.'

Oh God! It was like trying to pull your welly – or rather 'willy' in this case – out of a lake full of treacle and Superglue.

'I'm confused and I don't want to hurt you.'

'I'll wait.'

For fuck's sake! She was Limpet Woman. Her nails were digging into his skin. They'd actually left moon-marks! She was going to draw blood in a minute. When was his last tetanus shot?

'I'm sorry, Sue. You will thank me for this one day. I'm doing this for you more than me.'

He stood to go but she held on firm. He kissed her on the top of her head.

'Please don't cry, love. Don't throw your self-respect away on me or anyone, do you hear? You are worth so much more. Goodbye, and thank you for bringing some sweetness and light into my life. I'll miss you more than you will ever know.'

Milly Johnson

He extricated himself with a sharp tug and she collapsed onto the pub-table like a puppet with its strings severed. Phil made a hasty exit whilst her head was in her hands. The blast of cold Monday-night air as he opened the door hit him like a fresh morning shower. He was free.

Lou looked around her house and made a mental list. Clothes, make-up, treasure box, shoes, handbags, laptop, the recipe books, umbrella, radio alarm, couple of toilet rolls, some blankets. She streamlined it to basic essentials and the barest of emotional possessions. She wouldn't die if she didn't take her lovely dining-room curtains – they were just 'things' and she could buy more 'things'. She couldn't buy back what it would cost her to stay.

She made Phil venison for tea. Beautiful dark red slices with herby shallots and sweet potatoes and green beans sautéed with walnuts. It was even better than her lamb. She made chocolate and hazelnut sponge pudding with Chantilly cream which dribbled down Phil's chin as he devoured it with the greed of an all-conquering hero celebrating his final victory. She served him brandy and coffee and then, while she was clearing up, he went to sleep in the spare room for the very last time.

Tomorrow, Phil thought happily, he would smile at her and open his arms and she would run into them and everything would be back to wonderful normality with no more of this silly nonsense. The war was over – and he had won. Now he had all the spoils to look forward to.

Lou clicked the dial on the dishwasher for the last time.

Then, taking a coffee into the study, she logged onto the computer. *Your home is a mirror that reflects what is going on in your life*, reminded the words she had put on her screensaver. Well, once upon a time her home was cluttered and confused, but now it was clear and organized. Lou did what she had to do. It was two o'clock in the morning when she logged off and went up to bed.

Chapter 51

This was surely Phil's lucky day. Titanic Tuesday. Four brand new cars all on finance, a text message from Sue to say that she wouldn't be bothering him again but she would always treasure their special times, and Des was asking pertinent questions about the Classic Car business and would call round to the house later for five minutes. Yeah, well, Phil would only give him five minutes before chucking him out. He wasn't going to have his plans for him and Lou that night upset for anything. Fat Jack rang to say someone wanted them to find a Rolls Royce Silver Ghost – and tonight, he had goodness-knows-what to look forward to. Christmas had come fast and early – as would he, if he and his wife had a marathon make-up-sex session.

He had some *P.M. Autos* champers already on chill to take home with him, and rang up to order a huge bouquet from *Donny Badger's Floristry*, which he sent Bradley out to collect. The flowers were gorgeous, if pricy, but if he kept the receipt he could write them off against his tax, couldn't he? He'd casually ask Lou about that the next time she was doing his accounts.

★

'Honey, I'm home!' he boomed comically as he came through the door brandishing the bottle and assorted blooms, but there was no answer. The lights were on but no one appeared to be in. He called her name but there was no answer. *Where was she?* He went into the kitchen to plug in his mobile phone, and there he found the letter propped up against the charger. He opened it and read the words on the lined paper.

Phil, I've left you. I think you know why. Lou.

He looked around, expecting her to spring out from somewhere and yell, 'Surprise!' It didn't cross his mind that it could be true. Still full of disbelief, he went into their bedroom and paused for a moment before he opened their wardrobe doors. There followed a slight shift in his thinking when he discovered that her clothes were gone, and that her jewellery box and her make-up bag were no longer on the dressing-table, but that appeared to be all that was missing. He nodded and smiled. When wives left, they took half the house and the roof with them. *Touché.*

'I get it!' he said, grinning.

Lou wouldn't – *couldn't* leave this house and all these things she'd so carefully chosen over the years – and there was *no way* she would leave her new bathroom. Not after the battle she'd had to get it done. She was playing her own little game, showing him she had grown up a bit from last time and wasn't going to lie down without putting up a fight.

He checked his own wardrobe tentatively, though, just in case. His shirts weren't ripped up; his trousers didn't have the crotch cut out of them. No – if she really had left him, there would be more drama to it than this.

Phil defrosted one of Lou's superb chillis in the microwave and read the letter again. He'd had far too good a day for any silliness to spoil it, he thought, rubbing his hands together. My, there was going to be some red hot loving tonight when she turned up!

Lou carried the last of the boxes up into May's old flat. At least it wasn't as jarring on the eyes now that Tom and Deb had attacked it with the emulsion brush. She clicked on the electric fire, hoping the small room would heat up quickly as she felt chilled, both inside and out.

She set down the old cracket she had retrieved from the skip – it hadn't taken much sanding and waxing to give it a new lease of life – and rested her radio alarm clock on it. Pulling the curtain shut at the side of the bed, she plugged in the bedside light which she had just bought from Argos, along with a cheap double quilt and a pair of pillows. Switching on the radio for the comfort of some background noise, she unpacked some sheets and made up the bed, trying not to think about who might have slept there before her – although, was it in fact, possible *to* sleep on all those lumps? It could only be good for the back, she thought positively, and she was feeling remarkably positive in the circumstances.

She was just about to put the kettle on when someone pounded on the flat door. That was worrying, as no one could actually get to the door unless they came up through the café – and the café was all locked up.

'Who is it?' she asked, grabbing the breadknife from her box of basic supplies.

'Lou, is that you?' said Tom's voice.

She unlocked the door and he came in, followed by his faithful hound.

'I saw the light on and thought someone had broken in,' he said, looking around. 'What are you doing?'

'I'm, er, moving in,' she said with an embarrassed little smile.

'Moving in here?'

'I've left my husband,' Lou explained. Said out loud, the words made everything seem suddenly very real, very scary. She felt a bit wobbly and reached for the diversion of the kettle.

'Tea?' she said.

'Yes, I will, please,' said Tom slowly. 'So, hang on, you've left home and you're moving in here?'

'Yes,' said Lou, with her face turned away from him.

'Why here?'

'I've nowhere else to go,' said Lou with a shrug.

'Deb's, surely?'

'Deb's only got a tiny little place and I need to think. This place will be fine for now.'

'But Lou, it's cold and grotty. It's a storeroom, for Christ's sake.'

'It'll do. Honestly, I'll be fine.'

'There isn't even a wardrobe or a sofa.'

'There's a chair and a bed. It'll do until I get myself sorted out.'

Tom scratched his head in thought and then, having decided what to do, he grabbed one of her suitcases.

'Right, you're coming home with me. There's loads of room at the house.'

'No, I'm not.'

'Oh yes, you are. Now move it.'

'No, Tom,' said Lou decisively. 'It's really sweet of you, but no, I'm staying here. I want to be on my own.'

Satisfied that she wasn't playing at being serious, he put down the case and dropped heavily onto the chair, which creaked in shock. Lou passed a cup of tea to him. He took up half the room when he stood to take it from her. He was all work-dirty, he needed a shave, his hair was full of dust, he was gorgeous. Then her head went into reverse thrust and suddenly she wanted to go home to the familiarity of Phil and all her nice things and her big warm house. It was all very well when Miss Casserly leaped from stages at college hoping someone would catch her – which they always did – but the leaps got riskier as you got older. She felt as if she had jumped off the edge of the world this time, and realized halfway down how stupid she had been not to attach a bungee rope that could have taken her right back to where she started. In saying that, if it pinged back now, it would probably send her eyeballs into orbit.

'What are you having for tea?' Tom's eyes rested on a bag of crisps on the top of a box. 'I hope that's not it.'

She smiled a little at his concern. 'I'm not very hungry, Tom.'

'The workmen have started, you know. They'll be here at seven. They're ripping out stuff, you won't sleep past then.'

'I'll be OK. My eyes usually snap open at half-past six anyway.' She tried to joke but her throat went all croaky. Not that she imagined she was going to sleep much anyway.

'Lou, please, let me help you.' Tom's hand came out and at the moment of its contact with her arm, Lou stood up to top up her cup with hot water. *Please don't touch me,* she thought. She wasn't sure what that would release in her.

'I need to think, Tom, please. I'm all right, really. I just need to be alone.'

He took the hint, drained his cup and reluctantly stood. His head was less than six inches below the ceiling.

'OK, but I'm leaving Clooney. I won't take no for an answer on that one. He knows where to do what in the morning, when you let him out. I'll just whip him out now for you. He's been fed tonight and I'll feed him myself in the morning when I get into the office.'

Lou drew some warmth from the cup in her hands. The room was heating up from the bars on the electric fire, but she still felt cold, right down to the bone.

'Very well.' She allowed herself to be defeated on that point.

Tom returned ten minutes later with Clooney, a box of dog biscuits, a water bowl and the bean-bag bed that Tom kept for him in the ironmongery.

'Can't I change your mind?'

'No, you can't, Tom,' said Lou. 'And please don't tell Deb, not tonight. I'll ring her myself tomorrow. Please, promise me. I need space and she'd be round here like a flash.'

'You shouldn't be alone,' he said.

'I'm not alone.' She stroked Clooney's head fondly. 'You're leaving me this big bad burglar detergent.'

Detergent? He felt himself smiling inside at her Lou-ism, despite his concern. He wanted to pick her up and put her in his pocket.

'I do know what's best for me tonight. Really,' she said, in a voice that closed the subject.

She looked so little, so cold, so vulnerable, but he didn't try to touch her in any way. Her body was missiling out vibes that he was not to do so. He walked out as if in slow motion, giving her ample opportunity to change her mind. But she didn't.

Chapter 52

Clooney and Lou slept soundly, and yes, she had to admit, having him there was a big comfort. It was scarily quiet in the flat and the absence of streetlights made it very dark outside, but the big dog's snuffles in the night, his little yelps and twitches as he chased something fast, and probably rabbity, in his dreams took the edge off any fears. Plus it helped having a living presence in the room, especially one that she didn't have to put on a brave face for, who didn't fuss around her when she sat up in the middle of the night to stare out of the window at the stars and to whom she didn't need to explain why she was taking a bath at such an unearthly hour in the morning before climbing half-damp back into the lumpy, bumpy bed.

She couldn't sleep past six o'clock so she got up, had a coffee and dressed. Clooney got up with her and she took him outside where he went around to his usual spot of grass to do as nature intended. Lou gave him a few dog biscuits to tide over his tummy until Tom arrived. The builders were there at seven prompt, singing loudly to their radio, every rip and bang bringing her one step closer to their grand opening, but that thought gave Lou no thrill. She felt so numb she wondered if she were emotionally capable of feeling anything again.

Half an hour later, just as Lou had delivered four cups of tea to the builders, female shoes clattered up the stairs and there were no prizes for guessing whose they were.

'How crap a friend do you think it makes me feel, that you can't ask me for a bed for the night,' said Deb crossly.

Oh, that old chestnut, the guilt tactic, thought Lou with a wry smile.

'Coffee?'

'Damn right I want a coffee,' said Deb. 'Why didn't you tell me you were leaving Phil so quickly?'

'Because I just wanted to do it, not talk about it, Deb. Don't you see?'

Deb mumbled something whilst she was pouring milk into her cup.

'When did Tom phone you?' said Lou.

'Seven this morning.'

Lou shook her head with exasperation. At least he fulfilled his promise.

'You can't blame him – he's worried about you,' said Deb in his defence.

'Well, he shouldn't be. Why, what did he say?'

'He said "I'm worried about Lou".'

'Oh.'

'The bloke's in love with you – of course he's worried about you, you daft cow.'

Lou spilled her coffee all over herself and yelped.

'God, are you OK?' said Deb.

'No, I'm not!' said Lou, hopping about in pain. 'What did you say that for?'

Deb threw a tea-towel at Lou and went to make her friend another coffee.

'I'm not blind or thick,' she grumbled. 'You two might be, but I'm not.'

'Yeah, right. He's all over you like sliced bread, not me.'

'The expression is, "to be all over someone like a rash",' corrected Deb. 'Except he's not. He only wants to be my friend – and that certainly is not his primary intention in your case. Lou, the guy's eyes light up like a kid that's been told he's going to be locked in a Toys R Us overnight whenever he sees you.'

'Naw,' said Lou dismissively. And then: 'Do they? His eyes? Light up?'

'Yes,' said Deb. 'And vice versa, don't deny it. This is me you're talking to. I noticed how bloody relieved you were when you found out Tom and I weren't an item.'

'No, that's rubbish,' said Lou, convincing neither of them. 'He wouldn't anyway . . .'

'He wouldn't what? Fancy someone like you?' said Deb with a laugh. 'Well, here's news for you, Lou Winter: he does and that is because you are gorgeous and you're sweet and you're funny and you've got great knockers and beautiful eyes, and any bloke who got you should get on his knees and worship you like the sodding goddess you are, every night of his lucky life.'

Lou stared at her open-mouthed.

'Don't you dare cry, Lou Winter!' cried Deb fiercely.

'Then stop saying nice things,' said Lou, as her eyes started to fill up.

'I can't lie and tell you that I'm not over the moon about seeing you and that baldy knobhead split up, Lou, but I don't want to see you hurting and I don't want you to go through any of this on your own. I'm your friend. Use me, please. Come and stay with me in my bijou pad,' Deb pleaded, taking her hands.

Lou said, quietly but firmly, 'Please, Deb, I need to be on my own. I know what I'm doing. I want to be by myself. I have to get my head straight about things.' And when Deb gave her the same sort of look Tom had given her umpteen times the previous night, she added, 'Go on, go to work. I have to see my mother.'

Deb enfolded her in a comforting, sisterly hug.

'Don't let her talk you into anything that isn't right for you. Don't let any of us try to influence you.' Deb knew that, last time, she had been guilty of that one more than she cared to admit.

'I won't,' said Lou. Not this time.

By nine o'clock, Lou was on the telephone working her way through the listings for solicitors. She wanted an appointment that day. Number five on the list said that if she could get there for ten, there was a window with Beverley Brookes. Lou said she could and she did. First, she dropped Clooney off at the ironmonger's with Eddie. Tom, apparently, was on his way in. She didn't wait to see him; in fact, she positively avoided it. She didn't want the sight of him fuzzing up her thoughts.

At the solicitors, she cited 'unreasonable behaviour' as just cause. It seemed easier to prove than adultery and she had plenty of rock-solid back-up proof for that one. As she gave Beverley Brookes some cold examples of Phil's treatment of her over the past few years, she wondered how she had managed to stay sane through it all. When said aloud to a complete stranger, it sounded terrible, but when Beverley Brookes read it back to her, it was worse. How had she put up with so much for so long? When did hurt and betrayal – that Lou Casserly wouldn't have put up with in a million years – become the norm for Lou Winter?

Phil would get the divorce papers within twenty-one days, Beverley Brookes said as she shook Lou's hand on the way out.

Lou came out into a typical British summer's dull and drizzly day with the sudden realization that she had started divorce proceedings. It chilled her more than the weather did. And talking of chill, now it was time to tell her mother.

Phil had slept soundly although it was odd sleeping in that big bed without Lou. Her scent was still on the sheets, which made him feel rather horny. His arm hooked over the space where her body should have been. He knew she hadn't left permanently. Late last night, just in case, he had gone online and checked their joint bank account: it hadn't been touched. But just in case, he had transferred the funds over to his personal account. He wondered what she would have on the table for his tea tonight when she came out of her woman-sulk.

Chapter 53

Lou ordered a coffee and two crumpets in town. The first bite rolled around in her mouth as if it couldn't work out the way to the back of her throat. It took her a *Women by Women* magazine and two more coffees to realize she wasn't hungry, after all. Then she told herself off for unnecessary procrastination. Her brain knew she was doing it, even if the rest of her was trying to pretend it wasn't happening.

It was early afternoon when she got to her mother's house.

'This is a surprise,' said Renee. 'How come you're not working today?'

'Mum,' said Lou, standing on her mother's sheepskin rug. She had decided on the way there to lead into it gently.

'I've left my job and I've left Phil as well.'

Then again, the best-made plans . . .

Renee didn't say anything for a while. She digested the information, concluded that it was the truth, and then she reacted.

'Left your job? What on earth have you done that for?

Have you taken leave of your senses? And what do you mean, you've left Phil?'

'I left him yesterday afternoon.'

'But what for?'

'Because I don't love him any more. And he's having an affair.'

Renee twiddled her necklace. She was counting along the beads as if it were a rosary.

'Elouise, what are you playing at? Do you need a doctor?'

Even Lou was astounded by her mother's lack of sympathy. She had thought women of that generation and adultery were an oil-and-water mix, more so than her own generation.

'Mum, I'm not looking for your approval on this. I'm only telling you because you need to know I'm not at the old address any more and I figured you would probably want to know why. I'm not here to answer any questions about it. I know what I'm doing; I've instigated divorce proceedings.'

'But I thought you only left him yesterday!'

'Yes, but it's overdue by three years.'

'You were happy!'

'No, *he* was happy, *I* was sodding miserable!' Lou's voice crescendoed to its highest pitch.

'I can't believe it,' said Renee, dropping onto the sofa.

'Which bit? That Phil's having another affair?'

'No, that you're not thinking straight!' cried Renee.

'But I am, Mum. This is the first bit of straight thinking I've done in a long time.'

'Oh Elouise, he got caught sitting in a pub with someone. Once. You didn't catch them in bed together, did you? I bet you've got no proof this time either. I suppose that Deb being around isn't anything to do with it. Was it her again, stirring things up? Has it crossed your mind that she's jealous of what you've got?'

'What have I got, Mum?' demanded Lou, bordering closely on angry tears. 'I've got a pig of a man who can't keep it in his trousers, that's the sum of it.'

'You've got security, a lovely home, money in the bank, a husband with a growing business. Aren't you going on holiday soon as well?'

Lou laughed bitterly. That was typical of her mum – thinking of the creature comforts first. 'I can't believe it,' she said. 'I thought for once you'd be on my side.'

'I am on your side, Lou. That's why I don't want you to throw your life away,' said Renee, with something akin to panic.

'What am I throwing away that's so great, Mum?'

'Elouise,' said Renee, almost distraught, 'marriage is about riding the bad times. Have you looked at yourself to find out why he did it?'

'Why on earth would I do that?' asked Lou, with an incredulous laugh.

'Because . . .'

'Because what?'

'No, forget it,' said Renee.

'No, I won't forget it,' said Lou angrily. Let her have her say and get it over with. 'Because what, Mum, because WHAT?'

'Because that's what I had to do when your father did it to me!' cried Renee.

Lou didn't move. A pin-drop silence fell on the room, broken only by the soft tock-tock of the clock on the wall by the fire. Even when Lou tried to speak, no words came out. Her mouth moved soundlessly trying to form them, but they got hopelessly stuck behind the hurdle of her lips.

Renee took a linen handkerchief from up her sleeve and blew her nose with it.

'What do you mean?' said Lou eventually, on the faintest of breaths.

'I shouldn't have said anything. Forget it.'

But something like that couldn't be forgotten, could it? Something like that couldn't be stuffed back as if it had never happened?

'No, no, you have to tell me now.'

Please don't tell me.

Renee licked her dry lips. 'Your father had . . . an . . . We picked up the pieces. It was hard but we did it. We didn't throw it all away for a couple of rough years. It takes time and it was worth it. That's why I know your troubles will pass.'

'Dad did this to you?'

Lou couldn't take it in. Her beautiful, wonderful, kind, smiling father put her mum through this pain? Her dad, who had hugged her when she caught her first boyfriend snogging someone else and told her to forget him and move on because he wasn't good enough for a Casserly girl.

Renee didn't move, didn't look up, didn't make eye-contact.

Lou's stomach spasmed, not that there was anything in there to throw up. Her head went light and swimmy and she had to steady herself against the big oak dresser by the wall, ironically one that her dad had made.

Her dad and another woman?

Lou had to get out. The air in that room was thick and sucked dry of oxygen.

'I have to go,' she said, groping in her pocket for her keys.

'Elouise!' Renee called behind her, but Lou was already down the path and nearly at the car.

She drove blindly to the town park, got out of the car and followed the path up the hill to the folly, which her dad used to tell her was the 'Unleaning Tower of Pisa'. They'd had so many picnics on the grass there when she was little. Mum wasn't one for walking (being born in high heels) but Lou and her father and Murphy walked here a lot. He'd carry their picnic basket and they'd sit and open it here amongst the beds of scarlet tulips, and eat egg and cress sandwiches and Twiglets and the cakes that Lou had made, and wash it all down with Ribena for her, a flask of milky, sugary tea for her dad and a big bowl of water for Murphy. She felt close to her dad here. She could see him, stocky and big-shouldered with his large hands that were so gentle with plants and kind to animals. That was the dad she wanted to remember – not a dad who hurt hearts that loved him. Had she been attracted to Phil because she had sensed that deep down they were the same? No, no, no . . .

She felt as if someone had scooped out all her innards and replaced them with rocks. She wanted to be dead and not face the questions her head was throwing at her. No, not dead, because she might wake up on the other side with the same things going through her brain for eternity. She simply wanted to not exist, to slide out of everyone's consciousness, and for the hole she was in to close up completely over her, so she was nothing. Futures were taken away from people all the time, but Renee's disclosure had taken away her past – a past that should have been set in stone, unchangeable, a solid foundation. And now it was gone, crushed, and the rubble blown away.

It was quite dark when she realized she should go home, wherever that was. Her big comfortable house called. She could have a nice warm Keith Featherstone bath and crawl into bed beside Phil. Maybe it *would* be all right in time, as her mother said. They *had* been happy once, her mum was right. Well, content – was it the same thing? Lou didn't know.

She called in at the *White Rose* corner shop on the way back to the flat and bought a box of After Eights, a bottle of brandy, some kitchen roll and a set of drinks coasters. It was a ridiculous bag of shopping in the circumstances.

The silence was hard on her ears in the flat, so she clicked on the radio to release some music at a gentle volume, just to take it away. Then she twisted the top off the brandy and poured some into a cup before tossing it into her mouth. She didn't get the unravelling-of-the-day warmth that Phil seemed to get from the spirit; it merely burned the back of her throat. It gave her an excuse to sob.

It was late when Tom let himself into May's and he went cautiously up the stairs, hearing the melodic burr of the radio filter down through the café ceiling. He knocked gently, but when there was no answer, he pushed open the door and went in.

Lou was so locked in her grief, head in her hands, sobbing like a child that she wasn't conscious of another presence until Tom was a step away from her, when it was totally past the time when she might have salvaged any dignity. But Lou's pride was gone anyway. Everything was gone; she was hollow, empty, had nothing left within her that was capable of feeling anything but pain. He sat beside her on the bed and placed his arm around her shoulder, pulling her into him. She quickly wiped at the salty drops rolling down her face faster than she could clear them.

He noticed the brandy bottle, but there weren't enough of the contents gone to have caused any major damage.

'Can I get you anything?' he said softly.

'No,' she said, and laughed bitterly. 'Not unless you can get me a new dad.'

'A new dad?' he asked. 'Why a new dad?'

The story spilled out of her. Lou told him what a wonderful man her dad had been, and then she told him what Renee had said, and Tom used his thumbs to wipe away the tears she didn't think would ever stop. They were like giant facial windscreen wipers.

'Lou,' Tom said softly, 'your dad obviously loved you very much. You have to hang onto that.'

'Every time I've tried to visualize his face this afternoon, I can't. All I see is Phil.'

'Let me make you a cup of tea,' said Tom.

'I want another brandy. I want to get so drunk I pass out.' And Lou reached for the full mug on the table, but Tom snatched it away.

'All that's going to do is give you a blinding headache,' he said. 'Besides, I need that mug, so give it here.'

She let it go. She knew it was an angry, punishing act to throw a drink she didn't like at all down her throat. She wanted to lash out at Phil, at her mother and most of all at her father, but he wasn't there and never would be there to explain why he had smashed himself up in her heart. So the only available target to hurt was herself.

The radio was playing out ballads. The twangy guitar seemed to be directly attached to her tear ducts and wasn't helping her mood at all. Her dad was always listening to that sort of music. Tammy Wynette, Johnny Cash, June Carter, Dolly Parton. Phil obviously liked Dolly Parton, but for less musical reasons. *Dad. Phil. Dad. Phil. Dad.* They were the same man, a generation apart.

Some Country and Western woman with a smoky mountain voice had written a song especially for her and had chosen this moment to air it and torment her. The intro alone suggested it was going to go on about a broken heart and some man–bastard who had caused it. Lou lifted her eyes to the ceiling. Her heart felt physically capable of snapping like a biscuit.

Dance with me tonight, the woman sang. *Make everything all right . . .*

Lou was not in the mood to listen to a song like this, pulling the tears out of her soul, each one attached to the last.

'Dance with me,' said Tom instinctively, whilst he was waiting for the kettle to boil. 'Come on.'

'Don't be ridiculous,' said Lou, giving vent to a reflex laugh despite everything. Big Alan Flockton was the tallest bloke she had ever danced with at six foot three – in width as well as height. Not only had she felt a total prawn, but when the music stopped she found that every student within a 300-mile radius of the campus ball had been laughing.

'Come on, I mean it.'

But no one laughed now as Tom pulled her to her resisting feet and took her hand in his. She tugged it back, but he held on. He circled her waist with his arm and placed his cheek at the top of her head. A picture came to her of her dad teaching her to waltz in the front room to Engelbert Humperdinck. A sad song about loneliness.

> *You found me when my heart was close to breakin'.*
> *One dance with you and that was all it took.*
> *You're a chance I know that I'll be takin'.*
> *Sometimes you've got to leap before you look.*

They rocked gently, barely moving, his hand gripping hers – no, she wasn't going anywhere if he had anything to do with it. He pulled her closer still. She thought she felt his lips move in her hair.

> *I'd turned my back on lovin' and romancing.*
> *My life was cold and empty for a while.*
> *Then you took me in your arms and started dancing,*
> *And once again my heart began to smile.*

She didn't feel like a prawn now, she felt like china. This was wrong, though. She shouldn't be letting him hold her like this. But her body needed his warmth, his unthreatening affection, those lips in her hair.

Dance with me tonight . . . This had to be the final

chorus, and Lou hardly dared move in case she ended the moment.

... *And make everything all right. Dance with me, my darlin', one more time.*

He pulled slowly away from her when the song ended and took her face in his big hands.

'Lou,' he said, but the tone of his voice said much more.

His lips brushed against her salty cheek. He shouldn't be doing this, he knew, but when she didn't resist, he kissed her lightly. He felt her lips part in response as his touched the corner of her mouth, and then they fell full on hers, tentatively, before they made firmer contact. His arms came around her, hers were around him. His kiss took everything away, there was only her and him in this freshly white-painted universe – oh, and Kenny Rogers now singing 'Coward of the County'.

'Lou, I shouldn't say this, I know, but I can't help it. I've liked you – *really* liked you – for so long.'

'Tom . . .'

Hearing his name said in that way was enough for him to know he wasn't about to make the world's biggest plonker of himself.

She felt so wonderful in his arms, so warm, so right – but she was vulnerable and he didn't want to take advantage. But Lou was driving this and her need for what was happening between them was as great, if not greater, than his own.

A small chemical factory had exploded in Lou's brain and was detonating secondary incendiary devices all over her body where he touched her, and when they began to undress each other, feeling his skin next to hers made her shudder with delight. He was gentle with her, tentative, giving her a chance to back out at every step of the way, but she didn't – nor did she want to, because for once, Lou Winter was taking everything on offer. He felt so good, his hard, muscular body so different from Phil's soft belly, and even if common sense had prevailed, her starved heart wasn't going to stop this happening.

Waves of pleasure started washing over her as Tom entered her. She had never, *never* experienced anything as raw and powerful as this before. She couldn't remember ever feeling that made-love-to, or remember sex ever being such a *complete* experience, where everything – heart, skin, head – were screaming together on fire. And when it was over, he wrapped his great arms around her and pulled her into the warmth of his chest, his heart beating against her back – and together, in the lumpy, bumpy bed, they went to sleep.

Chapter 54

Of course he was gone the next morning, Lou expected nothing else. The indentation of his body was still there beside her, but the sheet was cold. Last night had been a beautiful escape, but it couldn't take away the smashed dreams and ugly truths that were waiting for her in the daylight. And now she had another problem to add to the pile – how to recover her precious friendship with Tom, who was no doubt too embarrassed to face her.

Lou curled into a foetal ball and closed her eyes for a moment, drawing on any available strength to get up and face the daunting task of their first meeting after the night. God knows what he must think of her, sleeping with another man when she had only just left her husband! They had crossed a line that was maybe never meant to be crossed. Was it possible to go back to how things were? How did you undo falling in love?

Just then, she heard the door to the café open and wheeze shut on the floor below. Footsteps thudded quickly up the stairs then the door opened and in walked Tom with two paper bags.

'Oh, it's you,' said Lou, sitting up but pulling the sheet as far up to her shoulders as she could get it. Her initial joy at seeing him slumped when she saw how difficult it was for him to make eye-contact with her.

'I bought you a bacon sandwich, although it's probably a bit cold now because I had to drive miles to get it,' he said. 'I thought you might be a bit . . . hungover.'

'I wasn't drunk,' she said, a little defensively.

'Well, I didn't know if you'd have regrets about waking up with a strange person then,' said Tom, in a pseudo-jolly voice, unpeeling his own sandwich from the bag.

'Why, do you?' asked Lou cautiously.

'I asked first.'

They both laughed gently.

'OK then, I'll answer first. No, I don't,' said Tom. 'Not one bit. And you're not strange, you're lovely.' He took her cheek in his hand and stroked it with his thumb and she leaned into it. Then, when he realized she wasn't going to say that it was all a huge mistake, he felt at liberty to kiss her gently on the mouth and whisper, 'Morning.'

'Morning,' she replied, trying to coordinate taking the sandwich out of the bag whilst keeping up the sheet at the same time. She wasn't hungry, but she wasn't going to tell him that after he'd gone to so much trouble to get it.

'Bit late for modesty,' said Tom. 'I've seen all you've got and done all sorts to it . . . them.'

She puffed out her cheeks in embarrassment and he released a huge roar of laughter. She had been so soft, like velvet. Women really didn't realize just what their soft skin did to a man.

'I was awake for a while this morning just lying next

to you,' said Tom. 'Watching you.'

Lou was horrified and it showed. 'Was I snoring?' she gasped. *Or worse, dribbling?*

'Don't be silly,' said Tom. 'But you were dreaming. I thought you'd got two butterflies caught under your eyelids.'

'Well, I've a lot going on in my brain,' said Lou with a little laugh.

'You started me thinking,' said Tom. 'Please don't bite my head off, but from what you were saying about your dad . . . and your mum . . .'

'Go on,' said Lou, feeling a bit as if she were in a dream where she was naked and everyone else in the room was dressed, which funnily enough they were.

'Sorry in advance for this. I'll just say it, shall I?'

'Yes, just say it.'

'Your mum . . . She couldn't be not telling you the truth, could she?'

'Why would she do that?' said Lou.

'Well, maybe she's worried you're making a mistake?'

'She *is* worried I'm making a mistake.'

Tom shook his head. 'I'm sorry, I shouldn't interfere. Strike it from the record. I don't know either your mum or your dad. I didn't mean to sound arrogant.'

But Lou knew them both very well and the seed of Tom's thought quickly took root in her subconscious.

'I'd get back in there with you, but I . . .' Tom wrestled with the order of the words in his head.

'Don't want to?' Lou suggested.

'No, I don't want to actually,' said Tom decisively. 'But not in the way you think, before you decide I'm a total bastard.'

'I understand,' said Lou, as little soldiers started to gather around her heart.

He grabbed hold of her hands. 'You don't see at all, do you? Lou, last night was fantastic. It was wonderful. And I've imagined it since the first time I saw you.'

'Rubbish! Have you?' said Lou, gob-smacked.

'OK, male chauvinist pig that I am, I thought, This woman hires and fills her own skips so she can't have a bloke around. And then I saw you didn't have a wedding ring on. I was about that far,' he held up a minuscule space between his thumb and forefinger, 'that far one day from asking you out for a meal and then you started talking about your husband being allergic to animals. I thought, That's that, then. She's married. End of.'

Lou was staring at him the way a baby owl looks at its first moon. Tom Broom smiled a big open sloppy smile.

'What I'm trying to say, in a really clumsy way, is that I want to court you, Lou. I want to snog on the sofa in front of a film and walk around the park and go to the pictures and then say goodnight to you on the doorstep and go home counting the minutes till I see you again.'

Lou looked into his shiny grey eyes. It could be a line. Phil had always been very good at staring you in the face and telling you lies. He had first got her into bed with a bluff line about 'respecting her enough to not want to go to bed with her too quickly', but she didn't think this was applicable in Tom Broom's case. She liked him so much – and this was exactly what she wanted to hear, because she needed space to do all the tasks that lay ahead of her. Plus, she was still married. Legally, if nothing else.

'Thank you,' she said. 'I appreciate that.'

He sighed with deep relief. Telling someone that you insist on giving her space after a night like they'd just had sounded like a line. He wasn't sure if she'd believe his intentions were selfless. If she only knew how much he had to hold himself back from jumping on her there and then and repeating the previous night all over again, albeit without the Country and Western soundtrack.

'Tom?'

'Yes, sweetheart?'

'You've totally mashed my sandwich.'

He looked down. He had squashed it in Lou's hands by holding them so tight. She didn't mind because it gave her a legitimate excuse not to eat it without hurting his feelings.

Tom laughed and kissed her with an apology and a goodbye combined. He asked her if she would be OK. Did she want him to go with her anywhere? Could he do anything for her? Lou smiled and said she was fine and after he left her, his caring stayed with her, like a big, snuggly, invisible coat that she would wear all day. Though the seed that he had planted regarding her parents had grown to beanstalk proportions by the time she arrived at her mother's house.

Lou didn't knock. She marched in to find her mother getting ready to go out.

Timidly Renee asked, 'Hello, love. Are you feeling better this morning?' She was fiddling with the clasp of her watch, which gave her an excuse not to look directly at Lou.

Lou had decided on a strong opening gambit. It had worked with Victorianna so there was no reason to think it wouldn't be just as effective with her mother, who was of a similar mould. 'It was all lies, wasn't it? About Dad?' she bluffed. 'I know.'

Even Lou wasn't prepared for her mother to cave in so quickly. Renee slumped heavily down on the sofa, as if someone had just whipped out her backbone. She covered her face with her hands.

'Elouise, I'm sorry. I don't know what came over me.'

Which meant what?

'Mum?'

'You don't know what you're throwing away.'

'What are you saying, Mum?'

Renee grabbed Lou's hands. 'I thought if I said it, you might not leave him. It will turn out all right, you'll see. Don't be silly and throw away everything you have on a whim. You're so well set-up with Phil.'

Lou struggled to take in what Renee was saying. Surely she hadn't been so sick as to lie like that and insult her dad's memory? She wasn't sure now what were lies and what was the truth. But, deep down, Lou Winter did know her dad.

'He didn't do it, did he? Dad didn't play around. You just said that to make me change my mind about Phil, didn't you?'

'Elouise, I'm sorry. I knew your dad wouldn't mind me saying it if it meant you would be happy in the end.'

A horrible thought popped into Lou's head.

'You weren't going to tell me, were you? If I hadn't come round now and confronted you, you were just going to let me keep on believing he was a bastard, like Phil.'

'I was going to tell you. Really I was. I was going to ring you when I came back from the hairdresser's.'

'The hairdresser's!' repeated Lou, incensed. She pulled her hands away from Renee and pushed her fingers deep into the redness of her hair. 'I could have crashed my car driving away from here yesterday! I've been going out of my mind all night, and you were planning to let me know *after you came back from the hairdresser's!*'

Hot tears of rage came unwanted and she flicked them away. 'How could you, Mum? How could you desecrate Dad's name like that?'

'You don't understand!'

'Too right I don't.'

'I was doing it for the best.'

Lou laughed hard and spat out bitterly, 'Whose best, Mum? Because it certainly wasn't for mine.'

'Yes, for your best!' cried Renee. 'I don't want you to be alone and poor. I want you to have nice things and holidays abroad and to make something of yourself.'

'You never loved Dad, did you? You couldn't have, if his memory is that cheap to you.'

'Of course I did,' said Renee, sobbing now, but to Lou these were 'found-out' tears, not ones of regret.

In one clear, crystallized moment she saw how much her parents' matrimonial template was echoed in her own. Had she copied this, thinking it was how marriages were? One partner taking all the other had to give, one partner jumping through hoops of fire to make the other one happy? One partner always destined to be on the begging end?

'Dad did everything for you that was important, Mum. He loved us with all his heart, he supported us, he even agreed to those silly bloody names you gave us. He did everything, except buy you a big fancy house so you could show off to your friends. You'd have loved him then, wouldn't you – if he'd been grafting twenty-four hours a day to get you your four-bedroomed detached house with a snooker room?'

'You're wrong,' said Renee, with so weak a protest that Lou knew she was right. Each revelation brought up another, for Lou, like a box of tissues.

'And I was just like him, wasn't I? Such a great disappointment because my priority was being happy and not making other people envious. I could never do anything right for you, could I, however much I tried? I was "wasting my time" on the cookery course that I loved but, wow, it was OK when I got a nice, well-paid job in something respectable like accounts, even though I hated it.'

'Accounts was a far better career choice for you, you must see that,' tried Renee. 'Where's the money in catering?'

'Money, money, money!' Lou clenched her fists and growled. 'Do you know, I wonder now if the big attraction of Phil was that I'd actually found someone you approved of. I'd actually pleased you for once! And what a novelty that was 'cos I was never the right size, my hair was never the right colour, my interests weren't the right sort . . . But then I met a bloke who was going places and who could give me all the fancy stuff my dad didn't give you – *and that was all that mattered*. Wasn't it?'

'Phil's not a bad man,' sniffled Renee. 'There are always two sides to every story.'

'You're so lucky that you never had anyone who treated you badly, Mum,' said Lou. 'You have no idea how few times I've smiled in these last three years. Dad treated you like a queen and you couldn't possibly have appreciated it because you are so shallow. What a total waste of a good man's love.'

'I did love him,' Renee protested. 'In my own way I loved him very much.'

Lou turned away in disgust. Her mother might as well have done a Prince Charles and added, 'Whatever love means.'

'You don't know what love is!' Lou cried. 'Love isn't a double garage and three P and O holidays a year. No wonder you prefer Victorianna, with her manor house and her rich boring partner and her holidays in Cape Cod.'

'I always loved you both the same,' Renee protested weepily.

Her mother looked small and pathetic, sobbing away into her pretty lace handkerchief, but Lou knew the tears were for no one but herself. Lou was spent. She didn't want to cry any more. Something had shifted within her heart, as if a rock that had been pressing against it for many years had suddenly moved to the side and let a long-forgotten chamber breathe once again. She would never have her mother's full approval, but she didn't need it. She was a big girl now – Shaun Casserly's big girl. And an OK, decent person.

Drying her eyes, Renee dredged up a limping line of defence. 'When did you ever take the time to show me you loved me?' she accused. 'When did you go clothes shopping with me or . . . or . . . do my nails for me or anything, like Victorianna did? You talk about *you* feeling unloved – well, what about *me*? You never loved me as much as you loved your dad.'

Lou opened her mouth. She would have liked to have told her mother all about one very special manicure – the one when her rings mysteriously went missing. But tempting as it was, that would be doing what her mother had tried to do to her – take away her past, tarnish the shining image of her darling baby, and Lou, despite everything, didn't want to hurt her like that.

'Oh, but I do love you, Mum. You don't understand how much,' said Lou, and she left her mother to her self-pity and her forthcoming cut and blow-dry.

Chapter 55

There were no signs of life at 1, The Faringdales as Phil keyed in the burglar alarm code: no evidence that Lou had even been back to collect some stuff, which was encouraging. Oh well, he thought, if she wants to play silly buggers then I'll make it all the harder for her to come back. She wouldn't be able to stay away from the luxury of his financial support and a house with all the mod-cons for too long. A weekend in Deb's poky flat sleeping on a couch would soon have her crawling back. He had no doubt that was where she was holed up – and she couldn't stay at her mother's as Renee would nag too much. Lou would be back all right, and probably in the next couple of hours. She didn't have the guts to leave, and he'd seen to it that she didn't have access to any money in their joint account. That would smoke her out, if nothing else.

Sighing, he switched on the sports channel, poured himself a stiff one and picked up the Indian takeaway menu. He rang for samosas, a chicken bhuna and a couple of stuffed naans to be delivered as soon as possible.

★

Lou arrived at Deb's with a carrier bag and rang the bell.

'Ah, the cavalry with our Chinese banquet. Welcome!' said Deb, ushering her friend inside. 'How are you?'

'I'll tell you when I've unpacked.'

'You're staying?' gasped Deb with glee.

'Unpacked the fried rice, I mean. No, I'm staying put at May's flat for now.'

'You're mad, Lou.'

'After all that's happened to me in the last few days, I'd be mad if I wasn't mad.'

'Anything else happened?'

'Mum told me Dad was unfaithful. I found out she was lying. Oh, and I slept with Tom.'

Deb grabbed the carrier bag. 'You get the plates, I'll open the plonk,' she said quickly.

Lou told her everything.

'Bloody Norah. All that in two days!' said Deb, through a face-full of prawn crackers.

'Yes.'

'You've swept with Mr Broom!'

'Very funny.'

'And how do you feel?'

'As if I've been thrown in a spin-drier.'

'I bet you felt as if you were sat on one last night!'

'It was better than that,' said Lou with a grin.

'Wow, you and Tom Broom,' said Deb, shaking her head in thrilled amazement. 'Is he in proportion?'

'Deb!'

'I'm your best friend and, as such, there are no sacred details about your boyfriend.'

Boyfriend. That word made the infatuated-teenage-girl smile slide from her face.

'What's the matter?' said Deb, watching it wither.

'I'm married. I'm having an affair. It's so wrong.'

'Well, you're not really having an affair, are you?' Deb said reasonably. 'You're not cheating on Phil because you've left him. You're free. You just have to deal with the technicalities of that decision now and get unmarried.'

'Yes,' said Lou, not sounding totally convinced. She wasn't even sure if Phil realized his marriage was at an end. Knowing him, he wouldn't really believe that she could have found the guts to leave him, which made her marriage still 'live' in her opinion. At least until he found out what else she had done behind his back.

'Anyway, back to the juicy bits. How nice was last night?'

Lou nodded. 'Lovely.'

'And *is* he in proportion?'

'Give over, you mucky tart.'

'Talking of penises, have you heard from Phil?'

'No, but I think I might soon,' said Lou. 'After what I did.'

'What have you done?' asked Deb, stuffing in a piece of prawn toast.

Lou told her that bit too and Deb listened with fascinated shock. Who would ever have thought her mild little friend had it in her?

Lou slept so soundly in the lumpy bumpy bed above *Ma's Café* that the noise from the builders didn't wake her until an hour after they had started work. They were singing 'Bohemian Rhapsody' downstairs in a chorus and Lou smiled. She was getting quite fond of the little flat. It was a clean, fresh space – a sanctuary – just what her head needed. But it could only be a matter of hours before Phil rang. She was surprised he hadn't done so already, to demand a meeting there and then. The thought of going back to The Faringdales filled her with dread, but she wouldn't meet him here and spoil the positive air in this space.

The builders downstairs were blowing wolf whistles and taking the mick out of someone. She realized who and why a minute later when there was a knock on the door and she opened it to find Tom, standing there with a bouquet of pink and white flowers.

'Good morning, gorgeous,' he said, sweeping her to him with his free arm. 'I missed you last night.'

'I missed you too,' she said and they kissed, with tongues, and it was rather lovely, give or take the angle her neck had to bend in order to enjoy it.

'I'll have to go and buy a vase, unless you've got a couple of spare milk bottles,' said Lou, sniffing the blooms.

'No need,' he said. 'They come in a bag of water. You just put them on the table and admire them. Easy.'

'I don't deserve you,' Lou was going to say, but she stopped herself. Maybe she did deserve him. Maybe what she didn't deserve was to be treated like rubbish by anyone any more.

'Can I take you out to dinner?' Tom asked.

Lou smiled but she was shaking her head too. 'This is awkward,' she said. 'I wouldn't want to be . . . seen . . . out.'

'With a big ugly monster like me?' Tom finished off.

'No, not at all, and you know I don't mean that.'

'It's OK, I understand,' said Tom. 'You wouldn't enjoy yourself out on the town with another man just after you've filed for divorce.'

Lou stared open-mouthed at him. It wasn't a myth then – there really were blokes who understood the female mentality.

'Yes,' she said slowly. 'It doesn't feel right being out on the town. I wouldn't want to rub Phil's nose in it, if he found out.'

'Didn't stop him doing it to you, though,' said Tom.

'In what way?' said Lou.

'Flaunting another woman when you could have—' He realized his mistake immediately.

'What woman?' asked Lou, stiffening.

Tom's mouth opened and shut like a distressed goldfish.

'Tom?'

Tom Broom was a man of straight lines and for that reason he felt he could do nothing other than come clean and hope for the best. He plonked himself down on her bed and patted the seat beside him, but she wouldn't sit.

'Deb saw him with someone,' said Tom. 'She was worried sick about you. She didn't know what to do for the best.'

'She should have told me,' said Lou coldly. Tom reached for her hand but she shrugged him off.

'Listen, Lou – she really didn't know what to do for the best. I didn't either.'

'So that's what all those concerned little looks you

were giving me were about then,' said Lou crossly. 'You both knew and neither of you thought to tell me I was being cuckooed in public.'

Any other time and Tom would have smiled at that, but Lou was hurting and it made him want to wrap her up in his arms and hug her tightly. 'Lou. Think about what happened last time when Deb told you. I found her breaking her heart because trying to stick a brave face on in front of you just got too much. I made her tell me what the matter was. You didn't see the state she was in. She was terrified of smashing up your life all over again. Please don't tell her I told you. I don't want you to fall out with her about this.' He rubbed his forehead. 'God, I'm so crap at covering stuff up.'

Lou took a long, hard look at him and a great warm feeling washed over her because she was so highly regarded by two people like this. Two lovely, dear people, who hated lies and deceit and had tried their best to protect her from them. She lifted Tom's face and kissed him.

'Can I come round tonight? I'll cook for you,' she said.

'Oh God, yes, please,' he said, pulling her into his arms and then he kissed her to a serenade of 'Crazy Little Thing Called Love' from the workmen below them.

Chapter 56

'Leave it with me, Jack. I'll get the monies transferred now,' said Phil to the gruff voice on the other end of the telephone. 'I'll just give the bank a tinkle. Ring you back in a bit, mate.'

He hung up and Tannoyed his secretary, telling her to go out and get him a bacon and sausage sandwich from the shop around the corner. *Where the fuck was Lou?* He had expected her to be back in the house by now. The washing was piling up and the freezer stocks were fast diminishing. There were no welcoming smells from the oven to greet him when he got home, plus he'd done something to the central heating and thrown all the settings out. Not only was the house dark when he got home, but it was hot enough to grow bananas in. And he was sick of the bloody microwave 'tinging' that his meal was ready. All plans of a cosy reconciliation were now gone. He was already wondering if he should resurrect his relationship with Sue Shoesmith and carry on with teaching Lou a lesson when she deigned to come back – whenever that would be.

He hit the fast-dial button for the bank and went through the security questions that confirmed his identity. Then he gave instructions for some monies to be transferred over to Fat Jack's account. The woman at the bank kept him on hold for an eternity, listening to what felt like the whole repertoire of Take That. And when she eventually came back to him, he listened in frustrated disbelief to what she had to say.

'You must have that wrong, love,' he argued. 'There's plenty of money in that account to cover this transfer. More than enough.'

Where did they get the sodding staff for these places – Bimbos Incorporated? He was put on hold once again whilst Gary Barlow lamented his non-ability to commit to his bird, and just when he was about to slam down the phone and go storming into the branch in person, she came back to him with her information. Phil listened in jaw-dropped horror.

'When? Who? *How* much?'

Phil put down the phone before his shaking hand dropped it. It appeared that lamb roasts were not going to be on the agenda for the foreseeable future.

He hadn't wanted to ring first, but she had left him no choice.

Lou saw Phil's name flash up on the mobile. She took a deep breath and pressed connect.

'Lou?' he said, as calmly as his adrenaline levels would allow.

'Phil,' she said, as calmly as her adrenaline levels would allow.

'Where are you? What's going on?'

'I've left you. Didn't you get my note?'

OK, thought Phil, working through a process of logic. Deb had probably told her about seeing him with Sue after all, and she was really, *really* pissed off. He needed to stay calm and pitch this correctly. What was that proverb again? Let something go and eventually it'll come back to you. Hopefully, with all the fucking money it had ripped out of your business account.

'Yes, I got your note, Lou.' He used her name, women liked that, so he used it again. 'Lou, I know you're angry, love, but don't do anything hasty. I haven't changed the locks or anything stupid like that, so you can come home any time. Please, I know you want space to think . . .'

'I've done all the thinking I want to,' said Lou, wondering when he was going to mention the business account money. She wasn't stupid – she knew that was the only thing that would have caused him to ring her.

'Lou, I'm not going to harass you but please, promise me you will take some more time to mull things over. Just think some more – that's all I ask.'

'Phil . . .'

'*Please.*'

The word sounded very genuine and it threw her. Maybe he needed a little time too, she thought – to come to terms with the fact that she wasn't coming back. So kindly she said, 'OK.'

'That's all I wanted to say. Bye, love.'

'Bye.'

Phil knew by the soft way she said that single word that she still wanted him.

She just felt the need to stamp her foot a bit. He gave her a fortnight max. Then he'd review his tactics.

That evening, after a delicious pork and mustard casserole, Lou stood up to leave. Tom tried to pull her back down onto the sofa where they had spent three solid hours talking. His eyes were glazed over from the effort of trying not to touch her.

'I have to go, Tom,' she smiled.

'Lou, can we just pretend I never said I wanted to do all this courting stuff. I can't stand it. I want you to stay.' He caught her arm and despite her giggling protest, he rolled her underneath him. 'Please, Lou, stay or I'll squash you flat. No pressure of course.'

The combination of her wriggling and giggling beneath him was turning him on so much he had to let her go before he exploded and blew up the new sofa. She was all flushed and her hair was stuck up all over the place.

'I hate you, Tom Broom,' she smiled, getting well out of his way.

'Move in,' he said, gently this time. 'I'm forty next month. That could be your birthday present to me.'

'Tom . . .'

'Don't go. *Per favore, non andartene, bella signora . . .*'

'That's not fair, using Italian! Below the belt, Tom Broom.'

'I know, I know,' he conceded, reaching for her hand and playing with her fingers, anticipating what she was going to say. He knew Lou had her values, and despite his frustration, Tom loved her all the more for them. Yes, he loved her. Thank God Phil Winter was such a total fool.

As if he had transmitted that name psychically to her she said, 'Phil phoned me today.'

Tom bristled. 'What for?'

'He wanted to give me some time to think about

what I was doing,' said Lou indifferently, although her tone did nothing to stop Tom's smile drying up faster than a raindrop on the sun.

'And do you need time?' he asked softly.

Lou came forward to give him a reassuring hug.

'Do you think I'd be here with you if I needed time? Phil is as tight as a duck's backside without a paddle,' she said. 'His reason for phoning was purely financial, though he didn't say it. He doesn't fool me. Right, I'm going home.'

'I hate you going back to that place,' said Tom. 'Do you want to take Clooney?'

Clooney's ears pricked up in his basket in the hallway at the sound of his name.

'No, he's all warm and comfortable here,' said Lou.

She got the car keys from her bag and Tom took her out to the car and kissed her goodbye with a snog that made every nerve from her brain to her big toes sigh.

Deb had said Phil was a manipulative cunning fox, thought Tom as he waved Lou off, and it very much appeared as if he had started mounting his offensive to win her back. Tom was worried.

Chapter 57

Phil finished the call to the travel agent in a foul mood. The fortnight deadline he had mentally given Lou to come to her senses was now up and there was no sign whatsoever of her returning. He had left it to the very last minute before cancelling the holiday they should have been taking tomorrow. It would have been worth losing a couple of grand if she turned up that night with her suitcase packed full of sarongs, but it didn't look very likely now. In saying that, no divorce papers had arrived, which cheered him slightly. Then he thought of the money she had taken out of the business account and he was thrown back into a place of frustration again. How ironic it was that this non-affair could spell the end of his marriage, when the others hadn't. They'd survived the Susan Peach thing beautifully, but Lou had known nothing about the one-night stand at a sales conference early in their marriage. That was his first fall from grace and he had felt so guilty and awful about enjoying the thrill of this encounter that he had tried to make it up to Lou by telling her they could start trying for a family if she wanted. Thank goodness nothing had come of that. Then there was a near-miss with that old bird in Corfu, whose name escaped him even if the vision of her grave-yard teeth would stay with him for ever. He'd had the luck of the devil that night for it would have been a tragedy to lose his marriage for a much-regretted and drunken bonk against an olive tree.

He had, out of respect for Lou, worn a condom every time though. Plus he didn't want to get one up the duff and relive the whole Sharon nightmare all over again. Talking of which, he had better write out that cheque for her and the brats and have done with it. Now what sort of flowers did Lou like again?

Just before lunch, Bradley said there was a pretty woman who'd asked to see him privately in his office. Phil smiled the smile of the victorious. *I knew it*, he thought, expecting to find a contrite Lou with her tail between her legs. But his smile soon dropped when he saw that the 'pretty woman' was Moon-Loon Michelle with those legs that he felt sure would glow in ultra-violet light, and mutton-dressed-as-lamb boots. He led her into the office out of staff earshot and politely offered her a coffee which he hoped she would refuse. She didn't, but he felt obliged to accommodate her, seeing as she'd brought him the present of a big Tupperware carton – although he wished he'd known it was only homemade bloody cornflake buns before he'd invited her into his inner sanctum.

'Is it true Lou's left you?' Michelle asked, wandering slowly around his office.

Pretty? He needed to get Bradley an emergency eye-test.

'No, of course it's not true,' said Phil indignantly.

'We're just giving each other some space for a while. Lou has a few problems.'

'She's got a shop in the Townend, hasn't she?' said Michelle. 'A café, isn't it?'

'Yes,' said Phil, even though he hadn't a clue. He wondered what the hell Michelle was doing here and why she was asking all these questions. 'Who on earth told you she'd left me?' he said.

'One of the builders who is working at the café has a sister who goes to my therapy group. He said she was living up above it.'

Oh, that was where she was staying, was it? Well, the novelty of slumming it in a hovel must be nearly at an end, thank goodness.

'Therapy, eh?' said Phil absently.

'Women in Crisis,' said Michelle.

What a surprise.

'I just came to see if you were OK,' said Michelle, attempting a bright smile. She wasn't bad-looking when her face cracked, thought Phil, although he suspected that was rarer than Halley's Comet.

'I'm fine,' said Phil, who had been considerably better since the new cleaner started a few days ago. It saved him having to learn how to try and decipher the mysteries of the washer-drier, and she'd fixed the central heating. Miserable bugger, though – she had exacted extra money for the pigsty she'd had to tackle when she first arrived and muttered the words 'environmental health' a few too many times for his liking. And no, she didn't cook, was the answer to his question.

'I think she's mad, for the record,' said Michelle, looking at him without blinking.

'Well, she hasn't left me. She'll be back soon.' Phil made that point clear.

'If you want to talk, you know, I'm a good listener,' said Michelle.

'Thanks, but I don't have anything to talk about,' said Phil with a smile that cloaked the 'bugger off' vibes he was firing at her.

'If you want any help around the house, I'm here for you.'

'I've got a cleaner,' said Phil, throwing out even stronger vibes.

'We could go out for a meal if you wanted some . . . company.' She put a sinister emphasis on that last word.

'I'm so busy here, I've hardly time,' said Phil, 'but thanks for offering. Very kind of you.'

'Phil. If you're free, I am. We could stay in and I can comfort you.'

Phil scrunched up his face in thought. Was she saying what he thought she was saying?

'Come again?' he asked, with a need for further clari-fication.

'If you like,' said Michelle seductively. She was behind him now, kneading her fingers into his stiff shoulders.

'Whoa fucking whoa!' said Phil, standing up and shrugging her off.

'Well, it might just make her change her mind if she sees someone else has moved in on her man,' said Michelle.

'No way, lady!' said Phil, feeling like he had suddenly been transported into a bad dream. 'Anyway, aren't you supposed to be one of Lou's mates?'

'Was,' said Michelle, with her lip wobbling. 'She threw me away as well as you.'

'She hasn't thrown me away!' God, where was a big crucifix when you needed one? 'And that's just sick, trying to make her jealous. I think you'd better go, love.' In the direction of the nearest strait-jacket shop.

'I don't want a relationship, you know. You've had an affair before – it wouldn't be the first time. She doesn't have to know.'

'You're nuts. Piss off, please.'

Michelle swung her bag onto her shoulder and stormed out of the office with chilli-hot tears stinging her eyes. The feeling of rejection never failed to reduce her to rubble, especially when she had just been rejected by someone who had as few sexual morals as Phil Winter. At least this new therapy group was helping her to work through things. She had made a new special friend there too who was coming round for tea that night. They'd have a good no-holds-barred natter about this later on. Her name was Sue – she'd looked a bit like Lou with her green, green eyes. Sue was having a really tough time too. She had just been dumped by this married bloke who didn't want to hurt her. An infinitely more decent bloke than a man like Phil Winter could ever hope to be.

Phil got a coffee to steady his nerves. Shagging one of Lou's mates was not on – besides which, she was too skinny with crap tits. Lou's sister had tried to seduce him a few times too, the saucy bitch, rubbing up against him and sticking her breasts in his face when Lou wasn't around. Actually, thinking about it, she did it when Lou *was* around. He knew he could have had her any time – that was enough for his ego. But even Phil Winter had his morals.

*

Across town, a massive Italian coffee-machine was spurting into action, and soon the aroma of raspberries reached Lou's receptive nostrils.

Now that *is* a winner, she thought, and one that definitely wouldn't be joining the coconut-meringue-flavoured coffee on the reject list. She had found she could only test a few at a time as her taste-buds got confused. The previous day she had realized it was time to stop when she thought she was drinking 'crème brûlée' flavour only to find out it was 'midnight mint'. She turned round to hear a gentle knock on the front door. A small, well-wrapped up figure was peering through the glass. Her mother. Lou felt her adrenaline start to pump. She tried to stay calm as she unlocked the door and Renee walked tentatively in.

'Hello,' she said, with a watery, nervous smile.

'Hello, Mum,' said Lou, and they gave each other a dry kiss on the cheek.

'How are you?' asked Renee.

'Fine,' said Lou. 'And yourself?'

'Not too bad, not too bad,' said Renee, looking around her at the stark black and white décor rather than try to make eye-contact with her daughter. 'It looks very nice in here.'

'Well, we had a good set of lads working for us. They've done wonders. We've still got the kitchen part to finish off, though. There's new stuff arriving every day.'

'Are you going to put some pictures up on the wall as well?' Renee asked.

'Yes – big black and white photographs. They're on order,' Lou answered, with a prickly tone.

'Oh, that'll be nice,' said Renee.

Blimey! thought Lou. That was edging dangerously close to a positive comment.

'Would you like a coffee?' she offered. 'I'm just testing out some raspberry truffle flavour. That's what you can probably smell.'

'That sounds nice,' said Renee. She sat down stiffly on one of the black cushioned benches and Lou brought over a full cup for her.

'I've just been in town getting some bits in for our trip to America,' Renee told Lou, slipping off her gloves.

'Yes, it'll be nice for you,' said Lou. 'Are you looking forward to it?'

'Oh yes,' Renee said politely and took a sip. Then: 'This is very nice.'

They sat in silence for a little while as Lou tried to think of something to say that didn't have the word 'nice' in it.

'Where have you been staying then?' said Renee. She was speaking like a little girl on her best behaviour. Lou found herself about to temper the truth before her mind told her to say it as it was.

'Upstairs here.'

'Here?' said Renee, with some incredulity, but she sat quickly on what she might instinctively have said, and asked instead, 'Is there much room?'

'No, but it'll do for now. I'll find somewhere more permanent to live soon.'

Renee opened her mouth to say something and closed it again so Lou spoke it for her. 'Yes, Mum, I do know what I'm doing.'

'I was just going to say you could have come home to

me,' said Renee quietly. 'I know you wouldn't have wanted to, but your bedroom will always be your bedroom if you need it.'

'Thank you, Mum,' said Lou, a little shamefacedly after that. Her mother looked so dreadfully uncomfortable that Lou was forced to appreciate how much courage it must have taken her to come there, especially after how they left things last time. Renee was still huddled up in her thin tweed coat and her little furry hat, and as Lou looked at the hands holding the cup, with their thin one-ply-skin, she noticed just how old her mother was getting. She didn't want to fight with her, whatever had passed between them. They were just two very different people and they always would be.

What's more, over the past couple of weeks, Lou had also been remembering the woman who ripped plasters off her five-year-old knee with a 'one-two-three-The-Beverley-Sisters' chant to distract her from the sudden sting. The woman who always had a cooked tea on the table for her when she came home from school and nagged her to eat her broccoli, long before it was recognized as a superfood. And the woman who made sure she never went to school with unpolished shoes, unbrushed hair or school shirts that weren't whiter than a high-definition Persil advert. And the woman who had dragged herself out of bed with flu to watch Lou's part in the primary-school nativity – as Herod. (She never had Victorianna's blonde ringlets that landed her the more glamorous angel parts.) Renee was, after all – as imperfect as she was, as annoying as she was – her mother.

'I've just been trying out a cheesecake recipe. Incredibly low-fat, but retaining most of the taste, or so

I hope,' said Lou, cutting off a small slice and holding up the plate. 'Want some?'

'I'm not one for cakes, Lou.'

'It's only a little slice and I'd appreciate your opinion,' said Lou.

'Oh!' said Renee.

I've surprised her, thought Lou, with as much surprise as she had inadvertently caused. Maybe she was right too about some things. Maybe I don't make her feel special.

Lou came to sit down at the bench with two plates of cheesecake.

'It's very nice,' said Renee, licking her spoon. 'Very creamy.'

'Does it taste lemony enough to you?' said Lou.

Renee tasted some more. 'You could afford to add a bit more lemon. It's a bit . . . tame.'

'Yes, I think you're right,' said Lou, sampling her cake again. 'If you help me perfect this, I'll name it after you,' she promised with a half-smile.

'Like Anna Pavlova!' said Renee. 'And Dame Nelly Melba.'

'And Doreen Banana Split,' said Lou.

Renee was concentrating too hard to get the joke. She took another dainty forkful. 'If you want my opinion . . .' she said, looking at Lou carefully to see if she really did, and Lou affirmed this with an eager nod. '. . . I think your base could do with a touch of ginger as well. No wait – maybe cardamom or walnut – to set off the flavour of your lemon.'

Lou took a forkful and tried to imagine the taste of that. Renee did the same.

'I think you're right, Mum,' said Lou. 'Thank you.'

Renee looked at her daughter and smiled. Shaun's leaf-green eyes looked back at her.

'I do love you, you know,' said Renee, coughing back a throatful of tears that suddenly blindsided her. 'And I am proud of you.'

'I love you too, Mum.'

They carried on eating, mother and daughter, Lou's first customers in her beautiful new half-finished coffee shop.

CHAPTER 58

'Lou, my love, I've got to move. I've got the most awful cramp,' said Tom, gently shifting a sleeping Lou over and standing up to dance away the grip in his leg.

'Sorry,' said Lou, stretching, and then she noticed the time and bounced to her feet. 'I'd better go, otherwise I'll never get up tomorrow.'

Letting Lou go back to the flat intact after the thoughts Tom was having about her almost did his head in. He knew she had her reasons for keeping him at arm's length, but was it a cover for her cooling off? In the last couple of weeks she had seemed to yawn an awful lot, which hadn't exactly put him at ease. She'd blamed it on the physical tiredness of not only assisting the workmen to clean up, but also helping some little old lady to clear out her house. He had been rather touched that evening when she had fallen asleep on him during the big snuggly film-watching session, but in the last half-hour he'd had a visit from a few bad-thought fairies who insisted on tormenting him with a distinctly more negative perspective.

'One last cuddle,' said Tom, and pulled her down on the sofa again. He held her face in his hands and smiled at her.

'Lou, you have eyes like emeralds, has anyone ever told you?'

Lou gave a little laugh.

'Did I say something funny?' said Tom, trying to discreetly adjust his trousers.

'It's just that Phil used to say that Sharon – you know, the one he had the twins with – had eyes like sapphires. It just struck me as a strange parallel,' said Lou, then she realized what she had said and slapped her hand over her mouth. 'God, what am I saying? I'm sorry, Tom, that was insensitive.'

'It's OK,' said Tom, who was thinking that Phil was still very much on her mind. His arms closed around her and he enjoyed the nearness of her whilst he had her. However long that would be for.

'Did you ever see Sharon?' he asked.

'Once, at Christmas, when we were in Meadowhall.'

'And was she as gorgeous as he made out?'

'She was, like a Swede. That's a Bjorn Borg sort of Swede, not a turnip.'

'I guessed,' said Tom with a smile. Then: 'What, she looked like Bjorn Borg?'

'No, silly,' said Lou digging him in the ribs. 'She was very pretty, with striking Nordic colouring – and the children were so like her too, except they had really beautiful brown eyes. Don't know who they got those from, though, because Phil's are blue too and so are everyone's in his family. Anyway, Phil just looked straight through them as if they didn't exist. It was so odd – horrible, actually. I couldn't get it out of my head for ages.'

'I can't imagine how anyone could do that to their own children,' said Tom.

'Me neither. Anyway, are you ready for your Brando in the morning?' asked Lou, changing the subject. Deb was unveiling her Brando creation first thing tomorrow. Odd time to have cake, but Deb had insisted on the timing.

'Course I am,' said Tom, pulling Lou even nearer to him. She felt so good, he couldn't bear it if she went back to Phil. Tom had already assumed that Phil wouldn't give her the quickie divorce she wanted and the battle would be bloody when he responded to the petition. *Unless he wins her back first.* Tom tried to chase that thought away. He had a feeling of dread which he couldn't quite shake off that this relationship really was too good to last. They sat there for a while just being together, the comfortable quietness broken only by the crackle of the fire logs. Tom couldn't ever remember feeling so happy or so sad at the same time.

The next morning Phil was feeling positive. That was, until the jolly, whistling postman delivered a long stiff envelope into his hands as he was locking the front door. *Cripwell, Oliver & Clapham – Solicitors* it said on the corner. He ripped it open to find that Lou had filed for divorce. He couldn't believe it. *Why?* It was a question that haunted him on the drive to the showroom as his brain tried to make sense of her actions. Eventually, it came up with the answer: his wife had gone too far and now she didn't know how to turn back without a bit of help. As such, he was still convinced the situation wasn't beyond the pale. He had slept well and was thinking positive thoughts – like today was one day nearer to his wife coming home to him. He missed her. Not just because she kept the house clean or cooked great meals, he simply missed her presence in his life. He hadn't realized just how much she oiled his wheels. On the day she came home, he'd fill the bedroom with flowers for her. He'd book a table in a restaurant. He'd cancel Fat Jack and Maureen and Celia coming around at Christmas. They were OK, he and Lou. Really – he could recover this with a bit of effort.

At the other side of town, Tom and Lou were sitting in the café with their hands over their eyes awaiting the arrival of the Brando.

'Da da!' announced Deb. 'Now you can look!'

Tom and Lou opened their eyes to see, not a monster cake but two huge ciabatta rolls stuffed with ham, egg, slices of sausage, mushrooms, and a basil-smelling tomato dressing that sent their salivary glands into overdrive.

'Everything grilled in a splash of olive oil, just to give people a chance at surviving it.' Deb sighed. She wished her mam could have been here to see this. She would have been in her element.

'Wow,' said Lou.

'I thought it was going to be pudding, not that I'm in the slightest bit put off,' said Tom, who didn't wait for an invitation to tuck in.

'Well,' hummed Deb, 'it just seemed like too good a name to pass up. A bit classier than a "belt-buster", don't you think? Talking of which, you should see our new uniforms. We're going to have to decide on a name for this café soon because we'll have to get logos stitched on them.'

Tom's eyes opened wide. 'You've got uniforms?'

'Black mini-dresses with stockings and six-inch heels,' said Deb.

OK, he knew she was joking, but the idea of Lou in that get-up hit the spot rather instantly. Deb guessed it had by the wriggle he did in his seat and laughed. She also noticed Lou was a little more reticent about tucking in.

'Come on, Lou, get that sausage down your throat. Ho ho.'

Lou didn't speak. She picked up her knife and fork and stared at the plate, then dropped them and ran upstairs, holding her mouth.

Tom looked at Deb.

'Hmmm. I thought she's been looking a bit pale,' said Deb.

'I'll go after her,' said Tom, wiping his mouth, but Deb pushed him down into his seat.

'Romantic as your intentions are, Tom, when a woman's vomiting, she likes a little privacy. It's a total myth that they like you holding their hair back whilst you're watching them spew their guts up.'

'Has she said anything to you – you know, about *him*?' Tom asked, his heart fluttering unpleasantly.

'Only that the solicitor said the divorce papers have been posted and Phil should get them today. She's bound to be a bit worried, Tom. It'll just be a touch of stress.'

'I'm terrified she'll go back to him, Deb. I'm scared I'm too boring for her.'

'What on earth makes you think that?'

'She keeps dropping off to sleep on me for a start.'

'Don't talk wet. We're knackered, the pair of us,' although she said that for Tom's benefit, because Deb could hardly sleep with all the adrenaline zipping around her system. 'Cut her some slack, Tom. She's totally besotted with you but she's been through a lot recently. There's nothing to worry about, I'd put my life savings on it. All three pounds fifty of them!'

They heard the faint rumble of the upstairs toilet being flushed.

'Besides which, if she goes back to him, I'll make her into these sausages and fry her up for lorry drivers,' Deb went on, giving him her biggest encouraging smile.

Tom managed a little laugh, but he wasn't feeling the slightest bit jolly inside.

Five minutes later, Lou came back downstairs to two sympathetic faces.

'You OK?' asked Deb, giving her friend's arm a stroke.

'Yes, much better,' said Lou. 'Sorry about that – I've ruined your grand launch.'

'It's fine,' said Deb, popping a slice of tomato-drenched sausage into her mouth from Lou's plate. 'Waste not, want not. Here, have a cup of tea.'

'Thanks, but I just want a glass of water.'

'You've been overdoing things,' said Deb. 'You need to get back to bed for a rest. Doesn't she, Tom?'

'Yes, she does,' nodded Tom, who had a head full of thoughts he really didn't want.

'No chance,' said Lou. 'We've got stacks of things to do and the sooner we finish them, the sooner we open. Plus I've promised another one of Mrs Serafinska's friends that I'll pop in and see her about some clutter-clearing, although God knows when I'll get around to doing that.'

'Well, May seemed to manage this place on her own,'

said Deb. 'We can always get some part-time help in if you want to go clutter-clearing.'

'That's hardly fair on you, is it?' said Lou.

'Well, I don't see why not,' said Deb. 'If you want to go off and shift rubbish sometimes, you go right ahead and do it. We're living out our dreams, Lou; we have to go with the flow. Think about it: if you hadn't started clearing up your life in the first place, we might not be here. I think we owe the powers-that-be a little respect in this matter.'

'You don't half talk some rubbish yourself at times,' grinned Lou, 'although, if I do the occasional job, I'll obviously plough the money back into the café – OK?'

'Whatever makes you happy, buddy,' Deb grinned back.

Lou had more interest in the pastry side of the business. It had already been arranged that she would make the cakes for the afternoon coffee shop whilst Deb ran the breakfast side. Deb was quite looking forward to being a more glamorous version of May in a roomful of rough men.

Lou's mobile went off just as they were clearing up the plates. The look on her face told Tom and Deb who it was even before she said his name.

'Hello Phil,' said Lou quietly. She was awfully drained-looking, thought Tom and Deb simultaneously.

'Yes, I think a meeting would be a good idea now.'

Tom rubbed the back of his neck.

'No, I'll come over to you . . . Yes, ten o'clock – at our house,' said Lou in the same quiet tone. 'See you tomorrow morning, then. Bye.'

Our house, Tom thought.

Lou threw the phone down and immediately ran upstairs again with her hand across her mouth. Tom knew how she felt.

Mid-morning, the plumber turned up to connect their newly-arrived monster dishwasher to the water supply. Lou hadn't stopped scrubbing and cleaning since Tom had left and Deb was worried about her. She was looking more and more ghost-like with every passing half-hour. She hadn't eaten or drunk anything all day except some water, which she had only just managed to hang onto.

'Don't worry, I'll be better when my meeting with Phil is over and done with,' Lou answered her concerns. 'I think he will have convinced himself that I'll be worrying myself sick overnight about the divorce papers landing and I'll take one look at him tomorrow and cave in.'

'Tom thinks you're going to,' said Deb.

'What? Go back to Phil? Not a chance!' said Lou, discreetly scratching her breast.

'Why do you keep doing that?' said Deb.

'My bra's killing me,' said Lou. 'It's rubbing me like hell.'

'Is it new?'

'No, that's the weird thing. It's not just this bra, it's all of them.'

'Have you changed your washing powder?'

'Nope.'

'When was your last period?'

'Don't be ridiculous,' said Lou, knowing where this conversation was going.

'Have you missed?'

'Yes, but who could blame me with all that's been going on?'

'OK,' said Deb.

She nipped out a little later, saying she was going to get some more teabags. Lou put on the kettle in her absence and had an instant coffee. It tasted unpleasant. That was all she needed – to have gone off coffee.

Phil took the afternoon off and called in at the supermarket for a cake mix. Jane Asher? he thought. No chuffing chance! It looked far too professional so he plumped for a Bettermix Instant Victoria Sponge in a nice cheap packet. It turned out a bit too well when he made it, but he cocked it up nicely on the icing. It looked quite pathetic, really, when he had added the little sweetie decorations – just the thing to pull at a woman's heartstrings. Lou would never be able to resist it, anyway.

As he put on the last smartie, the text beeped. It was from Sue British Racing Green Eyes. YOU EVIL LYING BAS-TARD it said. Now what the hell was that all about?

Deb came back in to find Lou taking a breather on a chair.

'Here, this might help,' she said, and tossed Lou the paper bag.

Lou tipped out the contents and gave Deb a quizzical look.

'Of course you are joking!'

Deb nodded towards it. 'I think you should take the test, Lou.'

Lou shoved the pregnancy test back in the bag. 'I've got a virus, that's all,' she said.

'Take the test, Lou. Call it a hunch. If it's negative I'll stick my head in that new dishwasher for making you do this, but just do it and get it over with.'

'How can I be pregnant, Deb? Talk sense.'

'Lou, I don't know and you may not be, but being sick, late periods, being constantly tired and having sore boobs, well . . . Find out for sure, though, will you?'

Lou sighed and was about to take it upstairs when Deb coughed.

'We have toilets here downstairs, you know. Very nice toilets too, thanks to the builders.'

'I know, I just wanted to keep them new.'

'Lou, get in the Ladies and don't be silly.'

Lou disappeared with her box. Deb waited outside for what seemed ages before Lou emerged looking like Frosty the Snowman with anaemia. The tears were rolling down her face and she reached for Deb.

'Oh hell,' said Deb, coming forwards. 'Lou, I'm sorry. I hate myself now. I just thought, with all your symptoms and—'

'Deb, it's positive,' said Lou. 'I did both tests and they both came up positive.'

She showed Deb the blue lines in the confirmation boxes on the tests. 'I have got it right, haven't I? That does mean . . .'

'Yes – yes!'

'What if they're faulty?'

'Both of them? No chance. Lou – you're pregnant.'

'I can't be!'

'According to those tests you bloody well are!'

They both just stood there, hardly daring to move in case they chased away the blue lines.

'Could it be Phil's baby?' asked Deb, cringing as she said it.

'It's not possible – I haven't slept with Phil in ages,' said Lou. 'It has to be Tom's.'

'Thank God for that,' said Deb, crossing herself internally.

Oh God, Tom! What on earth would he say? thought Lou. After one incident of love-making with him, she had fallen pregnant. *Would he feel that she had trapped him? Like Phil had with Sharon?* She was pregnant! She clung onto Deb for comfort. She didn't know whether to laugh or cry so she plumped for both.

'What do I tell Tom?'

'I'd say "Tom, I'm pregnant". I think you'll find that's all you need to say for now.'

'Deb, I'm pregnant!'

'Lou, you're pregnant!'

They both screamed and hugged each other and started dancing and bouncing around, like a pair of spaced-out Tiggers.

That was how Tom found them five minutes later when he called in to see if Lou was feeling any better.

Chapter 59

That evening, Tom lay back on the sofa grinning and in his arms lay Lou, also grinning. They had grinned so much, their facial muscles hurt.

'A baby next spring,' said Tom dreamily. 'Season of new birth – could that be any more perfect?'

'I didn't know how you'd take it,' said Lou, 'seeing as we've only slept together once.'

'Don't remind me,' said Tom with amused sarcasm. 'Move in tonight then you can sleep in my bed and let me be all gentle with you.'

That sounded awfully tempting, thought Lou, as something coursed through her veins which felt rather like very strong sweet wine. But not yet.

'Please, Tom, I need to finish off my business with Phil first, totally and completely,' said Lou. 'I don't have affairs. I'm not that sort of person. It doesn't sit well with me to do things this way round.'

'We're going to have a baby together, isn't that finished enough for you?' Tom asked. His voice had a wobble in it that she hadn't heard before.

'No,' said Lou. 'Give me one more day. Just one. Then we can plan for us.'

Tom nodded, pretending to understand. Was she playing for time? Giving Phil the chance to win her back? What if he rolled out a major charm offensive tomorrow? Phil Winter was so confident, so *cocksure*. He cuddled Lou until she had to leave his arms because she felt queasy again. Her hormones were all over the place. She was ripe for being manipulated. What if Phil played on that and convinced her that the best place was there with him in his big warm house and big warm bed? Tom knew this wasn't logical – after all, Lou was carrying his child. But feeling something and knowing something were totally different things.

Lou came back down the stairs and resumed her place snuggled up next to him. He put his hand on her tummy. He wanted his baby to get used to knowing he was close.

'I still can't believe it,' said Tom.

'*You* can't believe it!' said Lou. 'Not that I want to bring Phil into this, but the amount of accidents we had – and nothing – and only once with you and then "bingo".'

Phil again. Tom tried to laugh off his name being brought into their intimate moment by rubbing his nails imperiously on his shirt.

'Well, I must have supersperm.'

'What sex would you like?' asked Lou.

'Any sort of sex, I'm busting for it.'

'No – what flavour baby would you like, you nut?' said Lou, hitting him with a cushion.

'Honestly, Lou, I know it's a cliché, but as long as it's OK, I really don't mind.' *What if she went back to Phil and he never saw his child?*

'I've decided that if Phil wants to put up a fight tomorrow, I'll just get the divorce when I can. He isn't going to settle for a quickie and I'm not going to let myself get worked up about it.'

'I'd settle for a quickie,' said Tom, dodging the cushion again. He wrapped his arms around her tightly, savouring her . . . just in case this was the last time. The thought of her seeing Phil tomorrow terrified him. He hadn't wanted to come over all caveman but he was built to protect, it was just the way God had made him, and he was far too old and set in his ways to fight against it. He wanted to go with her tomorrow but of course she had said no.

'What if we had twins? One of each,' said Lou. 'Phil's twins were really beautiful.'

Phil Phil Phil.

'I don't think we'll be having blonde, brown-eyed kids, though – do you?' said Tom, shaking his black hair at her, fighting back the nervous, almost tearful tremor in his voice.

'No, I don't think so,' laughed Lou gently.

As they sat, each with their thoughts, Tom suddenly started muttering to himself. 'No, we can't, can we?' he murmured. 'No way. I'm sure that's right. Of course, of course. How stupid!'

'What are you on about?' said Lou.

'Wait a minute.' He unwrapped himself from Lou, bolted quickly out of the room and came back a few minutes later carrying a huge encyclopedia and grinning widely.

'Lou, I think you might get your quickie divorce after all,' he said. Taking a pad out of the dresser drawer, he started to draw little coloured circles on it. All this stopping at the petting stage had obviously sent him a bit loopy, Lou thought.

She realized she would have to make love to him very soon in order to save his mental health.

Chapter 60

The next morning, Lou checked herself in the mirror and added a little more rouge to her pale cheeks. She hoped the remission of morning sickness would last until this dreaded task was over. In saying that, the prospect of 'morning sickness' still thrilled her, because it was under the umbrella of pregnancy symptoms and she was quite prepared to suffer double, even treble sickness tonight, but *please God* just let her get through this morning with some dignity.

She felt pretty good, actually. She applied some red lipstick for courage and nodded at her reflection. She was ready.

1, The Faringdales looked different somehow. She felt no emotional attachment to the house she had moved into as a bride. It was hard to believe she had lived there for ten years. Her life there seemed a million light years away, even though four months ago, she had not even thought of clearing out a drawer or ever heard of Tom Broom. When she got to the front door, the instinct wasn't even there to walk straight in. It was no longer her home. She knocked and Phil opened it and brought her in effusively.

How long was it since he had seen her? She looked like Lou, but different. It sounded nuts to say it, but she looked like an older version of the young spirited Lou he had fallen in love with – the Lou she would have naturally grown into, had she not been worn down by his treatment of her.

'How are you, love?' he said. She wasn't wearing her wedding ring, he noticed.

'I'm fine,' said Lou. 'How are you?' He was wearing his wedding ring, she noticed.

'I've made tea,' he said, in the manner of a small child who was showing off a pasta picture to his mam. Lou let him pour her a cup. He'd got the best china out of the cabinet. It was his mother's tea-set – an heirloom that, ordinarily, wouldn't have come out for a visiting Monarch.

'I've left the milk and the sugar out,' he said, pointing to a bowl and a jug.

'Thanks, but I don't take either in tea,' said Lou.

Bollocks, thought Phil. They'd been together ten years – how come he didn't know that?

He got out the cake. It couldn't have been more obvious that he'd made it if he'd iced *Made by Phil* on it. She wasn't fooled by his trying-so-hard gesture. Did he think she was that easy to manipulate? Probably – because she *had* been that easy to manipulate in the past, hadn't she?

'Would you like a slice?'

'Thanks, but not for me. I appreciate you making it, though.'

Good, she's noticed. He smiled inside, but outwardly forced himself to look disappointed. Lou felt nothing and moved the conversation forwards.

'So, to business,' she said.

'Lou, you can't be serious. Come on, love, this has gone far enough. What can I do to make this right?' said Phil, flashing his best disarming smile. 'Come home, Lou, I miss you.'

'Phil. You miss your clothes washed, you miss your meals cooked, you miss . . . having your basic needs met. You don't miss *me*.'

'Yes, I do, Lou. Honest I do.'

This Lou was gorgeous. He could understand why it worked for people to take some time out in their marriage if they managed to find perspective like this.

Phil clicked his fingers. It suddenly came to him what this was *really* all about.

'This is about that Sue, isn't it?' he said.

'Yes,' said Lou. She wondered which Sue he was referring to, but really it didn't matter. Both Sues had played their parts in the downfall of her marriage, along with Phil – and herself.

'But, love, that was all sorted years ago!'

Ah, he meant the first Sue. 'No, it wasn't. You never even said sorry, Phil.'

'It was me that went to see her and told her not to press charges when you belted her!' Phil's voice rose in frustration. 'It was me that got you out of that mess. Didn't that say everything you needed to know?'

'No, it didn't.'

'I'm sorry, then. I'm sorry I put you through all that. It was the biggest mistake of my life.'

Lou drew in a big breath. Hearing that he was sorry changed nothing. It was all too late.

'Phil, I want you to sign the papers and for us both to get on with our lives.'

'Lou, I can't do that.'

Lou stayed calm. She should have known he would battle her on this point.

'You'll be wondering, of course, why I took the money from the business account.'

'Well, er, yes, I was, a bit.'

'I took the approximate value of *your* house as it stands now.'

'*Our* house,' he corrected.

'I subtracted the amount that you paid for it before we were married,' Lou went on, ignoring him. 'I added on a fair figure, I think, for the value of the fixtures and fittings and divided by two, and that's what I took out of the business account.'

'That's very cold for you, Lou,' said Phil, affecting bewilderment now.

Lou went on, 'If you don't agree with the figures, we can always let the courts decide. I think they'll find that I'm also entitled to half your business and a substantial proportion of your pension, but I don't intend to claim that. You can guarantee that because we'll sign for a full and final settlement. I've been a lot fairer than any judge would be.'

'You, lady, are guilty of fraud,' said Phil, trying to tie down his anger.

That was the second time she'd been accused of that recently, Lou thought with an inner giggle. She might soon have to consider getting plastic surgery, a false passport and a one-way ticket to Acapulco.

'Let's face it, Phil, you would have stopped my access to the joint account and denied me anything at all, had I not taken it first. This way at least I save you having to spend half of your savings on solicitors' fees. As it stands, we're sorted financially. The rest is just paperwork.'

He picked up his trusty mobile menacingly. The whites of his eyes were very startling against his traffic-light-red face.

'I could ring the Fraud Squad right now.'

'Go right ahead. But remember, you gave me authority to transfer monies. If I'd really wanted to defraud you, I'd have taken the lot. I only took my fair share. I could lie and say you gave me the money and then changed your mind. And if you want to talk about fraud . . .'

Lou pulled out two computer disks from her handbag and threw them on the table. 'This one has your up-to-date accounts for the last ten years. This one has your *real* up-to-date accounts. I could send the taxman both. I'm sure they'd find enough discrepancies to keep them in a permanent job, charging day-to-day interest on the shortfall alone. Obviously these aren't the only copies. You'll get those when the divorce is final.'

Phil's face suffused with even more blood. He looked like a red cabbage. He felt as if he was in a maze and every entrance was blocked off. Maybe not every one – he still had one trump card left. There was one thing over which he still had control.

'Well, you can wait for your divorce for bloody ever,' he snarled.

But Lou didn't even blink. She had to be on drugs, thought Phil. Some freaky herbal equivalent of Valium.

'I'll make you a deal,' she said, crossing her legs.

He couldn't remember her having legs like that.

'Sign the papers now and let me take them in, and I'll refund you over thirty thousand pounds with immediate effect.'

She got her chequebook out of her bag and clicked on her pen.

'How much over thirty thousand pounds?' said Phil with a grumbling interest.

'You'll have to gamble and find out.'

'What, and trust you?'

She held out the pen to him.

Thirty thousand quid was a lot of money and even now he knew Lou would be as good as her word. He hated to admit it, but he wasn't going to win this one so damage limitation was his only option. He didn't know this supremely confident and sexy woman in his kitchen. She was a very desirable stranger, though.

'I wasn't unfaithful to you after that Peach woman, you know,' he tried.

'It doesn't matter now if you were or you weren't,' said Lou. 'It was never just about another woman.'

He opened his mouth to ask what the hell else it was all about then, but some wiser part within made him shut it. He had been a total bastard to Lou, if he faced it. There were birds *before* Susan Peach. And he hadn't exactly been there for her during that fake pregnancy episode. His life with Lou flashed past him in a few lousy seconds and it hit him then what was really happening and why. Lou was leaving him, really leaving him. His marriage was ending, his control was slipping and he felt a seismic panic rumble through him.

'Lou, come on,' he said, a tremble in his voice. 'Me and you, we'll go on for ever. Remember what we used to say about you and me going on for ever?'

Lou remembered. She remembered being curled up in his arms talking through the life they were going to live, a forever life of warmth and mutual support, before he snatched back his dreams and feasted on them and left her with only the crumbs he thought to spare her.

'Phil . . .'

'Look, Lou, let's start again. Let's renew our vows. You always wanted to go to Italy, didn't you? We could get married in Rome. I'll write to the Pope and ask him to officiate at the wedding, how about that then?'

He laughed with an edge of desperation, the words tumbling out of his mouth, snagging on his throat, and Lou pitied him. He hadn't seen this coming at all; he really did think they were going to be Fat Jack and Maureen part II.

'No, Phil,' she said slowly, but decisively. She didn't want to go to Italy with him. He didn't *belong* there with her. 'Please, sign the papers.'

'I just wanted it to be back like it was between us, Lou. I might have been a bit heavy-handed, but we were so good together once, weren't we? We could be again. That's all I wanted. I thought I was a good husband. I've never hit you, have I? I'm not mean with my money, am I? I buy you flowers, don't I? We have great holidays – five-star always. And look at our house – it's gorgeous. This kitchen cost twenty-eight grand Lou – all for you.'

He could be a good husband, he knew he could. Better than most. And he was still on the way up so there was so much more to come for them. But Lou looked anything but impressed by his marital CV. She was shaking her head slowly and he *knew* he'd slipped from her heart. He'd gone too far. Their clock couldn't be turned back.

Like an accelerated course in grief, Phil had gone through denial, anger, and sadness that morning – and all that was left for him now was acceptance.

He sighed, took the pen, got the divorce papers out of the envelope and signed them quickly, trying not to think what he was doing. Lou checked them over and tucked them into her bag, then she rested her chequebook on her knee and scribbled. Finally she stood to go, handing him over a folded cheque.

'Thanks for the tea,' she said, even though she hadn't touched it. Phil seemed such a stranger, part of an old life which was now ended – a life that could have been so much better for them both if only they had tried harder. Oh yes, *both* of them – for she had played her own part in the downfall of her marriage. Like Maureen, she'd *let* her husband do those things to her. She didn't stop them happening. She'd allowed him more than his fair share of the sunlight and let him push her deep into the shadows. Thank goodness she hadn't left it too late to walk away.

As Phil's hand came out for the cheque he said quietly, 'I love you, Lou Winter. Please don't throw us away.'

Lou's breath caught in her throat. He sounded so desperate, so pitiable.

'You wouldn't have treated me like you did if you'd really loved me,' she said, surprising herself with the strength in her voice.

'I do love you. In my own way, I love you so much.'

In my own way. There was nothing more to be said. It was so over.

'Goodbye, Phil.'

As Lou walked out of 1, The Faringdales for the last time, she didn't look behind her to see Phil standing in the window watching her go, his eyes glassy with tears. She got in the car, slipped off the handbrake and drove off. Then she pulled up around the corner and sobbed.

Phil watched her go. He couldn't articulate the feelings inside him as she and her silver car drove out of his life for ever. There was something big blocking his windpipe that wouldn't be coughed away. He'd been so caught up in the moment that he had forgotten all about the cheque, which he now picked up – to find that it was totally blank on the cheque side. Then he noticed two things – the first that the printed name on the cheque was *Ms E.A. Casserly*, the second was the writing on the back of the cheque.

Blue eyes + blue eyes = brown eyes. Not very likely.

He stared at it for a full minute wondering whether to get in his car and chase Lou and ask her what the hell she was playing at when she had promised him thirty grand. Then his brain began to work with the facts available. He remembered something he'd seen on the television – some medical thing – *Casualty*. Or was it a documentary? Family secrets coming to light when a father offered a kidney to save the life of his son. There was a connection with the colour of eyes that he couldn't quite remember. Then it started to come to him as through a fog. *The bitch. The bloody duplicitous sneaky bitch!!*

His soon-to-be ex-wife was forgotten as he made a frenzied leap for the telephone and stabbed in the short dial to the bank.

'Which department, please?' asked the switchboard lady.

'I want to stop a cheque – NOW!' said Phil.

Chapter 61

'I wish you'd sit down, you're doing my head in,' said Deb, putting the newly washed crockery in the cupboards. 'You must have walked ten miles in here this morning. You'll be wearing grooves in the tiles in a bit.' But she was only gently cross with him. She had been where he was, worrying that Phil would work his magic. But Lou was different now. She'd found her old Casserly spark.

'She's later than I thought she'd be,' said Tom, raking his fingers through his over-long hair. It needed a cut. Did he look scruffy, up against Phil's neatness?

'She's got a lot to discuss with him,' said Deb calmly.

'What if he tries to talk her round?' Tom fretted, sitting at last, although his leg seemed to have developed St Vitus's Dance.

'He probably will.' Deb held up an arresting finger as his mouth opened to speak. 'Phil isn't coming in at night to a wonderful home-cooked meal or a basketful of clean socks, so of course he's going to try and talk her round. But Lou isn't a fool, Tom.' *Not any more.*

'He's a used-car salesman. He'll have highly honed manipulation skills,' said Tom, getting up again to repace. He could imagine the sort of tricks Phil would try. He would have a whole repertoire of sweet words and seduction techniques. He imagined Phil Winter was a man who had no concept of losing. One who would play hard and strike low to get what he wanted.

'Lou's eyes are wide open. She sees him for what he is. She's not going to leave you for someone like him.'

But 'someone like him' was legally bracketed to Lou. It would be so much easier for her to be lulled back home to Phil than ride the rough terrain of a divorce.

Tom caught sight of his reflection in the glass of a picture and felt suddenly outclassed. What was he? A big, rough bloke in an overall who had a job moving other people's rubbish and lived in a house that had no wallpaper, hardly any curtains and one carpet so far. OK, he had a solid business and property, but Phil out-ranked him on all fronts with his polished suit, killer smile, fleets of posh cars, pots of ready money, swanky wardrobe, big house and the persuasive powers of a snake-charmer. How could a glorified scrap-man compete with all that?

Lou opened the door and he saw straight away that she had been crying.

'You OK?' he said. He'd barely got the second word out before she moved into his arms to savour the wonderful smell and feel of him. He tried not to squeeze her too hard as the relief washed over him like a warm tide.

'How are things?' asked Deb, winking at Tom and mouthing, *Told you so.*

'OK, I think,' said Lou. 'The stupid hormones don't help. I just need to go upstairs for a bit.'

'To think?' said Tom, tentatively.

'To change into something nice and elasticky around my stomach,' said Lou.

'Oh,' said Tom. 'Can I get you anything, love?'

'A cup of orange juice and four cardboard boxes would be good,' said Lou.

'God, her funny cravings have started already,' said Deb, turning to switch on the kettle. 'Would you like them with or without jam?'

'Whatever Tom would like, seeing as they're going to be sitting in his house,' Lou announced. 'I'm moving in with him today, you see.'

Tom said nothing but stood there with his mouth wide open in shock.

'You wanton hussy,' said Deb.

'I'm glad you approve,' said Lou.

'I most certainly do,' said Deb.

Epilogue

'Happy Anniversary, partner!' Deb raised her mug of tea and clinked it against Lou's.

'Congratulations to you, Miss Devine. And may it be the first of many,' smiled Lou.

'I can't believe it's been a year.'

'Yes, a fair bit has happened, hasn't it. Biscotti?' Lou proffered the glass jar full of biscuits.

'Don't mind if I do. I'm in the mood for a good dunk.'

'Aren't you always?'

'Dirty cow!'

They laughed together as business colleagues and best friends. Both dressed in their black uniforms with their company logo above the breast. They hadn't used the name *Casa Nostra* – they'd agreed on a different name, a perfect one: *Mamma's. Ma's Café* was so well-known, they had merely Italianized it. It seemed, for many reasons, so very right.

'You need a bigger uniform,' Deb said. 'Your boobs are getting even more massive. We'll need an extension to the building at this rate.'

'It's my milk,' said Lou. 'Franco must be nearby.'

Right on cue, Tom Broom with a papoose carrying his black-haired baby son came shivering from the early chill of the morning into the bright, warm café. At his heels was his faithful dog who was as good as glued to the baby.

'By heck, it was warmer than this on Christmas morning,' he said. Franco was asleep, though, snuggled against his dad's thumping heartbeat.

'Here, have a cuppa,' said Deb, adding cheekily, 'No, please, don't offer me any money, it's on the house.'

Tom tutted and sat carefully down, as did Clooney. It might not have been environmentally friendly to have dogs in the place, but a few of the truckers travelled with them and the dogs were as welcome as their masters in a special section of the cafe. Whilst Lou had been on her very short maternity leave, they'd employed a relative of May's to help out. She was obsessively clean and animals or no animals, the place was constantly shining like a new pin. They'd had to keep her on – she was too good to let go.

'A year,' mused Lou again.

The same thought passed through both women's minds. A year ago today they'd been standing in exactly the same place, shaking with excitement and fear too. What if no one turned up? What if the scruffy old cara-van on the dual carriageway that doled out greasy bacon butties had absorbed all their clientèle in the weeks *Ma's Café* was closed, and refused to hand it back? Their fridges had been bursting with breakfast foods, most of it delivered by Karen's dad; the griddles, pots and pans were ready to start cooking, and the cakes were on dis-play in a beautiful rotating cabinet ready for the

afternoon clientèle. Huge, fresh gâteaux – ranging from
the 'Marco' (tiramisú flavoured with white icing), so rich
that it defeated even Tom on test – to the light lemon
and cardamom 'TortaRenee'; and in jars on the shelves
sat twenty different sorts of coffee ranging from 'Butter
Toffee' to 'Summer Pudding'.

They'd opened the red, green and white Italian flag
blinds at 6 a.m. precisely, to find no one waiting. Lou's
heart had sunk into her boots, and even big hard Debra
Devine looked close to tears.

Then, from nowhere, like the zombies in *Dawn of the
Dead*, only pinker and infinitely more benign, lumber-
jack shirts and denim jackets began to head across the car
park towards them, and lorries and vans and cars started
to turn onto their land.

And the only thing both of them could think of to say
was, '*Mamma bloody mia!*'

And now it was a year on, and Deb was having the
flirtatious time of her life behind that counter and her
best friend had been on an Italian honeymoon, acquired
a husband and given birth to a son – in that order. Lou's
eyes were still full of Venetian sunshine, and a certain
gentleman of Italian extraction was managing to keep
the brightness burning there quite adequately.

The planned phasing-out of the breakfast side of the
business hadn't happened. It was too popular, and
though it shouldn't under any circumstances have
worked that the afternoon tea set sat comfortably
amongst big hairy-arsed lorry drivers, both worlds met
and colluded in fabulous harmony. Little old ladies, business folk, students and men built like barn doors all
tucked into Brando breakfasts in the mornings and then,

in the afternoons, devoured the most wonderful cakes. *Mamma's*, it was reported in the local – then national – press, was the most bizarre place in the world and had to be seen and experienced. They'd even had the *Morning Coffee* TV team down there. The presenter Drusilla Durham had sat with Lou for nearly two hours after the cameras had stopped rolling. She'd been fascinated by Lou's clutter-clearing adventure and had left with a full notepad, a roll of binliners and the hope in her heart that she'd find the same fire that blazed in Lou Broom's eyes.

Tom suddenly clicked his fingers. 'I meant to tell you. I've just seen Phil.'

'Oh, where was he?' said Lou.

'Driving. He looked very intense.'

'Doesn't he always?' said Deb, heading for the loo before the rush of customers started.

Deb would never forgive him, but Lou wasn't his enemy. He had given her the quickie divorce she'd asked for in the end, and even sent lots of her things around in big boxes. On the top was a letter wishing her well that must have taken a big gulping down of pride to write. And he thanked her for alerting him to the fact that Sharon's children probably weren't his. The eye formula wasn't as simple as Tom remembered it from his biology lessons at school – that two blue-eyed people couldn't have brown-eyed children – but it was a strong enough basis for Phil to demand a DNA test. This had revealed that he was not the twins' father, after all.

'He'll be happy enough with his lot,' said Lou. 'He has his car business and that's all he really needs. Now me – I feel as if I own the whole world because of what I've got.'

'And let's look at what you *have* got, Lou: a nocturnal greedy little son, a big ugly skip man and a daft dog named after George Clooney.'

The daft dog in question lifted an ear, then dropped it and settled his head back in his paws with a happy sigh.

'And what have *you* got, Mr Broom? A plump little midget who bakes buns.'

'You're all I could ever want, Mrs Broom. *Angelo mio, ti amo passionatamente.*'

'Take me to bed, Mr Broom.' The eyes of Shaun Casserly's daughter glittered Irish-green and mischievously at him.

'You are so for it when you get home, Mrs Broom.

'I'm not sure I can wait that long, Mr Broom.'

'Trust me, it'll be worth it,' said Tom Broom – who later hijacked his wife at their front door, lifted her effortlessly, Prince-Charming-style into his arms, and carried her upstairs.